Jane Linfoot writes fun, flirty, bestselling romantic fiction with feisty heroines and a bit of an edge. Writing romance is cool because she gets to wear pretty shoes instead of wellies. She lives in a mountain kingdom in Derbyshire, where her family and pets are kind enough to ignore the domestic chaos. Happily, they are in walking distance of a supermarket. Jane loves hearts, flowers, happy endings, all things vintage, and most things French. When she's not on Facebook, and can't find an excuse for shopping, she'll be walking or gardening. On days when she wants to be really scared, she rides a tandem.

🐦 @janelinfoot
🅵 /JaneLinfoot2
www.janelinfoot.co.uk

Also by Jane Linfoot

Love at the Little Wedding Shop by the Sea

Jane Linfoot

OneMoreChapter

One More Chapter
a division of HarperCollins*Publishers*
The News Building
1 London Bridge Street
London SE1 9GF

www.harpercollins.co.uk

This paperback edition 2020
2

First published in Great Britain in ebook format by
HarperCollins*Publishers* 2020

A catalogue record for this book
is available from the British Library

Ebook ISBN: 978-0-00-840810-7
Paperback ISBN: 978-0-00-840809-1

Set in Birka by Palimpsest Book Production Ltd, Falkirk
Stirlingshire

Printed and bound in Great Britain by
CPI Group (UK) Ltd, Croydon CR0 4YY

For Yoyo, my wonderful Old English Sheepdog,
beside me all day, every day.
25.3.2004 – 26.5.2020

Sometimes good things fall apart so better things can fall together.

—Marilyn Monroe

FEBRUARY

Chapter 1

Friday, Valentine's Day.
The Harbourside, St Aidan, Cornwall.
Early birds and aftershocks.

It's a boy!

There are certain significant moments in life you know you're going to relive again and again. As those three small words bounce off my phone screen and resonate around inside my skull, I'm on the edge of a huge crowd of people with one of my oldest friends, Poppy, at my elbow, but I couldn't feel any more alone. It's the sting of the salty wind on my cheeks that's being etched on my memory, the blackness of the water lapping against the quay, the dark lines of boat masts etched against the sky. The curve of lights out around the bay edge.

Even when you know a metaphorical tidal wave is coming your way, it's still hard to predict how it will demolish you. I expected this would blow my heart apart, but it actually hits way lower. It's nothing like the thousand tiny glass shards in my chest I was braced for, more a boot in my bowel.

All the same, I'd still rather know than not.

When your closest friend and business partner accidentally hooks up with your fiancé – well, *my* fiancé – then they decide that's how it should have been all along. And then seal the deal with a baby.

This baby.

Let's just say, this text from Lucy, our maternity-cover office assistant, is the latest in a year of seismic shocks.

In case you hadn't already guessed, this is all playing out in tiny St Aidan on the furthest edge of Cornwall where the land meets the sea. Where the higgledy-piggledy cottages that start at the edge of the cobbles stack up the hillside in shadowy lines behind me. It's somehow ironic that we're out on this freezing February night waiting for a firework display to begin; that this tiny baby who's turned my life upside down for the last few months has now claimed the Brides by the Sea Valentine's Day celebrations as his own too.

Poppy is next to me, pulling her Barbour jacket closed against the slice of the wind, stamping her feet as we wait. 'Everything okay, Milla? You're lucky to find a signal down here.'

I'm watching the strings of lights in the distance along the prom being lashed by a gale. Pushing my phone back into my pocket, I say, 'Phoebe's had a boy.'

'The baby's here already?' Poppy's eyebrows shoot upwards in horror the same way they have ever since we played together as kids growing up in Rose Hill village, a few miles inland from here. 'But first babies never arrive on time! The last two weeks waiting like a beached whale are what prepares you for every-thing ahead.' She had her son Gabe two years ago, so she's an expert. She's also enjoying a rare night out on her own, but seeing as she's Brides by the Sea's cake baker, this counts as work rather than pleasure.

'Phoebe won't put up with lateness, especially not from a baby.' Realistically she was never going to let herself get to the size of an elephant. Even with something as unpredictable as childbirth, she's the kind of person who plans scrupulously and always comes up smelling of roses. And she's good at it too. Like popping her baby out on Valentine's Day, exactly a year to the day after she and my ex, Ben, got together – it takes a special kind of very dedicated control-freak to pull that off.

'Christmas effing crackers, that wasn't in the plan was it?'

I'm shaking my head at Poppy. 'I haven't even turned the bed down at my Airbnb yet.' Okay, admittedly I've been at the wedding shop catching up with everyone since I arrived earlier this afternoon. But somehow, I'd counted on having more time to settle in. Get myself ready. Put my hard hat on.

It's odd to think that this time last year I still had a fiancé and the flat we shared. Then, somewhere around midnight, my whole life plummeted to oblivion – in a *Titanic*-hits-the-iceberg kind of way. I'll save the goriest details for later. But, just like the iceberg, I did not see this one coming. I'd been Phoebe's head bridesmaid when she'd got married six years earlier and our business had sprung from us organising her wedding, so it was natural that I'd support her when her husband Harry walked out. And when she was suddenly left without a partner for the black-tie Valentine's ball we'd paid a fortune for her to go to, I didn't think twice about lending her my fiancé Ben. They were my two most trusted people, in business and in life. The last thing I imagined was them ending up in bed together when she'd been so meticulous about showing me the separate rooms on the booking.

What's the old saying? One kiss is all it takes. Admittedly it was a bit more than that. A lot more. Enough to throw a wrecking ball through my relationship with Ben. But we were all very adult about it. Or at least, they were. However much I kicked and yelled, it wasn't going to help – the damage was done, what I'd had was already gone. He moved his stuff around the corner into her place. And we went on from there.

But after those long years literally spending all my waking hours scrambling to make a go of our Brides Go West wedding company, and borrowing to the hilt, I couldn't afford to let the business slide and lose that as well. But it was more than that. As my life imploded and my self-esteem went with it, Brides Go West became my one refuge. I might feel like a worm in every other area, but an award-winning business lets me hold my head high. Phoebe and Ben might have whipped every other meta-phorical carpet out from under me, but I refuse to let them run away with the business too.

So, for the last nine months I've watched Phoebe's bump growing across the office desk like a slow-motion horror movie. In the end I decided if I actually had to be there for the birth, my screams were going to be louder than the ones coming from the labour ward. So after a whole year of gritting my teeth so hard they're stumps of their former selves, I left town for a couple of weeks around the baby's due date.

Poppy's arm slides around my shoulder. 'You do know you are worth more than this?' Her voice is low in my ear. 'It might feel like the end of the world now ...'

I've heard it so many times I can finish it myself. '... *but it will get better*.' The problem is, deep down, I can't imagine ever getting to a place where there isn't a stone in my gut and my chest isn't aching. When I can look at a wedding dress and not have my mouth fill with the taste of sour lemons. Which isn't the most practical thing to happen when I write about the damn things most days on our blog.

Poppy lets out a groan. 'Sorry, it's not the best timing, but you're about to meet Gary and Ken. They're doing a great job giving out flyers for our Brides by the Sea cocktail event later, but they're insatiably curious too.' She pulls a face. 'Remember what it's like in small-town St Aidan?'

I grimace. 'Where everybody knows, and everybody cares?' It's very different from Bristol where I've been happily anonymous for the last twelve years. As a teenager growing up here, I dodged the worst of the spotlight because my mum was ill and I was her carer. When you barely leave the house, you become pretty invisible. But even if I don't recognise many of the faces in the crowd here tonight, the reason I've run back here now is to be with my oldest friends.

As Poppy and I are both in the wedding business, we're often in touch. And as my life unravelled, Poppy's the one who's been there for me, texting and messaging. And she was the one who literally saved my sanity when she suggested I take this working holiday. I know if Ben were the last guy in the world on a desert island, I'd actually have to make a boat and leave. And that's saying a lot from me, who came bottom of the class in woodwork. But however much I don't want Ben anymore, this baby moment is still so monumental it's a relief to be three hours down the road.

'So who are Ken and Gary?' So far as I can see they have great taste in tight, spangly shorts and are experts at elbowing their way through a crowd while rocking their Cupid costumes.

'They run a highly decorated local B&B, and they're also stars of the Hungry Shark's karaoke nights and the Chamber of Commerce.'

I shake my head. 'They were never going to let a fancy-dress Valentine's pub crawl pass quietly.'

Poppy calls to them as they wriggle into our space on the

cobbles. 'Hello, you two, you're the only men I know who can wear so little red lamé and make it work.'

The smaller, portlier one fans his fingers in front of his face. 'Thanks, Poppy, you're a sweetheart, as ever.' He turns to me and flutters eyelashes so long they have to be fake. 'You're from Brides Go West, aren't you? We saw you getting out of your van earlier.'

'Also known as Milla Fenton.' This is where I have to admit I've half borrowed/half absconded with the works vehicle, although it was actually mine to start with. As it's got two-foot-high light-up letters on the top, it's not exactly subtle.

'Lovely to meet you, Milla, there's a lot of vintage camper envy going on here. We've always wanted pink paintwork and our names in lights, haven't we, Ken?' He turns to Poppy. 'So, do tell, is this another of Jess's protégés coming to sprinkle her fairy dust on Brides by the Sea?'

As if he hasn't got enough of my attention already with his all-over sequined T-shirt and matching wings, Ken grabs my arm. 'It's the most wonderful shop Jess has created here, four floors of bridal gorgeousness overlooking the sea!'

I'm about to tell him the shop's a big favourite of our Brides Go West blog followers too, but Gary carries on seamlessly. 'Poppy's the cake maker there. The five-tier confection she made for us was Cornwall's first EVER naked wedding cake. But you probably know that?'

Ken and Gary seem to ask non-stop questions with no space for answers, but Poppy finally dives in. 'Milla's here for a couple of weeks to help with social media and to set up some special wedding fairs for the Brides by the Sea anniversary.'

Gary's eyes are popping. 'Fabulous and even more fabulous! Ten years since Jess took over the whole building, how amazing is that?'

Ken's carrying on. 'And a whole year of birthday celebrations starting with tonight's fireworks ... did you know they're actually Jess's Valentine's present from her fiancé Bart?'

Gary gives a sigh. 'He's our favourite pirate – handsome and loaded, she can't go wrong there. We wouldn't have thrown him out of our bed would we, Ken?'

Ken gives a shudder. 'Speak for yourself, Gaz, he's years too old for me. But who'd have thought? He offers her diamonds, and she asks for fireworks instead ...'

As if on cue, a huge boom echoes across the bay, and a cascade of multi-coloured stars arches up, then shimmers down the sky and falls into the sea.

Poppy's murmuring in my ear. 'They're letting them off from pontoons anchored out beyond the harbour. Watch out for the Valentine-themed ones too.' Her smile widens. 'Jess and Bart are down the front, if she chose this over a Tiffany necklace, we should be in for a spectacular display.'

As the explosions rock through my body and the wind splits the coloured reflections on the water into a thousand mirrored fragments, the people around me huddling deep into their padded jackets are letting out gasps and wows. Again and again the starbursts rip through the blue velvet sky above the bay. And as I listen to the swish of the waves rushing up the beach underneath the fireworks' bangs, I'm remembering how final it felt as I pushed the keys of our flat through the estate agent's letterbox earlier this morning. It's as if I'm watching my old life disintegrating into pieces high above me. I couldn't cry then, but now, in the dark, my tears are flowing too fast to wipe them away.

As I take a moment to dip in my bag for a dry hanky and look back at the boats on the harbour, there's a lone figure leaning against a mast. So maybe I'm not the only person in the world on their own tonight. It just feels that way.

Poppy nudges me. 'We must be close to the end, don't miss the best bit.'

As I look back up at the sky, there's a volley of booms above the waves and the heavens fill with red heart-shaped outlines that sparkle and crackle. Then there's a final rattle of explosions and they all drift downwards. As they sink behind the line where the sky meets the water and everyone starts to cheer, it feels a lot more bitter than sweet for me.

My phone beeps and this time Poppy's watching me. 'More news?'

I nod. Then, as I read, my saliva turns sour again. 'Hunter Benedict, 2.8kg.'

Poppy's brow furrows. 'If it's upsetting you, why not switch it off?'

I push my phone away and pull out another tissue. Ugly nose-blowing is one of Phoebe's worst hates but right now I'm past caring. I can't help my wail either. 'Hunter was my name, I bagged it first. I know I found it on her wellies, but it still feels like she's stolen it.' Baby names are a whole minefield of rules I've only dipped my toe into since I turned thirty and it seems like our entire friendship group apart from me suddenly got pregnant. You can't call a baby the same name as any other child you've ever heard of, but at least for people like me where children are lightyears away, it's still possible to stake an advance claim. Or it should be if your friends aren't completely disrespectful. This feels like Phoebe's final wave of the finger.

Poppy's hugging me again. 'Pinching your name is outrageous.'

'It bloody is.' I'm staring at the black smudges on the hanky, knowing there's worse on my face. 'I might go back to the van for a moment.'

Poppy links arms with me. 'Don't worry, we've got a few minutes before we need to be back at the shop. I'm in charge of cocktails so the bar will open when we get there.' We break away from the crowd and hurry to where the van is tucked away beyond a line of fishermen's cottages at the end of the quay.

'Okay, time for repairs.' I open the door and heave myself into the driver's seat, and peer into the rearview mirror.

As Poppy joins me from the passenger side, she's staring around the inside of the van. 'Even though it's dark, how cool is this interior?'

As I scrub away my panda eyes and dab at the blotches on my cheeks, I'm already feeling calmer. 'I still love the pink-and-white-checked seats.'

Poppy passes me a lippy from her pocket. 'Here, try this – fuchsia gives you a lift every time.' She's biting her lip as she watches me put it on. 'I know today's been the crappest, with handing in your keys and the baby coming. But at least that's the worst over.'

I look sideways at her in the half light. 'You're going to tell me it's time for a new start?'

'Well isn't it? St Aidan is heaving, the singles club is out there running wild.' Her face twists into a grin. 'It would be a shame to waste the opportunity.'

As I let out a breath, I'm sorry to flatten the mood. 'The last thing I want is another boyfriend.'

She laughs. 'Who said anything about committing? It just feels like it's time for you to stop being sad and get back to having a good time.'

I blow. 'We both know Ben is a tosser and I'm better off

without him. But am I ready to hit the world and party?' I really don't think so.

Her eyebrows edge upwards. 'How about your challenge for this evening is to collect five kisses?'

I can't believe how impossible that sounds. 'When I was twenty-one and first went to Bristol I'd have done it in five seconds. Now I feel I'd struggle if I had five years.'

Poppy's eyes are wide. 'This is so much worse than I thought. Let's set a more achievable target – how about one kiss, and all evening to claim it?' She sends me a wink. 'It's dark, you'll never see them again. And it's a watershed – once you've crossed the making-out bridge you'll be able to get on with the rest of your life.'

'I—I—I …' It's all sounding very 'old-style hen party'. Someone should tell her, hens have moved on, these days they don't get smashed, they do self-care. If she'd suggested kick-starting my new life with a massage therapy afternoon at The Harbourside Hotel, I'd be so much more up for it.

She's wiggling her eyebrows, which is never a good sign. 'Hunk coming our way now, he looks like he'll do nicely. Get your window down and shout him over.' She's sitting up straighter. 'In fact, no need, he's coming straight for us!'

As he saunters our way, what I'm getting is dark hair blowing in the gale. Shadowy cheekbones. A chunky sweater inside an open windcheater jacket.

I'm muttering. 'Considering the weather, it seems like someone's completely missed the point of wind wear.'

Poppy's hissing back. 'You can't write him off because he hasn't done up his coat, I need a better excuse than that.'

I reach for the window winder. Being vintage, they're the keep-fit, do-it-yourself version. By the time the glass slides down far enough for me to speak, I'm breathless from the exertion. 'Anything we can do to help you?' However much he's making a beeline towards us, I'm confident there won't be.

Poppy lets out a low laugh behind me. 'You'll have to be more direct than that to score.'

He clears his throat. 'Sorry, I couldn't help noticing your van when you parked it earlier.'

I'm used to comments, we get them all the time. 'The pink was deliberate. Hopefully it sidesteps dirty white and dated cream but still shouts *bride* really tastefully.'

He's blinking at me. 'Sorry, I'm not talking about the colour. You've parked in the boat owners' area – if you don't display a permit the wardens will ticket you.'

Poppy gives a low laugh. 'Bribing traffic wardens by snogging their faces off? It might sound desperate, but I wouldn't disallow it.'

I shut out Poppy and concentrate on the guy. I was up at six this morning, taking the last of my stuff out of the flat and putting it into storage. It's been a hell of a day. All topped off with Phoebe stealing my effing baby name. I'm just not ready for another argument. 'Well, if you'd like to step a yard to your right, I'll get the hell out of your precious owners' area and find somewhere else to park.' I haven't got the first idea where, it's a surprise it's this crowded.

He's shaking his head. 'You don't have to move. I've brought you a visitor parking pass. So long as you bring it back to *Snow Goose* before you leave town, you're welcome to use it.'

'You're offering to lend me a permit?' I'm picking my jaw up off the car mats.

He gives a small cough. 'It's us against the wardens down here, I'm happy to help out.' The permit's already so far through the window that all I can do is grasp it and drop it on the dash.

'Thanks a lot. I'll be sure to return it.' My voice jolts as Poppy jabs me in the side.

She's hissing in my ear. 'Go on, ask him – if you don't, I will ...'

'Great, well, thanks again. *Snow Goose*, got it, I'll drop it back.' This is me dismissing him and it's worked because he's waving and backing away.

But Poppy's like lightning. She's already out, across the cobbles, and murmuring in his ear. Talk about sitting targets – as he turns around to the open window there's literally nowhere for me to go.

This time he's laughing. 'Someone in need of a Valentine's kiss? I'm sure I can help out with that too.'

It's one of those instant decisions. I could make a dash for the crowd, but if I escape this time, I'll only get ambushed later. At least here there's only Poppy to see it. So long as she takes the permit back for me, I'll never have to set eyes on him again. So I make my spine rigid, screw my eyes closed. Pinch my lips together for the quickest of pecks.

But somehow his hand is behind my head, and as he comes in sideways through the open window his delicious scent is a split second ahead of him. And when his lips hit mine they're not hard and cold, they're soft and persuasive, like warm chocolate. As I give in and go with him, it's like there's a super-heated tornado rushing through my body. It can't be more than thirty seconds – thirty seconds of what? Pure, undiluted, liquid pleasure. With an overtone of lust that leaves me clutching the steering wheel to steady myself. Enough to say, when he pulls away he leaves me breathless and open-mouthed.

'Wow!' That's every last molecule of Poppy's lippy demolished.

And for anyone wanting marks out of ten – I'd have to go with a straight fifteen.

'Thanks for that.' He lets out a low laugh as he backs across the cobbles. 'Anything else I can help with, you know where to find me.'

'You've already done more than enough.'

But Poppy's hopping up and down, her eyes popping. 'We're serving free cakes and cocktails at Brides by the Sea ...' she glances at her watch '... any time around now. Up the hill, and turn right into the mews. If you'd like to come you're very welcome?'

'The wedding shop?' For a moment his eyes light up, but then he shakes his head. 'Sorry, there's somewhere else I need to be.'

'But – but – but ...'

I can see Poppy's going to push this, so I jump in. 'We totally understand. Fireworks and cheating the parking wardens, that's more than enough excitement for one day.' Quite apart from never wanting to see him again, there's no way I want to have to stare across a room at him knocking back pitchers of Sex on the Beach. In the same way that both Chris Hemsworth or Hugh Jackman are sizzling but you might not necessarily want them dangled in front of you in the same room, especially if you weren't in the best place in your life to take advantage. I mean, every woman has her limits. And I think I've found mine.

His lips are curving into a smile. 'In that case, I won't say *see you later*.'

That's good for me. I call after him, 'In that case, neither will I.'

Poppy's leaning her bum on the end of the van, watching him disappear into the shadows. 'From the grin on your face, we can safely say that was instant gratification?'

I'm laughing. 'Hell yes. Those permits are like gold dust. Mr Snow Goose just saved me from two weeks of parking nightmares.'

Poppy's shouting. 'That's not what I mean, and you know it!' She lowers her voice again. 'But you do feel like you made that whole new "somewhere over the rainbow" start?'

I'm shaking my head now too. 'Pops, it was twenty seconds ...'

She's not letting this go. 'It was SO closer to a minute!'

'As if a few seconds could change anything.'

'But it has, hasn't it?' Her stare is so intense it's like she's peering into my head. 'Tell me what you're thinking!'

Phoebe stole my fiancé, and now they have a baby. Sure, my heart was banging so hard the van was shaking just before, but it's going to take more than one kiss to mend my broken life. Not that I want to go back to serving coffee. It's just that now weddings are trigger points for me rather than my destination happy place. In the long term, for the sake of my sanity, I could do with a change of direction. Ideally, I need a career change.

But I'm staying totally quiet on all of that for now. 'I'm thinking, if we don't leave in the next ten seconds, you're going to have some very impatient cocktail customers.'

She's laughing. 'And I'm thinking some time in St Aidan is exactly what you need to shake you up and turn you around.'

I have to say, as we hurry up the steep, winding street towards the shop, my heart is pounding in a way that has to be down to more than us racing up a killer of a hill. I can't remember when I last felt this alive.

Chapter 2

Friday, Valentine's Day.
Brides by the Sea, St Aidan.
Cranberries and camper vans.

'So what can I tempt you with? Tie-me-up-tie-me-down? Hanky-panky? A Kiss on the Lips?'

Half an hour after Poppy and I arrive at the shop and I slosh drinks into glasses from tall glass jugs, any inner howling in my head is being drowned out by a room full of revellers. And in case anyone thinks this is me channelling my inner sex-goddess, I'm shouting about the delights of the Valentine's cocktails on offer.

With every group of guests who push their way in from the cobbled mews outside, the salt-laden gusts are blowing in straight off the sea, catching the chandeliers, making their crystals flash, ruffling the chiffon on the snowy dresses beneath the hanging strings of paper hearts and tiny studded fairy lights in the window. At one time this would have had my heart racing too, now it just gives me an ache in the pit of my stomach. But obviously I do my best to hide that.

As another wave of people unwrapping their scarves walks in, I turn to Poppy who's next to me behind the drinks table. 'Where are they all coming from?'

Poppy laughs. 'I told you, St Aidan Singles Club events are huge. And we're dishing out free stuff so everyone will call in here. As Jess says, it's never too early to bring a single person aspiring to be part of a couple to a wedding shop.'

It's no surprise. This is the kind of long, hard-nosed game Jess plays. In her eyes every unattached adult downing Poppy's complimentary cocktails and cupcakes tonight is a potential bride or groom down the line. It's the same determination Jess had when she came here fourteen years ago with a divorce settlement and an idea to sell flowers from one tiny room in the basement. And we can all see how well that turned out.

Poppy laughs again. 'The customers are only meant to be here for long enough to get a glimpse inside the shop. Don't worry, they'll be off to the next stop at the Hungry Shark before you can say Love on the Rocks.'

I don't need to worry too much about what I'm shouting from the chalkboard menu either, because I'm only doing this for two minutes while Jess grabs some more mint sprigs and whooshes some potential husbands-to-be upstairs for a quick look at the Groom Room. My real allocated job here is much more my thing – taking Polaroid pictures of happy couples on the loveseat that's nestled in the corner by the fitting room. This is so when the customers sober up tomorrow, they've got something to remind them to shop at Brides by the Sea when the time comes. And so when they write their names and emails on the back of the pictures we keep, the shop gets to grow the customer contacts list.

This is how it always is with Phoebe and our wedding fairs too. She's our queenly front-of-house figurehead, like the swan gliding above the water. Meanwhile, I'm the frantic swan feet, rushing around out of sight making things work. But, as Phoebe's fond of saying, that way we both play to our strengths.

Poppy's swishing her blonde ponytail, ramming cherries onto sticks like there's no tomorrow. 'Blame Jess for the cocktails, she got a bit carried away. Any other day, it's Prosecco all the way, so the spills don't show.' As Poppy's been the shop's wedding cake maker for ten years, the whole town knows how delicious her baking is. It's no surprise there's a scramble for her cupcake towers with their mouthwatering swirls of pastel buttercream and heart-shaped sprinkles.

I nod at her as I brush the cupcake crumbs off my boob shelf. 'You can spill anything you like on me. These sequins are very forgiving – I'll just wipe them clean.'

Poppy laughs. 'You make a very cute cherub, even though I say it myself.'

I'm smoothing down the pale apricot mini-jumpsuit I borrowed from the bridesmaids' sale rail this afternoon. Dressing me as a cherub was Poppy's attempt to cheer me up, and as the baby news hadn't hit then, I was happy to go along with it. As for the rest of what I'm wearing, it goes downhill from the all-over sequins. Looking back, it was one of those times when going wild got the better of us. I've got an oversized cupid's bow wedged across my boobs. I also have wings, a sling full of arrows, and laurel leaves stuck in my hair. Truly, don't ask me where the laurel comes in.

I pick up another two jugs and wave them at the sea of padded jackets in front of us. 'Anyone for a Screw on the Drive or a Heart Attack? And the cupcakes are lavender, white chocolate, and vanilla buttercream.' I grab another two for myself and mumble at Poppy as I pop one in my mouth. 'Bite-sized cakes are so practical when you're serving.'

As she leans towards me, she's waving a tissue. 'Two things – first, there's lipstick in your ear.'

I let out a groan as she wipes it off. 'How the hell did that get there?'

'We both know the answer to that.' She lets her grin go. 'And second – on the same subject – the guy from *Snow Goose* just walked in.'

'WHAT?!' My gulp is big enough to suck in the whole cupcake I'm holding. Then the paper case hits the back of my throat and next thing I know I'm choking then sneezing the whole lot into Poppy's well-placed tissue. She hands me a second one so I can wipe the last of the crumbs off my eyebrows. On Phoebe's scale of misdemeanours, this would get a similar score to vomming on my feet. I swear, I only did that twice, and never in front of our bridal customers.

The good bit tonight is that at the crucial moment I managed to drop to my knees so the worst has been hidden behind the bar table. But it leaves me looking up at Poppy.

She's talking down to me through clenched teeth. 'Don't look now ...' which is completely unnecessary as I've no chance of a view '... but he's flying this way ...' her eyes are as big as flower buckets '... and the eagle – er, goose – has landed ...'

I can keep quiet and let Poppy do her worst up above, or I can stand up and do this for myself. I shake my fingers through the dangly bits of my hair in the hope of a bit of volume to hide behind and pop my head up over the table edge.

'Hey! I thought you were going elsewhere?' Listen to me! I sound as up-myself as Phoebe.

The guy pulls a face. 'Luckily for you, I met two men who wouldn't take no for an answer.' In the light he's even more beautiful than in the dark, in a lived-in kind of a way. His face is lean with the sort of bone structure and stubble shadows you mainly see on Vogue models. And somehow I just know that there's a body to match underneath the effortlessly stylish denim jeans and dark hand-knitted sweater.

I shoot Poppy a sideways glance as I finally stagger to my feet. 'Just checking stock levels down there.'

As he moves forward, his eyes lock with mine. 'And I came to say how much I enjoyed the fireworks.'

As the words sink in, I'm staring at his lips. Thinking about catching my fingers in those tawny-brown tousled waves. Remembering how I slid my tongue over his teeth. Thinking of the explosions in my gut, and how he must have felt them too. My mouth is dropping open but nothing's coming out.

Poppy stands on my toe. 'Weren't the rockets amazing?'

Rockets? *Those* fireworks ... Of course, that's what he's talking about. 'Yay to the amazing bangs – and those hearts floating down the sky!' I'm frantically wiping my hands on my backside, moving this on before I make any more of a tool of myself. 'What can I pour you? Anything on the chalkboard, we've got it all.'

There's a definite spark in his eye. 'I was wondering what would have happened earlier if I'd passed over a full resident's parking permit rather than a visitor's one.' His lips are twisting as he scans the handwriting. 'If this is what's on offer, I think I got my answer.'

I don't flinch. Instead, I fix my eyes on the Diesel logo on the front of his coat. 'So what's it to be, an Unleash Your Libido or a Lovebite?'

'What do you recommend?' As his sooty lashes lift there's a flash of dark grey iris softened by the glint of a tease.

'Er ...' As our eyes lock again, my heart thuds to a halt and a shiver zips down my spine as I remember the rush as our mouths collided. I catch a waft of his scent across the table and I'm thanking my lucky stars for the sequin shield covering my boobs. However thick the padding on my T-shirt bra is, it's no match for a dark gaze like that. And I'm only opening and closing my mouth because no one's asked me that yet.

Poppy comes to my rescue. 'We're drinking non-alcoholic Rhubarb and Rose.'

'But that's for wimps.' My voice jumps into action, spurred on by the spark in his eye and the need to get this over fast. 'I reckon you should try the Love Potion No. 9.'

Poppy turns on me. 'Is that even a thing?'

I hitch my cupid bow back into place on my shoulder, fill up a jam jar, toss in a cucumber slice and a spoonful of berries, push in a striped paper straw and push it towards him. 'It is now. There you go! Enjoy!' *Then get the hell out of here.*

This time his lips curve all the way to a smile. And of course the teeth are going to match the rest of the package. Why wouldn't they? In the same way that dark chocolate voice of his sounds exactly as he tasted. 'So is this the bit where I give you my heart?'

'Excuse me?'

Poppy's nudge lands in my ribs as she hisses. 'The drinks voucher he's holding – take it off him, Milla.'

I swallow hard, curse silently at how much I'm showing myself up, and make my beam really, really bright. 'Great.' But as my fingers reach the paper he whips it away.

There's a low laugh. 'One more strawberry then I promise, it's all yours.'

I'm shaking my head. In the wedding business you have to be super-polite, every second. As Phoebe has reminded me most days for the last six years, you need to look like you're having the most fun, but there's simply no place for messing about. As this evening is more of a random free-for-all, just this once I let myself go. 'Another strawberry? Talk about demanding customers!'

He's properly laughing now and turning the twinkle in his eyes up to max. 'I just sailed in after a month at sea, I need all the nutrients I can get.'

Unbelievable. Just my luck to hit on a superman. 'And I just drove all the way from Gloucestershire, but I'm not about to inhale all the fruit.'

He's still grinning, but this time he's looking straight at me with the kind of smile that turns your insides to molten toffee. 'Which saves me asking. I thought I recognised a Bristol burr.'

My eyes snap open. 'I *so* don't have one of those, thanks all the same.' I'm so desperate to move him on I push the whole bowl of strawberries at him. 'Take as much fruit as you need. And if you're going to collapse due to vitamin deficiency, please don't mess up the displays.'

He scoops a strawberry into his drink and pushes another into his mouth – ah, those teeth again. Then he hands me his heart and his face splits into a grin. 'One heart, be sure you look after it. And watch you don't drop your quiver.'

The best I can do is widen my eyes as I try to work out what the hell he's talking about.

He's raised an eyebrow now. 'Your arrow pouch – it's called a quiver. And I'm no archery expert, but it looks like yours is about to fall off.' His grin splits even further. 'If cupid loses his ammunition, you're not going to have many takers for your pictures.'

Don't you just hate it when guys come over like they know so much more than you?

I roll my eyes upwards to the chandelier. 'I wasn't planning on taking aim, my bow is purely decorative.'

'In which case I'll leave you to dish out your Lovebites.' There's one cocked eyebrow and he might be laughing. 'I'll catch you later.'

As he saunters off into the crush of brightly coloured padded jackets and flushed cheeks, I turn to Poppy. 'He took his time.'

Poppy's grin is wider still. 'And you don't think he hung around because there was so much flirting going on?'

'What? With *me*?!' Surely, she can't be serious? 'Whatever happened before, you know I'm done with men.'

She's biting her lip. 'He liked the starter so much he came straight back for more.' The way she peers into my eyes, it's like she's trying to look inside my soul. 'If you wanted to take things further there, I guarantee he wouldn't refuse.'

For a second the pit of my stomach turns to syrup. Then I land right back in the real world and come to my senses. Of course I bloody wouldn't be up for anything of the kind. What is my body thinking? But before I can let out my full scream of protest Jess comes into view, her wide-leg linen trousers flapping as her loafers clip clop on the floorboards.

Her eyes are shining as she comes towards us. 'However much Ken and Gary are stretching it with those hot pants, they're excelling themselves at getting the crowds in.' As she smooths her aqua chiffon blouse, her laser gaze is directed straight at me. 'Here, take some mint to your lovely friend over there. Four weeks at sea, he must be in need of some greens.'

That's the funny thing about Jess – wherever she is in the building, she still knows what's going on. Who else would pick up on windcheater guy from two floors away?

But luckily I'm spared that, because Jess starts clinking a

spoon very loudly on a cocktail jug. The moment the buzz in the room dies down she clears her throat. 'So, a *very* big welcome to the first of our anniversary celebrations and our first ever joint event with the singles club. As most of you know, here at Brides by the Sea we've always waved the flag for solo flyers ...' She pauses to beam around at everyone.

This isn't just a sales pitch, it's actually true. For years after the shop opened the team here were all single, independent, and happy to stay that way. It's only in the last couple of years that one by one, despite not looking, they've unexpectedly found their happy-ever-after partners – even her.

Jess's grin moves seamlessly into an eye roll at her roguish and rather crumpled fiancé, Bart, who is leaning a shoulder on the whisper-grey wall. Not only did he give her the fireworks, he also happens to own a fabulous stately home in Rose Hill.

She carries on. 'Lately, Brides by the Sea has been like cupid dust for couples. So make the most of that while you're here this Valentine's Day! Take a leaf out of my book – be brave and give love a chance!'

There's cheering and clapping around the room. Jess is a pro when to comes to working a crowd. She knows exactly the right moment to start again. 'At Brides by the Sea we always like to offer you something special ...' She waits to get everyone's attention. 'Anyone who has their photo taken by Milla tonight and put up on our Valentine's Day board can come and claim a ten percent discount ...' she pauses for effect, '... at any point in the future. Regardless of who you're getting married to.'

As Poppy grins at me she's shaking her head. 'That's Jess for you, she wouldn't let a tiny detail like someone being with a different partner down the line get in the way of a sale.'

Jess is gazing around the room like an empress surveying her subjects. 'So there's no time to lose! Get those bottoms on the loveseat and your photos on the board!' She whips around and fixes me with her gaze. 'What are you waiting for, Milla? Grab that camera and get snapping!'

I'd be more pleased about this if I hadn't just glimpsed the back of a Diesel windcheater still in the room.

By the time the crowd thins out a lot later, I've lost count of how many Polaroid film packs I've got through and the corkboard hanging on the shop wall is covered in cute retro-tint photos. Poppy came to help too, which was great, all the way to the last customer. But truly, I could do without the eyebrow action she's giving me as she ushers windcheater guy into the corner. By the time he finally sidles towards the curve of the white-painted seat, his coat is over his arm. I'm staring at a dark, hand-knitted jumper and frantically checking around to see if he's got anyone with him.

'So is it ...' not meaning to discriminate against people on their own, but for the sake of the picture I need to check '... just you?' Behind him Poppy's eyebrows have switched into overdrive.

He pulls a face. 'It was, last time I checked. That's still good for the discount?'

Poppy jumps in. 'No worries there.'

He laughs. 'If I'm planning a big spend, I can't say no to an offer like that.'

Poppy's eyes widen. 'Maybe you should be having a chat with Jess?'

His nose wrinkles. 'I do have quite a few weddings on the horizon. But there's no rush.'

I can't ignore a boast that's even bigger than his yacht one. 'Well, let's hope all your wives will be very happy.' As for where the hell that came from, I'm as shocked as anyone. I don't wait for a reaction, instead, I nod at the loveseat and lift the camera. 'Well, make yourself comfortable for now, I'm ready when you are.' I'm just lining up the angle when there's a whoosh from across the room and the camera is wrenched out of my hands.

As Jess shoulders me out of the way, she's beaming down at windcheater man. 'It'll spoil the composition if we don't use the whole seat. Why don't you pop on there too, Milla?'

If I wasn't so surprised, I'd already have given her a thousand very good reasons. As it is, the best I can do is to grab hold of Poppy and drag her down with me. 'One of us either side of you, how's that?' I flash a smile at Jess. 'Three for the price of two. What's not to like?'

It's only as we wedge our hips down between the chair arms that I realise my big mistake. With two on the seat there'd have been space for a gap between us. As three of us crash down there's a muffled crack somewhere under my bottom, but so long as the seat's holding up I'm not mentioning it. As I aim for my best selfie face I'm rammed so hard against a certain woolly jumper that I'm not only getting the pattern of the stitches printed on my skin through my playsuit, I can also feel every single torso muscle underneath it.

'Big smiles all round!' Jess is properly purring. 'Then hold that for a couple more clicks. Okay, it's in the can. You can relax!'

All I can say is, it's good that I've spent the last year perfecting smiling when I'm hating every second. A guy's arm extending around my waist isn't what I'd meant to allow in my life again, even if it does ease the crush. And I hadn't planned to have stubble pressing against my cheek either. As for his delicious scent, with a lungful instead of my earlier noseful I'm practically passing out. I'm also close enough to see I wasn't the only one with pink smudges on my ear.

Poppy is first to unwedge herself. 'Hey, nice aftershave. Is that Paco Rabanne?'

As I try to stand up, there's a resistance that's a lot more than my hair wisps catching in his beard. Then, instead of an answer to Poppy's fragrance question, there's a loud squawk. Windcheater guy yelps and clutches his side as I'm finally on my feet.

His voice rises in protest as he points at a stick that's appearing from the loose knit of his jumper. 'Hey, Cupid, I thought you said you weren't firing? You just scored a bull's-eye!'

Oh crap. My stomach drops so fast I feel sick. When I look down at my pouch my arrows are splintered and I'm definitely one short. At least that clears up what the cracking sound was. On balance, the seat collapsing under our weight might have been better. 'I'm so, so sorry! Have I impaled you? Are you hurt?'

He lifts his sweater and stares at his ribs. 'No worries, it's only a scratch.'

There's the six pack I already knew about. As for the bronzed stomach I get an eyeful of as well, that's just another given that goes with the territory. Then I take in a slick of red sliding downwards, huge and bright against his tan. 'Shit, you're *bleeding*!'

You know that thing with emergencies? Sometimes you freeze. And sometimes you leap into action but it's like someone else is moving your limbs. That's what happens to me now. Before I know it, I've jumped up and snatched a handful of tissues from the mother-of-the-bride decorated hanky box. By the time I'm back my hand is already so far up his jumper to mop up the blood that most of my arm's disappeared too.

I'm not sure if it's due to the warmth inside his sweater or the flush of embarrassment, but, whatever, I'm super-heated, puce, and there are sweat rivers trickling down inside my sequins.

Sera, the dress designer, wanders over, her thumbs through the belt loops of the ripped denim shorts she always wears. She pushes back an armful of sun-streaked curls and laughs as she starts to gather up the blood-streaked hankies. 'What's going on here? It looks like something out of *Call the Midwife*. Hang on, I'll get the first-aid box.'

Windcheater guy's shaking his head. 'I just sailed the Atlantic single-handed, I think I can manage without the paramedics.' As he turns to look up at me, he's grinning. 'In any case, I'm being very well looked after here.'

Don't ask me how, but I manage to grab more tissues with my spare hand, and ram them into his. But in the end it's just easier to let him lean back and pull up his top, while I take the largest plaster in the box from Sera and stick it into place.

He lets his top drop again and passes me a piece of splintered stick. 'You were firing with a broken arrow, no wonder you were six inches too low. If you're aiming for my heart, you'll have to try again.'

I'm smiling like a crazy person despite wishing I could crawl into a hole. 'Maybe next year?' Like I'll be around – of course I damn well won't.

It's definitely not that he's smouldering – that's just the colour of his eyes. 'I might have sailed off into the sunset by then.' As he stands and squares up to me, I can't be the only one to have noticed the width of his shoulders. His low-slung jeans. The bulge below that scuffed leather belt. 'One last chance to take aim while I'm stationary … It's a lot harder to hit a moving target.'

I snap my eyes shut to close out the view, then flash back at him. 'And it's even more impossible if I'm driving at top speed in the opposite direction.' Hashtag, camper van in a hurry, me getting the hell out of here. Just saying.

Jess is beaming. 'Except you might not be, Milla.'

'Cupid's honour, I will.' That's one thing I'm certain of.

She narrows one eye. 'I'm pretty confident I may be changing your mind on that very soon.'

Windcheater guy chimes in too. 'If you're sticking around then keep the permit as long as you want.'

Jess spins round to windcheater guy. 'So if you're all plastered up, unless you'd like to propose to anyone here right now and get the bridal ball rolling, we'll look forward to seeing you again when you're back to claim your discount. Anything and everything to do with weddings, we take it on. Remember, no job too large or too small!'

He ignores her immediate challenge, but his lips twist again. 'I'll see you very soon then.' He hesitates. 'Unless I can tempt you to carry on at mine? It's not my yacht, but it's big enough for all of us. I can soon whip up some rum and banana pancakes with cream and toffee sauce. You're very welcome to come aboard.'

I watch Jess weighing it up. Even though she's with Bart, she's never one to turn down offers from dreamboats, especially ones with their own sea-going transport.

She sounds a lot more decided than I expected. 'We're actually having a small private function here later, so sadly we'll have to pass on that one.'

That's Jess speaking for herself but using the royal "we". In my head I'm already digging into a stack of pancakes with lashings of whipped cream. 'Well maybe I could ...'

Jess lets out a cry. 'A private party with you as guest of honour,

Milla.' She lets out a husky laugh. 'Be in the studio in half an hour's time, I've a proposition for you.'

We all know that's not a tone you argue with. And I'm bracing myself for what she's going to hit me with. Because however much I dislike what she might suggest, I'm not sure I'll be strong enough to resist.

But on the plus side, I've got through tonight without too much wailing in public. I have slightly impaled a customer, but I've managed not to spill drinks on anyone. And even though I'm a crappy cupid, it's probably better that my arrow didn't score a direct hit on windcheater guy's heart. I'm in enough trouble with that one as it is.

Chapter 3

Friday, Valentine's Day.
The Studio, Brides by the Sea, St Aidan.
Bubbles and big bangs.

'I'd love to be heading into our anniversary year with business looking up not down, Milla, but like everyone else, we've felt the squeeze lately.'

Poppy, Jess, and I have climbed the narrow winding stairs leading from the downstairs showroom to the studio, crossed the creaking waxed-wood floor, and now we're peering out of the small square panes of the sash window at the far end of the room. Far below, the dark ripples of the water are giving way to pale lines of breakers as they slide backwards and forwards up the beach. And after the upbeat whoosh of free cocktails, the truth feels like a chilly wind. I know the fun has gone out of weddings for me for a totally different reason but where the industry was seriously overheating seven years ago, now it's entering an ice age. I'm just surprised a rock-solid outfit like Jess's is feeling the effects.

'You're surely not telling me Brides by the Sea is in trouble?'

Jess raises an eyebrow. 'We never use the "t" word here, Milla. Even when a mother-of-the-groom chopped too much off the bottom of a beautiful bridal dress the night before the wedding, we called it an issue not a disaster.'

Poppy's face crumples. 'Truly, that must have been the worst night, but I missed it because I was in hospital with fake contractions.' She turns to me. 'Didn't you do a blog piece about it afterwards?'

I'm nodding. 'It did feature in my tips for taking care with dress alterations. It would be less of a problem now since the most forward-thinking Bristol brides are showing ankles.'

Poppy blows out a breath. 'The point was, everyone pulled together and by morning they came through smiling.'

Jess nods. 'Just as we will this time.'

As I look around the white-painted walls of the studio, the half-finished dresses hanging on rails are silky in the pools of light from hanging shades. There are fragments of lace scattered across the work area, and sketches and scraps of pictures covering the pinboard and I'm already thinking what a gift of a piece the studio will make for my Brides Go West wedding blog. It was Poppy who gave me a scoop introduction for a blog piece a few years ago when celebrity Josie Redman chose Sera, Jess's main designer, to make her wedding dress. It's always been one of my favourite bridal shops to visit.

Better still, the shop is the perfect inspiration for copy in winter when there are fewer real weddings to feature. I write all the Brides Go West social media content, so I'm always on the lookout for pretty things to photograph and new angles for pieces. By the time I've trawled every corner here I'll have inspiration to keep our followers clicking through until more weddings start up again in the spring.

Jess may have put a flute of Prosecco in my hand, but we're in the same business. She watches the bubbles rising in her glass and the bow on the low neck of her chiffon blouse heaves as she takes a breath. 'It's no secret – in a global economic slow-down, weddings are the first casualty.'

I usually leave conversations like this to Phoebe. Talking about anything global makes me feel like someone else is moving my mouth. 'Most people just don't have the cash to splash anymore.'

'In a nutshell, Milla, that's my point exactly.' Jess taps a pale russet nail on the windowsill. 'Weddings without limits took the shop to fabulous places but we have to face it – those heady days are over.'

I know exactly what she means. 'Suppliers used to fight to get a place at our wedding fairs, but lately a lot of them can't afford it. In the city now it's more about budgets than blow-outs. And being kind to the planet, of course.'

Jess's stare is intense. 'This is why you're invaluable, Milla. Whatever the cosmopolitan brides are embracing will be trending here next season.'

I smile. 'Meghan certainly turned the bridal mindset upside down when she walked down the aisle in that classically simple dress of hers. And more and more brides are going for gowns like Ellie Goulding's, with high necks and statement sleeves.' Sensing Jess nodding, I'm throwing it all in. 'But today's couples think about every penny before they spend it. And when they do, vegan menus are big, silent discos are popping up everywhere, and some couples are even going alcohol-free.'

Poppy's nodding in agreement. 'That's true. We had one of those over Christmas at Daisy Hill Farm. They had afternoon tea, then it was berry cordial all the way until home time.'

Jess has her disgusted-of-St-Aidan face on and her voice rises to a rant. 'This is what we're up against – pinching the pennies, lace-free and no booze! How bloody boring is that?' She blows out a breath. 'The good part is, people will always get married. We've always offered our brides amazing value and the most startlingly beautiful, exquisite products. If there are fewer brides per square mile, we'll simply have to expand our reach.' She pauses to give me a piercing stare 'Which is where you and your alchemy come in, Milla.'

'My *what*?' Just when I'm giving myself silent cheers for keeping up, my patchy education comes back to haunt me. I've never quite got over being the only person in any room without a single exam under their belt. The thing is, back then, missing the exams happened without me noticing. But there are big gaps in my knowledge. It's the strangest thing – when you do know something, it's often no big deal; when you don't, the chasm between you and everyone else is huge.

As a teenager, when Mum was ill, she never actually asked me to stay home. Her illness started as a tingle in her fingers and ended in total paralysis. At first, all we noticed was her stumbling. But as her condition got worse, she needed me there to look after her and I couldn't do anything else. So long as my younger brothers went to school, that was all that mattered to me.

If it happened now, I'm sure there would be social workers chasing me down. But back then the teachers understood we were struggling and were kind enough not to cause us any more grief. I was a write-off. The important thing was that my mum saw my brothers come through with straight A's before we lost her.

Looking after my mum certainly gave me a strong stomach for the grittier side of life. Her illness was always two jumps ahead of us; as she was able to do less and less, I always felt like I was failing. And when it was all over, everyone assumed it would be a relief. But the only way I can describe it is that it felt like someone had split my chest open with an axe, then wrenched my heart out.

Somehow I stumbled my way to Bristol, and when all I had to do was work forty-five hours a week, and I could sleep whenever I wasn't clubbing, it felt like a part-time job. But gradually it dawned on me that there's a lot more to life than being capable. Being able to balance a bed pan and a breakfast tray while sticking on morphine patches and sorting out hospital transport only takes you so far.

But that's why it was so great for me when I accidentally hit on the wedding promotion business. My only claims to self-taught fame are knowing Photoshop inside out and being able to build a webpage in my sleep, and both of those were invaluable for the blog side of the work. With the wedding knowledge I've gathered along the way, I've somehow become an accidental expert in an area I adore. When it comes to weddings, I can hold my own with anyone, and I can't tell you how great that feels. As for discussions like this one, I'd usually have Phoebe around for backup. We might have been in an equal partnership, but we both know she's the one in charge. And that's why, in spite of everything, a part of me is still wishing she were here now – simply because she'd smooth through a meeting like this standing on her head.

'Hard times call for an inventive approach, Milla.' Jess is tapping her nail on her glass. 'This is why we're desperate for your input with the Faceplant side.'

Poppy stifles a smile. 'That's Jess's affectionate name for Facebook.'

I catch Poppy's wink from behind a dressmaker's dummy and take my chance to slide back into the conversation. 'I can certainly do a lot with your social media.' It's barely there, so it won't be hard.

Jess is nodding back. 'And the anniversary wedding fairs you're helping us organise will boost business too.'

'Absolutely.' That's one of Phoebe's favourite words; she says it all the time. It seems to be working for me here, even though I can't quite make myself smooth through to the snorty *bah* she always does after it.

But doing the fairs for Jess is another of my comfort zones, thanks to my long lists of fabulous suppliers and exhibitors all over the south west, built up over the years since Phoebe got married. Messaging them and signing enough of them up for the shows shouldn't be too difficult. Until I find a new career, I'm going all-out with the blog and adding in some fairs for Jess.

Jess is giving me a searching stare. 'Poppy tells me Phoebe is usually the frontwoman for the fairs you do.'

I'm nodding. 'And obviously you and the shop staff will be fronting these ones.'

Jess's nostrils are flaring. 'We're very keen on professional development here. It'll be good for you to try that role too.' She obviously has no idea about my total inability to look impressive or tidy, or she wouldn't be suggesting this.

I'm not actually sure I could stay straight-faced for an entire day either, but I'm too professional to mention that now. 'Brill. Anything to do with weddings, I'm always up for a challenge.' I'd never get a chance like that with Phoebe, that's for sure. And if I think of it as a possible launchpad to a new career, I can put up with the pain.

As I glance at my phone, I see this has taken all of two minutes. Not that I've got any particular reason to go, because however many pictures of whipped cream and pancakes there are flashing through my head, I won't be heading for the harbourside. But I might persuade Poppy to nip down to the Hungry Shark with me after all. 'So if that's everything ...?'

Jess is laughing. 'I'm sorry if you're anxious to finish what you started with Nic Trendell, but I allocated us half an hour. That means there's twenty-three minutes of talking left to do.'

I'm frowning. 'I'm not sure I know anyone called Nic Trendell.'

As Jess flips a Polaroid photo out of her trouser pocket, I see Poppy and me laughing at the camera with windcheater guy jammed between us. I let out a shudder. Barely two hours ago I was pashing his face off; I could do without the everlasting reminder.

'The man from the loveseat wearing the Jean Paul Gaultier spray, remember? Not many guys can carry off the extreme version. Did you hear he sailed the Atlantic too?' Jess beams as she pushes the photo into my palm. 'I snapped an extra in case you wanted your own copy.'

It seems rude to say I'd be more likely to want to eat my own head, so I wrinkle my nose at Poppy, try not to think about the way my heart was clattering earlier in the van, and drop it in my bag. Then, to show I'm grateful I down my Prosecco in one, so I'm ready to run when the moment's right. Which wasn't a great idea because before my flute hits the coaster on the cutting table, Jess has it fully topped up again.

'So that's one Nic I definitely won't be getting to know.' Along with every other one in the world.

Jess lets out a chortle. 'I doubt you'd be too comfortable stowing away on his yacht. If it fits in the harbour here, it can't be that luxurious.' She turns to me again. 'So if all Poppy's cottages are full for half-term, where are you staying?'

Like a lot of other things, I'm glossing over this. As comfy accommodation goes, it's a total disaster. 'It's called The Loft.' The reviews from last July were dazzling, but I totally missed the ones saying that in February the gale howls through it so hard you'd get less windburn sleeping on the beach. I was there for all of five minutes earlier and that was nearly enough to give me frostbite.

Jess half closes one eye. 'That's the place with the draughts, isn't it?' Her nostrils flare again. 'When I first came here, I'd just split from my ex and I slept on the floor of the flower store. It wasn't great, but at least it means I recognise a person in need when I see one.' Jess pats my hand. 'When times are really tough, it usually means they're about to get better.'

My mum used to say something very similar. *Always believe something wonderful is about to happen, Milla. Then it will.*

I'm just glad she isn't here to see what a mess I've made of everything. But her voice is so real in my head it has me biting my lip and swallowing hard. I'm used to holding it together, but Jess being kind is making me crumble. I can't possibly start to cry now when I'm trying so hard to look serious and capable.

Poppy's smiling too, and she comes close enough to give my hand a little squeeze. 'What Jess wants to say is that she's happy to let you use the little attic flat here whenever you need it. Starting now.'

At least the shock stops my tears. 'Not the one with the sloping ceilings and the little round windows?' It's where Poppy stayed a few years ago, and I've often called in since when she's been doing her baking there.

Poppy's laughing. 'You'd have to promise to work as a cupcake taster too.'

'But that would be brilliant. Thank you so much.' My smile

widens as I think of the next couple of weeks curled up snug on a sofa, the scent of Poppy's chocolate muffins wafting through from the kitchen, instead of freezing my bum off in The Loft.

Jess nods. 'Why not have it for the next few months?'

My stomach has dropped. Running the fairs for the shop will mean I'll be visiting more this year, but when I planned my trip I was thinking ten days was a long time to be away from the city. Much as I love the thought of St Aidan as a bolthole, it's pretty much the end of my world, not the centre.

Poppy's nudging me. 'It's only until you get back on your feet again. Weren't we saying earlier how great new starts can be?' Thankfully she doesn't catch my eye.

Jess is beaming and seems to have missed that my cheeks have flushed beetroot red. 'If you had the attic as a base, you'd be on the spot for the other consultancy work I had in mind too.'

'Consultancy?' If I'm repeating it in a really high voice, it's only because it sounds more suited to Phoebe than me.

Poppy's laughing again. 'No need to panic, Mills. It's hard to find an actual job description for what Jess is thinking of.' She sends me another wink.

Jess is purring. 'Brides by the Sea is planning to offer a bespoke "go the extra mile" service to couples. And you're our number one candidate for the work.'

I'm confused. 'But what does it mean?'

Jess's eyes are shining. 'The whole point is that we'll only know what's needed when people actually ask. But it will be very exclusive, and it has the potential to super-charge our turnover.'

My insides are fluttering with the sudden uncertainty. 'You mean exclusive as in ... expensive?'

Jess nods. 'Any service this tailored has to come at a price. Obviously we'll take our cut, but you'll be very well remunerated. And it's supremely flexible too.'

Poppy's nodding frantically now. 'In other words, the pay will be fantastic, you'll never be bored, and you can fit the jobs around your other commitments.'

When I think of being at the far end of Cornwall, hours from lovely, buzzing Bristol, light years from fabulous London, on a bit of land sticking out into the sea, there's a shudder thudding down my spine – and not in a good way. But I'm also thinking about the money I borrowed from my brothers when we expanded Brides Go West. Even though they say they're loaded and what does a few grand each matter anyway, it would be so great to pay that back. And even if it's not where I'd ideally choose to be, if we're talking about widening my wedding experience, this could be another huge opportunity. If I'm dreaming of flying away from weddings altogether, this could give me the wings I need. So long as I can stomach a double dose of weddings in the meantime, which I'm not sure I can.

Jess is holding my gaze. 'As for upcoming jobs, they're superconfidential – but we've got a bride whose best friends are across the world and unavailable. She simply wants a right-hand woman on the day.'

Poppy's face is eager. 'It's like being head bridesmaid, but without the dress. You've done that before, haven't you?'

I'm nodding. 'Me being chief bridesmaid for Phoebe was the start of Brides Go West.' It all grew from the blog I did called My Best Friend's Wedding. We'd only met the year before at Costa, but by the time Phoebe said 'I do' we were both hooked on weddings. Growing the blog and running fairs was a great way to leave the coffee machines behind and do what we loved instead. Which is exactly the kind of lifestyle leap I'm looking for now. If I've done it once, it should be possible again.

Jess's eyes are shining now. 'How about you start there and we'll take each new job as it comes after that?'

I'm thinking of that tiny kitchen in the sky with the bright blue cupboards. And the cash. But from somewhere else there's a fantasy of a thought that if I take this offer, at some point down the line, I may never have to see Phoebe or Ben ever again. And if that's the final clincher that pushes me over the edge, I'll never know. But for some reason I'm hearing my own voice from a distance saying:

'Great, I'll take them both – the work, and the flat!' Then my sensible self catches up. 'At least until spring.' A few weeks away from Bristol ... even I should be able to manage that. As for the extra dose of all things bridal? Well, sometimes to get where you want, you have to suffer first. So long as I think of it like that, I can grit my teeth and put up with it.

'So, welcome to Brides by the Sea, Milla. I promise you won't regret this.' Jess is sloshing more fizz into our glasses. 'Didn't I tell you you'd be leaving the bad times behind? And you know what else we need to work on? You feeling like you have to say yes to everyone, all the time!'

The irony isn't lost on me. But as Sera appears to ask if we're ready to join the party downstairs it feels like a done deal.

Chapter 4

Saturday, one week later.
The attic flat, Brides by the Sea.
Desert islands and muffin tops.

A whole week later, as I ease open my eyes and let in the pale light of another morning in the little attic flat, I'm listening to the cries of seagulls wheeling high above and the distant crash of waves on the shore below. If I'm missing the rumble of the traffic, it's only what I expected. I left here for Bristol when I was twenty-one ... when we lost Mum. It's not a thing you ever get over, but after a few blurry years you learn how to hold yourself together every time you re-remember, instead of falling apart. The noise of the city and numbing my brain at the all-night dance clubs somehow helped me cope with the gaping chasm where Mum should have been; if I'd stayed around here, I might just have walked into the sea.

As I push back the duvet, kneel on the high bed under the low sloping ceiling, and lean towards the round porthole window, I shudder at the resounding emptiness of all that ocean. It's no less desolate or uncomfortable than it was the first morning. There's just such a jarring contrast compared to where I've come from, and the flat I've left behind forever.

The old place was clunky and Victorian. Not all the rooms were nicely decorated and some of the plaster was flaking, but at least they were ours. When we moved in, a part of me felt like it was so amazing it had to be too good to be true ... which turned out to be pretty accurate, because in the end it was.

The things I liked most about that flat, other people couldn't see. I adored the constant revving of the engines from the road outside, in the same way people here lap up the noise of the sea. Far from being a problem, the wail of sirens in the early hours was a reminder that I was surrounded by civilisation. I loved that there were twenty all-night takeaways within a few hundred steps of the door, that I never had to worry about going hungry or shopping ahead. Of only being around the corner from a major A&E department. Not that I ever used it myself. I suppose it's a hangover from when my mum was ill, and we were at the hospital so often that I came to view it as the place that always sorted out our crises. As a healthy person, it's always great to know if you break your leg or have a heart attack, you're only ever two minutes away from being saved. You can't under-estimate how secure that made me feel.

As I peer past chimney pots and shiny slate roofs, the immense stretch of blue-black sea far below is scratched with dashes of white foam, and the layers of clouds above it are almost as dark. But if the outside seems so wild, the cosiness inside more than makes up for that. Like now, the delicious smell of coffee and vanilla drifting past my nose is so intense I could almost have my bed in the kitchen. I'm about to go and investigate when there's a tap on the door.

Poppy's head appears first, then a laden tray and her pink stripy apron. 'I've got drinks and white chocolate muffins here if it's not too early for breakfast?'

I can't hold back my smile as I take in the size of the muffin stack. 'You know I'm always ready for cake, but you don't have to wait on me.'

Poppy's nose wrinkles. 'You're technically still on holiday so being spoiled is fine. I've been here since six this morning doing final cupcake designs for a wedding reception next week, so I'm ready for a break.' She grabs a mug, takes a sip of her drink, and her muffin is already peeled.

'Go on, tell me every last drooly detail ...'

She grins. 'It's a drive-in-movie 50s-themed wedding party in a school gym. Think red checked paper cupcake cases, pink, baby-blue, and mint-green icing piped to look like ice cream, all finished with tiny triangle wafers and luscious fresh black cherries with bendy stalks. The main food is hot dogs served from a van with real ice cream sundaes delivered by waitresses on roller skates.'

'St Aidan brides know how to party!' I take a slug of coffee and peel back my own muffin paper. 'And when I finally get up, I promise I'll be dedicating my entire day to uploading my pictures from Brides by the Sea to Pinterest and pimping the Insta account.'

As well as taking photos all around the shop, I've also spent a lot of the last week pulling together lists of wedding suppliers around St Aidan and contacting a long list of venues all around the south west as potential hosts for Jess's special wedding fairs, so I reckon I'm due some playtime.

When Poppy looks over the top of her gold, spotty I'd-rather-be-drinking-prosecco mug she's giving a sheepish shrug. 'That's my other good-morning news. Jess has another customer for the special request service, they're popping in for a chat with you both later.'

'Wow, that was quick.' I'd counted on longer to work myself up to this.

Poppy glances at her phone and winks. 'Once our Jess gets an idea, she doesn't mess about. They'll be here in forty minutes, that's loads of time to get ready.'

As I close my teeth onto my first deliciously sweet mouthful of muffin, I'm kicking myself for not unpacking yet. But bringing in anything more than an overnight bag felt like too much of a commitment. 'Damn. My smart clothes are still in the van by the harbour.'

I'm making them sound better than they are. They're not beautifully laundered and pressed designer pieces, folded into matching suitcases of descending sizes, like Phoebe's would be. They're mostly strewn across the van floor and falling out of bin bags. And it's pointless pretending this is all down to the move because I may as well come clean here – wardrobe chaos is a natural failing. And, incidentally, one of the long list of reasons Phoebe came up with for why Ben would prefer her to me. Sad to say, my slipping bow and broken Valentine's arrows are pretty much how it is. And talking of quivers, as I've been around town all week without catching even the smallest glimpse of windcheater guy, I'm hoping he's sailed off into the sunset and taken his perfect pecs and the very disturbing rest with him.

Poppy's looking down at yesterday's skirt and top, in a heap on the polished boards where they fell as I got into bed. 'They'll do fine, you know you always look fabulous.'

My lips spread into a grin. 'Phoebe wouldn't agree. She tells me off all the time for having creases in the wrong places.'

Poppy laughs. 'Stop worrying about what Phoebe says! In sleepy St Aidan, a little bit of city style goes a long way.' She pops the last bit of her muffin into her mouth and finishes her drink. 'I'd better dash. If you need me, I'll be up and down putting cake into the car. There's loads of hot water for a shower.'

'Brill.'

As Poppy backs out of the room, she slides my clothes onto a hanger and hooks it over the copper-pipe clothes rail. 'The creases will have dropped out by the time you come out of the bathroom. I'll tell Jess you'll be down soon.'

As for St Aidan being sleepy, I'd say it's wide awake this morning. By the time I've coiled up my hair and let the steaming shower spray pummel my back, I'm refreshed and ready to go too. A few minutes later I'm in my T-shirt and pants hurrying back to the kitchen for a last cup of coffee and the rest of the muffins before I get properly dressed. Let's face it, this is my first face-to-face client meeting at the shop, I'm going to need all the calories I can get.

I'm halfway – well, two steps – back across the landing heading for a comfy seat when I hear a bump, which is strange as Poppy last clattered downstairs a while ago. As I nudge open the living room door, I'm looking at the usual – blue sofas, porthole windows, stripy rug – but what I see this side of the big vase of dusky blue anemones makes me freeze. When Poppy was running through the operating instructions for the flat she mentioned lots of things, but I swear a guy stripping off by the coffee table wasn't one of them.

Excuse me …

His shirt has hit the floor, and he's hopping around in his socks, getting out of his trousers too.

What the hell!

It hits me that I'm moving my mouth but there's no actual sound coming out.

As he whips round to face me, my gaze locks on some rather

fitted Calvin Klein undies and what Phoebe would have referred to – with very tight lips – as his lunchbox.

Denim blue has to be the sexiest colour of all in that it shows every line and contour. Which makes it even more embarrassing that my eyes are welded to that when there's a whole six feet and more of guy I could be looking at.

When I finally manage to yank my eyes upwards, at first I'm held up by the line of hair running up a very flat stomach. Then I finally get past that, leapfrog his navel, and come to some super-tanned abs. I'm seeing if I can actually count six in this pack when my gaze slides sideways. As my eyes come to rest on a jagged red scar just below his ribs, my heart stops banging and contracts so hard it feels like it's disappeared entirely.

Of all the lunchboxes in all the world, this one has to land here.

'It is Milla, isn't it?' His mouth curves into a grin. 'So this is where you've been hiding. I wondered where you'd gone.'

As my indignance rises, I finally get my act together 'What the hell are you doing?'

'I could ask you the same thing.' This is windcheater guy; he's not going to hold off on the backchat. 'Oliver had a bit of a crush in Groomswear so he sent me up to the overspill attic changing area. He warned me Poppy was up here baking, but he didn't mention there would be barely-dressed women up here too.'

Damn. This far I've been so bedazzled by his bare skin, I totally forgot about mine. 'Sorry to disappoint you but there's only me. And where I come from, a sleeping T-shirt and shorts counts as fully clothed, not undressed.'

In his anchor-print socks and Calvin's he's in no position to judge, even if my briefs are exactly what it says on the tin. No doubt they'd be huge on someone whose bottom was smaller, but on me they're teeny. It's also worth mentioning that they don't go with my top either. The joy of mismatching pyjamas is one advantage I've totally rocked since being single. Ben getting picky about tops and bottoms and pairs going together is one bit of the relationship I was not sad to wave goodbye to.

But back in the attic, just to be on the safe side, I yank my top down, keep my eyes low, and definitely don't dwell on how Nic's got exactly the right amount of hair on his thighs to make your insides melt. I slam my eyes closed before I get to thinking how it would feel to run my fingernails over the pale strip of skin on the inside of his leg. If he'd be ticklish. Or just super-appreciative.

From his low laugh, I wonder if he's read my mind. 'There's no need to stalk me, Milla. If you want me to take my shirt off, you only have to ask ...' The smile he's holding back breaks free again.

'Dream on, mate.' There's male beauty we don't mind appreciating even when it takes us by surprise on Saturday morning. And then there's knowing you've got a body to die for and assuming every girl wants a piece of it. Which is way less attractive.

'If you'd like to see more of me this week, I'll mostly be down at the harbour. Just ask for Nic Trendell.' His eyes spark for a moment, then he looks away and snatches a glance at his watch. 'And much as I'd love to stay, I'm due at my next appointment.'

'Fabulous.' It's totally not. If my feet weren't welded to the spot, there's no way I'd be watching him pick up his denim shirt from the sofa. Or notice that as he takes an inordinate amount of time to do up the buttons, I'm back to letting out mental *phwoars* at how taut those thighs are. Or be picking my jaw off the floor as I watch him pull up his jeans and zip in.

If there's an upside, it's that you can't feel guilty for mentally undressing a guy when he's already stripped off in front of you. And if there's a sense of anticlimax, not relief, as he finally buckles his belt and tucks in his shirt, there's no way I thought that.

He's picking some smart navy trousers off the floor and sliding a white shirt onto a hanger. Pulling a face at the jacket that follows. 'I'd take ocean-going waterproofs over satin lapels every time myself, but at least the fit's perfect.' He dives past me towards the door. 'Let's make sure we have breakfast together very soon.'

I'm ignoring the butterfly storm in my chest that his offer unleashes. Instead I growl softly, 'Over my dead body.'

He's not the only person in the world with a busy Saturday morning. Below, the shop is buzzing. I'm in a hurry too, but before I open my mouth to say so, he's already out of the door and bounding down the stairs. Hopefully to the other side of town. Or better still, a whole lot further.

As for me, I need to smooth out my skirt, paint on some eyebrows, then start hoping like hell that whatever request is coming my way, it's something tiny that will be over very fast.

Chapter 5

Later the same Saturday.
The Style File, Brides by the Sea.
Special offers and discount codes.

'Talk about a coup for our Special Request service, Milla! Even with the ten percent discount claim this one is *huge*!'

This is Jess a few minutes later. And as she marches me down the stairs and into the wonderful basement department known as The Style File, my stomach is quaking more with every exclamation.

I've lost count of the hours I've spent down here this last week. I've put my personal discomfort to one side and pointed my camera at everything from clusters of candles to flowers in pots, past vintage dressing tables reinvented as wedding cake stands and themed place settings, to light-up signs saying L-O-V-E. There's so much bridal pretty crammed between the chalky lime-washed and bare brickwork walls my memory stick is bursting.

Jess steers me to a metal table by the big French doors and clinks down a bottle and three glasses. 'No need to look so worried, Milla. Have a glass of fizz and relax.'

As we sit down in the warmth of a sun splash and I look

past a tiny outside courtyard full of lanterns to a tiny patch of iron-grey sea beyond, I know it'll take more than a few bubbles to calm me down.

'A big job ... in what way?' In theory, I should be able to handle anything wedding-related, but there's the pressure of doing it in a new setting. I'd assumed that being a bride's right-hand woman was as big as the job was going to get. We've been emailing each other this week; Calista is super-friendly, extra pretty – judging by her Insta photos – and rocking the cool New Yorker thing, and the most she's asked for so far is my dress size and that I carry her tissues for her.

It's a measure of my state of high-alert and how anxious I am to make a good impression that I'm rubbing at a scuff on my kitten heels. Usually I wouldn't give scruffy shoes a second thought, let alone try to hide them, but I'm desperate not to let Jess down here. And much as I'd rather not know the details of the upcoming job if it's huge enough to put me outside my comfort zone, I'd rather find out the worst before the customer arrives.

When Jess lowers her voice so the others can't hear, it's breathy with excitement. 'We have a very charming but clueless gentleman who's wanting to put together his very own *Don't Tell the Bride!* wedding.' She pauses to pop the cork and passes me a full glass. 'He needs you to hold his hand all the way from now until the big day in July.'

One partner taking sole charge may be great for shock-value TV, but in real life not so much. 'It'll be fine if he's easy-going. If he's in any way picky, early summer could prove pretty impossible.'

That's the catch about the wedding world – the run-up times are traditionally very long because perfection can't be hurried.

Couples book venues as much as three years ahead and dresses are ordered in September for delivery the following spring. A fast-track wedding is fine for anyone happy to take what's left over but you have to be prepared to compromise.

On the other hand, there can be advantages to fast-tracking. I can't say I'd recommend the kind of endless engagement that Ben and I had, where years went by and he always found another excuse not to set a date. Looking back, I'm sure the only reason we bought the flat was so he had yet another reason to avoid the wedding.

'Impossible's not an attitude we ever have in this shop, Milla.' Jess is snapping and wagging her finger, then she's back to a purr. 'It's wonderful to have uptake for our Special Request service so soon. And better still, he's willing to pay top money for a top job.'

'It's a big responsibility! I hadn't planned on this length of commitment.' The sound of my wail tells me how much I don't want to be here for so long. As for working so closely on a real-life wedding, that's another thing that has those horribly familiar, invisible steel fingers closing around my gut.

'This would work wonders for putting you on the map, Milla. We both know you can deliver on this.' She pulls a crystal-covered pen and pad out of her pocket, scribbles, and pushes the paper towards me. 'See if this estimate of earnings sweetens it any.'

As I take in the long row of figures after the pound sign, my wide eyes stretch. 'But that's an enormous amount!' Ridiculous even. The calculator in my brain is clicking. If I added in other jobs alongside, a lump like that would go a long way towards paying off my brothers. But cash isn't everything.

She nods. 'It's only in line with the demands of the job. But just think, after this you'd be a fully proven solo wedding planner, and a lot less beholden to Phoebe. It's worth taking on, if only for that.' Her eyes are gleaming, then her face lights up even more. 'And here he is now. Such a shame it turns out he's spoken-for after all, but he's going to be a dream for you to work with all the same.'

As I turn my jaw drops and my stomach follows it. The shirt and jeans coming towards me are very familiar, but at least the Calvin's are covered this time around.

If there's a stab in my chest as the implications hit me, I'm not admitting to it. It doesn't matter a jot to me if he's taken or not when I've got no interest in him or anyone else in a romantic way. In fact, him being off the market makes life a whole lot easier – at least it'll get Poppy off my case.

At the same time, I want the ground to open up and swallow me, because if he's this spoken-for I can't imagine what Poppy can have said to bully him into that kiss last week. I mean, what kind of engaged guy gives out Valentine's kisses to anyone who asks? Although I may have answered my own question earlier. Up in the flat he certainly acted like he was God's gift to women. And I have to take some responsibility for how long that kiss went on; if I hadn't had a year's drought and pulled him in, it might have been over in a nanosecond.

And that's before we get to all the over-exposure that just happened in the attic. As for Poppy and me crushing him onto the loveseat ...! If the bride sees that photo of the three of us, the wedding could be over before it began. Then, as he walks the whole length of the room, I'm desperately trying to ditch the version of myself who just flashed him and find the one who's up to the job.

'Good morning, Mr Trendell ... again.' Apart from my stran-gled hedgehog impression, I just about nail it.

Jess ups her purr from kitten to tiger. 'Come and sit down, Nic. We've found you the perfect person to guide you all the way from now until the big day.' She nods at me. 'You and Milla have already met, haven't you?'

I'm straight in behind her to cover that one up. 'And *Don't Tell the Bride!* too ... how much fun is that?' My whoop is so loud, I'm definitely overcompensating. 'Not much time, but don't worry, we'll nail it.'

Nic's pulling a face. 'I'd call it anything but fun myself.' He shakes his head. 'People entrust me with multi-million-pound vessels every day of the week at my boat piloting agency, but I have no idea where to start with this.' It's hard to believe that the long-faced groom who's turned up here is the same jokey guy I saw way too much of barely ten minutes ago. He must have switched to his getting-married persona on his way down the stairs, because one thing's for sure; this version of Mr Trendell wouldn't have been dishing out snogs willy-nilly.

Jess's nostrils flare. 'I'm afraid it takes a lot more knowledge to put on a wedding than to drive a yacht, Nic!' She's looking at him as if she'd like to eat him. 'But if you're looking for expert help you won't find better than Milla.'

I have zero idea about boats, but Jess is right about the size of this; more importantly, as it's sinking in how much time I'll have to spend with the groom, my body's getting sweatier and my feet are getting colder.

Nic's clearing his throat. 'What I do know is, this is the most important day of two people's lives. There's absolutely no room for error.'

Last time he saw me in the shop I was pouring out love potions – or more probably spilling them. I've got ten seconds to convince him I can up my game from that. 'Weddings are our business. I promise we're trained to deliver excellence in high-stakes situations.' At least that's given me a few minutes' leeway to decide if I can actually face this. And big mistake number one is that I didn't even think about putting my Spanx on. If I'd known this was coming, I'd have trussed myself up to be more impressive and less wobbly.

As Jess narrows her eyes, I can see she's as aware of Nic's doubtful expression as I am. 'And that's exactly why we've chosen Milla for you. Her appreciation of the latest trends is second to none, she knows weddings and suppliers inside-out.'

It would be easier for Jess if she was pulling me out of a bag all fresh and new but Nic Trendell's already seen a lot more of me than she realises. Begging for kisses in a car park. Prancing around in a mini-jumpsuit and wings. Stuffing my arm up his jumper after I accidentally stabbed him. I can hardly blame him for thinking twice – it's a big ask for me to move on from that lot and reinvent myself as a shiny professional who commands shedloads of cash.

Nic's wrinkling his nose. 'I always employ top-flight personnel for the agency.'

Jess's jaw is clenched. 'As we do here.'

Sometimes it pays to get things out into the open rather than trying to hide them. As I turn to Nic, I make my smile extra bright. 'I know I missed with my arrow, and my pyjama bottoms didn't go with my top. And I appreciate fewer sequins and longer skirts would be classier on a daily basis ...'

He stops to give a shrug. 'If I'm being brutally honest, I'm worried about much bigger issues here than kittens chasing pompoms.'

So he did see my pants. Damn!

Which means he also saw my legs all the way up to my

bottom and possibly beyond. And I know I didn't stint on the similar view of him. But how can I ever come back from that? And that's before we even get to the bit where I tried to eat his face off.

'I fail to see the relevance of sleepwear!' Jess's eyebrows are somewhere around her hairline.

I'm almost squeaking. 'On the upside, I'm really strong on the fun elements, which are the bits the guests will remember and talk about forever.'

Nic pulls in a breath. 'Okay, let's take this back to a more professional place. In the day job I employ hard-hitting, practical people, and I'd like to do the same here.' The way he's frowning at my feet it seems he's not impressed by the lack of heels. 'So how about courses or certificates? Put my mind at rest, Milla, tell me about those.'

My heart plummets because he couldn't have asked me a worse question. As for my shoes, I knew I should have gone for the super-high ones that really make me look like I can kick ass as well as Phoebe does. If it hadn't been for four flights of stairs I would have. I'm so totally sunk here that I'm opening and closing my mouth and nothing's coming out. But Jess is staring at Nic like he's about two inches tall.

'With all due respect, Nic, we're talking brides here, not harbour tugs. In this industry it's experience, capability, and a huge capacity for hard work that are the keys to success. Paper rarely comes into it.' Her sniff couldn't be any more condescending. 'I'm completely confident that Milla will deliver all the way from the save-the-date cards to the going-home taxis.'

Nic tilts his head. 'Save the what?'

I jump in to explain to cover for Jess's eye roll. 'They're cards you send to the guests in advance. But first you need a guest list. And with your tight schedule you'll have to sort the dress and the caterers, like, yesterday.'

'Okay.' From Nic's bemused stare it's clear he has no idea about any of it. He swallows and as he speaks his voice is low and dry. 'Getting this right is the biggest responsibility of my entire life. I can't afford to gamble here.'

I have one chance to show him I'm up to this; if he's this desperate for some super-executive I'll have to haul out my most sophisticated side. I sit up really straight in my chair and take a huge breath to try to make myself as tall as Phoebe, but all that happens is my merino knit jumper gets really tight so my boobs stick so far out Mr Trendell's eyes almost pop out.

So I abandon that and concentrate on my lower half. I try to cross and uncross my legs a couple of times like Phoebe does so effortlessly, but with shorter legs it's a lot less elegant. In fact, it isn't working at all. In the end, all that happens is my pencil skirt rides up really high and ends up like a tourniquet around my thighs, and worse still, I have a horrible feeling that Nic got yet another unscheduled view of my pants. By the time I've realigned the split in my pleather skirt, his face is fully buried in his hands.

After what feels like forever, he looks up and blows out a breath. 'Cards on the table, my ideal person specification would be someone more like you, Jess.'

Jess looks as if she might explode. 'However much you're willing to throw at the problem, Nic, you couldn't afford me.'

This is my time to bow out gracefully. 'I know I could deliver you a wonderful day, Mr Trendell, but if you've set your heart on someone with a stack of certificates, that's obviously not me.'

He pulls a face. 'Thank you for your honesty, Milla.'

As I stand up and collect my squishy velvet bag from the

floor, I'm kicking myself again. As two faces turn to me their mouths are hanging open.

'When you do find her though, don't hang around. Get straight on to choosing a venue; July is a popular time.' I have no idea why I'm still going, but I throw in a last thought for sisterly solidarity. 'And remember, modern hens definitely prefer spa days to blow-up willies. Oh, and good luck ... you'll certainly need lots of that!'

I have the whole length of The Style File to listen to my pointy heels clicking on the wooden boards and thank my lucky stars that it's nothing to do with me anymore. Then I remember I've just waved goodbye to a whole wodge of cash. And possibly the attic flat too. But at least I've saved myself from six months of wall-to-wall weddings. And I'll be saved from seeing Nic Trendall ever again. If that last thought is making me feel even a little bit disappointed, I won't be admitting it. Even to myself.

MARCH

Chapter 6

Saturday, one week later.
St Aidan school gym.
Shark attacks and second chances.

'You know the best thing about tonight, Milla?'
     It's a week later and Poppy's shouting at me as we cross the car park to the school, and I'm taking a wild guess and yelling back at her. 'The roller skates?'

She's shaking her head at me. 'It's that getting this last-minute request for wedding help means you can get straight on with the next job. And wave picky Mr Trendell and his arsey attitude out to sea.'

We both know there's no comparison between this job and the one I spectacularly failed to clinch last week, but it's nice of her to say. As for how much I let the side down with that, so far no one's made me feel bad about it. Jess just said in a very matter-of-fact way that my confidence needed a reboot and we'd talk about it later. Although, I have no idea what she means by that because this is nothing to do with confidence. It's back to the age-old stumbling block – me not ever being good enough to match up to expectations due to not having qualifications. However hard Phoebe worked at making me just like her, in reality people can tell the difference between the tower of power she was and the squashed-up version that's me. And Phoebe never missed a chance to point out my abysmal lack of paper-work. And now it's tripped me up again.

I mean, maybe I didn't want the job in any case. But despite Nic implying I'm a lightweight, I know I could have done it standing on my head with a blindfold on. At least this way I'm saved from having him looking down on me.

I'm shouting back to Poppy now. 'And remind me whose wedding it is tonight?' As we're pretty much crashing their party, it might be useful to know.

'Dave and Betty, better known locally as Danny and Sandy. She's head of Year 12, and the whole sixth form is invited. That's why they've gone with the High School theme and they're having the party here. But they're from further along the coast so there won't be too many people here we know.' If this is her way of reassuring me we're not going to run into Nic Trendell, I'm happy to cross that off my worry list.

I have to admit as we bounce along beside excited hordes of girls and women in their full, brightly coloured skirts, and guys flicking their Elvis quiffs, it's a long way from the quiet Saturday evening I'd anticipated.

Poppy's best friend, Immie, has also been roped in, and she jabs me in the ribs. 'And as you've kindly volunteered as desig-nated driver, Milla, expect Pops and me to cut loose!'

Immie looks after the holiday cottages at Daisy Hill Farm where Poppy lives with Rafe. I've known her my whole life too and she's always been the same – as wide as she is tall, telling it like it is. Taking on the world for her friends, while drinking Cornwall dry and whooping it to the max – the same way she's stepped in tonight. Although it sounds like leaving the dads in charge at home has gone to her head. If she's whirling her Barbour jacket in the air this early, we could all be in trouble.

There's another jab from Immie. 'You do know your van's getting more attention than those swanky American cars parked by the entrance, Milla.'

I laugh. 'There's no hiding it, I'm a driving advert for matrimony wherever I go.' More's the pity.

Immie wrinkles her nose. 'I know that pink you've painted it is supposed to be feminine, but it does remind me of fanny pads.' This is Immie. She doesn't hold back, but that's part of the whole honesty package. When I was at home with Mum, and not going to school, there was never a day when she didn't drop by. There was always shopping from her gran, or a snippet of goss from the school bus, or a magazine for Mum, passed on from one of her many aunties. Obviously we had carers coming in and out, and Poppy and her mum always came round with baking too. But along with them Immie was my main link to the outside world. So, after the way she kept me sane then, she can be as rude as she likes about my paint job.

Poppy's rolling her eyes at me. 'She won't be grumbling when you deliver us home. And with that light-up sign right along the roof, however plastered she is, she should get in the right van.'

Poppy said to me earlier, as she hauled me off the sofa, that Immie wouldn't have been her first choice to serve cocktails on roller skates at a wedding. At Daisy Hill events she's mostly back-of-house and under strict instructions not to swear in front of the guests. But thanks to the Falmouth Roller Derby team having a dodgy takeaway last night, they've been dropping like flies all day. The call for extra bodies to skate around adding atmosphere to the wedding party was less of a special request, more a howl of desperation. And as the bride is a friend of Jess's from way back, this is a favour rather than a big-money job. So here we are, swishing our ponytails, rocking our red pouts, and literally ready to roll.

As Poppy swings the door open, we can hear the sound of a twangy guitar and the first bars of *Baby I Love You*. 'The spare skates and clothes are in the changing rooms, we'll have to do the best we can.'

I pull a face at her. 'Seeing as none of us have skated for twenty years, I'd say the dresses are the least of our problems.'

Poppy sniffs. 'Don't worry about skating, it's exactly the same principle as Jilly's dance spectaculars when we were young. You do remember those?'

'As if I'd forget.' Along with every girl in Rose Hill, we spent our Saturdays doing dance classes at the village hall. And at the regular shows, so long as there was one fabulous dancer pirou-etting across the stage and sliding into the splits, all the rest of us had to do was arrange our feet and stand still, and people naturally assumed we could all do the same. 'So we hang on to the walls and leave the flashy stuff to the real skaters?'

Poppy's grinning. 'That's it.'

Except the next ten minutes prove me wrong. The skater dresses turn out to be skimpy stretchy cheerleader dresses rather than 50s-style knee-length ones in unflattering shades of dayglow, which probably wasn't even invented back then. As for me thinking I'd get the biggest because I'm the tallest by half an inch and the most curvy – wrong! In the end, Immie claims the longest due to having the widest waist, and I'm left with a skirt that's marginally shorter than my pyjama top and jaw-droppingly pink in the worst way.

Immie's waving her arms about, wildly shaking the silver foil pompoms on elastic bands on her wrists. 'These are going to play havoc when I'm sinking my pints, they'll dangle in the beer.'

Poppy's biting her lip the way she does when she's trying not to laugh. 'All ready to skate into the party then?'

I'm staring down at boots two sizes too small. 'I might do better if I could feel my feet.' Then I flick my frown to a beam. 'But – yay! Let's go for it!'

As we start to inch our way along, hanging off the changing room hooks, Poppy lets out a moan. 'This isn't anything like when we messed around in the village as kids.'

A nanosecond later, my feet whoosh from under me and my bottom thuds onto the lino. 'It's the wheels – these pro skates are extra whizzy!' That's my excuse and I'm sticking to it.

Another thud, and Immie lands beside me. 'With floors this smooth we're buggered.'

Put it this way – without one of the Falmouth skaters to open the door for us we'd never have made it out into the gym.

She grins at us as we pass. 'We're so grateful. Just leave the fast work to us! Have fun, don't over stretch!'

'We won't!' We're crawling past her on our hands and knees, exchanging WTF? glances.

Poppy hisses. 'Stay like this, and skirt around the edge?'

Immie's nodding. 'Head straight for the bar. It's down the front, by the wedding cake and the drive-in cars.'

No idea how she's so good at her directions when all we can see are a forest of legs, pumps, and sneakers, but I add my bit. 'Anywhere near the cherry muffins is good.'

As wedding parties go, it's a bit back-to-front. During the hot dogs and mass dancing, we sit at a group of tables with black-and-white-checked table cloths, and pretty floral decorations made from pink carnations in sundae glasses. We stick out our skates so people can see them, waggle our pompoms and say 'howdy' to the guys, who all seem to be in white T-shirts and tight jeans, making their way for beers and bottles of coke. This also gives Immie a chance to get well ahead on her beer-drinking while I make a dent in the muffin stack and the ice-cream sundaes.

The bride and groom are the spitting image of the stars from *Grease* and halfway through the evening, Betty/Sandy nips out and swaps her white knee-length lace and tulle wedding dress for some slinky black satin capri-pants that are so tight and shiny they could have been sprayed on. And then, even though they've already been rocking all night, they have their first dance, to *You're the One That I Want*, *wooohoooohoo* which couldn't have been any more fabulously choreographed. And it's so amazing, they do five encores.

By which time, someone's reminded us there are brake pads on the toes of the skates, so we finally attempt to move. Immie goes closer to the bar, and Poppy and I manage to tiptoe across enough open floor to admire the pastel-coloured buttercream rosette piping and the jiving bride and groom on top of the gorgeous four-tier cake she made, which will take centre stage in the cake cutting ceremony very shortly.

Then we find ourselves a very shiny turquoise blue convertible car, drape ourselves over it, and try to look obvious.

I grin at Poppy as I watch the real skaters swirling between bodies at top speed, skating backwards, spinning to a halt with their trays of drinks and ice creams. 'This is great.' My arm's wedged over the car window so it's like I'm superglued. 'If we jiggle our pompoms in time to the music, we look like we're pros taking a breather.'

Poppy shakes her head in mock despair. 'We're marginally

better than cardboard cutouts. But we were available, we are here, and better still, everyone knows we're flying the flag for Jess's new Special Request service.'

'And good luck to Mr T, I hope he finds himself the wedding planner he deserves.' I held it in as we arrived, but now I care less. 'He might find it hard, everyone decent will already be booked.'

'Which is why he should have snapped you up when he had the chance.' Poppy's eyebrows move up. 'You do know I saw him earlier?'

My stomach had no reason to drop like a high-speed lift. 'Really!?' With the hugest effort I yank my voice down so low I totally sound like I give no shits. Which is exactly the result I want. 'What the hell's he doing here?'

'Same as everyone else except us – he must have been invited.' Poppy pulls a face. 'Sorry, I'd have said before, but I didn't want to ruin your evening.'

'Like I'd let any guy SPOIL MY NIGHT!' It would be way more convincing if it wasn't a shriek. I cover up that I've just done a scan right around the hall to check and failed to find him by moving on fast. 'So, what's Immie doing?' I may be wrong, but beyond the cake table, she appears to be zig-zagging across the horizon between the bar and the jukebox.

Poppy's eyebrows close together. 'I'd say she's in that happy place where she's had enough beer to make her forget she can't skate – and not enough to stop her legs working.'

I couldn't have asked for a better diversion. 'It's wonderful what people can do when they lose their inhibitions. She's just picked up a full tray of ice-cream sundaes too.'

'Wonderful – or maybe not?' Poppy's face crumples. 'Hold on tight, she's heading this way!'

By some miracle, Immie is accelerating towards us heading straight for the car. But at the last minute she spins around, reverses, wedges her bottom neatly past the open car door and into the empty back seat. And as she sinks down her tray of sundaes comes to rest lightly on her knee.

'Fancy footwork, or what? Roller skates and Rock Dance beer, what a combo!'

Poppy's groaning under her breath. 'Give me strength. She's so out of practice with her drinking she's totally off her face.' Then she hangs onto the car wing mirror and edges forwards. 'Let me take the tray, Immie.'

Immie lurches backwards into the car. 'Like toad bollocks you will! These are ALL mine!'

Poppy's wild eyes say it's way worse than she thought, but her voice is soothing. 'No one's trying to steal your ice cream, Immie.'

Immie gives a snort. 'Too right!' A second later, who knows how, she's back on her feet, tray in hand, sundae glasses still upright. 'You'll have to catch me first, good luck with your speed skating.'

From where she was standing Immie could have set off at three hundred and fifty different angles, and skated off into the oblivion of the crowd with no more risk than a splat of ice cream on a T-shirt, or at worst a bill for cleaning a couple of dresses from Iron Maidens down in the village. Except she doesn't do that. Instead she sets off like she's in an Olympic pursuit race. But worse still, she's heading straight for the cake table.

It isn't like there's a choice. Either way, something's going to get very broken here. I'd just rather it wasn't the cake Poppy spent all week making. So I throw myself forwards and launch myself after Immie. I'm on skates, I'm out of control too, and none of this is precision judgement. But somehow, I'm able to draw level with Immie and hurl myself onto my back and into her path just short of the cake table. As her skates ram into my thigh, she throws her tray upwards and the sundae glasses rise and trace arcs in the air as they start to fall again. Immie's body thumps down across me, then the sundae glasses and ice cream scoops come raining down on my chest and face.

Immie comes to first. 'Thundering crab arses, Milla! What the hell are you playing at? You nearly demolished the cake there!'

I've got Immie's full weight crushing my hips, her foil pompom is in my ear. And wiping a lump of ice cream out of my eyes is a lot less fun than it sounds. As for what it's done to my mascara, Panda-face here I come again. But then someone comes and rolls Immie off, and I'm lying here staring up at the criss-cross strings of hanging flower-stem decorations and fairy lights with the gym ceiling far above.

For a moment I close my eyes. And when I open them again, I'm hoping to see Poppy laughing down at me. But instead I'm looking up at the kind of dark eyes and sooty lashes I'd hoped never to see again.

'Mr Trendell.'

His lips are twisting. 'That was a spectacular save you made there, Ms Fenton. You showed a natural instinct for averting disaster back there. Perhaps my rejection last week was a little hasty.'

I'm shaking my head. 'No Nic, anyone could have done it. I'm just less drunk than everyone else because I'm on effing wheels, that's all.'

He wrinkles his nose. 'Maybe you could do my job after all?'

'Absolutely not.' On principle, quite apart from anything else.

As I lick my lips and the taste of strawberries and cream explodes onto my tongue, I'm making a mental note to head straight for the pink sundaes as soon as I'm on my feet. Then I have a thought. 'So I take it you haven't found your perfect planner yet?'

He's blowing out his lips. 'Turns out they're a lot rarer than day skippers.'

I wipe a glob of cream out of my nostril. 'So, have you checked everyone?'

He blows out a breath. 'Everyone on the approved list Jess gave me, which apparently is anyone who's any good. I've been at it all week.'

I have no idea why Jess would hand him over to the opposition. As I'm scraping seven sundaes worth of cream off my boobs, I have to point it out. 'This is how I am at the moment, like a magnet for disasters. Truly, you wouldn't want me anywhere near your wedding.'

He's frowning down at me. 'Sure, the gym is knee-deep in ice cream and bodies. But if this were the Trendell reception, at least we'd still have a cake. For me that counts as a result.' He blows out a breath. 'You're the one who said there's no time to lose. At least step in and get it going for me. How about you start by showing me those venues you mentioned?'

'If you were the last man on earth … In any case, it's not as straightforward as it seems. Venues will be the same as planners; anything worth having will already have gone.'

'I'll pay double.' Don't you just hate these people who think qualifications and money make the world go round?

'Cash isn't everything.' I'm about to add, *sorry, but I'm not for sale* when another voice cuts in.

'Make it triple and I think we can confidently call that a deal,

Mr Trendell.' It's Jess, and her laugh is husky. 'Monday morning at nine. Don't be late, we'll make a start.'

'I'll be at the shop.' He's holding out his hand to help me up.

But I've already rolled over. And by the time I'm pushing myself up from all fours to wobble onto my skates he's gone, and I'm face to face with Jess's legs.

'Brilliant save, Milla, marvellous work.' Even though Jess has gone as far as navy cigarette pants and a tailored denim jacket, she still looks exactly the same as she does every day in the shop. 'And I see it's game on with Nic! Well done for that too.'

My heart's sinking. 'Really? After everything he said?'

'He needs us and we're going to come through for him.'

'We are?'

'What's more, when you ace it you'll feel so much better.' She's smiling down at me. 'You're not on your own, Milla. We'll all be here to help you.'

And I need this like a hole in my tights. Because after all my efforts to avoid it, here I am helping organise a short-notice wedding that's guaranteed to be a disaster, which won't be great for my reputation. If this is what Jess meant about talking about it later, well I'm the fool again. Because worse than all of that, I'll be working for Nic Trendell. And from the way my pulse was racing when he looked down at me just before, I'm really not sure that's a good idea.

Chapter 7

'So we knew the Harbourside Hotel might not be "the one".
But seeing it gives us a good baseline to start from.'

Even if the morning sunlight has turned the sea to a shimmering carpet of turquoise sequins, I can think of better things to face first thing on a Monday than Nic Trendall at a wedding venue. And I admit, acing it with the first viewing would have been too much to ask for as well as a sunny day.

If I was worried that once we were on our own Nic might bring up our unfortunate Valentine's night encounter on the harbourside, I needn't have been. If he hasn't mentioned it by now, I seriously doubt he will, so it's a relief to know it was as insignificant for him as it was for me. That he's put it firmly behind him, and forgotten it as much as I have. It's also good to note there's not the tiniest a hint of flirting on his part either. Today's version is full-on serious groom.

Jess was as good as her word with the help, too – she's set up today's itinerary so all I have to do is drive us from one place to the next, then state the obvious. Easy-peasy. As Jess says, with the great hourly rate, how can we go wrong? But it's not the next five months of her life she's giving away.

'So onwards and upwards!' And I know I'm talking like an arse – it always happens when I'm nervous. 'Any more reactions from you, Nic?'

My handbag's between us on the bench seat of the van and Nic's looking like he's pretty close to puking into it. I have to say, if he did I'd happily join him. I've had this really unnerving sensation in my stomach ever since we set off which has to be down to how anxious I am. Like a million dragonfly wings fluttering just above my dress belt, crossed with how you feel those times you have too many coffees and your heart starts racing.

He fiddles with his seatbelt as I pull out of the car park. 'I hate to sound picky.' Which is exactly what people say when they're going to be. 'But it just felt very ordinary. And there were a hell of a lot of steps.'

'Unfortunately, that's what you get with a cliff-top hotel with access to the beach.' Just saying. In my cheeriest voice. As for it not being special, it's all relative. Realistically, if he's used to yacht clubs in the Caribbean, we're going to struggle to surprise him in St Aidan.

'So, anything you're looking for especially?' More information now could save us a lot of unnecessary miles, which could be a factor as I glance sideways at his dark hair and strong jawline. When you think of all the grooms in Cornwall, it's just my luck to get a sizzler. Not that I objectify. But while a hottie will be great for my portfolio pictures, what's less great is my immediate – and very uncharacteristic – animal impulse to leap on him and bonk his socks off. I'm personally blaming that bit on the snog we've completely forgotten about and won't ever be thinking about again. While simultaneously wanting to shake him for being such hard work so soon after we've begun.

He wrinkles his nose. 'You show me all the best places and I'll know when I see the right one.'

Which is about as much use as a chocolate tea pot. If this is how cooperative he is, the search will be endless.

Luckily there are lots of options at Poppy's place where we're heading next. If we pull in Rose Hill Manor which belongs to Jess's partner Bart, we'll have offered a whole array of viewings at a variety of price points. Okay, it's an insider job, but the masterplan is that we look super-efficient. And with so many fab places on offer we may even clinch a booking.

As I steer around the station roundabout and out along the coast road, I'm blinking past the sun visor at the shine off the water. 'So the next venues are twenty minutes inland.' And I won't be sharing that that's where I grew up. But the drive is a great chance to do a spot of digging. If he won't respond to straight questions, I need to try another way.

'So you're in the boat business.' I'm wracking my brains for the right name for what he does. 'Did you mention a nautical piloting agency?'

He looks like he's woken up at last. 'Nicolson Trendell is run from my phone and one small office near Penzance.' He gives a shrug. 'I have the same slogan as Jess – no job too small or too large. We do everything from rowing tourists across the harbour to taking millionaires and their super yachts around the southern oceans.'

I'd expected to be yawning but instead my jaw's sagging with surprise. 'And *Snow Goose*?'

A grin flashes across his face. 'That's one job I fitted in myself.

Her owner wanted her brought back from the States, and now he wants me to stay onboard until he uses her again.'

'And you get *paid* for that?' As I take in his nod beyond my elbow I can't hold in my shock. 'So has *Snow Goose* got a bathroom then?' I've always wondered how Captain Jack Sparrow managed, I might as well find out.

'The facilities onboard are basic, but mostly I use the very nice shower block behind the harbour master's office.' Out of the corner of my eye his lips could be twitching. 'There might not always be a power shower, but I have total freedom and worldwide travel, plenty of fresh air and challenges, and no two days are ever the same.'

'Except when you're sitting in St Aidan harbour.' Just saying. He's been here weeks now. And if I sound a bit like I'm picking him up on every little thing, I am. Because however much we're charging him, it's not enough. To be brutally honest, I'm still annoyed that he thought I wasn't good enough for him first time around.

'You got me there.' He's smiling to himself now.

I grab my opportunity and go for it. 'So does the bride sail too?'

His smile widens. 'She loves it even more than I do.'

Result! I start my mental list with 'tanned and outdoorsy'. Just like him. Add in 'doesn't mind teensy bathrooms'. But before I get to remark how much they have in common, he's crossing his ankles and carrying on.

'From what I've seen so far, weddings don't sound like anything I'll have an aptitude for.' It's a shame he's already so negative.

I pull a face. 'In which case, I suggest you start learning. The details are what make the day.'

His face drops. 'You can't be serious?'

I can't help teasing him. 'They don't give marriage certificates out to people unless they put the hours in.'

He's straight back at me. 'And have you got one of those? I mean, are you?'

'Am I what? Married? *Me*?!' I'm so surprised, I stop steering and bump up the verge. Then I straighten up and flash him a smile. 'Not at the moment. So I haven't even got that piece of paper.'

I'm not going to go into how long my wedding to Ben was pending and how many hours of wedding planning practice I had there. How I woke up every New Year's Day for five years and vowed that this would be the year. How with every new effort I'd search out better and more impressive venues, each time hoping this would be the one to get Ben onboard and keep him there. But the pattern was always the same. He was all for it on the first visit, but by the time we came to book I'd lost him. Then I'd be back to looking again.

'So what about that other thing ... the one with the ring?'

I can't help my high voice. 'Even for a guy, that's vague.' For a groom it's spectacular, but to be fair when it comes to men having areas of wedding blankness, nothing will surprise me. 'You mean the engagement?'

'The one with the special hand?'

I flex my fingers on the steering wheel. 'Third finger left side.' A year on there's still an indentation where my own ring used to be.

'So how about that?'

As I look sideways and meet that dark gaze, I'm answering when I don't mean to. 'Only once.' I shuffle in my seat. Remind myself he's paying for my expertise not my life details. 'Ancient history. It came to nothing and it's way too complicated to go into.'

'So there's a story to tell?'

'Definitely not today.' Definitely not to him. And thankfully, the sign for Rose Hill village is coming up. 'Not far now.' The way this is going I can't get there fast enough.

I swing the van into the pretty main street with its neat cottages, and can't help smiling because the pots of pansies on the pavement by the brightly painted front doors are still so much the same as they always were my whole childhood. As we pass the end of the narrow lane where our cottage was, there's the same surprise I always feel as it slides by. This is where I spent all my time until I was twenty-one, and yet apart from still being friends with Poppy and Immie, there's very little trace now that we were ever here at all.

But one flash of those familiar grey-stone house fronts with their small-paned sash windows is enough to bring the memories rushing back. How they were pretty much all we saw for the years we were housebound. How the world shrank to the size of our front room as my mum was less able to do things. How determined and full of fight my mum was to begin with. How by the end that strength had ebbed into mute acceptance.

'Everything okay, Milla?'

I jump as Nic's deep voice penetrates my daze. 'Fine. Just hoping you'll like what's coming next.'

As we leave the village behind and roll down the lane towards the farm entrance, there's a tingle zithering down my back as the hand-painted signs come into view. Finding lovely things to say about Poppy's venue won't be hard at all.

Something about doing this now brings it all back to me. There is a poignancy to it all. All those bursting feelings of optimism and hope I had when I first had an engagement ring on my finger and started to search for a venue. How naive and young and hopeful I was back then. I try to forget the sting and make myself upbeat again to launch into my pitch.

'So, Daisy Hill Farm! In summer the pasture bursts with flowers, ox-eye daisies and buttercups waft in the wind.' There should still be a few left by July. 'Whether you go for a formal marquee or a laid-back tipi vibe, you won't find anywhere more beautiful for a meadow wedding.' I'm giving silent cheers, because I didn't let Poppy down at all with that.

Nic sends me a sheepish look. 'Sorry, I should have said earlier – definitely no fields.'

My stomach drops so far it hits the road, but I make my beam bright. 'My fault, I should have checked.' And now I will. 'So are we actually ruling out everything farm-related, or just big expanses of grass?'

The face he pulls wouldn't fill anyone with hope. 'We may as well see the rest now we're here.'

As I drive up the cobbled courtyard past the farmhouse and pull to a halt by the picturesque stone barns and cluster of holiday cottages at the top of the slope, I'm hoping Poppy's got some baking waiting in the kitchen. I know my initial expectations were maybe too high, but when it's going downhill this fast I'll definitely be needing a buttercream fix.

As the van doors clang closed behind us, a gust of freezing air wafts up my skirt and makes me wish I'd chosen something thicker than this flimsy crepe tea dress. 'Fingers crossed, it should be a lot warmer in July.'

He gives a grunt. 'Let's hope so.'

Today I've put on my boots with the highest heels, so I'm at least three inches more impressive than I was on Saturday, even if I'm staggering a bit. Mostly I'm trying not to catch the heels in the cracks between the pavers, but there's still time to take in the lovely grey-painted windows as I wobble towards the Wedding Barn. Poppy's told us to help ourselves, so I push my shoulder against the huge oak entrance door and shove hard. As I lead the way into a space as big as a cathedral I pause to give Nic a chance to take it all in.

'It's equally magical filled with fairy lights or flowers, perfect for a surfer theme or a transformation to a ski resort.'

Until the break-up I'd have been literally gushing here, now I'm having to force myself. But it's worth pushing myself, because a wedding here would work well for all of us. For Poppy, to get a booking. For Nic, because there would be so many of us around to look after him. And for me, because it would get me off the hook so neatly.

He blows through his teeth. 'It's a shame about those cobbles.'

And that came from left field to surprise me. 'The ones outside?'

He nods. 'They're way too rustic, you could barely walk on them. Sorry, but we can't have that.' It's not much, but the wrinkles in his brow say the rest.

'So that's another straight "no"?' I take in another nod and kick myself for not walking better. 'And it's brilliant to be ticking them off the list so fast.' I line up another fixed smile and stagger back across the offending cobbles. I mean, they go up and down, but isn't that part of the charm? Realistically, if I can stand up on them in these boots, anyone can. 'Let's grab a drink with Poppy, then we'll try the main house we passed on the way in. There are stone flags down there, they're much easier on the legs.'

Walking into Poppy's kitchen you always get a wonderful

smell of baking, and today we're hit by a wall of warmth from the Aga and a smell of chocolate that's so intense I can almost taste the air as I inhale it.

I grin at Poppy as she waves from the sink. 'Double chocolate muffins?'

She nods. 'Too right! There's a fresh pot of coffee, so help yourselves.' Then she smiles at Nic. 'Viewing venues is always hard work, I thought a cocoa fix might help.'

I fill three mugs and take them over to the huge plank kitchen table. Noticing Nic's frown, I have to ask. 'For someone ripping through the venues, you're very quiet. Is everything okay?' I watch his throat move as he swallows.

He's three shades paler than he was. 'I hadn't counted on it taking this much time.'

If we're barely an hour in and he's flagging, it's not a great sign for the next few months. This is the guy who, thirty minutes ago, was up for seeing every beautiful venue in the South West. I need to get him to be more open about what's going on here. I can't do a good job if I don't have the full picture, so however reluctant he is, I'm going to have to lean on him harder. And even though I'd find it easier not to know who he's marrying, I'm going to have to interrogate him sooner rather than later. As every approach has so far failed, I need to be more imaginative.

'Have some of Poppy's cake.' I push the muffin stack towards him and take one myself. As I sink my teeth into the dense velvety sponge the tension in my neck falls away.

When Poppy comes to sit down, she's laughing. 'Two muffins in as many seconds? You don't need to tell me how it's going.'

I'm already peeling the paper off my next one. I turn to Nic and congratulate myself on the next veiled question. 'I think we can safely say the future Mrs Trendell isn't a fan of mud?'

Nic blinks. 'She's not the kind of woman to call herself Mrs, she'll definitely stick to Ms.'

Even better than a proper answer! I'm suddenly on a roll. 'And does the future Ms Whatever have a first name?'

'Elfie – short for Elfinor. But mostly we call her Pixie.'

As Poppy and I exchange glances we don't need a description, because the name says it all – she's a waif. And suddenly this shadowy person has sprung to life. She has to be one of those truly amazing people who are so tiny and delicate they barely exist. I take an extra large bite of muffin. Whatever that pang in my chest, it's nothing to do with another fleeting flashback to that kiss I can barely remember. Hell no! I'm really not wishing it were me instead of her.

Now I'm facing him, I'm getting the full benefit of the intelligence in those dark eyes, the flickering changes in his expression as he considers. The muffins seem to be working their magic, so I'm firing out more questions.

'So is Elfie hard to please? I mean, will it be difficult for you to make choices she agrees with?' For my money, with a groom this stressed she's got to be a nightmare. Not that I'm biased; I'm actually being very careful to have no opinion either way.

Nic shrugs. 'She's never taken much interest in weddings, but she hates people looking at her. Left to herself I doubt she'd even bother.'

I add a few more to my bride list: indifferent, reluctant, super-thin, not keen on wellies. Then I'm forcing myself to picture them together but even when I let her slip back to being a shadow it's quite hard to get him to put his arms around her. When he does it isn't face to face. They're side by side at the washbasin, cleaning their teeth. And the most I get him to do is one hand flopped over her shoulder. Which might seem unrealistic but it's probably more than Ben ever did to me. Then as I push myself to think of them moving out of the bathroom and climbing into their super-king-sized bed together I get as far as the Egyptian cotton sheets and featherlight down duvet from The White Company and I swallow so fast I choke on my cake. Once I get my breath back, I decide to stop the pictures for now.

'That's very helpful to know.' I'm trying to be gentle yet persistent. 'But is Elfie happy about it?' That sounds so challenging now it's out, I'm immediately back-tracking. 'I mean, weddings are hard work to put together, but they're fun and fabulous too.'

'And?' Nic's wrinkling his nose.

'It's a lot for you to take on by yourself.' I brace myself to go in for a last stab at the truth. 'Right now, I'm picking up a lot more angst from you than bliss. Not judging. Just wondering if there's anything extra we can do to help at all?'

He rubs his chin. 'On balance, I'd say, carry on as you are.'

Which takes us right back to where we started. Thank you, Nic. Except we have learned something crucial – however hard I imagined this was going to be, times it by ten. Or maybe a hundred.

I push the last of my muffin in, make sure I swallow without choking this time, then pull out another bright smile. 'Lucky we've saved the most grown-up venue here until last. Even the most reticent couples fall in love with this one.' *Reticent* is a politer word than fussy. Or demanding. Whatever he's looking for, and however unfocused his thinking is, what's up next might well make him fall in love. I pick up a last muffin. 'Ready to take a look at the old farmhouse?'

Chapter 8

Later on Monday.
On the way to Rose Hill Manor.
Cloudy skies and puddle suits.

So, how did our third viewing go? In and out, and another rejection pretty much covers it. And now Nic and I are back in the van, heading down from the farm courtyard towards the road and Rose Hill Manor.

If I'm slightly wound up, it's only because after four straight rejections I'm struggling to get any meaningful feedback from Nic at all. Poppy's simply-restored Georgian farmhouse was my trump card. It held Nic's interest for a good half hour, all the way past the grand piano, the monumental fireplace and the orangery. Then he saw the bride's changing room, mumbled about it being 'too tight', and we were back in the yard before you could say 'impossible client'. Which is why, for the next attempt, Poppy's following behind us in her Landy, to give me some much-needed backup. And hopefully a few tips on how to get more out of Nic.

I've decided it's best not to give Rose Hill Manor any advance build-up either. I've saved it until last because it's the jewel in today's selection, so the plan is that I'll just let the house slide into view around the last twist of the tree-lined approach. Then let the mellow, welcoming façade with its random small-paned windows, and the big, shiny slate roofs and the lakeside setting capture Nic's heart all by themselves. I'm counting on him being instantly wowed. I'll have gone partway to proving myself. And we'll all go home happy.

I'm too tired for more questions, and I can't risk exposing him to my girly songs either, so instead of flicking on my CD player I lean forward and tap the address into the sat nav. It's less than a mile down the road, but I'd rather take instructions from the sat nav lady than listen to the kind of personal-life interrogation I was getting from Nic on the way here.

'Turn right in two hundred yards.'

How I'd hoped she'd keep Nic quiet I have no idea. Take him into a wedding venue and he's like a mute. Put him in a vehicle, set off down the road, and even having to compete with the sat nav lady, there's no shutting him up.

'You know the trouble with sat navs? People turn them on and switch off their brains.'

My smile's wry. 'I've already proved I don't have a brain, so that won't be a problem for me, will it?'

He shakes his head but he's still going. 'A friend of mine got one letter wrong tapping in the post code and ended up in Norwich instead of Nottingham.'

I mentally roll my eyes. 'That sounds like the original urban legend, and this is the country not the town.' Just saying, I'm not going to add it to my very long list of anxieties.

'Another couple typed Carpi instead of Capri and ended up four hundred miles away at the totally wrong end of Italy.' From his snort he clearly thinks it's funny.

'I know where I am, I lived here over half my life.' If I was less stressed, I'd never have let that out.

'Really?' His eyebrows shoot up. 'Why didn't you say that earlier? More to the point, why the hell do you need the sat nav then?'

Obviously, I'm blanking that. And obviously, I know the way. But it's one of those funny things – when you've been away for a while you forget the details of the bends and turns. And it's easy to have a momentary mind blank about where you are. Like the other day coming out of St Aidan, I completely missed the coast road and ended up cutting across country and getting horribly lost. Which definitely won't be happening here, because even though lately I've come in from the other direction, I know I simply have to turn right, go past another little crossroads, and then it's a couple of hundred yards on the left. However low Nic's opinion of me is, even I should be able to get this right and maybe claw myself to a better place.

'And there was that other couple who did what the sat nav said and ended up just driving into a lake. I mean, who would do that? You'd think they'd have seen the water, engaged their brains, and stopped.'

'Turn left in fifty yards … in fifty yards you will have reached your destination. Turn left … turn left …'

I grit my teeth. 'Would you please just shut the eff up about driving into bloody lakes and let me concentrate.' There's a phantom Phoebe, frowning over my shoulder, tutting. Telling the customers what I think is another no-no.

In my head I'm remembering more trees. But it's quite possible Jess might've cut them down. Have you noticed how tetchy these sat nav women get if you don't do what they say fast enough? As for having Mr Trendell on my case too … I spot the gap in the hedge, the open gate. Bring out my most decisive driving, pull on the steering wheel and accelerate into the turn.

It's only as the tarmac runs out into grass instead of gravel that my tummy gives a little flutter of doubt, but by now it's too late. As the grass opens up and I realise that I'm going totally wrong here, my stomach cartwheels and I jump on the brakes. But all that happens is we're skidding forwards down a slope. Then, as the ground levels and we slide to a halt, I feel the steering wheel get heavy and immovable.

Damn, damn, damn. Of all the effs!

I look across at Nic and keep my tone very calm and my smile very bright. 'Excuse me, I think I may have turned too early there. One moment, I'll just get out and check exactly where we are before I turn around.'

'Exactly in a field by the looks of it.' What's worse, he sounds like he's holding back a laugh.

I fling open the door. 'It doesn't take a prize navigator to work that out.' There's no need for me to lose it completely. If I keep cool, I can breeze my way through this. 'It won't be a problem, I'll just reverse back out into the road.'

The last thing I need is to listen to another bloody urban legend. Or worse still, him crowing about me joining the ranks of disengaged brains. If I leap down onto the grass at least I'll look like I've got this situation under control. But when I land on the grass it isn't as firm as I was expecting. My boots sink straight in and before I know it there's muddy water sluicing halfway up my calves. I shiver as the freezing liquid seeps through the seams and all the way to my toes. And as I'm standing there, I take in the van tyres, buried up to their axles in mud too.

And as if that wasn't bad enough, when I look up, Nic's sliding across the front seat of the van and he's staring down at me from the driver's door.

'What I was going to say was, *wait, Milla, it could be muddy*.'

I scowl up at him. 'How is it, always being right? Did you need a degree for that?'

He doesn't actually answer that. 'If your feet are stuck, it might help to grab hold of the van.'

I need to look like I've got this. 'Stuck feet … who, me? I don't think so.' I wobble, throw out my arms to get my balance and try to move my leg sideways and you know what? He's bloody right again. My best bet is to lunge forward and cling onto the door. It's only when I've got both hands locked onto the interior door handle that I feel more stable.

Nic's not hanging back with the instructions. 'Okay, hold it there.'

'Like I've got any choice.'

He's frowning. 'It's so much windier down here. Let's hope the next venue isn't exposed to the prevailing westerlies.'

The weather's not uppermost on my mind right now. 'I thought sailors liked wind.'

He pulls a face. 'It has to be the right sort, in the right place.'

Of course. I glance down at my dress, billowing out behind me, then up at the clouds tearing across the sky. 'Well, it's gale-force out here now and there's no blow-away brides today, not that I can see.'

He cranes his neck and stares up through the windscreen at the sky. 'Flukey too.'

'Excuse me?'

'That's when the wind is prone to abrupt changes of direction.'

If he spouts any more irrelevant meteorological trivia, I

might just scream. Except, right on cue, the wind turns. One minute it's buffeting my face, the next it's slapping me in the back. Then there's one almighty flap, and instead of streaming out behind me, my skirt passes my ears and flies upwards over my head. If I had two hands free, I'd be able to control the thrashing fabric. As it is, with my hands clamped to the door holding me upright, I have no chance. I can hear Nic's voice over the roar of air.

'Are you okay down there?' He's practically hanging out of the van now and there's a rumble in his throat that could almost be a laugh.

'How is this funny?'

'It isn't. Obviously.' He's easing down from the seat now, and even though we're standing in what feels like a hurricane, when he lands right next to me in my personal space the wind doesn't blow his scent away anything like fast enough. 'I just seem to be seeing more of your legs today than I am wedding venues.'

'What?'

'Like, now. And before in the van ...' He takes in my appalled gape. 'Sorry, there's a slit in your skirt and they were there, I couldn't help noticing.'

'You didn't have to *look*.'

He reaches up above my head, catches my skirt and yanks it down. 'There, is that better?'

'Marginally. But none of this is good.' I mean, he's a groom, he shouldn't be looking like he's about to grin. More to the point, my only hope of clawing back any credibility here is by keeping this serious. I clear my throat. 'I think you should be more respectful, that's all.'

'Okay, I'm sorry. It won't happen again.' As he looks away, I'm pretty certain I catch a smirk.

'It'd better not.' I'd find it easier if he wasn't still hanging on to my skirt.

'And, truly ...'

I'm bracing myself for what's coming. If it's some derogatory comment about women drivers, I might just push him in the swamp too.

As he clears his throat, his grin fades. 'I'm very sorry, this is all my fault for messing about. If I hadn't been distracting you, we'd be at the manor now. I take full responsibility for this one, what must you think of me?'

That he's a knob is the short answer. But as he's the client, I keep that to myself and instead let my eyes pop open with the shock. 'Really?' He's flipped from hideous and annoying to apologetic as fast as the wind's changing direction.

'Obviously I'll pay for the recovery vehicles to come out. And for any damage to your van too.'

I can't believe how concerned and reasonable he's being. Nice even. Helpful. None of them were on my groom's list earlier. 'That might not be necessary.' As an engine roars out in the lane, the tension in my shoulders eases. 'That's Poppy. I don't want to count my chickens, but I think she has a winch on the Landy.'

He's staring at me in disbelief. 'You know what a winch does?'

'You don't have to be so patronising.' All those rainy summer festivals paying to have the camper towed out of fields suddenly seem worthwhile, if only for this. 'Not only that, I know where my towing bracket is too.'

Nic's laughing. 'That goes a long way towards making up for those missing qualifications of yours. Two minutes from now we'll be back out on the lane and you can have a second try at turning into the right gateway. Then we can all see your star venue.'

I know I should be grateful for how accommodating he's been here. But it would be so much easier if he wasn't such a super-brain. Everything other than weddings, he seems to be an expert. And now he's being reasonable and considerate as well, it makes it ten times worse. As for those soulful, puppy-dog eyes and that deep reverberation in his voice when he sounds remorseful. Let's just say, he was a whole lot easier to handle when he was just plain awkward.

I've already lost count of the number of times I've regretted ever setting eyes on that windcheater of his. And as I watch Poppy chugging towards us in her Land Rover something tells me, this won't be the last.

Chapter 9

Later that Monday.
At Rose Hill Manor.
Winter gardens and hit singles.

For once Nic isn't right – it takes way longer than two minutes to pull the van free. In fact, we wouldn't have done it at all without him. Poppy and me are all about girl power, but I reckon even Beyoncé would have struggled here. Nic's one of those guys, like the farm workers, who effortlessly knows what machines are for and how to use them, which Poppy and I were grateful for. And he did it all without once being condescending. Even if Poppy and I knew the basic principles of 'hitch up and pull', it's useful to have experienced hands that know exactly which switches to push when.

After how negative Nic's been all morning, it would have been no surprise if things had gone downhill at the speed of jumping off a cliff. They do say putting someone in a tricky situation is a fast-forward way to show you a person's true character, and as Nic lay jammed under the rear axle, he showed us a whole new, less arsey side to his personality. He also had the same thing going on as Mel Gibson in *Braveheart*, where the muddier he got the bigger his phwoar factor became. Which was less good news for me. But, hell, if it means getting my van out of the mud, I'm happy to deal with a racing heart rate.

And then, rather than turning up at Rose Hill Manor looking like we're on a mud run, we whip back to Poppy's for a clean-up while Rafe's farm guys very kindly hose down the van for me.

By the time we go again, the paintwork is back to being all pink and beautiful and I'm wearing Poppy's tights and some borrowed hiking boots, so I'm certainly rocking the chunky foot style. And this time – just to be sure – we're travelling in convoy, with Poppy leading the way.

As we wind down the lane, I've given up caring so much that I flick the CD player on and tap my fingers to the sound of *Always on My Mind*.

Nic lets out a squawk. 'The Pet Shop Boys?'

'It's upbeat and wedding-y. What's not to like?' It's also one of the tracks off my mum's favourite Get Up and Dance playlist. She loved to party, and when she reached the stage when she couldn't move or talk anymore and all she could do was lie on her back, listening to it never failed to cheer her up. Quite a few of those tracks have made it onto this CD I made. It used to be my personal challenge to sneak it past Phoebe; at some point in every wedding fair I'd always lift the mood with my upbeat compilation of less obvious love songs.

I flash Nic a fierce stare. 'I love trashy pop and I refuse to apologise for that.' The fast tempo and words of regret are just what I need to bolster me for what's ahead.

Nic's eyes are wide with surprise. 'It's not a criticism, I just haven't heard them lately.'

I blink away my own prickles, relax slightly. Then stick with my plan to let the house make its own impression. As we approach the manor entrance for the second time, I bump the CD onto the next track and turn up the volume so the words to *This Is It* are reverberating off the side of the van and hopefully lodging themselves in Nic's head.

He shuffles in his seat. 'And now a subliminal message from Melba Moore?'

I ignore that, take the turn and edge along between the avenue of trees towards the manor. But even though I fade the music at the vital moment, we're suddenly back to how we were before driving into the bog. The most I get from Nic is a sniff as he shifts the position of his legs – which I'm definitely not noticing or looking at because I'm way too busy steering. Seriously, I've run off the road once already, I can't risk it happening again. And even if Nic is unmoved by the low slant of the afternoon sun turning the stone on the front of the house to the colour of warm honey, at least I enjoy it.

As we pull up beside Poppy's Landy, next to a front door flanked by bay trees in hammered lead boxes, I can't tell if Nic's lack of any comment at all is because he doesn't like it, or because I've overdone the music and numbed his brain entirely. If it's simply down to mud fatigue, no one could blame him.

As we get blown towards the front door, I'm trying to stay relaxed and light. 'So, this is where Jess and Bart live, but Poppy's manager, Kip, takes charge of weddings here.'

Having Poppy grinning at me from behind Nic makes me feel so much better. Her squeeze on my elbow lets me know she hasn't forgotten that a few summers ago when the venue was first open, I once brought Ben to a wedding fair here put on by Brides by the Sea. Obviously that day, as soon as I'd got enough notes and pictures for a piece on the blog, I headed straight for the sweet table and Ben ended up flat out on the lawn by the beer gazebo. Which was very much the pattern we followed.

Needless to say, unlike lots of other couples, we didn't make a booking.

I make sure my skirt is nipped firmly in place between my knees, then give Nic a bright smile. 'So, the main house opens onto lawns that roll down to the lake.' I only have a few more minutes to clinch this, so I'm not holding back. 'Even from out here you can see it offers the perfect combo – a wonderful party venue that will give you amazing photographs too.'

Nic's nodding. Which has to be a good sign, doesn't it? 'In terms of the space to move around, this certainly looks much better than anywhere else we've seen.'

'Wow, did I hear a "certainly"?' I give Poppy a nudge. 'That's the best I've had all day.' It's great to be part of a double act.

Her eyebrows have gone into overdrive as she reaches for the handle on the huge front door. 'So we might have a contender here?'

He did say he'd know it as soon as he saw it, and my heart's already lifted.

He pauses for so long I'm making silent bets if he'll say, *abso-bloody-lutely*, or *sure thing*. He doesn't even need to be that fancy – a simple yes would do fine.

He clears his throat. 'What I was actually going to say was, lovely as it is, I don't think there's much point going in, because it won't be in the running.'

I'm picking my jaw up off the floor. 'Excuse me, Nic, but I don't get it. You made it clear you can afford the manor – and not many people can. Jess has made what's usually completely unattainable these days very available, especially for you. It's out-of-this-world amazing. And you're NOT EVEN GOING INSIDE?' I know Poppy's giving me throat cutting signals, but I can't help my frustration from spilling over.

She's got her best bride-soothing voice on. 'So maybe you could share exactly what it is that didn't wow you?'

I'm trying to pull this back, asking myself where the hell we went wrong.

Nic pulls down the corners of his mouth. 'I know I asked for somewhere with better circulation spaces than the farm, but Pixie just isn't an ostentatious person. That sweeping drive, the whole country estate, stately home feel – she wouldn't be comfortable here at all.'

'Great.' I say. 'Good for Elfinor!' And bummer for us. 'The more of a picture we get of her likes and dislikes, the easier it'll be.'

Which probably isn't true either. As I know to my cost with Ben, choosing a wedding venue isn't an exact science. Sometimes nothing suits. And back then we didn't have time constraints either.

Nic's jaw clenches again. 'I'm really not meaning to be awkward.'

'And if we're making you feel like you are, we're really not doing our job.' I'm starting to think he was right to doubt me. Here I was thinking I knew it all, and he's just proving I haven't got the first clue.

Then he lets out a long sigh. 'If anyone deserves to have the perfect wedding day, it's Pixie. More than anyone else I know. That's why I have to get this right.'

There's a note of desperation in his voice. But beneath it, the tremor and the depth of love is so deep, my heart's actually aching for him. And suddenly I understand. I swallow hard and without even thinking, the next thing I know I'm smiling and patting his hand. 'I really promise, we'll do our best to give her that.' And then I come to my professional senses and whip my hand away.

I'm not sure I ever heard a tenth of that amount of love in Ben's voice. Not that I'm comparing. Just thinking anyone bringing out that much love from a man is one lucky woman.

Poppy gives his arm a squeeze. 'You bet we will!'

'That means you'll show me more venues? Let me into the secrets of the wedding cheat sheet?'

From how it's gone so far, he'd be mad to want more. 'I've totally failed to show you anything remotely close to what you're looking for. I've also managed to drive into a bog and cover you from head to toe in mud.'

He's biting his lip. 'I already told you, that was down to me.'

If he hadn't just wrung our hearts out, I wouldn't be saying this. 'Leave it with me.' Everything today was me at the top of my game. Another day might be even more disastrous.

He just smiles the kind of smile that makes your heart melt. 'I was hoping you'd say that.'

'And you might want to work on a guest list.' I haven't mentioned it before, but we can't take this forward without a better idea of numbers.

Nic gives a cheeky salute. 'Aye, aye, cap'n, I'll get straight onto it.'

'I'm booked in to visit some wedding fair venues later this week too.' That came out before I'd thought it through. Probably on the same sympathy wave that had me signing up for more of this hell. But do I really want to complicate those appointments? 'I doubt you'll be free at such short notice.'

Nic shrugs. 'Any time this week is good for me.'

My heart drops. So many miles to keep my eyes on the road rather than on those legs. And that's before we get to how distracting his conversations are. And how much he loves this Elfinor person.

Poppy's beaming at me. 'Great plan. It'll save you having to make two trips, Mills.' I don't have to tell you what her eyebrows are doing. 'At least this way you can rule a whole lot more places in – or out.'

And my week ahead just went downhill very fast! All I'm banking on is that the more I see Mr Trendell, the more his ridiculously attractive exterior will fade. With any luck, by the end of next week he'll be so familiar, I won't even be noticing he's there at all.

Chapter 10

**The next Monday.
In the Style File at Brides by the Sea.
Dog chews and pots of gold.**

As I push through the doors to The Style File early on Monday a week later there's a welcome scuffle of paws as Ivy's dog Merwyn dashes across to greet me.

'Morning, Merwyn, how are you today?'

He gives me a woof, runs two laps around the desk, then curls up back on his cushion again.

Ivy's pops up from behind a pile of boxes. 'That's an extra big hello, Milla, you haven't been to see us for ages.'

I catch a glimpse of the glasses she's unpacking. 'Is that a rainbow table you're working on?' I love this latest trend of oranges and blues and pinks and greens because the burst of vibrant brights are like my mum personified. When most of the other cottages in the village had their walls painted in tasteful shades of sand and hints of beige, Mum's colour palette was taken straight off the Beatles' *Sergeant Pepper* album cover.

Ivy pulls the tissue paper off a bright orange tumbler and puts it down next to a pink one. 'Don't you just love the popping colours?'

I give Merwyn a last pat and slip a folder into the counter drawer. 'Meanwhile, I've been to the furthest corners of Devon and Cornwall in search of wedding fair venues – with Mr Trendall in tow too.' At least I've been spared having him in the van with me. It took one visit for him to realise arriving after I'd finished my meetings with the owners saved him getting bored out of his brain.

Ivy's nodding. 'And how did that go?'

'We got to see some amazing places. Needless to say, Nic rejected most of them before he even got inside.'

So much for me worrying about seeing too much of him; in the end I barely saw him at all. Though I have to admit, I dismissed some places as fast as he did once I saw them in real life.

'We crossed another twenty-odd venues off the list for Nic's wedding, but at least I've got some strong possibilities for us.' And none of it was wasted for me because it's all great material for blog pieces.

Ivy nods. 'I've had a word with Bill, and he's definitely up for bringing the Cockle Shell Castle gin to the fairs.' This is one woman whose life actually sounds more like a fairy tale than the things themselves – she's come to live with her new partner Bill in his castle around the bay. And as if that wasn't enough, he also owns a gin distillery!

'Great, I'll add you to my exhibitor list. I saw your posters too. Design-your-own-gin-cocktail taster evenings will go down a storm with brides and grooms.'

Ivy gives a grimace. 'So Nic's still holding off on the decisions?'

I grin back. 'He's due down here any moment, I'm hoping The Style File will give him a wedding reboot.'

Ivy laughs. 'Trying to shock him into coming off the fence?'

'If he doesn't get off it soon he'll still be there on the wedding day.' As I hear a clattering on the stairs my tummy gives a little jump. 'This will be him now.'

I'm bracing myself just in case the dragonflies in my tummy go too wild, but when the door swings open instead of wind-blown curls and a moody frown I'm staring at stylishly cut blonde hair and some startlingly blue eyes.

I rush in to do the talking because I'm nearest the door. 'Can I help you?' Behind the desk, Merwyn's re-opened one eye and his little tail is tapping on his blue velvet cushion.

The guy's face breaks into a boyish grin. 'I'm looking for Milla?'

Ivy's looking through a bright turquoise glass as she calls across. 'Then you're in the right place. How come you always get the best-looking grooms, Milla?'

He's already stepping forward and grasping my hand. 'Great to meet you, Milla.' Then he squats down and lets Merwyn sniff his fingers. 'And who's this?'

I smile. 'That's our part time design advisor, Merwyn.'

'Good choice of cushion, Merwyn, I'm liking the pompom trim. So long as you never dribble on my shoes, I'm sure we'll get along fine. 'When he stands and pulls himself up to his full height he's towering over me. 'I have to confess, I'm not actually a groom. I'm Casper Jonston, from ...' he flicks a card out of his trouser pocket '... Here Comes the (B)Ride! What do you think of the little brackets around the B? I wanted to say what we did without being too in your face.'

'They're fab!' Faced with his bounce I have to add more. 'And so ironic! And that rustic font is very on-trend too.' I can't tell you the hours Phoebe and I agonised over getting the perfect feel for our lettering. That's why it's lovely to see someone else get it so right.

His beam widens. 'Pleased you appreciate them. I heard you're on the lookout for wedding fair exhibitors?' He was dishing out smiles before, but this time he adds in a row of very white teeth too. 'We're brand-new, we do the coolest rides for brides, you have to put us in your shows.'

With a perfect pitch like that, I could hardly refuse. 'So, tell me about your cars?' The fine tweed suit and brown roll-neck jumper he's wearing are the sharpest I've seen yet in St Aidan. When I take in the taper of his trousers, I'm extra pleased I made the effort to squeeze into my tightest pencil skirt and highest heels.

With his direct blue gaze, he's giving me every bit of his attention. 'We major in quirky and vintage, cuteness with a touch of class.' Despite the stubble that's almost a beard you can see there are dimples in his cheeks. 'We have bubble cars, Hillman imps, all kinds of convertibles. And the all-time favourite – our ubiquitous aqua-blue camper van.'

He's slender but athletic, mid-twenties at a guess, given the enthusiasm, and light years younger than me. It's funny that not long ago no one younger than us had got their shit together at all. Yet now the thirty-something businesspeople are all work-weary and the hungry ones coming through are the babes like Casper here.

'If that's a VW bay camper, I'll say snap! Only, mine's pink.'

He's pointing at me. 'Let me take a wild guess ... you're the bride going west with her name in lights?'

Ivy's eyes light up. 'That makes you camper van twins!'

Casper sends me a wink. 'I've been working as a chalet

host until now, but I've left the slopes and I'm here until autumn, and fully committed to taking bookings for next year too.'

His eagerness is so engaging I'm jumping in to help. 'Well let's hope we can fill your diary. And maybe I could feature your cars on my wedding blog too?'

His eyes widen. 'You have a blog?' You have to love this generation – it's the level of reaction I'd usually get from a guy my age when they discover my bra size has a D in it. 'In that case, let me buy you lunch and show you the cars!'

'Great!' It's out before I think. 'And I can run you through the terms for the fairs and tell you the likely venues.'

He's looking at his watch. 'I could make it for one if you're free later?'

I pick a shop card off the desk, scribble my details on the back and hand it to him. 'Sorry, I'm busy today, but message me and we'll arrange another time.'

He stoops to give Merwyn's ear a last tickle then turns towards the door. 'I'll look forward to lunch then. And we can compare campers too.'

I stick up both my thumbs then hope it's not totally uncool for twenty-somethings to do that. 'Good plan.'

I'm just re-arranging my messy bun when I realise the door never closed, and Nic's striding towards me.

'So what was he doing here?'

Ivy laughs. 'That was Milla's next date.'

For someone so laid-back, Nic stiffens. 'I thought you said you didn't have a boyfriend?'

As if it's any of his business. 'No, what I think I said was, I didn't have a fiancé.' And then I remember – I'd hardly have been grabbing strangers on Valentine's day if I wasn't single. And there's also whatever Poppy said to force him into that sympathy make-out.

Nic's opening and closing his mouth. 'But that was Casper Jonston, he can barely be twenty?'

Ivy catches my eye and grins. 'A lot of women find younger men more attentive.'

I'm biting back my smile, nodding at the fur pile on the cushion. 'Merwyn seemed to like him.'

Nic gives a sniff. 'So, now I'm here are you going to introduce me properly?'

Damn for overlooking the formalities, Phoebe would never have made that mistake. I find my brightest smile to compensate. 'Nic, this is Ivy, she recently joined the team from London. And she's working on a carnival-themed table.'

Ivy waves, but Nic's shaking his head. 'Ivy and I met weeks ago, Milla, I'm talking about the little guy on the cushion.'

'Right.' I'm picking my jaw up off the floor as it sinks in. 'Sorry, Nic, if you'd like to step behind the counter – Merwyn, come and meet Nic.'

As Merwyn hears the word 'come' his ears prick up. A second later he's leaped to his feet, lunged, and now he's on his hind legs, head in Nic's hands, enjoying the ear rub of his life.

I have to give out the warnings. 'Watch out, he might dribble on your shoes!'

'Isn't slobber what dogs are all about?' Nic gives an eye roll as he gently returns Merwyn to his bed.

'I had no idea you'd be a dog person.' We always had dogs growing up and I had assumed Ben and I would get one once we had our own place. But when it came down to it I had more chance of persuading him to book a wedding than commit to a dog.

Nic pulls a face. 'Dogs don't fit with my current lifestyle, but that doesn't mean I don't appreciate them.'

I can't help saying it. 'Let's hope you'll take your lead from Merwyn today – he's great at snappy decisions.' We could certainly do with some of those. 'And to help with that, Ivy and I have found you the perfect tool.' Today's secret weapon is already halfway out of the drawer, but Nic's frowning at me.

'You do know they're not his cars?'

'Excuse me?'

There's that head shake again. 'He swans around in them, but whatever he tells you, they belong to his dad.'

'You're still talking about Casper?' I don't want to give the game away, but at the same time, I can't let the opportunity go. 'If you do fancy any of his cars for your wedding transport, he'll probably have availability?'

Nic's looking at me as if I'm crazy. 'Don't be taken in! Casper never sticks around, he'll be long gone by April, let alone the summer.'

'In which case, let's move on to my other surprise.' I whip out the folder and shove it where he can't possibly avoid looking at it.

'The complete wedding organiser?' His face crumples. 'But isn't that what you are?'

I ignore that. 'All the bridal essentials inside one cover.' The manliest version was dark blue with berries, knowing how much he values paper, he should love it. 'There are checklists and countdown calendars, it's even got a ziplock pocket.' Bigging that up because it's the kind of detail guys go for.

'It's very thick.'

Hurrah if he's finally getting his head around the size of the job. 'It's actually very concise. It will be a good way for you to keep up with what's coming at you, and lock down all the information in one place.'

'If it's a ziplock pocket, I hope it's waterproof.'

Is that the only thing he can say? 'Why, are you planning to throw it in the harbour?'

He gives a shrug. 'Accidents happen when you live on a boat.'

I place it firmly in his hands, then stride past him. 'So while you're here, let me whizz a few things past you so those check-lists make more sense.'

He's still frowning, only this time he's staring at my feet. 'Have you seen the height of your heels? How did you even get down the stairs?'

I ignore that he's trying to distract me from the job and pull out my best client smile. 'Funnily enough, I did look at my shoes when I put them on. Vertiginous stilettos are something we high-flying women learn to get used to.' At least he's noticed I made the effort, so it hasn't been a waste. There's no way I'm telling him my toes are numb, or that I took the shoes off to make the dash down four flights. 'Maybe we could take a look at stationery first?'

Nic holds up a finger. 'Or better still, this might be a good time for my surprise?'

'So what's that?' I can't see he's carrying anything.

His lips are twitching. 'You should find it in your inbox if you open the attachment.'

I grab my phone from the counter and as I get to what he's talking about my jaw is dropping. 'Amazing! We have a guest list!' As I open the file and scroll down pages and pages of names and details my heart is hitting the floor. 'Well, a list this size definitely rules out micro weddings!' And a lot more venues too, given the numbers.

He gives a shrug. 'If Pixie insists on inviting her entire basket-ball squad it was never going to be small, was it?'

Eighty-plus living breathing guests have suddenly made it feel a whole lot more real. 'It's great we're finally out of the starting blocks!' There I go, sounding like a total arse again under pressure. And not only is Pixie a waif, she's a sporty one too, which puts her in the superwoman league. The total oppo-site of everything I am. 'And what better time to look at our pinboard to see what other couples have been choosing for their invitations.'

'Lead the way but mind you don't fall, it's a long way down.' He's very close behind me now. 'And are you sure those spikes are safe to walk in with a dog around?'

I ignore the cheek and take a few very deliberate steps towards a stand-up easel covered in examples. 'Most brides leave us an invitation or save-the-date card for other people to get ideas. You don't have to stick with cards, couples send out on everything from fridge magnets to cupcakes. See if any catch your eye?' The last thing I'm expecting is for him to dive straight in, but a second later he's flicked out a card.

'This one looks interesting.'

Ivy hurries over from her table. 'Sorry, that's not an invitation, those are flyers for our design-your-own-wedding-cocktail evening.'

It's no surprise that he's passed over reams of invitations and homed in on the one mention of alcohol. 'Ivy helps with marketing for the Cockle Shell Castle gin distillery, it's a promo-tional event she's putting on for brides and grooms.' The kind couples get to come to once they've put the work in, and nailed down every other item on the checklist. When all they're left with is the fun stuff to fill in the last weeks while they're kicking their heels waiting for the big day to arrive. Given Nic's time-frame and attitude, I seriously doubt he'll make it to that point.

Ivy smiles at him. 'Why not take a flyer? It can be the first thing in your folder.'

'Thanks.' He crumples the paper into his windcheater pocket, which kind of shows what we're dealing with here.

'Seeing as that went really well, let's move on to some of the themed areas.' I take a deep breath, knowing it's a long shot. 'So have you had any ideas of themes you might choose? Like the 50s theme in the gym.'

'What?' His stare is totally blank. 'Isn't that the stuff I'm employing you for?'

I purse my lips. 'Absolutely.' Phoebe's rule number fifty-six: act like the customer is right even when they're wrong. 'But I'd usually take direction from the couple. So, tossing out a few ideas here, tropical themes are big this year, country garden always works well, or you could go with something nautical or sporty?'

'It all sounds so crass.' He's making the kind of face he'd pull if he'd sucked on a lemon dipped in vinegar. 'What's wrong with simply having a wedding?'

I blow out a breath. 'You did say you want the most amazing day for Elfinor?'

'You mean Pixie?' He shoots me a sideways glance. 'No one ever calls her by her full name, it doesn't sound like her at all.'

Point taken. Wrist slapped. I take a breath and go again. 'Even if you only choose a colour to stick to, then everything will hang together so much better.' There's no hope of walking him round the different areas let alone getting him to see what he prefers. But I'm not giving up. 'Or you could have all the colours! Ivy's putting together a "colour pop" table now, with all those zingy shades. She's already hung a hundred lanterns over the table, then she's adding in the glasses and plates and napkins and flowers in colour waves and it's going to look sensational.'

But he's already glazed over. 'You'll have to count me out of this bit.' He looks at his watch. 'Sorry, but if that's everything I could do with heading off now.'

'Just before you do ...' I hadn't counted on this being such a spectacular fail – if anything he's less engaged than he was. 'Please, just have a look around ... I mean everywhere ...' The wave of my arm passes right around the entire expansive, style-laden basement. 'It might just be one little sign saying "wish upon a star", a close-up photo of a diamond ring on the wall, a crate of tulips, or a single sprig of eucalyptus for a buttonhole. But try to find me one thing you think Elfinor ...' I give a little choke '... or Elfie – would like.' I point my finger at him. 'Go, go, GO!'

I hold my breath and tiptoe back to the desk, exchanging eye rolls with Ivy as I pass. To his credit, he takes a lot longer than I expect. It's a good ten minutes later when he finally saunters back to the desk.

'So did you find your thing?' I'm not hopeful.

He nods. 'More than that. Actually, there are two.'

I feel myself brighten. 'Great. So what are they?'

He stares at me. 'The Cockle Shell Castle gin. And the dog.'

I'm blinking. 'You mean Merwyn?' He's on the floor at my feet and he opens an eye.

'That's the one. She'd like both of those.' He gives a shrug. 'The rest, not so much.'

My mum always said to celebrate the victories, however small. So I will. 'Okay, well, let's say high five to that!' I raise my hand and step forward to where Nic's standing just at the side of the desk.

It shouldn't be hard. I mean, it's a tiny hand smack. One small, inconsequential meeting of palms in mid-air, as managed by most people over the age of two. But maybe the size of my stride is a little bit optimistic for the length of my legs and the narrowness of my skirt. And I certainly hadn't counted on my second foot not following my first. But somehow the spike of my heel gets caught up in the pompom braid at the edge of Merwyn's cushion, and where there should be a quick tap of palms as I do a swift dip forwards and back again, instead there's a loud ripping sound. Before I know what's happening my nose is lunging forward heading straight for Nic's knees. Actually, that's another optimistic view. On reflection, knees would be fine. The exact spot I'm heading for is so much worse – in one second's time I'll be doing a face-plant on his lunch box and then probably roll straight over to demolish the save-the-date easel, possibly taking in a cake table too.

I open my mouth to warn everyone what's happening, but I'm halfway through the 'waaaaaaaaaaaaahhh' when everything stops, because Nic leaps forwards and breaks my fall. So instead of making my full arc to flat on my face, I end up still standing, with my face crushed against his chest and my hips grinding his groin.

It takes a few seconds to register that the reason I can't move is because his arms are entirely wrapped around me.

'Everything okay there, Milla?' Ivy's heading over, and even though she's using her best shop assistant voice I can hear the laughter breaking through.

I twist my neck, pull the strands of my messy up-do free from Nic's stubble. Try not to listen to the sound of whoever's heart is banging like a very loud drum, block out the wonderful man-smell atmosphere inside the windcheater, push my fists against his chest, and force myself away.

'Grief, Milla!' As I step back, Nic's groaning. 'Are you okay?'

'Absolutely!' Seeing I've just hurled myself at the groom, I'm keeping this as corporate as I can. 'Thank you so much for breaking my fall. Next time you might like to do your coat up.'

Nic's wincing. 'Next time, it might be safer to lose a couple of inches off the heels?'

I'm appalled at the thought. It's not like I'm rocking the professional bit here as it is. How much worse will I be with less height? 'Maybe, in the interests of the job. I mean, a wedding organiser with a broken leg won't be any good to you, will she? There's just so much more to trip up on here than in Bristol.'

Nic's biting his lip. 'If you're okay, I really do have to rush?'

'I'm fine.' Everything's abso-bloody-lutely fine. Or it will be when he's gone. 'I'll see you soon.' Except maybe I need a reality check. I just chucked myself at the groom – again! My stomach feels like a big wheel. None of this is fine.

He's halfway through the door when he turns. 'Grab me a couple of tickets for the gin event.' He gives a low laugh. 'You can add them to my bill.'

I blow out a breath and turn to Ivy. 'Two tickets. Did you get that?' I have no idea why my chest just imploded. 'Looks like we're finally getting to meet the elusive Elfinor.'

'Elfinor?' Ivy tucks a strand of her sleek dark bob behind her ear and grins at me. 'I thought he said her name was Pixie?'

And it's only as we listen to Nic's footsteps echoing from the stairwell that we see – he's left his wedding folder lying on the desk.

Chapter 11

Thursday, ten days later.
Sera's studio at Brides by the Sea.
Transatlantic flyers and white lies.

'Two days before my wedding, and we're remaking the dress. This is why everyone told me long-distance wedding planning was a mistake.'

Another day, another bride! And this is Calista, my next Special Request job, now known as Cally, since I hugged her five minutes ago. She's standing in a column of white satin in the studio, peering through the curtain of her dark hair. On the floor below her, Sera is kneeling, dipping in and out of her pin box, while Poppy, Holly, and I look on. And judging from how wide open and bright Cally's dark blue eyes are and the size of her wail, I'd say her wedding nerves are starting to kick in.

'It can't have been easy ... organising every detail ... from New York.' Sera's mumbling as she works, tweaking the satin of the bodice as she moves around, gently flicking Cally's silky waves out of the way as she goes.

Cally runs her hand over the soft shine where one hip bone sticks out into the slip. 'The dress was the simple bit. I'd seen your designs, you were happy to ship. I'd have been laughing all the way to the aisle if it hadn't been for this last hiccough.'

Sera steps back, hitches up her ragged denim shorts, and puts one scuffed Doc Marten boot on top of the other as she surveys her work. Then she glances over her shoulder at the lightest whisper of an over dress on the hanger behind her. 'Luckily for us, when your seamstress took in the satin underdress two months ago she didn't cut off the fabric. Now we've let it out again, it's just a matter of refitting. And with the looser lace layers over it, all cinched in with that gorgeous beaded belt, truly, we've got this.'

Cally smiles down and wriggles her toes in her vintage gold heels. 'It's my own fault for getting ahead of myself with the alterations then putting all those inches on my waist and boobs.' I think we're all relieved she's relaxed enough to joke about this.

Now she's here in person, there's so much I want to ask. 'But when you were already in a wedding destination as cool as New York, why fly all the way to Cornwall?'

Cally pulls a face. 'Nigel's family would never have agreed to an American wedding. They're sceptical enough as it is.' Her accent might be gentle and sophisticated, but the way she wrinkles her nose is just plain cute. 'This is mostly their show. All our plans got overruled, especially the numbers and the cake.'

Poppy's beside me, still clutching the box of cupcake samples she brought down for final approval. 'At least you get to choose the cupcakes.'

Cally lets out a sigh. 'And I hung on to my gold theme. And we'll definitely be doing our first dance to The Supremes, because that's what was playing when we met. It's a good thing I'm marrying the loveliest guy on the planet, because there's not a trace left of the low-key wedding we planned.'

Poppy looks around at the rest of us. 'His mum insisted on an exact copy of Nigel's parents' cake – five tiers, plaster columns and royal icing made the old-fashioned way.'

Cally's shaking her head. 'No offense to your baking Poppy, but so many tons of dark fruit cake and icing that sets like rock? I hope a hundred and fifty guests are ready to break their teeth!'

I'm picking my jaw up off the floor, and mouthing at Poppy? 'A hundred and fifty people?'

Poppy's whispering back. 'It's grown so big they'll need every bit of that cake! And it's at the Waterfront Marina Hotel, no less.'

Cally stares at her. 'You've been there? The Andersons are part owners but so far I've only seen it in pictures – so how is it?'

Poppy hesitates. 'Er ...'

Cally's smile has gone. 'Please, I need you to be honest.'

I pick up the baton. 'It's like a country club by the sea, a little bit starchy ... but the service and the setting are wonderful.'

Poppy nods. 'Imagine your most upmarket yacht club collided with Buckingham Palace – well, that.'

Cally bunches up her mouth. 'It's sounds like Nigel's parents all over.'

Sera grins up from where she's bending over examining the waistline. 'It doesn't get any posher than a groom with five Christian names.'

I can't hold it in. 'So who are you marrying?' Maybe I should have asked before.

Cally laughs. 'Nigel Henry Peter Avalon Ivanhoe Anderson. Believe me, he's a sweetheart, it's just his family who are a little bit *ew* about him getting hitched to a yank instead of an English rose. His mum's so posh she's practically royal, she's been so much worse since Meghan and Harry moved to the States.' Cally winces. 'It's all a bit of a battlefield, they assume I'm only marrying Nigel because he's rich.'

'And are you?' Sorry, but it will help to know; she wouldn't be the first woman to marry for the love of a yacht club.

Calista's laugh is surprisingly husky for someone so slender. 'Hell no, I'm a New York attorney, I have quite enough money of my own. In any case, Nigel's a second son so the acres won't be coming to him. That's the only reason he managed to escape and work in the States. But that's why the family have an iron grip on the arrangements.'

Over the years I've come to understand – not every wedding is blissful and romantic. Wedding days are wired to be exciting and heart-filled, but add in strong characters with opposing ideas, and they quickly become power struggles. There are a lot more horror stories than you'd imagine.

This is another thing I've been dying to ask. 'Is anyone on your side coming – apart from me?'

Cally gives a wistful smile. 'I'm an only child, my mum's asthma is too bad for her to fly, and my two best women friends are seven and eight months pregnant. We're having the wedding party we really want once we go back home again.' She lets out a sigh. 'I ended up pouring my heart out to Jess one day on the phone, and her idea of having you to help, Milla, has saved my sanity.'

'You can definitely count on us.' Forget carrying tissues, I might be taking out the mother of the groom.

Cally puts a hand on her waist. 'I might have managed, if it weren't for ...' She breaks off and looks at the tape measure hanging around Sera's neck.

I step in because it's happened to me so often this last year. 'We all know what it's like to hit the cookie dough Haagen Dazs to bust the stress and wake up ten pounds heavier.' Actually, looking round at the other lean people in the room, they probably don't know at all, but whatever.

Cally winces, then she lowers her voice. 'Actually, it's top secret – but I'm pregnant. It wasn't planned but we're really happy. I just didn't count on expanding so fast.' As she pushes back her hair there are sweat beads on her forehead. 'But his family can't know, or they'll only think it's proof I've trapped him.' Her voice is rising. 'His mum is already frosty – one whiff of this and she'll turn into the ice queen.'

It's one tiny 'p' word, but it's still enough to bring all the awful memories from nine months ago flooding back. But even so, my heart goes out to Cally. 'How have you been feeling?' I mean, the first three months are notorious, even superwoman Phoebe didn't escape the all-day nausea. 'Are you drinking plenty of ginger tea and nibbling on bread sticks?'

That sunny morning last summer when I came into the office with the usual takeaway coffees, and instead of diving on them Phoebe just winced … then marched out. Then came back an hour and a half later looking like death and sipping a bottle of iced Fentimans lemonade. That's another moment etched on my brain like a silver nitrate photo negative.

Before that I think Phoebe was scared that Ben might wake up one day and slip straight back to where he'd come from. But even though the pregnancy finally slammed the door on Ben ever changing his mind, and however desperate she'd been to make it happen, I still suspect that on that particular day the enormity stunned her before it delighted her.

She confirmed the news later that week by throwing a Clearblue pregnancy test stick in the office bin, then sat for a full three hours before she finally went off to pee a second time and left me alone with it. After everything that had come before, this was like an extra kick in the guts. For a while, the only way I could cope with it was to pretend it wasn't happening.

Cally's eyes are lighting up. 'You didn't say you had kids, Milla?'

I can feel Poppy at my side giving my elbow a sympathetic squeeze. And standing there in the studio it hits me how much I wanted that to be me.

I take a moment. Swallow hard. 'No, it was someone I shared an office with.' Poor Cally, it's not her fault. 'You're safe with me though, I know all the cheats.'

Needless to say Phoebe turned out to be the kind of pregnant person who couldn't lift a finger and had to have every last cream cracker carried to her. It wasn't that I wanted Ben back – I didn't. But rather than me being reminded every time she retched or went pale that she was getting the cosy family I'd wanted, it was in everyone's interest for me to keep her feeling as well as I could. A constant supply of ice cubes to suck, mint tea, ginger thins – you name it, I tried it. And thanks to looking after my mum for all those years, mostly I was successful. So long as I could keep her as close to normal as possible, until she started to show it gave me another few months to get my head around it all.

Cally gives a shudder. 'All I can eat so far is chocolate cake which is why I've piled on the pounds.'

'So you mentioned you'd like me to carry your tissues on Saturday?'

Her grin is rueful. 'There's a Gucci bag over there full of my favourite snacks. Can you carry that too?'

'Of course.' So much for thinking this was going to be straight forward. But if anyone needs a wingman, it's Cally. She's one of those women who are so open and honest and lovely, she deserves a perfect day.

Sera's looking over to me. 'Your dress is waiting over there, Milla.'

Cally pulls a face. 'Fingers crossed yours fits better than mine.'

I'm puzzled by the floor length cover on the rail, because Cally mentioned cocktail length. 'I was expecting a short one?'

Cally wrinkles her nose again. 'Me too. Then Sera showed me a full-length dark champagne satin with over layers of burnished gold lace and tulle in your size and I couldn't resist.' She sends me an anxious smile. 'So long as you don't mind an upgrade to official bridesmaid?'

It's more the leap to what sounds like a Cinderella ball dress I'm surprised at, but I can't say that. Sera's dresses are amazing, but ballgowns aren't exactly my thing. 'Whatever works for you.' So long as I can wear my control pants, I don't give a damn, and at least I'm being paid.

Sera laughs. 'Have a look and try it on. Then we'll pop Cally's next layer over.'

'Great.' I'm almost at the hanging rail when Cally recalls the last of the details. 'And the taxi will be here to pick you up at seven-thirty sharp on Saturday morning.'

I let out a squeak. 'That early?'

'The ceremony is at twelve, we don't want to be rushed. You have a suite booked to stay over at the hotel. And I'll email you the final order of the day, so you know what's coming.'

'Lovely.' My stomach is clenching with each new piece of information. I should be used to dawn starts, we're always doing them with the wedding fairs.

She's still going. 'Oh, and I can't drink, but no one can know. So if you could help out with that too?'

First hauling round industrial quantities of biscuits, now tipping champers on the pot plants. 'Whatever it takes, I'll sort it.'

As I reach to unzip the dress cover, I'm bracing myself for the worst. If I end up looking glitzier than a chandelier, at least it's only for a day.

Chapter 12

Saturday, two days later.
The attic at Brides by the Sea.
Another unhappy landing.

I was kidding myself about the daybreak starts. However much I'm used to them, waking early enough to be ready and down on the street for seven-thirty means getting up in the middle of the night and is every bit as agonising as it sounds. Just saying. In case anyone thought this was easy money. Three large mugs of coffee, four croissants and a shower later, I'm just beginning to wake up.

As for the bridesmaid's dress, I'm reminded of my mum's favourite saying – there's always a bright side, the trick is to find it. Except I didn't have to look hard to find it this time. Far from being the bridesmaid's outfit from hell, the dress nestling in Cally's bag was pretty enough for a princess. Better still, there's something about the lightness of the lace and the folds of the satin slip that makes me look as if I'm barely there – so that's not just any old princess, it's a princess three sizes smaller than me!

The gold high-heeled sandals and fake fur stole are also lovely, but with so much fab stuff there's bound to be a downside. The first catch is that the dipping neckline at the back of the dress means my knee-to-boob control pants are definitely out, and I end up in a more minor pair, doubled over so they end on my hip bone. Catch two is that the dress would be perfect for someone without boobs, but on me it's a lot more 'chesty' than I'd choose for myself.

But let's keep this real. The guests are Nigel's parents' friends – I won't know anyone so me venturing out minus Spanks, with enough cleavage on show to make people's eyes water, matters less.

Right now I'm bare-faced, clean-scrubbed, and heading for the stairs with my overnight case, Cally's Gucci bag over one shoulder, holding the dress bag so high in the air I've already got arm ache. The plan is I'll have my hair and make-up done and get ready with Cally at the hotel. I've added a few key items to the pudding-filled essentials bag – mint hot chocolate, iced gems, and Tangfastics. At seven-fifteen sharp I make it all the way to the bottom of the four flights of stairs without breaking my neck and head out into the salty morning air. There's no sign of the taxi in the mews, so I go as far as the corner of the road that winds up from the harbour and do a final check to be sure I've got everything.

'Taxi for Ms Fenton?'

I look up from where I'm burrowing deep in the Gucci bag. 'Thanks, that's me.'

'Everything okay there?' The driver's out of the sleek black car and standing next to my bag pile.

'Fine, except I can't find ...' What's missing is my box of emergency nappy bags which must still be sitting on the kitchen table in the attic. I'm agonising because I lost count of the times a well-placed plastic bag saved us when Phoebe was throwing up. Four floors is a long way to run, but on the other hand I could be kicking myself later if I don't have them with me. 'Sorry, I've left something important behind, that's all.'

'We can't have that. If you're off to the Waterside you need every bit of your finery.' The driver smiles as he takes the dress from me. 'Take your time, I'll load this lot onto the back seat while you fetch what you've forgotten.'

'I'll be two minutes.'

As I hare back towards the shop, my feet are slithering on the Mews cobbles. Then inside the door I kick off my heels and sprint for the stairs. By the time I reach the top floor I've got a stitch and my throat is burning. There's a fleeting second where I take in that the smell is less Poppy's baking, more of something I can only put down to the taxi driver's good taste in body spray. When I dive into the kitchen I put my hand straight on the bags and turn straight around. I'm hurtling blindly back across the landing when I collide with something large and warm and solid.

As I come to my senses the chest my cheek is rammed against is bare, and I'm looking down on one very muscular, very naked thigh. And a very skimpy striped towel.

'Milla, what are you doing here?'

I can't decide if it's better or worse that it's Nic. At least this time I have the advantage of wearing a slim leather skirt, a loose shirt, and a teddy coat more than he is.

'It might come as surprise, but this is where I live.' I let out a snort. 'So what's your story this time? In my flat without clothes again – it's never a great look.'

As I stagger backwards, I'm already trying to wipe out how it felt to bury my fingertips in his biceps. The implant of his body crushed against mine. The heat of his skin. How goddam good he smells.

His shrug isn't anywhere near guilty enough. 'Jess brought me up through the basement a few minutes ago. I bumped into her down at the harbour and I'd just found out that the boat owner showers were out of action. She took pity and offered me this one.'

'Great.'

'That is okay? I mean, I wasn't expecting ...' As he leans one shoulder on the wall, he's obviously completely unbothered by everything that's on show. 'Jess implied you were away for the weekend.'

'I was ... I will be ... I am.' My eyes have snagged on the flat planes of his stomach. The low-slung towel. The bulge I just collided with. Then as I drag in a full lungful of his scent it hits me – I'm in a hurry here.

He's still standing in front of me, blinking. 'That's what's different – you're so small today. And pale but extra pretty.' He pauses to push his hair back off his forehead. 'And where are your shoes?'

For someone standing there in the buff he's way too relaxed. Maybe it's all those years hanging out on deck on tropical oceans. Or maybe this is what guys are like when they're fully committed. When they're well and truly spoken-for. If he were mine, I'm not sure I'd be comfortable with him colliding bare-chested into random women on upstairs landings, but that's the thing – he's a million miles away from mine. I need to stop thinking like that.

Which is all the more reason I can't stand around listening to his random ranting. 'Actually, I need to go.'

He's frowning at my hand. 'So what's with the nappy sacks?'

I drag in a breath. 'Don't ask.'

His brow crumples, then his face clears. 'Wait a minute, have you got a baby? Is this with the engaged guy?'

'No, definitely no baby.' I'm shaking my head. 'It's a long story. One for another time.'

He gives a grunt. 'I'm not falling for that twice. You still haven't told me about the last one yet?'

I'm going to have to get past him to reach the stairs, and something tells me he won't be moving until I do. 'I spent five years planning a wedding that didn't happen. Is that long enough for you?'

'Crap, Milla, I'm sorry.'

I make my voice light. 'It's fine, I picked up the pieces, we all moved on.'

His brows close. 'That must be hard when you're in the trade.'

I'm waving the box at him, aware there's a taxi waiting downstairs. 'And the bags are wedding business too, but someone else's. Now, if you'll excuse me ...' I'm screaming inside at how like Phoebe I sound.

'So many weddings!' He's laughing now and his eyes are sparkling. 'Of course, I forgot, every day's a wedding day at Brides by the Sea.'

'Great soundbite. But I am working, I really do have to rush.' I'd rather not push past him with so little space and so much of him on view, but thankfully he steps back into the living room doorway. 'And you need to get dressed.' Just reminding him, as he seems to have forgotten.

The corners of his eyes crinkle. 'I'm actually on my way into the shower ...'

So he's going to get naked, not dressed. That's one blank I did not ask my brain to fill in. And I could do without the sudden burst of dragonflies in my chest too. At this rate I'm going to need the nappy sacks before Cally.

From the way he's standing there grinning at me it's clear he's enjoying this. 'Well, after this extra special start to the day, you have a great wedding. And a lovely weekend.'

I'm shouting up from halfway down the first flight of stairs. 'Back at you.'

'And watch out for sundaes and waitresses on roller skates.'

I'd tell him to eff off for that, but I'm already too far away. In any case, when I think of what's in store for me today, on balance I might choose the ice cream.

Chapter 13

Later on Saturday.
At the Waterfront Marina Hotel.
Portion control and musical differences.

The first view I get of the grey façade of the hotel is against an expanse of glassy, dark green sea. The chunky stone, the repeating windows and the sheer scale of the hotel building is so palatial, pretty much all that's missing is Her Majesty. But then, where Buckingham Palace would be sitting in acres of royal gardens, the massive sweeping lawns here run straight out into a small private marina where the glittery broken water beside the jetties is filled with shiny cruisers and a few over-sized yachts with very tall masts.

Around the front, the taxi draws up outside some wide stone steps topped by columns that flank an entrance portico. Even before we slide to a halt there are doormen in bright blue jackets, their pinstripe trousers brushing the car wings, poised and ready to open the car doors.

The next three hours flash by, with a few exceptions where small shocks make time stand still. Like when we find out the posies are double the size of the ones Cally ordered, that the roses have changed to lilies, and the string quartet has been swapped for an orchestra. And when Nigel's mum, Patricia, bursts in to inspect us, and she calls St Aidan a dump. Then there's my first glass of champagne that goes out of the window and onto the heads of some guests down below having a cheeky cigarette.

That's the thing about wedding mornings – however many light years you allow at the start, by the end it's always a rush. But we're here now, and I'm whispering to Cally outside the ceremony room, keeping her calm.

'It looks like most of Cornwall is in there.'

Holly, the photographer for the day, has gone in ahead of us to join Jules, dropping my bag off for me under my seat on her way, and I'm filling in the seconds as we wait outside the huge double doors. We've already noted that the taffeta chair covers and chiffon bows are the right colour of burnished gold and now we're peeping past a monumental triple pedestal floral arrangement that's so huge it would suit a lamp post more than a hotel to the sea of dark jackets and exotic hats beyond.

'And I barely know any of them.' Cally blows out a breath and clutches her tummy. 'I feel sick.'

'So long as it's only nerves.' I give her hand another squeeze. 'The moment you hear the *Truly Madly Deeply* entrance music start up you'll be fine.' We were singing it at the tops of our voices in the lift on the way down to keep Cally calm. *I'll be your dream, I'll be your wish, I'll be your fantasy* ... You don't get a more romantic opening line than that.

Penny the coordinator comes to join us. 'The Master of Ceremonies is announcing you now, if you're ready.' I give Cally's fingers a last squeeze then Penny gets hold of my shoulders and squares me up to the doorway. 'So, here comes the bridesmaid, remember to walk nice and slowly. One, two, three ... off you go!'

I've got one foot moving forwards through the air when Cally's fingers clamp on my shoulder.

'Wait!' She rounds on the wedding coordinator. 'It's the wrong music! That's not Savage Garden!'

I let out a groan. 'Oh, crap, of course it's not.'

Penny's eyes pop open. 'Savage *what*? Patricia was definite about Vivaldi's *Four Seasons*.' She's shaking her head. 'If there were fewer guests, you'd have had the full orchestra not the CD.'

And eye-rolls to that! I'm looking at Cally. 'Do you mind?'

Cally pulls a face. 'It's not ideal, but I'm here because I love Nigel ...'

Sure, it's a first-world problem, but I'm so cross I'm talking through clenched teeth. 'But it's Cally's day, Penny. It's down to you to get this right for her.'

Penny's shrugging. 'Sure, I could stop it and we can go again when I find the right music ... but it will totally spoil it.' Her hiss hangs like a threat in the air, then she adds another blow. 'By which time the registrars will be out of time too.'

And then there's a forceful shove in the small of my back, and with no input from me my legs are moving and the ceremony is happening regardless.

As I carefully put one foot in front of the other my sandals are sinking into a regal maroon carpet stretched along a very, very long aisle and there are so many faces on both sides, all turning to look at me. And instead of Cally's dreamy wishes and fantasies she's getting very uptight and rather screechy violins.

Then I catch a glimpse of the blond head that must be Nigel and take in his broad shoulders, and as he turns his face breaks into the warmest smile. If that's what's waiting for Cally, I suddenly see why she doesn't mind about any of the rest. Hands up anyone else who wouldn't mind marrying Chris Hemsworth's body double.

You've no idea how long it takes me to walk the length of the room. By the time I'm far enough forward to see the registrars, Vivaldi is really ramping it up. As I draw level with the awesome Nigel, I send him a little hello wave and a thumbs up because I know how beautiful Cally looks. Then I get straight on with checking what the hell Patricia's done to the buttonholes. So long as you overlook the gold-sprayed berry bunches, they seem to be pretty close to the white roses and eucalyptus sprigs Cally's expecting.

In terms of wedding stress my tummy's had a fair few lurches this morning. But as I spot the satin underneath Nigel's buttonhole my heart does a little pause again. It's only short, but it's long enough to nudge my brain and send my head into overdrive rattling through the memory banks for where I've seen a similar lapel before. And as a groomsman appears to point me to a seat on my own on the left-hand front row and I get a full frontal view of his finery, it finally clicks – I saw a suit like this the first time I caught Nic stripping off in my living room.

I'd take ocean-going waterproofs over satin lapels every time …

As the words echo round my skull, I'm desperately trying to sneak a look at the line of groomsmen across the aisle. In keeping with the size of Patricia's vision, there are effing loads of them. But just because Nic had the suit doesn't mean he's at this wedding. There's no need for panic because obviously he's in St Aidan; I saw him there only this morning.

And then Cally arrives beside me, the violins finally fade, and Nigel steps forward. And when I look across the gap he's left and I get a view straight across to the best man, my stomach officially leaves the building. I take a huge gulp of air, but for some reason my lungs seem to have stopped working. Somehow, I manage to pull myself together enough to step forward and take Cally's bouquet from her.

The best man is Nic.

I think I may just die here and now and be done with it. Of all the weddings in the world, he has to turn up at this one. And when I sneak a little sideways peek it's ten times worse than I thought. Because instead of looking normally hot, with his dark hair and stubble set off against the black satin lapels, the sizzle is off the scale.

What's more, he's bound to have the perfect Mrs Pixie-face here too. Believe me, it's totally unfair for me to be in the same room as someone like that without my biggest power pants on. But however huge my personal disasters are, I need to blank them out. I'm working for Cally here; she's what I need to focus on.

When I look at her standing next to Nigel, there's more colour in her cheeks than I've seen all morning, but to be safe, as soon as I'm settled in my velvet high-backed chair I dip into my bag, twist out a nappy sack and scrunch it into my fist. As I perch on the edge of my seat, my eyes locked on Cally, listening to the registrars welcoming everyone, two things hit me. First, how very much in love Cally and Nigel are. Standing side by side now it's as if they're lighting each other up. And, on seeing that radiant glow in their faces, the second bombshell hits – I've finally given up hoping that this will ever happen to me.

Listening to people in brightly coloured dresses coming up to the front to do readings, I'm so thrilled for Cally and Nigel, but at the same time there's this core of solid sadness buried deep inside me. That's the drawback with weddings. If you're heading for one yourself, they couldn't be any more exciting or exhilarating. But if you've kicked love into touch like I have, they tend to drag you down.

Then Nic produces the rings and as they both slide them on, the tension in their bodies visibly eases. Then as they say their little speeches to each other and Nigel promises to adore Cally forever but not to leave his socks on the bedroom floor and everybody laughs, I glance sideways. And suddenly my eyes lock with Nic's. The look he's sending me is half grin, half eye-roll, and for a fraction of a second it's as if we're the only ones in the room. I'm just wishing it hadn't made my heart contract quite so hard when I notice his eyebrows have shot up and that he's jerking his head. As I follow the direction of his nod down to the floor I spot what he's looking at and my stomach jumps again.

There I was, dreamily sitting there. But all Nic is doing is getting me to notice the small purple tin that's dropped out of my bag and is gently rolling across the wooden floor towards Cally, Nigel, and the registrars. I make a dive for it but Nic's already on it too and no need to guess who gets there first. One stride, Nic scoops it up and as I clamber back up onto my seat again he's pushing it into my hand and sliding onto the chair next to me.

He's breathing in my ear. 'Chocolate pudding in the ceremony, Milla, whatever next?' He's biting his lip, but it could be covering a smile. 'And you might want to readjust ...' he nods towards my chest then lowers his voice even more 'Flash that lot at Nigel's elderly uncles and they may just expire on the spot.'

It's only when I look downwards that I realise quite how much boob got away with the dive to save the chocolate pudding. 'Shit!' I slam my hand over my mouth to catch my groan, readjust my bra, slap down my tit tape and feel my cheeks burning.

Nic dips forward again and this time he snatches up the nappy bag drifting across the floor, and hands that to me too. 'Also yours? Be good, I'll see you in a bit.'

I'm talking out of the corner of my mouth. 'Not if I see you first.' Believe me, after the amount of cleavage I've just forced into his face, I'll be keeping well away.

He gives a low chuckle in my ear. 'Head bridesmaid and best man are joined at the hip for the day, I thought you'd know that?' A moment later he's across the aisle back in his seat, and then the registrars are at the bit where they declare them man and wife and tell Nigel to kiss the bride.

And then, damn me, Nic's right again, because next thing I know, he's behind me steering me over to join Nigel and Cally so we can all huddle in and sign the marriage register.

As he pulls out a chair for me, his eyes narrow. 'So why the bag? You do know we're throwing confetti not nappy sacks?'

I'm hissing at him and beaming at Holly's lens all at the same time. 'Of course, I know, I'm a wedding expert.' Except, having sent a runaway chocolate pudding bowling into the ceremony, I'm maybe less of a hot shot than I should be. Which just means I've got to concentrate even harder at getting things right for the rest of the day. Especially if Nic's here watching my every move.

Chapter 14

Even later on Saturday.
The Waterfront Marina Hotel.
Beach huts and queen's speeches.

It's the start of a very long day, but somehow we get through it. First there's a champagne reception with canapes that runs seamlessly alongside approximately a thousand photo opportunities. The high point is the confetti tunnel of white rose petals down by the jetties, when the sun comes out and turns the water so glittery behind the multi-coloured boats that it's got more sparkle than the champagne.

We're actually so busy rushing around that for the first couple of hours Cally avoiding alcohol isn't an issue. Due to the wind, I'm constantly on call holding her dress in place and rearranging escaping clumps of her hair-do. Meanwhile Nic's away organising the groomsmen to round up the guests needed for the pictures, so until we assemble for the banquet, I barely see him. And once we move through to the oak-lined banqueting hall with the snowy white cloths and glittering silverware, the seating plan means I'm between Cally and Nigel's dad, while Nic's at the other end of the table between Nigel and Patricia. So I make it through the whole day and hardly see Nic at all.

The six-course meal and waiters with orders to keep everyone's glasses full is a challenge. But, luckily, I love oysters enough to eat my plate and Cally's too. I manage to whip her seafood vol-au-vent out of the way before she retches, and a quick substitution with a chocolate pudding concealed in a ramekin dish gets her back on track again.

With all the iced water Cally's sipping we'd overlooked how often she was going to need to pee, but nipping out when you want is a bride's privilege and every half hour ties in nicely with my drinks disposal system. Luckily my bag is big enough to hold some plastic pint glasses I come across in the corridor on the way to the loos, and I dump the fizz into those under cover of the long white damask tablecloths. So long as I don't jump about too much on the way to the Ladies, it's job done.

The meal goes on for what feels like forever, but after the cheese, sweets, and coffee we roll straight through to the speeches, with Nigel's dad kicking off to welcome everyone, then Nigel who talks about how he fell for Cally the first time he saw her at a salsa class when he first went to work in New York, then Nic has everyone in stitches with stories about sailing mishaps he and Nigel had.

By the time we move through to the ballroom to cut the cake, it's already been dark for a couple of hours. There are doors right along the seaward side of the room leading to an illuminated terrace with views out to the inky darkness of the water beyond, and the distant trail of lights out along the nearby headland.

I look at my phone as we make our way under a ceiling made out of hundreds of draped gold ribbons and smile at Cally. 'Four hours on the dance floor, then you'll have cracked it!' We're coasting nicely towards the end of a very successful and sober day.

'Thanks to your chocolate puddings, I've had my best day yet.' Her face softens into a grimace. 'I just hope you aren't counting.'

I laugh. 'As if I'd do that.' I thought twelve would be way more than we'd need. The way she's powering through them, I only hope we've got enough to last the night.

Then, as we collect around the snowdrop-white tower of Poppy's cake, champagne glasses in hand again, waiting to toast the same miniature bride and groom Nigel's parents had on their cake, I hit my first big problem. I drop my bag on a nearby chair, but the next thing I know the gap between me and it is filled with a crush of excited guests, all pushing to get a better view. Even if I could reach my bag, without the yards of damask table cloths to hide under my hands are in full view. If I start throwing drinks into my bag here, even the drunkest people are going to notice.

Cally turns to me with a full glass. 'Could you possibly hold this for me, Milla?'

It's approximately the twentieth time today, but I give her the same beam I have every other time I've taken her drink from her. 'Of course.'

There's only one thing for it. I take one look at my own full flute, turn towards the wall, and down the contents in one. I'm retching at how sour it is, but I brace myself and as Cally hands me hers I down that too, and pass her my empty one. I'm so busy giving a silent cheer for how easily we got over that hurdle I miss that there's a waiter leaning in from across the cake table. Before I know it, both the damn glasses are full again.

Cally's staring at hers. 'Oops. Same again, Milla?'

'Absolutely.' I fire them down, and this time I keep the empties firmly out of sight behind my back. Four glasses of fizz in as many seconds? It's a good thing champagne doesn't go to my head. But there's a catch, because suddenly Holly's here, sliding her shoulder bag onto the floor.

A moment later she's springing forward, camera in hand. 'Okay, grab your glasses guys! Let's take a few shots of you toasting this glorious cake before you cut it.'

And five minutes later, that makes six. Which only goes to prove how well we did earlier; if I'd been doing this all day I'd be legless by now. As it is, I'm solid as a rock. Barely feeling dizzy at all. Except when I dip down to get my bag when the cake is cut and the crowds have moved away, the room sways a bit.

I make my way to an open door to assess the damage, hoping the fresh air will help ease the vague spin in my head when Nic arrives at my elbow.

'You might want to go easy on the fizz there, Milla. Happy Hour's coming up next.'

Damn that he saw. And damn again that he's right, though for once I couldn't agree more – I'd much rather not have all that fizz onboard. 'Where does Happy Hour come in? It's the first dance, then a dancing free-for-all?' At least it was the last time I sat on the loo and consulted the running order I've felt-tipped on my leg. It's so useful, I've barely used the list in my bag.

He shrugs. 'Dancing for whoever wants it and cocktails for the rest of us.' He's nodding at a guy with a violin flicking through the music on his stand. 'Can you honestly see people making shapes on the dance floor if the orchestra sticks to Stravinsky?'

I'm opening my mouth to protest that Cally definitely wants a disco, when Nic's hand lands on my arm and his eyebrows go into overdrive. When I look over my shoulder and follow his gaze, Patricia is heading straight for us, her jewel-encrusted coat flowing behind her.

From the sharpness of her eyes, I can only assume she's been tipping all her champers away too. 'Nicolson, you must tell me how you and Nigel know ...' She nods at me 'I mean, Calista tells me you three met as teenagers?'

I'm gawping. 'Nicolson?' Cally and I are about to be totally stuffed here.

Nic laughs at Patricia. 'Milla's always known me as Nic.' He gives a cough. 'Over the years, that is. You could say we bonded over ice cream.'

If he'd said we'd met eating cow pats, Patricia couldn't look any more disgusted as she rounds on me again. 'I suppose you were working in one of those common little ice cream kiosks on the beach?'

I refuse to lie. 'A lot of people in St Aidan do.' Obviously, I didn't, because I was looking after Mum.

Nic's lips are twitching. 'You should see the party trick she does with soft scoop and sundae glasses – that's why we call her Milla Vanilla.'

Patricia sniffs. 'Well, boys will be boys!' She's moving off. 'I'm pleased we've sorted that one out, Nicolson. And thank heavens you grew up and left all that behind you.'

I blow out a breath as I watch her back disappearing across the room. 'Thanks for covering for me.'

Nic's calling after her. 'All we'll need is a tray and some roller skates, Patricia, and she'll do it for you ...'

I jab him on the arm. 'Nicolson T, you are one bad man.'

Nic's biting back his grin as he turns to me again. 'What a pity she rushed off.' He rubs his chin as he watches her go. 'Anderson family survival rule number one: never let Patricia intimidate you.'

I wince. 'I feel smaller than a worm around all these moneyed people.'

He's staring at me open-mouthed. 'I thought you loved all the trappings?'

I can't believe I'm hearing this. 'Why ever would you think that?'

He's staring at me. 'Because you're a hundred times more designer than everyone else in St Aidan.'

'Says the guy in the tux with satin lapels.' I sniff. 'Looking effortlessly stylish is a must for running wedding fairs, but it's mostly hell to achieve.' I've only got this far due to Phoebe's iron will.

He pulls in a breath. 'Who'd have thought? So maybe you and I don't need pretence to feel okay about ourselves.' His eyes are dark and he's looking very deeply into mine. 'You're every bit as good as them and more, Milla. Never forget that.'

It's kind of him to try to make me feel better. He isn't to know that a deep gaze like that turns my insides to trifle. 'Thanks for the best man personal-guru advice.'

He's nodding. 'You're more than welcome. What matters is, Nige is one of the good guys – if supporting him means putting up with his arsey family, I'm happy to do that.' He flashes me a grin. 'It's only a day after all. And despite Patricia's orders about keeping the bow ties on all evening, I'm about to lose mine.'

'Aren't you the rebel?' As I watch him loosen the black satin and undo the top button of his shirt, he's practically edible. I'm not sure if it's down to the double dose of oysters, inhaling so much champagne, or him trying to help, but 'dangerously attractive' just lurched to 'having big trouble keeping my hands off' which is bad news for all the reasons. I mean, for a start I'm working. But he's also somebody else's fiancé – he couldn't be any more off limits.

Worse still, as I reach for my bag and hook it over my arm, he's sliding his hand behind my back. 'Come on, we need to be next to the dance floor, so we're ready for when Nige and Cally finish their first dance.'

'Sorry?' I'm shivering as the sleeve of his jacket rubs against the exposed skin of my back.

He's looking even more pleased with himself than usual. 'I've studied the best man guide – my next job is to dance with you.'

It's a relief he's making it sound like a chore. 'I'm sure no one will notice if we skip that.' If my tummy's doing cartwheels simply staring up at his throat, there's no way I can let him whirl me around the dance floor. In any case, I'm waiting for the right moment to find out where the hell Elfie is, so I'm moving this on. 'So anything from today you'd consider choosing yourself?'

His nose wrinkles. 'I've enjoyed hearing the sea.' His frown deepens. 'And your dress is great. Especially the front bit.'

I'm appalled. 'For eff's sake, Nic, that's not what you should be noticing.'

He shrugs as we arrive at the dance floor. 'What? You were the one who asked.'

I ignore him and smile at Cally waiting by the dance floor. 'All ready for the best bit?'

Nigel's looking at her doubtfully. 'Should we really be doing all the lifts?'

She's looking up at him. 'We've got to do those, they're my favourite part.'

As the Master of Ceremonies comes up to the microphone stand next to the musicians, his voice booms out around the room. 'If I can have your attention please, ladies and gentlemen ... we're moving on to the first dance. Will you please give a big hand for the Bournemouth Symphony Players who will be providing our music for the remainder of this evening.'

Nige lets out a groan. 'What? Surely not them again?'

Cally wails. 'What happened to my disco?'

I hiss at Penny. 'These two are dancing to The Supremes, and this time we're NOT BACKING DOWN!'

Penny's talking through gritted teeth and looking like she'd like to throttle me. 'Not according to Patricia. You do know any change will ruin the moment?'

I'm glaring at her. 'You aren't pulling that one again.'

The players have lifted their bows and the violin notes are already drifting across the room. I've watched for the last eight hours as Nigel and Cally have had every choice they've made for their day overruled. It's definitely not my style, but something about Patricia's sneering and Penny's refusal to give an inch has made my blood fizz. Add in those six glasses of champagne, and I'm already over at the mic stand.

I have to say, I only win the fight for the mic because the Master of Ceremonies isn't expecting me to wrestle him. Before he thinks to tighten his grip, the mic is in my hand. And as I hold the flat of my palm up and glare at the orchestra the notes gradually stop. I ignore the 150 other open-mouthed faces staring at me like they want to nuke me, and drag in a breath.

'Okay, so listen up ... er ... ladies and gentlemen, Nigel's dad, Patricia. I think we all agree that Patricia's wedding organisation has been totally fabulous. But the stars of today are actually Cally and Nigel – and the good news is, we'll be having their choice for your entertainment tonight: first *they're* going to be dancing to *You Can't Hurry Love* by The Supremes, and after that *you'll* all be dancing the night away to my personal collection of wedding party bangers.' I dip into my bag and hold my CD high in the air. 'Track twenty-three, Penny, please. Take it away, Mr and Mrs Anderson!'

I look out at the audience expecting at least one person to inadvertently clap, but instead there's only a gaping awkward silence, the swish of Patricia's coat tails as she whooshes off into the next room, and the distant sound of waves crashing out on the beach. But then Penny scuffles away to a cupboard in the wall, and Nigel and Cally move into the centre of the space on the floor. It feels like we're waiting forever. Then suddenly, coming from the speaker stacks at the side of the room there's the first, low, rhythmical beat of the drums, and the clink, clink, clink of a tambourine. And then, as the singing starts, Nigel and Cally are dancing together, shimmying across the floor. It's bouncy, it's catchy, it's light, and it's the most fun thing we've heard all day. *You can't hurry love, you just have to wait, love don't come easy, it's a game of give and take …*

Nigel holds Cally at arm's length, then pulls her in to him again. At first they're smiling, then as he twirls her around and sweeps her backwards down to the floor then whips her up again, they start to laugh. It's barely two and a half minutes, but they move across the room, twirling, spinning, making small steps, then big runs. One swift movement twists fluidly into the next as if they're joined by an invisible thread. When he throws her into the air and flips her over I can't help gasping along with everyone else.

I murmur to Nic. 'Oh my, she's so athletic.' Then I kick myself for giving him the opening. This is usually where he'd tell me how Pixie-face does flick flacks and tumbles in her sleep, and how she's actually on the Olympic gymnastics team for the floor routine. And I'm actually ready to feel so sick in anticipation of it that I'll be reaching for one of my dedicated purple sacks. But he doesn't.

Instead he gives a wistful smile. 'She's certainly been great for freeing Nige from his mother's snares. If anyone had told us he'd ever dance like that, neither of us would have believed them.'

And then as the track ends, Nigel slides Cally backwards down onto the floor. Then he pulls her up again and into his arms and kisses her, and the room goes wild. People are stamping and clapping and whooping, and there are shouts of 'Encore, encore'.

But Cally comes across the floor, and still leading Nigel by the finger she takes the mic. She's a little breathless as she speaks and she's smiling straight at me. 'Thanks for making our day with that, Milla, and thank you all for coming. Now, it's over to all of you – get on the dance floor and show us your moves!'

Nic's staring down at me, his head tilted as he listens for the notes coming through the speakers. 'What's next then – The Pet Shop Boys?'

I'm surprised he remembered. 'Unless she's got it on shuffle, it should be *Is this the Way to Amarillo?*.'

Nic pulls a face. 'Can't we ask for something better for our dance?'

'Like what?' I had no idea he'd be so picky or have an opinion when he usually doesn't.

'Roxy Music, *Jealous Guy* would work, or Bon Jovi, *Always* ...'

The guy certainly knows his way around power ballads. Due to how out of control my dragonflies are today, both of those would be worst-nightmare tracks for me. 'Or *Tiger Feet* perhaps?' It's the slowest I can handle.

Nic's shaking his head. 'Not suitable at all.'

As *Amarillo* begins, I'm watching all Nigel's parents' friends flooding into the space, and jiving around. But at the side by one of the open doors to the terrace, I'm also watching Cally leaning against Nigel.

Nic's prompting me. 'Come on, you'll have to do better than that.'

I'm biting my lip. 'How do you think Cally looks?'

He gives a shrug. 'The same as she always does ... with a bit more lace.'

I'm already two steps away. 'Give me a moment. She's not usually that white.' That particular shade of ghostly green means we've got five seconds, tops. As I hurl myself towards her, I'm diving in my bag. 'Everything okay, Cally?'

She's already clasping her hand to her mouth.

'Let's get some fresh air.' Arguing over dance tracks when I should have been on Cally's case ... what the hell was I thinking? As I propel her out onto the terrace, I'm fumbling to open up a nappy sack. 'Here, take this ...'

But I'm too slow. Even as I shove the open plastic bag at her she jack knifes in the middle, heaves, and the stream of dark chocolate vomit completely misses the bag and lands in a trail right down the front of her wedding dress.

'Oh crap.' This fail is all down to me. If my reactions hadn't been dulled by the champers, if I hadn't let my attention slip off Cally and onto Nic, I'd have been on it. My job for the day was to be ready for disasters and avert them, not pick up the pieces.

Cally groans. 'Look at me, Milla! What the hell am I going to do?'

I'm thinking the same, but I can't say that. Instead, I call back to Holly who has followed us as far as the doorway. 'Tell Nigel we're off for a quick toilet stop.' I turn to Cally. 'If we whip you round the outside and straight upstairs, no one will be any the wiser.'

She blows out a breath. 'I shouldn't have made Nigel tip me upside down. He knew we were pushing it.'

After eleven chocolate puddings most people would have barfed without being tipped upside down, but I can't say that. 'Don't worry, Cally, it's only a bit of sick. I'm your bridesmaid for the day, I've got this.'

I've got no idea what I'm going to do. But someone has to sort it, and this one's down to me.

Chapter 15

Later still that Saturday.
The Waterfront Marina Hotel.
Salvage teams and rescue remedy.

'So brides change dresses?'

This is Nic and I'm looking over his shoulder from the bar where we're sitting with Cally and Nigel, watching the dancing guests across the room and pondering our umpteenth cocktail. Put it this way, Nigel's parents' friends would never have been jumping around this enthusiastically to cellos and clarinets. And considering how happy Nic's been to blank out all things bridal thus far, surely a few more hours' silence would not have been too much to hope for from him.

I give a silent groan. 'Why the sudden interest, Nic?' As Cally and I seem to be getting away with our makeshift mix-and-match outfit swaps, it's hardly the ideal moment for him to start scrutinising the details.

To have any hope of Cally saving the dress to wear again in New York, the only option was to seal the whole lot in a plastic bag and courier it straight over to Iron Maiden's dry cleaners in St Aidan for an immediate emergency clean. Which left Cally coming out of the shower ten minutes later with a pair of seam-free Calvin Klein pants, two nipple shields and the belt which by some miracle escaped the carnage.

Sacrifice and resourcefulness are what being a bridesmaid is about. So I whipped my lace dress straight off and handed over my satin underdress. You could probably fit two of Cally inside mine, but after we'd made pleats in the side seams, and pulled it all together with the beaded belt clasped around her ribs, thanks to the beautiful bias cut of Sera's dresses the fabric fell in folds like a lustrous waterfall. The super-sophisticated dark cream satin was set off so wonderfully by the tiny gold shaded beads of the belt, there was very little to give away that this wasn't what had been planned all along.

Which left me with one see-through lace over-layer for myself. I added the cream slip I'd been wearing under my make-up robe, turned inside out to hide the silver #TeamBride printing. With my cleavage hidden inside the slip, it was one of those swings and roundabout times, when masses more leg on show through the lace is nothing like as bad as it could be now my boobs are properly under wraps. Unless I turn up for the evening reception in my pleather skirt, this is as good as it's going to get. Since we've been back perching at the cocktail bar, Cally's already had loads of compliments on her outfit change, so that's our story and we're sticking to it. If you say something enough times with conviction, you start to believe it too. As for finding the bright side, yet again, we were damned lucky.

And that's the other tricky thing. Where everyone on #TeamBride is in on Cally's secret, Nige hasn't yet shared it with anyone on #TeamGroom. If Nic had half an idea what was going on here, he might shut up.

He stares at me over his cocktail as he swirls the blue liquid with the stick. 'Do you know how contrary you are, Milla?'

'Excuse me?' My gasp is so big I hiccough. 'That's quite a challenging statement, Nicolson, you might need to back it up.'

He looks completely certain of himself. 'You spend weeks pressuring me to take notice of weddings, then the moment I do, you don't want to know. It's the same with your heels.'

'How do shoes come into this?' My voice is an octave higher than I'm expecting. I'll put that down to the shock and quite a few too many margaritas.

He pulls a face. 'Every guy appreciates a heel, but the second I flag up that yours are extreme enough to constitute a danger in the workplace, you come back in higher ones still.' He takes a sip of his drink. 'How you haven't broken your neck on those shop stairs I'll never know.'

'Years of practice.' I'm not going to tell him how hard it's been, or that I've taken them off when he's not around. But it's sinking in how wrong I've had this. And if I've got this totally back-to-front, what else have I ballsed up? I'm smiling very brightly. 'As Phoebe says, a heel can never be too high.'

Nic frowns. 'And who the hell is Phoebe?'

Strange how I'd momentarily forgotten he didn't know her. 'She's my super-intelligent business partner – the one with all the knowledge.'

'And have you ever considered the possibility that your "super" esteemed colleague Phoebe is talking bollocks?'

I'm staring at him. 'Totally not.' I have to throw it in because I know he'll be impressed. 'She's got qualifications.'

'What, diplomas in bullshit?' He's still not done. 'Anyway, back to you being contrary, I have one best man duty left today, and now you refuse to go anywhere near the dance floor.'

Which is something else entirely. The trouble with that is, however infuriating and spoken-for Nic might be in real life, and however rude he is, thanks to me having the old mojito goggles clamped firmly over my eyes, with every new cocktail I knock back Nic and his tux are becoming more and more delicious ... to the point of being irresistible. Right now, all I'm getting are the hollows of his cheeks and the stubble shadows on his jaw. And the dent at the base of his throat that looks like it's crying out for me to put my finger in it. And possibly my tongue too.

Whatever my intentions of skipping Happy Hour, there have been more than a few cocktails. Cally's and my latest arrangement is simple, fool proof, and guaranteed to work. We sit together with our drinks between us. I sip from alternate glasses and Cally waves hers around but doesn't drink from either, and both drinks gradually disappear. Sure, I'm drinking when I hadn't intended to. But the night is almost over, so as long as I pace myself, it's a considered risk I'm happy to take. And if I'm brutally honest, when I threw back the first cocktail, the ache in my chest for my own lost wedding eased so much I couldn't wait to start on the next. The only unforeseen drawback is the horribly misdirected alcohol-induced urges I'm getting. And the floor in the loos that was swaying uncontrollably last time we went. But that's way better now we're back sitting down on our bar chairs again.

As for this irrational compulsion to hurl myself at a guy, I can't say it's anything I've ever felt before, even in my wildest partying years. Lots of couples talk about the time when they couldn't keep their hands off each other, but I always assumed Ben and I had sidestepped that because when we got together it wasn't as if our eyes met across a crowded room and we were helpless to resist. It was more that we got inadvertently roped together and dragged along because of where Phoebe was going.

As a teenager she'd done that ridiculous thing where she decided she'd be married by the time she was twenty-six come hell or high water. As she'd just blown out twenty-five candles on her birthday cake and was still flying solo, she was ramping up the effort. Panicking even.

Phoebe, always on the lookout for available talent over the Costa counter, had offered Ben and Harry free coffee if they came back at the end of our shift. So it was nothing to do with instant attraction, but more that all four of us randomly ended up at a table and went on to hang out together.

To start with, we went everywhere as a foursome simply because Phoebe wasn't confident that Harry would go out without Ben. And, strange as it seemed, our pairing off was as simple as the sides of the table we sat on that first Saturday afternoon when the guys got their large Americanos on the house.

At the time, Phoebe had her eyes set so firmly on an engage-ment and a wedding that she wasn't taking that much notice of the guys themselves beyond them being tall enough and working in management. But, true to form, she made it happen – within six months she'd got her ring and a year after that she had her husband. And all before she turned twenty-seven. She was also right about Harry and Ben taking their leads from each other. The weekend after Phoebe and Harry's wedding, Ben turned up with a ring for me too. And the rest, as they say, is history. Ben and I set off on the longest engagement known to man, and Phoebe and Harry settled into the marriage that Harry would walk away from five years later.

As I sit sipping – then slugging – from my alternate glasses and fighting the urge to jump on the best man, I can't help questioning what the hell is going on. Champers is famous for

making you buzzy. Or maybe it's the tux. Although, that's immediately rubbished, because the other guys in identical tuxes aren't
getting my vibrations going at all. If I Google 'drinks that make
you horny' tomorrow and find tequila's the top of the list, at
least that will explain it. But for now, I can't be too careful; I've
already committed an epic fail letting Cally throw up on her
dress instead of in a bag. After ending up on the floor in a pile
of ice cream at the last wedding, if I make an alcohol-fuelled
lunge and start dry humping the (already spoken-for) best man
at this one, I have an idea my extra work for Jess could come
to a very swift end.

As dancing with him is totally out of the question without
me completely embarrassing myself, I'm safer going back to Nic's
first question.

'Some brides change dresses for a more sophisticated look in
the evening and I think you'll agree, Cally's nailed that.' I didn't
mean my forced laugh to be quite so hysterical. 'You know what
we women are like – any excuse for a new dress.'

For a guy looking at women's bridal wear for the first time,
he's very quick to sum up. 'Well, hers is better than before, but
yours isn't so good.'

'Since when did you become Falmouth's foremost fashion
guru?'

He's doing that annoying, nonchalant shrugging thing again.
'I've got eyes, that's all. Cally's dress tonight is a lot like yours
this afternoon, but with less wow factor.'

I'm shaking my head, hoping Cally didn't hear that. 'Shit, Nic,
don't diss the bride.'

He's pulling down the corners of his mouth as he protests.
'I'm only telling the truth. And what the hell have you done to
yours?'

There's a thousand per cent less breast on show for starters, which is the last thing he should have on his radar. 'I've changed to a warmer version in case the evening turns chilly.'

'They both look awesome. But, given the choice, I'd go for the first one.' He's pursing his lips. 'Just saying.'

I'm inwardly rolling my eyes but outwardly sounding super-professional and upbeat. 'Well, great you're getting some practice. We'll know to head straight for the slash-to-the-waist styles when the time comes for you to choose.'

He's looking at me, tilting his head on one side. 'You do know you're drinking Cally's cocktail there, not yours?'

Ouch. And damn. It's my turn to sound like I don't give any shits. 'Really?'

The lines on his forehead deepen. 'That's the second time I've seen you doing that.'

'Oops.' If he's only spotted it twice, I'm actually doing a great job.

He shrugs. 'I know with your past that weddings must be hard for you, but binge drinking isn't the answer.'

I'm so surprised I gulp the rest of my cocktail in one. '*I'm okay. Really!*'

He coughs. 'If I know Patricia, these will be double strength.'

If he's intending to be insulting, he's succeeded. 'What is this, best man chore number fifty-four, stop the bridesmaid getting rat-arsed?'

He closes his eyes. 'This is coming from the best place.'

I blink back at him. 'And this is coming from an even better one – Nic, I'm not drunk, shut the eff up and get off my case.' It comes out so loudly that there are people on the dance floor looking round. I try to look relaxed but when I lean forward to stir my cocktail, somehow my stick completely misses the glass.

'Let's talk about something else.' He leans back on his chair, which is pretty disastrous too. 'So how do you and Cally know each other? I thought you just arrived from Bristol?'

'Hmmm ...' I'm trying to wrench my eyes off the uninter-rupted view of his zip area.

He's still going. 'And this morning – why did you say you were off to work?'

'When did the questions get so hard?' I was hoping not to ask, but it's all I have left to put him off. 'So where's – you know ...' I force myself to say it '... Elfie?'

It works, because his eyes snap open. 'Why are you asking that?'

'I just thought she'd be invited, that's all.'

'I told you, she's on an intensive course in Scotland. That's why I'm in total charge down here.'

As the walls beyond his head lurch alarmingly, I've got my hands flat on the high table trying to hold the room steadier. 'I suppose Elfie's just as great at dancing as Cally ...' It's like someone else is operating my mouth. But she has to be, given she's brilliant at everything else. Or maybe this is my desperate grasp for the truth to cut straight through my heart and force my outrageous libido back into line.

As I stare into his eyes, willing him to reply, his face clouds, then his jaw tenses. He's drumming his fingers, and as he takes a breath to answer, Nigel stands up and pulls Cally to her feet too.

'Come on, guys, if we don't dance soon, we might miss our chance.'

Cally rolls her eyes at me. 'A lull on the floor and Patricia will wheel the violins straight back in.'

Nic slides down from his chair and looks across to the dancers. 'So shall we?'

As my sandal hits the carpet I ignore his outstretched hand but as my leg lands it feels so wobbly it's like it belongs to someone else. 'I may need a bit of air.' That was me playing for time, but as the words come out my head is spinning

'Are you okay, Milla?'

I might be swaying as I duck to avoid Nic's arm coming around my back. But I just claimed I was sober, and he's super-judgmental so I'm hardly about to admit the room is whirling round so fast I feel like I'm on the waltzers.

And then Cally is pushing him out of the way. 'Let me take care of her, Nic.' She dips into my bag, and as we bolt for the door we're going so fast I know she's going to vomit again, but she's talking to me. 'Don't worry, Milla, it's all fine, we've got this.'

But it's all wrong, because as we trip through the doors and lurch out onto the terrace and the wind tries to tug our hair out by the roots, she's the one who's holding out the purple bag to me. And I'm flailing for the bag, but every time my hand goes out, it's not where it's supposed to be. Then there's a tap on my shoulder and it's spinning to check that tap that finally makes my head explode. And as I turn in slow motion it hits me that I'm the one who feels like puking here. But the bag has gone, and instead I'm throwing myself forward. Knowing I have to keep the vom off the bridesmaid's dress.

As the heave finally comes, I clamp my eyes shut, drop to my knees and dive for the floor. It's only as the heaves finally subside and I feel my cheek pressed up against smooth cool fabric that's wet and smells of sick, my fingers tangled in shoelaces, that it hits me. I may just have vommed on the best man's feet. And possibly his tux too.

Chapter 16

Sunday, the next day.
In my room at the Waterfront Marina Hotel.
Afters.

'Is that you, Nic?'

I open my eyes a crack, take in the dark-haired figure by the window sliding back the curtains who's definitely not from housekeeping. Then, as the sunlight floods across the carpet and my head splits open, I clamp them closed again very fast and moan. 'What's going on?'

Even if I can't think what the hell he's doing in my room, the good news is that the shirt and dark chinos are less of a challenge than yesterday's suit. The part that's not so brilliant is that the last thing I remember from last night is being sick on my hands, but how I made it to bed is a total blank. I know I'm about to feel mortified, but I'm not sure how much.

Nic's sounding very business-like. 'Patricia's ranting this morning, I made the executive decision we'd be safer to have breakfast up here.'

My heart's sinking. 'What annoyed her most?' The list is huge. I can't bring myself to say the actual words, but the bridesmaid barfing has to be close to the top. In terms of embarrassing myself, it doesn't get much worse.

Nic's eyebrows go up. 'You're lucky, Patricia was still too apoplectic about the lack of violin concertos to notice what was going on out on the terrace. And your party bangers worked their magic – there were oldies doing non-stop crazy dancing until the early hours. I've returned the CD, it's on the dressing table with your purple box.'

'Great.' At least that's flagged up that Patricia doesn't know, but I'm still not sure how he feels about getting puked on. For me trying my hardest to come across as a professional, it couldn't be a bigger disaster.

He's standing with his thumbs hooked through his belt loops, his eyes narrowing in query. 'What worries me more is a bridesmaid who's so disturbed at missing out on her own wedding she sets out to drink so much she travels with her own sick bags.'

Here we go! It had to happen. I'm opening and closing my mouth, thinking how to explain without dropping anyone in it. 'It wasn't like that.'

'Well maybe you'd like to tell me what it was like?'

'It's ...' It's impossible for me to come clean here. It's my job to protect Cally, not give away her secrets. And even though I'm rattling through my brain for excuses, none appear.

He's straight into the gap. 'Let me guess – it's another of your very complicated stories?'

I let out a sigh. 'Well, yes ... and no ...'

He gives a shrug. 'If you do decide you'd like to share your problems, I'm always here to listen.'

'Excuse me?' Even if I did have a problem, I can't think of anyone worse than Nic to talk to; he's judgemental, he looks down on me, and, apart from the day the van got stuck, he's one of the least sympathetic people I know.

'If you're hurting, talking might help.' His tone is so deep and sympathetic my stomach is starting to melt.

'It totally won't. Thanks all the same.'

He coughs. 'Our wedding manager will be a lot more useful to us if she's on the ball rather than tipsy.'

It hits me like a bucket of cold water – that's his only concern. I take a swift glance under the duvet and push myself up on my pillows to try to salvage a tiny bit of self-respect. 'Message received loud and clear, Nic. I'm exceedingly sorry for last night's mistakes, I can assure you I won't be repeating them.' If I end up talking like Phoebe to claw myself back to a more respectable place, it has to be done. As far as I can see in the gloom under the covers, I'm still wearing my slip which is a relief, but the cogs in my brain are starting to click. Sure, I blundered all over the place last night, but he's the one opening my curtains and that has to be wrong. 'What are you doing here, anyway?'

A shadow that could be guilt flickers across his face, then he laughs. 'I know I was banging on about dancing being my final task. But everyone knows the best man's last job of all is to spend the night with a bridesmaid.'

'*What?!*'

His smile fades. 'You were falling off your heels, I was the first in line to help you to your room, that's all.' He sends me a look. 'If they hadn't been so high I'm sure you'd have managed.'

At least he's not saying how off my face I was. Not remembering any of it isn't a great sign. 'You didn't have to ... carry me?' I'm so appalled at that thought it comes out as a squeak.

He's pulling a face. 'Sorry if that was too Tarzan for you, but it seemed the easiest way to get you up here fast.' This is getting so much worse. 'And once we were here you weren't in any state to be left on your own. So I took the sofa for the night, I hope that's okay too?'

'You did *what*?' None of this is okay.

His face is suddenly serious. 'You could have hurt yourself, I was hardly going to run off back to the party.' He rubs a thumb along his jaw. 'It's fine, I was happy to stay awake and check you were okay.'

My eyes snap open. 'So you haven't slept?'

He shrugs. 'It's not a big deal.'

It totally is. The poor guy must be knackered. 'Thank you so much. I'm so sorry.' I'm blinking my way through this step by step, then I hit the wall and my heart plummets. 'And what's Elfinor going to say about this?'

He gives a rueful smile. 'I'm sure Pix will understand.' He pulls a face. 'So long as it doesn't happen at her wedding ...'

'Hell yes ... no ... I mean ...' I can't believe how easily he's dismissing it. It must be incredible for them to be so sure of each other that it wouldn't even figure. And this time I'm truly grateful for her Pixie-halo, and for her being such an effing amazing human being. And to Nic too.

I ease up the vest strap that's dropped off my shoulder, and move on to the next chasm I've got to hurl myself across with Nic.

'So, what happened to the dress?' Let's face it, questions don't come much more awkward ... to ask or to answer.

Nic's eyes snap back into focus. 'Right – so, your dress and my tux were whisked off to Iron Maiden's cleaners in St Aidan first thing by courier.' There's another shrug. 'One of the perks of a five-star country club.'

My inner groan is so loud it bursts free. 'That bad?' That's not the news I was hoping for. Sick on the gravel outside is bad enough, but on clothes takes it to another – totally unacceptable – level. And I'm really more interested in how the hell I got undressed than the choice of cleaners.

He sniffs. 'Your hem took the brunt, my legs got the rest.' He smiles for a second then it falls away again. 'In case you're worried, I did help you take it off, but the most I saw was the writing on your leg, and only as far as the speeches.' He's still going. 'It was way less than you saw of me in the morning. In fact, I'd say we're pretty much even again.'

'Marvellous.' As I catch sight of my phone on the bedside table and squeeze it on I gasp. 'It can't be eleven thirty already. I need to say goodbye to Cally before they leave for Paris!'

Nic's shrugging again. 'Sorry to disappoint you, but Nige and Cally are long gone.' He's biting his lip. 'We did ask the airline if they'd postpone the flight until you woke up, but air traffic control wouldn't agree.'

I give him an eye roll for that. 'So that's that then.' There are so many reasons to kick myself – for stuffing last night up so spectacularly, for not waking up to wave them off, and now I've got the hangover from hell.

His face softens. 'Cally said to tell you she'll be in touch. And how grateful they both are for all your help.'

So at least my customer was happy. 'What's that noise?' I know I've been listening to the distant crash of waves on the beach in my sleep, but this particular water rush is closer and more constant.

'I'm running you a bath.' Nic's looking particularly pleased with himself as he darts towards to the en suite. 'That reminds me, which bath oil would you like? Pomegranate and ginseng, bergamot and hibiscus, or gin fizz and rose.'

'Anything but the gin.' I'm not sure anyone has ever run me a bath before. Is there no limit to this guy and his hidden talents?

A couple of minutes later he's back again, his shirt sleeves rolled up. As he drops a waffle robe on the bed and dries his hands on a super-fluffy towel I'm definitely not noticing how amazing his wrists are. Or wishing the bath was for both of us.

'So, your bath's almost ready, a French pastry breakfast with coffee will be here at twelve, and your taxi back to St Aidan is booked for one.' With precision like that he could almost pass for Phoebe.

'So what about you?' I'm sure he mentioned breakfast for us both. As for imagining a lift back with him might be nicer than a taxi ride, that thought was never one of mine.

He's looking at his watch. 'I'm pretty much bang on schedule.'

'I meant, what are you having for breakfast?' With those sculpted forearms, I'm guessing it'll be some kind of lean, carb-free, full English after porridge doused in chia seeds. Whatever, it's going to take ages to eat.

He grins at me and nods at a trolley full of shiny silver domes by the sofa. 'Catch up, Milla, I had mine hours ago, I'm heading off to the airport.'

'To wave them off?' I wouldn't mind skipping breakfast for that.

He's shaking his head. 'No, I'm flying out too.'

It comes out as a shriek. 'Flying? Flying *where*?'

'The Med.'

I can't believe what I'm hearing. 'But you can't go away! What about the wedding planning?'

'This delivery job's been booked in since last year. We worked Nigel's wedding around it and that has to take priority.' He's rubbing his jaw. 'In any case, we haven't exactly been moving forward.'

I have no idea why my neck is prickling. 'We can't possibly make progress if you're not even in the damned country.'

He's almost pouting. 'Cally organised her wedding from New York.'

'Yes, and look how that went! She got everything she didn't want!'

He's staring at me. 'They both had fun, love triumphed in the end. Isn't that what's important?'

However much I agree, I can't let him think he's right. 'Fine, but love won't come out on top if you don't book a venue, Nic.'

He's totally ignoring that. 'The break will do us good. I promise I'll put in the effort when I'm back.' He's so full of bullshit. And he's also backing towards the door. 'I'll see you in a couple of weeks then.'

'Two weeks?'

'Maybe three if the weather's good.'

If that's his attitude, why am I bothering? Everyone knows everything that goes on round here. The shop can't afford to ruin its reputation helping with a wedding that's a disaster because the groom organising it gives no shits at all. The sooner I make that clear, the better.

'If you want to carry on working with me, you're going to have to seriously up your game, Nicolson Trendell.'

He's almost in the corridor now. 'I'd say that makes two of us, Milla Vanilla.' He lets the words hang in the air for a second before he carries on. 'And if you wouldn't mind picking up my tux for me, it'll be ready Friday and it's already paid for.'

I'm picking my jaw up off the floor, dragging in enough breath to tell him where to get off. But the door closes, and he's gone.

APRIL

Chapter 17

Thursday, two and a half weeks later.
In the attic flat at Brides by the Sea.
Overkill and rearview mirrors.

One of the disconcerting things about weddings is that the days themselves are so emotion-filled you feel as if you could burst. But once they're over and the hangover finally clears you can end up feeling like a popped balloon.

Luckily for me, my 'incident' on the terrace doesn't seem to have gone any further than Cally, Nige, me and Nic. And everyone here knows about my blunders after I explained why both dresses were at the cleaners. However badly I stuffed up, a bouquet of spring flowers, hand tied with a gold satin bow, arrives for me from Cally on Monday and there's a 'thank you' postcard of the Eiffel Tower lit up at night that arrives in the post on Friday. On Saturday, I nip along to Iron Maiden's and both clean dresses are sent express delivery to New York. I hang Nic's suit on the back of the bedroom door, and that's that. Job done.

As for Nic disappearing so suddenly, I'm missing him and his reluctance to engage with anything wedding related about as much as a hole in the head. Better still, him being away has given me a chance to move up a gear with other things. We've

Jane Linfoot

got our first fair coming up. My pieces about the shop are generating loads of traffic on the Brides Go West blog and even though the posts about the Cornish venues are outside our usual area, they've been really popular too. So there's really no reason why I should be feeling as flat as I am.

I do admit that the for the first couple of weeks after Nic left, every time I heard footsteps on the stairs my heart did stop momentarily, thinking maybe he'd come back early. If I unzipped the suit cover of his tux to see if there were any lingering traces of his scent – there weren't – it was only now and again. But now he's been away three days short of three weeks without so much as a text, I've pretty much given up on him altogether. I'll be surprised if he even comes back at all.

If Nic ever does come back, this time around I need to be fully prepared and super-slick. So with that in mind, this afternoon I've asked Holly to show me pictures of weddings she's shot at places I haven't visited yet to give me a fast-forward view of what else is out there. And Ivy's coming to grab the opportunity to get to know the venues too.

There would have been acres more space in Holly's studio or the basement, but as Poppy's baking today we decided to squash in upstairs and be on hand for her samples. And Merwyn's here as well, lying at our feet on the rug. When he's snuffling around in his latest Fair Isle jumper, everything feels so much homelier.

Holly's next to Ivy on one sofa, flicking through pictures on her laptop as Poppy drops a tray of drinks and cake on the end of the coffee table. She flops down next to me on the other sofa with a muffin in her hand.

'These are apple with roasted almond topping. See what you think.' As we all reach out and sink our teeth into the warm sponge, she's leaning forward peering at the pictures I've been sorting through on my screen. 'So those are the famous tree-houses you visited?' As she runs a wedding venue, she's always interested in what else is out there.

I nod. 'It's a great place for a green wedding if the numbers aren't too big. At least, that's what I said in my blog piece.'

Poppy's giving me that hard stare she does. 'I hope you aren't throwing all your Cornish pieces away on the Brides Go West readers.' The twitch of her nose shows she doesn't approve. 'I just hate to see you always doing the work while all Phoebe does is sit back and count the clicks.'

I'm holding back my smile. 'I've actually decided to do a new blog, all of my own, for this area. I've got loads of material, but I wanted to ask you about names.'

Poppy pulls me into a hug. 'Genius, Milla, you have to do it! So, for names, think what's unique about Cornwall?'

Ivy flicks her dark bob behind her ear, crosses her fabulously long legs, and counts on her red polished fingertips. 'As someone who's just arrived, I'd say the wild windy shores, the surfers, the sunshine, the inky night skies, the stars, the castles ...'

Holly nudges her. 'Says the girl who lives in one ...'

I feel as if I'm about to burst. 'I've got it! Brides Go West is classy and upmarket. Meet her carefree, bohemian, salty-haired sister, Brides Go Wild!'

Holly's smiling as she tries out the words. 'Brides Go Wild? That's brill. It's similar enough to link the two, but they each have their own really strong identity.'

Poppy's laughing. 'They're actually like you and Phoebe personified. She's all urban and smart, while you're the relaxed beachy one.' She gives a rueful grimace. 'Or at least you were before she remade you as a total clone of herself.' That's the thing with old friends – they know you so well there's no pretending.

I'm smoothing my pencil skirt over my knees. 'Don't knock it, Pops. Getting me into a tweed suit and Pringle twinset was one of Phoebe's greatest achievements for our brand.'

Holly's cheeks are flushed with enthusiasm. 'I can't wait to see the Brides Go Wild version of Milla.' She retwists her haystack hair into a messy topknot. 'How about borrowing some of Sera's ripped shorts?'

Ivy's studying me through half closed eyes. 'Or maybe somewhere between. I think a nice denim midi, and some brown suede boots would work a treat with your light hair.'

Poppy's pulling me into a hug. 'That's your new blog and personal style decided then. Anything else before we move on to Holly's pictures?'

Ivy's waving a sheaf of papers. 'I've brought some flyers for our new made-to-measure wellbeing weekends at the castle. We're offering massage and beauty treatments, beach walks, shell collecting, star gazing, yoga and meditation, as well as the famous hot tub.'

I let out a sigh as I catch a glimpse of the twinkly turquoise sea through the little porthole window. 'You had me at treatments, that's so my kind of weekend.' I laugh, because I have to be honest. 'So long as there wasn't too much walking or exercise obviously. And I'd probably skip the yoga.'

Poppy's grin is indulgent. 'I love that you never change, Milla.'

I'm remembering why we're up here in the first place. 'If Nic ever comes back, we could definitely look at those for his hens.'

There's a loud cough and a tap on the door and as we hear the low growl of a husky male laugh we all sit up straight.

'Why might I not be coming back? I'm here aren't I?'

However many times I've seen Nic's face in my head over the last three weeks, the real thing appearing round the door of my living room makes me breathe in so hard I almost swallow my tongue.

'Nic, what the hell?' There's a dragonfly swarm beating in my chest, and my stomach feels like a washing machine that just kicked onto fast spin. And the only rational explanation is that now his wedding is careering towards me again at a hundred miles an hour, my adrenalin circuits are rebooting.

He's got the kind of laid-back air of someone just back from holiday who's still on slow-mo. 'I said three weeks and here I am, three days early.' He gives one of those shrugs he does. 'Jess sent me up. She said you were looking at venue photos, I hope that's okay?'

I definitely need to ask Jess to warn me before she springs him on us again. What's less okay is how extra-hot he looks. 'I take it you found the sun you were looking for?'

He rolls his eyes at me. 'Lovely to see you too, Milla. It's a wind tan, one of the hazards of Mediterranean sailing.'

'At least that saves us having to sit through your transatlantic name dropping.' I'm not sure why I'm feeling so prickly or why I'm still annoyed when it's weeks since he rushed off. 'I hope you remembered to moisturise.'

Poppy jumps up, squeezes past him, then nudges him towards the seat right next to me. 'I'm just off to check the oven. I'll bring you a tea, Nic, take my place next to Milla.'

It's not like there's space anywhere else, but it's not the best news. Sure, I was trying to check out his smell on the tux, but I was hoping for a teensy waft. The noseful I get as he drops down beside me now is way too overpowering. Combined with the whole sun-tanned sex-god vibe and his thigh rammed up against mine, it properly pushes me over the edge.

'In the attic with your clothes on, Nic, that's a first too.'

Poppy jerks to a halt in the doorway. 'Have I missed something?'

I'm kicking myself, and backtracking. 'Just a private joke.' That sounds even worse. 'I mean, it's completely public, obviously, or it is now everyone knows about it.'

Nic laughs. 'Milla has a knack for walking in on me naked, that's all.'

Holly's eyes are wide. 'Lucky Milla.'

Nic's still going. 'Whatever the rumours, we've only ever spent the night together once. And nothing happened.'

I'm staring at him. 'Nic, why not take a muffin and shut the eff up.' I know I started this sparring, but I didn't mean it to end up here. I shove a flyer at him. 'And this is for your wedding folder. We just found you your perfect hen party destination.' I turn to Ivy. 'Any chance we could drop by to check it out before we book?'

She beams. 'I'm in all afternoon tomorrow.'

Nic's obviously trying to prove he's back in the game. 'Great, how about we come around two.'

Merwyn's jumped up and he's staring at me, ears pricked. 'Did you hear the word "come"?'

A second later he's sprung up and he's lying, head in my lap, tail draped across Nic's jeans, pinning us together.

'Merwyn!' Ivy's on her feet, staring at my skirt and pale pink jumper.

'Don't scold him, he's fine.' It's actually lovely to have his warm silky head on my leg and I swear when he hears me say that his lips curl into a smile. 'And I know the skirt is Burberry, but unlike Phoebe's, this is from two seasons ago and I got it for a snip off eBay.'

Ivy sounds doubtful. 'If you're sure you're both okay like that?'

Nic's voice has softened as he pats Merwyn's bottom. 'We totally are.'

I'd rather I wasn't lumped in with that 'we', but whatever. It's Merwyn blissing us out, nothing more than that. I'm taking sideways glances at Nic, to make sure that the fizz effect has faded now I'm sober again. But what I've lost with the alcohol he's more than making up for with his bronzed cheekbones, the stubble shadows accentuating his jaw and the crinkles around his eyes when he smiles. The picture flashing past my eyes of me rubbing Ambre Solaire into his shoulder blades in sweeping strokes right down his back towards his bum aren't helping either. If anything, the phwoar factor's ten times worse, which I'm sure I'll get to grips with once the surprise dies down. The sooner he gets the hell out of my personal space and takes his toned thighs and T-shirt-clad torso with him the better. How the hell I'm going to concentrate on Holly's photos I have no idea.

Holly's turning her laptop screen towards us. 'We were just about to start our virtual venue tour, Nic, so if you're all ready, first up we've got The Mermaid Hotel.' We're looking at a bride by small-paned sash windows, and shots of a sheer glass extension running straight out onto sand dunes. 'This one's a beautiful mix of Georgian and contemporary, it's practically on the beach, and as you can see from this shot of Ken and Meriel's wedding, one of its biggest assets is the stairs where the bride makes her entrance.'

Ivy's leaning in. 'Wow, that's a proper Disney staircase. Her train rippling down the steps is almost as good as Megan's outside Windsor Abbey.'

I might as well explain to Nic. 'This is why you buy the dress to go with the venue.' For now I'll keep quiet about his fixation with plunging necklines.

He's already shaking his head. 'Great, point taken on the dress, but I already know that place. We'll pass on that one.'

No surprise there then. To be honest, it would have been more of a shock if he'd shown an interest. At least this way we're travelling fewer miles as we rattle through the options. Next, he rejects a lovely harbourside house, then an old lighthouse station, a boutique hotel or three, and a fabulous walled garden which was so quirky and beautiful I really thought it would have been in with a shout. By which time we're so virtually exhausted we break off for more tea and cake. Then we move swiftly on to an old printworks, an engine shed. Then more country barns than I have fingers, village halls, a marquee on a fake village green. Then a pub in a disused station, a handful of converted chapels and finally an aerodrome.

When Holly brings up a tipi resort with its own beach, it's a given that he's going to wave that away too. But he doesn't. Instead he says, 'Slow down a moment,' and then as he pours over every picture there's that little crease in the bit between his eyebrows and a concentration in his gaze I didn't know he was capable of. By the time he's scrutinising the inside of the reception tipi and murmuring about fairy lights, he's shifted Merwyn so he can lean closer to the screen. And despite everything, I'm suddenly wildly optimistic.

Holly flicks onto the next picture. 'And this is the bridal tipi.'

Nic's nodding. 'More of that consolidated gravel outside there too.' Even Merwyn rolls his eyes at that comment. But

Nic's a guy, he's bound to notice different things from the rest of us.

I let out a sigh because it's so romantic. 'That huge double bed is so much less obvious than a four poster.' Then, probably due to the pressure on my leg, I carry on. 'Look at those vintage prints on the eiderdown, and the gorgeous painted dressing table – that's what glamping is all about.'

Holly nods. 'And the bed looks out across a little private bay. Apparently, a lot of couples have an early morning swim next day.'

I hardly dare to breathe. 'And it's only twenty minutes along the coast from here, so that's great too.'

Nic's running his thumb across his jaw. 'So are there any photos of the en suite?'

Holly's frowning at him. 'As far as I remember, the tipis don't actually have bathrooms.'

He pulls a face. 'So what about the shower and loo?'

Holly shrugs. 'Those photos didn't make the wedding album. They're in a central block and the facilities are really lovely.'

Nic's leans back against the sofa cushions. 'What a shame, I thought we were onto a winner there.' And now he's rejecting it.

I'm not letting this go so easily. 'No venue is a hundred percent perfect, Nic. There will be elements of compromise with all of them.'

Nic sniffs. 'Without an en suite it definitely isn't going to work for us.'

Says the guy who uses the harbour master's showers and goes to the toilet on a bucket somewhere in the bilges. But he's the client; it's his call.

Holly's pursing her lips. 'I'm afraid that's the last of the bunch today.'

Ivy's trying to make up for the sense of disappointment. 'It hasn't been wasted. It's great for me to see the places brides talk about.'

I'm looking for the silver lining. 'And I've ticked at least another million places off the list and saved us a thousand miles of fruitless driving.' I let out a sigh. 'So it's back to the drawing board for me. I'll get my thinking cap on.'

As Nic moves to get up, he sends me a grin. 'Great, I'll see you in another three weeks then. Or maybe a month.'

My mouth drops open so far I'm almost hyperventilating. 'But – but – but ...' How the hell does he think we can organise anything if he's never here? I know it doesn't matter a jot to me if the stupid man doesn't get his wedding, but right now I'd like to push him in the harbour. And whatever happened to tomorrow?

As Merwyn jumps down and Nic stands up there's a sudden cold streak on my thigh where his leg has been. Then as Nic spins around to look at me, he's biting back his smile. 'Got you there, Milla Vanilla. What do you take me for? First you think I'm not coming back, now you think I'm going away again.' There's no answer to that. 'I'll call for you at one tomorrow.'

'Isn't that a bit early?'

'Not if we're walking.' His grin just got wider. 'Don't forget to bring your beach shoes.'

As for me imagining the view of his back in a towel rather than jeans as he walks out.

Please tell me I didn't just think that.

Chapter 18

Friday, the next day.
On St Aidan beach.
Raspberry ripples and vanilla skies.

Over the last seven years, as Phoebe has wound up the height of my heels, my leg muscles have shortened and my height to width ratio has improved. It's just another reason why I owe her – I used to be short and she gifted me an extra five inches. On the best days, teamed with my high courts, I kid myself my check wool cigarette pants and cashmere high neck give me a sleek outline. But marching along the tideline in the three-quid emergency Chelsea boots I grabbed earlier from the Cats' Protection charity shop, my calves screaming in protest at the flats, I'm seeing the world from a much lower perspective and feeling extra dumpy too. Not that I have much natural glamour or pride at the best of times underneath the sharp clothes Phoebe chose for me, but today I've left every last bit of both up in the attic.

Thanks to a sugar-fix stop at the Surf Shack beachside cafe to get us as far as the castle, I'm also waving a soft scoop ninety-nine cone with two flakes, raspberry sauce, and nut topping. Kicking the sand, and trying my best to cover the half mile around the bay without falling over my feet or getting my wildly blowing hair tangled in my ice cream.

As I'm the woman whose partner left her for someone else, I'd be the last person in the world to ever look at anyone who was spoken-for. I know there was that – *ahem* – incident where my mouth collided with Nic's on Valentine's night. But that was totally unrelated, and I swear I've buried that so deep in my memory files it's not even available to pull out and shudder at. Even less to remember the way the heat surged through my body like an incoming tropical tidal wave. And I know along the way I've had some misplaced shivers, but however strong they've been, even if I've acknowledged that they were there, they were probably just what every other woman in St Aidan was feeling in reaction to the hot guy from *Snow Goose*. I'm very uncomfortable admitting it and I'd never ever act on it. In any case, in real life if I was open to a guy, Nic would be leagues ahead of me.

So, bearing all that in mind, I'm watching Nic running ahead of me across the wavy ribs where the sea breeze has dried the sand into patterns. As he dips down and skims pebbles across the shallows it's typical that he can manage six skips of the stone on the water and hold an ice cream at the same time too. As he turns and shouts for approval he's got the kind of dream-boyfriend veneer you only ever find on the pages of Vogue fashion shoots and Mrs Hinch's Insta shots. I know it's all down to the stylists and the contouring, I'm totally not taken in.

That's the thing. In real life, boyfriends don't have curly hair ruffled by the on-shore wind. They don't stand silhouetted with the silver shine of the sea behind them looking so amazing your heart stands still. In the same way, how often do you get deep blue skies with fluffy clouds racing across them like they are today? When I think back to the years with Ben, I can't remember ever looking at the sky much at all. On the weekends when I didn't have wedding fairs, we'd spend most of our time at the flat clearing up my mayhem from the previous week. In other words, I'd rush through the place from top to bottom clearing up all my crap and then Ben would follow on behind me re-cleaning because I hadn't done it well enough. Obviously, he never made any mess at all because he was a tidy freak. When he wasn't at the gym, he'd spend his spare hours re-configuring his tie collection or tidying his cufflinks. So, believe me, I know how to spot the difference between real-life humdrum and outright fantasy.

'How's the ice cream, Milla Vanilla?'

As Nic arrives at my elbow I jump back to reality and give him the same. 'It's fab to have raspberry sauce again after so long, Knickerbocker Glory.'

Nic gives me a nudge. 'Knickerbocker Glory's a bit long for a nickname.'

'And Milla Vanilla isn't?' I roll my eyes and try again. 'You could be Columbus because you sail round the world? Or maybe Captain Kirk.' Don't knock how random this is, it's a great way to avoid more challenging topics.

Nic's staring at me as we walk. 'From the Starship Enterprise?'

I nod. 'I'm not an obsessive, but it's well known in Star Trek history that Kirk is the person who removes his shirt the most. There may be some parallels there.'

'And we're both in charge of our ships – I could go with that.' He laughs. 'It's good to see you with red cheeks today not green ones.'

That's exactly the kind of conversation bullet I was hoping to dodge here. 'Just what I need! A reminder of my fail *and* to hear that I'm scarlet.' I quicken my pace so we can get there before I go puce and he starts asking me if I've read *The Sober Diaries* or done any dependency workshops. But that only makes me even more breathless.

He's talking long easy strides beside me. 'I'm guessing that if we're widening the search for a venue we'll be eating a lot of ice cream over the next few weeks.'

Even though it's pounding from the exertion, my heart still manages to wither. Much as I love ice cream, lately I'm finding him even less comfortable to be with. And him talking weeks not days isn't encouraging either. I need to crack this venue search as soon as possible before we reach as far as London. 'Aren't there boats to deliver?'

'This is my priority; I'll be on it full time now until it's sorted.'

'Great.' It's not great at all. Now he's back, I can't think why I wasn't more delighted to see him go away.

He bobs to pick up a pebble and rubs it between his fingers. 'The trouble with walking on the beach without a dog is it always feels like something is missing. My mum and dad have a houseful, we need to borrow them.'

We don't agree on many issues, but he's right on this. 'We always had dogs when I was younger. They used to love the beach.'

'So are your parents still in Rose Hill?'

I swallow away a sudden rush of saliva, then move in to brush it off. 'My dad left when I was small, so he didn't ever figure, but my mum died eleven years ago.'

He lets out a long sigh. 'I'm so sorry, I wouldn't have asked if I'd known.'

Making other people feel okay is always my first job when they find out. 'It's fine. I'm more used to her being gone now.

But however long it is, I don't think about her any less – I still miss her every day.' Every hour actually.

His face creases. 'Poor Milla.'

My mum hated wallowers; I owe it to her to lift the mood again. 'She's never that far away. Most things I do, I can hear her voice in my head telling me what she thinks.' I send him a grin. 'She was so vibrant and alive, she'd hate us to be sad. Most of those party bangers came from what she called her "playlist to die for". She was never going to leave quietly, she had the whole village reverberating for months.'

'She sounds awesome.' He dips across and gives my elbow a squeeze, but I do a spurt in my speed trot and it's over before it's begun. 'That must be where you get it from.'

By the time my mum reached the stage where she couldn't move out of our living room, she took delight in arguing the toss with the village vicar when he visited, so usually he steered clear. And she never talked about heaven as real. Instead, she insisted she'd be crossing the proverbial rainbow bridge for pets, and finding our dogs and all the guinea pigs we ever had, along with the three rabbits who escaped, gambolling in a sunny meadow on the other side. And she always promised that whatever happened she'd always be here to watch over us kids. But there are times, like now, when I look up and see Merwyn haring along the beach towards us, snapping at the tangles of dried seaweed, and it really feels as if she's up there gently pulling the strings as she reclines on one of those fluffy clouds.

I slow down to a gasping walk and shout to Captain Kirk. 'Unless Ivy took a hearth rug out for a walk there could be a dog on his way to meet us.' I bend down and call. 'Mer-wyn!'

A moment later he hurtles at our legs and starts haring backwards and forwards, barking, jumping up at each of us in turn.

'Hey, take it easy, mate.' Nic puts a steadying hand on Merwyn's head, which works for a nanosecond before he belts off again to meet Ivy.

Ivy's got a beret pulled down over her ears and her blue fake fur collar pulled up against the horizontal gusts and she still looks like she came off a catwalk. Not in a stiff twig way like Phoebe, but in a vibrant, alive, beautiful way, like a dark Claudia Schiffer. Her face lights up as she greets us. 'I thought we could walk the last bit together, it's lovely coming in to the castle garden straight from the beach.' Her face breaks into a grin. 'Merwyn and I only came here full time in January, the novelty hasn't worn off yet.'

I'm racking through my memory banks as we follow her up the sand and past some bushes. 'I think I remember coming past here when we were children.' Then suddenly it's in front of us, and as we stare across a lawn to a wide building with end towers and battlements and light-grey stone walls, I'm gasping. 'It's like something out of a film, only better, because it's real.'

Ivy's looking shy. 'Welcome to Cockle Shell. This is the higgledy side of the cosiest castle in the world.' She nods at me. 'Truly, if you think it's amazing now you should see it in the moonlight. And it's lovely because inside it's even smaller than it looks from out here.' She's shaking out her keys, pointing towards a pergola. 'That's the terrace over there with the hot tub. Come around the side, and I'll take you in through the main door.'

I can't hold back my enthusiasm. 'This is idyllic. I can just imagine the hens rushing out onto the beach to make sandcastles.' I bet they'd love messing around in the rockpools too.

Our feet are scrunching on the gravel path as we go around the other side, then Ivy leads us out onto the lawn so we can see the front. 'This is the garden side with the proper symmetrical façade. It would be so lovely for hens to have afternoon tea on the lawn here in the summer.'

I can barely hold back my excitement as I take in walls that have been punched through with small paned windows, with a square tower at each end. 'Scones and jam and dainty cucumber sandwiches on vintage china plates in front of the castle ... it couldn't be any more perfect.'

Then she leads the way closer and pushes open the huge plank front door, and we follow her into the hall, with a huge chunky staircase and lovely flagstone floors and walls too. 'I first came here in December, and we had the hugest tree here decorated with shells and miniature gin bottles.'

'Who does Bill let it to usually?'

'He set out to specialise in stag parties. I ended up here styling the place for a festive let for a big family group, but that was a one-off.'

I'm straight in there. 'This will be fab for hens whatever the time of year.' I send her a wink. 'It's totally wasted on stags.'

'You could be right.' She laughs and pushes through a really wide door to a spacious room with a huge stone fireplace. 'It was quite spartan when I arrived, but we brought in more furniture to make it comfy over Christmas and it stayed.'

The room I'm staring around is huge. 'Do you look after all this on your own?'

She raises her eyebrows. 'Bill's dad and his mates from the Silver Surfers Club help out. They're not completely housetrained, but they're enthusiastic.' She stops for a moment by a steel console table. 'One thing – due to the thick walls most of the castle is internet-free with no phone signal.'

I'm looking at Nic to check. 'Is that okay?'

He's doing his puzzled frown. 'If I've had internet connection mid-Atlantic surely ...'

I glare at him. 'We're on land, Nic, we're talking women taking time out here.' It'll be just my luck if Elfinor's a hot-shot tycoon who can't ever be without her phone.

He looks at the ceiling then nods. 'Okay, fine.'

Ivy's smiling again. 'In that case, I'll show you the rest.'

We follow her through downstairs spaces as wide as galleries that are filled with velvet sofas and leather club chairs, catching glimpses through the windows to the sea and the distant curve of the bay. Then we move on to two more floors where the bedrooms all have simple framed four posters and sleek white bathrooms.

Then we come back to the ground floor again. I have to admit, Ivy had me with the scones and the towers. By the time we reach a stylish kitchen with a vast island unit, more sofas and floor-to-ceiling doors opening onto the paved hot tub area, I'm ecstatic. When I skim through the list of treatments on offer from the list she hands me, I'm beyond blown away.

I sigh to Ivy. 'Imagine a hot stone massage with views of the beach. Followed by a pedi and a long, lazy afternoon in the hot tub with a glass of fizz, then a night of girly games by the fire.' Obviously, due to the present company I miss out any reference to the obligatory downing of shots. As I turn to Nic I'm breathy, because it's such a lucky break to be offered this. 'Sleeps twenty, so that should be more than enough. If there's less of them they can forget the top floor. All that's left is to hope that Ivy's free weekends coincide with your dates.'

Ivy's eyes are wide. 'I checked with Bill, he's happy to offer you ten percent off.'

'Better and better!' I'm so excited I'm hugging myself.

I'm expecting Nic to whip out his phone to check his diary and commit before she changes her mind, but instead he hesitates. 'Could we find the hens somewhere more compact – I'm sure they'd be fine with less space?'

Out of womanly solidarity, I'm going to make sure his hens get the best. 'You cheapskating them into a mud run and a tenner behind the bar is not going to happen on my watch, Nic.'

His eyes flash in frustration. 'You know I wouldn't do that.'

Actually, I don't, but I'm not going to argue. Ivy saw yesterday how easily Nic dismisses places. If he's already crossed this off there's no point prolonging the visit, we need to get the hell out of here. 'If that's a definite "no", let's not take up any more of Ivy's afternoon.' As I march towards the hall my heart is sinking. If he's being this picky with the hens, what about the real venue? And it's all extra time I'll have to spend with him, when I'd rather not. I know the client's always right, but I might need to remind him. 'If you're rejecting quality like this, Nic, you're making the whole job impossible.'

I've stomped halfway across the very long wood plank floor before I realise he isn't following. As I look over my shoulder, he narrows his eyes.

'This isn't a rejection.'

I've just about had enough. 'I don't know what intergalactic universe you're flying through, Captain Kirk, but I think you just said the hens didn't deserve anywhere this big.'

He clears his throat. 'I don't want to waste this on the hens because I want it for something else.'

Now I get it, and I'm fuming. 'Nic Trendell, you are *not* stealing this for the stags!'

His lips are twitching. 'You don't think that's a great idea?'

I'm bursting. 'No, I bloody don't!'

His eyes are twinkling. 'No need to explode, I'm only winding you up. It's way better than that, Milla Vanilla – you may just have found the perfect wedding venue.'

'What?'

His mouth curves. 'The spaces are fabulous, the feel is exactly what I've been looking for. We're so close to the beach we can hear the waves breaking on the shore, we can see out across the whole bay. I told you I'd know it the minute I saw it – Cockle Shell Castle is the place.'

I'm swallowing my shock, trying to get to grips with this. Playing for time, thinking back to his pet hates. 'There certainly aren't any pesky cobbles or disgusting fields.'

His smile has spread to a grin. 'Better still, the lawns are smooth and firm, the gravel paths are in excellent order, and the stone flags and circulation space inside couldn't be better.'

'I can't argue with that.' What is this recurring obsession he has with damned floors?

He's eyeing me. 'It's a great party venue that's endlessly photogenic. See, I was taking notice – that was what you told me to look for, wasn't it?' He has me there. 'And best of all, Merwyn's here.' As he goes over to where Merwyn is lying on a velvet throw on the sofa, Merwyn's little tail bumps against the cushions. 'Every venue needs a dog like Merwyn.'

There are difficult clients. And then there are impossible ones like Nic. And I can't quite believe this is happening. 'There's only one problem.' I hate to be the one to break it to him. 'This isn't actually a venue.'

Nic's frowning. 'As if I'd let a little thing like that stand in my way. Pixie deserves the best, and this is it.'

If this had been a venue I'd visited with Ben, I'd have moved heaven and earth to get married here. But weddings are a specialist market. There are reasons why venues command hugely inflated prices. Stag weekends can be heavy duty, but a castle rammed with rampaging wedding guests who've been drinking all day would make a handful of stags look like a picnic.

I turn to Ivy. 'Have you ever considered hosting weddings here?'

Ivy gives a shrug. 'Bill looked into getting a license a while ago.' She pulls a face. 'But after his hard-to-please guests at Christmas he's discounted weddings altogether.'

I completely understand. 'They're not something you dip in and out of.'

Nic's hands are deep in the pockets of his windcheater and his jaw is jutting. 'I've considered every venue in the county, none of the others come close to this.'

I moan inwardly, then make my tone bright and light. 'But, Nic, if the owner isn't willing, it isn't even an option.'

He gives a sniff. 'I wouldn't be asking if it wasn't so important. Please, please, please, Milla – you have to make it happen.'

I'm opening and closing my mouth. 'B—b—b—but ...'

'So I'll leave it with you?' He raises an eyebrow.

I let out a wail of protest. 'But you said you were on this until it was sorted!'

He sends me a grin over his shoulder. 'You have a wonderful way of working your magic, Milla. See what you can do for us here.'

And as he strides through the door and we hear the front door slam behind him, all Ivy and I can do is blink at each other.

Chapter 19

The next Thursday.
At Cockle Shell Castle, in the distillery.
Ice buckets and recipes for success.

As the week goes on, I'm wishing I'd never taken Nic anywhere near the castle and I'm also kicking myself for ever having my bright idea for the hens. If I'd suggested a spa experience at the Harbourside Hotel they'd still have had a great time and life for the rest of us would have been so much less fraught.

Without getting too tied up with the details, Ivy asks her partner Bill if he's up for a wedding at the castle, and Bill comes straight back with the answer: 'Hell, no.'

Then Nic sends me a message reminding me that money's no object. But rather than tempting Bill to reconsider, that makes him shut down even more.

Which leads us all the way to the design-your-own-cocktail evening a week later in the coach house gin distillery at the castle, where it's less a case of 'shake your pompoms, it's Thursday', and more 'put your flak jackets on, anything could blow up here'.

I'm standing with Poppy by the Star Shower gin table, my compromise medium-heeled boots tapping on the polished concrete floor, hoping the new denim midi Ivy helped me pick from the slightly reduced section at Fat Face isn't too casual. As we build our first cocktail we're gazing up at the high sloping ceiling and the hewn stone walls and leafing through the prettiest recipe card suggestions on the table, waiting to move on to the boards of chopped herbs and fruit-filled garnish bowls.

Behind us, the distillery is rammed not only with brides and grooms, but with the entire staff of Brides by the Sea too. Lily and her other half, Kip, are just arriving, Jess and Bart just popped a bottle of champagne over by the copper cauldrons in the corner, and Holly and Rory are both in Cockle Shell Castle aprons offering suggestions to the more hesitant couples. Even Casper Jonston's turned up to tout for business for his wedding cars.

Poppy drops the spoon back in the ice bucket and turns to me. 'Anyway, where's your tame groom? Have you dared to let him off the leash?'

I laugh. 'He's gone to make a gimlet – under strict orders to drink his gin and stay well away from Bill.' Ivy said Bill might be persuaded, but it'll have to be at the right time, in the right way. 'If Mr Trendell does a macho rush he could blow his chances forever.'

Poppy shakes her head. 'Poor Nic.'

I have to say she's wasting her sympathy. 'There's nothing poor about Nic. He's first in line for the biggest pain-in-the-arse client of the year award.' For a million reasons, not least being how hot he's looking as I catch a glimpse of his slate grey eyes and dark stubble shadows over the bottle necks. And that's despite me staying strictly alcohol-free tonight.

I'm aware how great it would be for me if the venue search

ended here and now, which is why I'm ready to move heaven and earth to make it happen. I've also been thinking very hard about unrequited desire and fancying people you shouldn't. I reckon what I'm suffering from with Nic is a raging hormonal crush linked to me being celibate for over a year now.

Obviously, with my heart truly pulverised and my life in ruins, I'll be avoiding relationships like the plague for at least the next ten years, if not forever. But due to the human race being programmed to survive rather than die out every time someone gets cheated on, my libido still needs to flex now and again to keep in shape.

So whatever fake rushes I'm getting here, they're simply my primal urges limbering up while my shattered emotions stay fully protected. My personal survival mechanism has kicked in by making sure I'm getting the flutters for the most unattainable individual in St Aidan, if not England. They don't come any more out-of-reach than a groom fully besotted with his amazing bride-to-be. So it might be uncomfortable, and at times it might be agonising. But at least now I understand it I can dismiss it, knowing it will go away soon.

And to be fair, now I've found my explanation, I'm less disturbed and alarmed by the intensity of my physical reactions. Obviously, I'd give anything to make them stop, but at least I'm reassured that this isn't about me being a bad person. I'm completely confident it will dematerialise when Nic gets married and the job ends. And if that thought momentarily makes my insides freeze, it's just too bad.

I take a minute to admire the fabulous glass tables like the ones in the house, drop some viola flowers into my tumbler of special cordial, then peer into Poppy's scarlet flute. 'What are you going for?'

She reaches for a splash of fresh blackcurrant juice then tosses in a handful of red currants. 'A bramble base with a raspberry gin echo and a pink stripy umbrella.'

As I'm here more as a spectator than to join in, I didn't bother to look at the cordial label any further than it having a really pretty picture of dill and fennel. But whatever I'm drinking is so delicious it slips down really fast and I go straight back for the same again, but this time add raspberries and a mint leaf. As I only had a cheese muffin for dinner, I'm guessing my body craving the calories is why I'm feeling so thirsty. At the rate I'm knocking back the berries, I'll have had my five a day in no time.

As for Nic, I'm keeping watch while staying far enough away to avoid any unnecessary shivers, and for now he's safe with Rory and Bart. And Casper breezed past me earlier saying he's just back from Indonesia and let's connect later, which possibly explains his yellow shirt and why I never heard back from him about lunch.

It's ages later when I finally get back to Poppy again. And despite eating my body weight in fruit garnish, I'm seriously starting to get hunger wobbles. I'm standing with Poppy by the massive floor-to-ceiling window at the beach end of the building, staring out at the trail of lights along the bay, when Ivy arrives too.

Her eyes are shining. 'We've got lots of couples who are planning to use our gin in their wedding day cocktails, and loads more people have signed up to our mailing list.' Her sleek bob is almost black in the gentle light as she flicks it behind her ear. 'And one quick tip, Milla. If you're hoping to change Bill's mind at all, he's at his happiest in the distillery.'

'So now might be a good time?' I spin around to the table,

take another shot from the tap on my favourite juice urn and grab the last lime twist. 'Okay, I'm on it.'

Poppy's eyes are bright. 'And I'll come as backup.'

Three strides later we skid to a halt on the edge of the group of guys. I drag in a breath, screw up my courage, then reach up and tap Bill on the shoulder. 'If you've got a moment, Bill, I'm Milla, I organise the wedding fairs where you'll be showcasing your gin.'

Bill turns and smiles. 'Right, great to meet you, Milla. I can talk you through the manufacturing process if you'd like?'

'Lovely.' I have two seconds to launch before he does. 'I'm also Milla who wants to book the castle for a wedding – on behalf of my client, obviously. Actually, we're really desperate – it's so beautiful here.' I'm splurging more than I'd planned.

He's rubbing his jaw while his eyes narrow. 'Let me level with you, Milla – my Christmas let was a nightmare.' He gives the same kind of grimace he'd make if he sucked on one of Ivy's lemon slices. 'That's the last time I'll ever be blinded by pound signs.' So at least that confirms why Nic can't just wave his cheque book around and get what he wants.

I need to keep him talking. 'It's a shame to let one challenging client group put you off.'

Poppy's giving me a discrete double thumbs up for that behind her cocktail.

Bill's lips are tight. 'Weddings are a big deal, there's huge potential to let people down. And anyone who pays top dollar won't hesitate to take you to the cleaners if things go wrong.' He still sounds very raw. If only we'd come along six months earlier before he'd got his Christmas candles burned, we'd likely have swung it.

The remaining groups have both fanned out into half circles

now, the talking has stopped and everyone's openly listening in. From along the line of women, Immie waves her pint glass at him. 'So what you're saying, Bill, is that you can't be arsed with this wedding of Milla's!'

Bill shrugs. 'I'd rather stick to making gin and serving stags.'

Nic's brow wrinkles into a frown and as he steps towards Immie he lets out a squawk. 'Hey, I know you! You're the roller skate woman! What the hell are you doing here?'

Immie's reaching up and prodding Nic in the chest. 'Stop being a toad bollock, I could be about to save your arse here.' She turns to Bill. 'As for you – stop wimping out and open your mind for half a second ...'

The trick with Immie is to keep her energy positive so I jump in quickly. 'No offense, Bill, but what Immie is trying to say is that if she were here your bedrooms would run like clockwork.'

Now it's Bill's turn to frown at Immie. 'Why the hell would she be in my bedrooms?'

I risk a little eyebrow wiggle. 'She looks after the holiday lets at Daisy Hill Farm, they have loads of weddings a year there. I'm sure they'd be happy to help you out too.'

Bill's staring at Immie. 'Seriously?'

I'm smiling at Bill but, to be fair, I'm as surprised about how this is going as he is. It's like I've reconnected with the same bit of me that grabbed the mic at Cally's wedding. 'Poppy, Rafe, and their team have won Cornwall's Best Wedding Venue award ... er ... quite a few times now.'

Poppy's beaming at me. 'Absolutely true.'

I'm beaming. 'So there's your answer. If you want to host a wedding but lack the expertise, simply get the Daisy Hill guys over to manage the event for you.'

Bill's staring at me. 'It's that simple?'

I'm grinning at Bill. 'All the gain, none of the pain.' I have no idea where that came from either, so I try for something less crass and more corporate. 'It would certainly take the pressure off.'

Bill coughs. 'What you're forgetting is the castle is very old and prone to problems, like broken boilers and sticking door handles.'

I'm not going to let him back out over a doorknob, so I say what I've heard Poppy say so many times before. 'They do weddings every day – when things go wrong, they simply find a new way forward.'

Poppy's nodding too. 'It's often the things that don't go to plan that make the days especially memorable.'

I'm giving Bill a nudge. 'You wouldn't have to stop at one wedding either. You could do six a year, like they do at the manor.'

Poppy's straight in to back me up. 'That way they're really exclusive, we stay familiar with the venue, and we all do well out of them.'

Jess has joined us now and is chipping in. 'It's such a spectacular setting that you wouldn't even need to advertise. Brides by the Sea could handle all the bookings for you – our rates are very reasonable.' You have to admire the way Jess seizes every opportunity.

I have to close the deal. 'I'll take that as a yes then?'

Bill puts his hand up. 'Hang on, don't let's get too carried away.'

Immie lets out a triumphant shriek. 'Too late mate. This is St Aidan. We all pitch in and make things happen, that's how it works here.'

Jess is shouting over Poppy's head. 'Better still, Bart and I have been prevaricating too long. Getting married at Cockle Shell Castle would be way more practical for us than Klosters or St Kitts. We'll take the second of your six slots, Bill.'

Bill's opening and closing his mouth. 'B—b—but I haven't agreed.'

I reach forward and pat Bill on the arm. 'It's obviously such a great idea, I think they've decided for you. I'll be in touch to finalise the details in the morning, Bill.' I'm not one for speeches or proclamations, but as I look around the circle of smiling faces I realise I'm going to have to do more here.

Jess waves a champagne bottle. 'Let's all drink to that! Give us a toast, Milla.'

Casper's blond head pops up next to her. 'Don't forget, Here Comes the (B)Ride! will give you the coolest wedding cars in town.'

I've drunk so much lemonade, I'm going to be peeing for England tonight. I scuttle back to my favourite urn for a re-fill. I have zero idea how to do this properly, but I grab a chair and leap up onto it anyway. Now's my chance to set this in stone in front of as many people as possible, so I raise my glass. 'Here's to St Aidan's newest, most exclusive wedding venue! To Brides and Grooms at Cockle Shell Castle!' It feels like the more I throw in, the harder it will be for Bill to duck out of this later. 'And yay to Captain Kirk and his up-coming wedding day!' No idea why I called Nic that in front of everyone, but I throw back my head again, down my entire half pint, narrowly miss choking on a raspberry, but from the roar around the group it seems to have worked because everyone joins in.

As the shouting dies down, I'm still on the chair, and it's suddenly a lot more wobbly than before.

Nic's staring up at me. 'I thought you weren't drinking, Milla?'

'I'm not. Well, not apart from my specials.'

He stares up at the roof. 'And how many of those have you had?'

I screw my eyes closed and let the garnishes float past the insides of my eyelids just like I do with sheep jumping over a fence when I'm trying to drop off. 'Thirteen maybe.' Give or take a couple.

Nic's face crumples. 'I wish you'd told me you were still finding weddings difficult, rather than hitting the gin.'

'I'm drinking CORDIAL! From the thingy with the—' it's not helpful that I hiccough '—wafty leaves on the picture.'

Nic turns and comes back with my urn. 'This one?'

This time my hic comes out with my nod. 'Yu-p.'

'Jeez, Milla!' Nic's shaking his head. 'Sure, it's got ferns, but this is exactly what it says on the tin, extra strength gin infused with herbs.'

'But it can't be. It was on the leaf green fruit juice table.'

'No, Milla, those were the forest green speciality extra-strong spirits. I was using the alcohol-free table.'

'But what about your cocktails?'

He's shaking his head. 'Those can wait for another time. One of us needed to stay sober to get you home.'

As the words sink in, I let out a moan. 'Oh crap. On the upside it tasted totally fant ... fant ... fant ... fant ... abulous.' I'm not sure that's even a word. As for standing on a see-through chair, I can't recommend it. It's like those glass floors you get in tall, expensive buildings that no one can walk on because they give you vertigo – only worse. When I look down past the toes of my boots I can see straight through to the floor below and it's like when you paddle and the sea rushes past your feet and makes you dizzy. It's so bad I do one of those awful lurches, the ones that you get when you're dropping off to sleep and you feel like you've just fallen off a cliff.

I've almost found my balance point again when Nic yells. 'Milla, watch out!'

'Watch out? For *what*?' I spin round so fast to look, I might have been fine if the damned chair legs hadn't been made of jelly. As it is, the wobbling goes bananas, and the next thing I know I'm doing one of my dream falls through the air. Except, as the polished concrete rushes towards me at a hundred miles an hour, it suddenly hits me – I'm not asleep, I'm awake. The last things I see are the see-through chair arm, hurtling towards me and Nic's outstretched arms.

Then there's a final flash of yellow and everything goes black.

Chapter 20

Later on Thursday.
Outside Brides by the Sea.
Singalongs and softplay.

'Well, thanks for the lift back.'
          I'm in the passenger seat, watching as Nic turns into the mews and comes to a halt in front of Brides by the Sea.

He pulls on the handbrake, leans forward and rests his forearms on the steering wheel. 'And thank you for the in-car entertainment.'

Okay, I might have been singing along to *Uptown Girl*. Probably at the top of my voice. Lucky for him there was only time for two repeats.

'And I'm really sorry ... for all of it.' For landing in his arms when I fell off the damned chair. For knocking us off balance. As if getting accidentally off my face isn't bad enough, falling on top of my client when he manfully puts his body in the way as he tries to stop me smashing my skull on the floor – well that's unforgivable. Made all the worse by Casper diving in too. Don't ask why he thought jumping in with a rugby tackle so we all ended up in a heap on the concrete would be helpful.

Nic swallows. 'Given the successful outcome with the castle booking, I think we can overlook the rest.'

But I still want to make it clear. 'However it looks, I don't make a habit of getting wasted.' Thanks to the wind blasting straight off the beach and into my face, I'm a lot less wooshy than I was. A lot more back in the room.

He gives me a sideways glance. 'Only once every three weeks then.'

I roll my eyes. 'At work I'm usually much more—' I'm looking out at the mews, the stone washed in the yellow light from the street lamps, the shop window lit up and snowy with tulle, studded with tiny lights '—more careful. More ... not drunk.'

'I'll take your word for it.' Nic sniffs. 'I was going to suggest you came down to the boat for pancakes.'

That's not appropriate. For so many reasons. 'Truly, however hungry I am, that's never going to work. I doubt I'd make it onto the jetty without falling into the harbour.' I give a little shiver as I think about it and reach for the door handle. Me throwing myself at him once is enough for today. 'I'd better go up.'

As I bump my shoulder against the door to open it, his hand lands on my arm. 'Hang on, we don't want you in a heap on the cobbles. I'll come and help you out.'

That's the thing, people who haven't drunk anything can move so much faster than people who have. A split second later I'm still where I was and he's arrived at the open door. And even though I'm on the passenger side instead of in the driving seat, however much I'm trying for it not to be, it's still like Valentine's night revisited. You'd think after being crushed in a heap together I'd be over the scent of him, but another head-spinning waft blows over me.

'Right, let's do this.' I'm peering down at the pavement and getting ready to leap, but mostly all I can see is the front of Nic's shirt inside his open jacket. The denim of his jeans stretched tight across his thighs in the half light. The bulge of his Adams apple as he swallows.

'It's a long way down for someone who'd fall off the jetty.' He sends me a grin. 'Here, grab my hand.'

Even slightly drunk people know how to get out of a van – you put one arm on the dash handle and the other on the door post. If I'd done that, I'd have been fine. As it is, when I begin to lower myself and he grabs one of my hands, I'm done for. Again. This time my tumble is less spectacular but the result so much worse – I plummet downwards and he doesn't step backwards. So I simply body slam into him and end up rammed between him and the van seat. Fully engulfed in the heat from inside his coat, all I can hear is the sound of my heart hammering against my chest wall and the distant roar of the waves crashing far below us on the beach.

I'm staring up at him, and for however long he's staring down at me, it's like our eyes are locked. I hear the clatter of two hearts banging really loudly. And then someone – it could be me – lets out a groan. 'Oh frig.'

You don't need to ask – thanks to all the gin, my lust-ometer went off-the-scale quite a few hours ago. Due to my huge breath in, my boobs are practically bursting the buttons off the front of my dress and my knee's somehow rammed between his legs in a way that's terrible news for everything everywhere that's aching to be rubbed. It's as if time's standing still, my lungs feel like they're going to explode. And his face is dipping down towards mine, I'm closing my eyes, parting my lips, standing on tiptoe to reach ...

'Waaaaaaaaaaaaaaaaaaaaahhhh!' It takes a second to realise that squawk came from me.

Nic steps back, but now he's staring at me even harder. 'Everything okay, Milla?'

'Tiaras!' I'm winging it, filling the gaping chasm of embarrassment. I'm not sure, but I think I just threw myself at the bloody groom. Properly this time. If my override instinct hadn't kicked in, my tongue would be halfway down his throat by now. And where making out through a van window imposes its own limitations, when you're crushing your entire body against someone's pretty sizable erogenous zone, it's a lot harder to make excuses and pull out of it. 'And hair vines. And combs with pearls. Jess just ordered a fantabulous new range.'

He's looking bemused. 'And?'

'If your booking's nailed down, accessories are next. That's all.' I wriggle for the gap and make a leap towards the door to the attic stairway.

'Something else to look forward to.' His smile has to be ironic, but at least we're moving on.

'And thanks again for driving.'

He dangles the van keys. 'I'll park at the harbour and bring these back with me. It's probably best if I stay over, seeing how accident prone you are.'

I gulp so hard I almost swallow my tongue. 'What?'

He laughs. 'Anyone who can pull off that castle booking is worth hanging on to. We need to take extra good care of you.' He pauses for a cough. 'I can't possibly let you stay on your own. Especially if you're totalled.'

I pull myself up to my full height and point at my feet. 'Heels, not too high. A bit of sea air, my head's all clear again.'

'At least let me see you up the stairs?'

So I can end up jumping him in the kitchen instead? I'm holding my ground here. 'Totally not necessary.' It's amazing how sheer panic can sober you up. 'Drop the keys off at the shop in the morning. I'll message you about the booking.'

'Only if you're sure?'

'Oh, I totally am.'

And when I slam the shop door behind me, I'm not sure who's had the luckier escape. But one thing's certain – I can't carry on like this. I need to find a new plan.

Chapter 21

Until Bill accepts a deposit we're still treading carefully at the castle; *eggshells* doesn't come close – it's more like walking on meringues. It also makes sense to keep Nic well away until we've tied up the details. Everyone is busy with events over the Easter weekend, so first thing on Tuesday, Poppy and Kip meet me over at the castle with their files of brochures and price lists and contracts and happy couple letters to show to Bill. After another tour, we all sit around the kitchen table, and Bill and Ivy give their input on the quirks of the castle. Then Kip and Bill go off to make some calls to the council, and Ivy, Poppy, and I curl up on the kitchen sofas with Merwyn to sort out available dates. Ivy and Poppy search through their diaries to find days in July when Kip's team and the castle are both free. Meanwhile, I'm watching the frills of white breakers moving up onto the sand and looking out to the vast stretch of duck egg-blue sea streaked with jade beyond, thinking that this truly is a gem of a location.

As weekends are out, they quickly come up with some

weekday dates that work for both of them. I'm nipping in and out of the room where there's phone signal, messaging Nic to check which they'd prefer. As I listen for the distant ping of Nic's reply on my phone, I'm rubbing Merwyn's silky ears and eating Bill's warm raspberry muffins.

Ivy sips her coffee then puts down her mug. 'It's funny, Milla, I'm so used to seeing you and Nic together, I keep having to remind myself you're not the couple here.'

That's the last thing I want to hear, even as a joke, but I laugh it off. 'He's definitely marrying someone else.'

But once you stop to think about it, it's been one unfortunate episode after another with me and Nic. And I know Elfinor has a water-tight work reason for not being around, but it's still strange that she hasn't come to visit once. Having been with my own very reluctant fiancé who went on to commit the most spectacular fuck up, I hope Nic's not on his own – possibly unconscious – mission to push his wedding off the rails faster than he's arranging it. For his sake, I hope he's marrying the right person.

My stomach has dropped so far my throat feels hollow, but I keep my voice steady and my words slow. 'For the record, there are two things I've noticed about Nic. The first is him driving me wild by refusing to focus. And second is how truly devoted to his bride he is.' I throw in another thought to move them on and hope like hell they don't hark back to Valentine's Night. However much I think about it, I can't quite reconcile or excuse what happened there; I still feel uncomfortable about it from his side and mine. 'But I'm not the best person to ask, because I actually haven't got a clue what being in love actually feels like.' As I'm here with my good friends, this could be a good opportunity to get a few things straight in my head.

I didn't ever have any excitement or compulsion with Ben. Not in the way they talk about in the trashy songs anyway. It was all very matter of fact; our progress was logical rather than passion-based. We got engaged in the aftermath of Phoebe and Harry's wedding and with our leases ending at the same time it made sense to get a flat together so we could save for the future.

If I'd known how picky he was going to be about me leaving my micellar water on the bathroom shelf instead of in my bedroom drawer, and that however neatly I put away his boxers, he'd have to get them all out again and re-iron and refold them, I might have thought about it harder. The only real flutter of excitement I ever had was the first time we went into John Lewis to buy light bulbs together. But Ben took so long to decide on how many lumens and if we wanted warm white or cool, and then agonised for literally hours over the shape. By the time he'd filled the basket I'd lost the will to live.

I can see Ivy giving me a sideways glance so I need to explain. 'Poppy will tell you, I totally missed out on being a teenager because my mum was ill. I had the longest engagement known to man, and then he left me for someone else. When it comes to love I don't really have a clue.'

She's looking at me through narrowed eyes. 'Love's funny – it's not at all rational, you often don't have any choice about it.'

Poppy's nodding. 'It can be very chaotic. And it has all kinds of weird effects on your body too.'

Ivy's agreeing. 'You might deny it at first, but it has a power all of its own. It just grows and engulfs you.'

I have to be honest. 'The way you two are selling it, I'll definitely be giving it a miss.' It's also slightly unnerving to think that if I were comparing how I've felt lately, I'd be nodding. A lot.

Ivy laughs. 'That's the thing, I'm not sure you always have that option.' She holds her finger up as there's a low beep. 'In the meantime, that could be Nic for you now?'

'Let's see what he says.' I make a dash for the downstairs bedroom and grab my phone.

Pixie says yes to 2nd July!!

I ignore that my insides feel like they've been hit by the ice age and tap in my reply.

So we'll go ahead with that then?

He comes straight back.

Yup. So long as that roller skate destruction person isn't anywhere near.

Why am I sighing?

I said there would be compromises – that could be yours.

He's straight back.

Me not getting a Saturday is already a compromise!

I'll move this on before he thinks of any more conditions.

Any thoughts on save the date styles?

Straight back again.

I'll leave that to you.

No surprise there then.

Fine, I'll sort a few options and get back to you.

I go back through to Ivy and Poppy. 'They're going for July 2nd.'
Poppy shouts. 'Yay to that!'
I know I've explained this to my own satisfaction, but I might as well ask. 'So, one last question, where does insane lust fit into the love picture? I take it that's completely different?' *Asking for a friend here, obviously.*
Ivy laughs. 'In my experience I'd say they're pretty closely linked. When I first came to the castle, Bill annoyed the bejesus out of me, but I still fancied the pants off him.'
Poppy's agreeing again. 'Same with me and Rafie.'
Damn, damn, damn. 'Great.' My jaw's sagging with the shock. There's nothing good about it at all. But before I have time to properly beat myself up about it there are footsteps out in the hall and the guys come in.
'Obviously when I found out how delicious Bill's baking was, he made me much less cross.' Ivy looks up at Bill. 'I'm just explaining to Milla how we got together.'
Bill's laughing. 'I'm under no illusions, what clinched it was me making a cake that looked like Merwyn.'
Poppy's joining in. 'Never underestimate the power of chocolate buttercream.'
Kip puts his folder down on the table. 'We'll have to try that on the council. Bill already made an application to hold weddings last year, so the paperwork shouldn't take too long to come through.'

Poppy's wiggling her eyebrows at me. 'Which means you can move straight on to dresses and menus and styling, Milla.'

And the flowers and photographers and cars and a million other decisions that are going to take weeks to sort out. I know how much everyone's put in to make this happen so I'm beaming back at her because I can't do anything else. 'I can't wait!'

But the words are just a whisper because when I think of having to sort out all those things with Nic at my side, after what I've just been hearing, my stomach contracts so much I feel like I'm going to be sick.

As for how I'm going to handle the next three months – I need to acknowledge that, on every side, I'm in deep shit here. And I need to make some big changes.

Chapter 22

Later on Tuesday.
At Brides by the Sea.
Bigger pictures and even bigger ones.

'Remind me again why we need save-the-date cards?'
This is Nic, later that afternoon down in the styling department, reminding me why every step of this journey is so hard.

I've explained this to him so often, what does one more time matter? 'You send these to lock in your guests until you finalise the details for the main invitations.'

It's also underlining exactly why I've come to this decision: now that the all-important venue has been booked, due to what I'm calling in my head the 'ongoing workplace difficulties', these cards will be the last job I do for Nic.

When I came back from the castle to the shop, the first thing I did was to check how the rest of the Daisy Hill gang were fixed for Nic's date, and with the entire team on the job, I can step back knowing Nic will be in good hands – he'll still get the best service and the most amazing wedding. Bish bash bosh, that's how easy it is.

I spent the rest of the morning brooding over what Ivy had

said about thinking we were the ones getting married. As for their eye-opening revelations about love, I'm not even thinking about those. But as my mum used to say, *there's no smoke without fire, Milla*.

As I played around with the card designs, I knew I couldn't ignore the warning bells any more. If there's fire, you need to fight it. Pour water on it. Or in my case, bring in several engines with damn good hoses.

There's probably nothing at all in what could have been a throwaway comment. But, thinking about it, I should have been much less friendly towards Nic all along. I should have kept a better distance. Like, a couple of counties away would have been good. Obviously, my hidden feelings are leaking out. I'm more transparent than I thought and people are perceptive. The only thing to do is to distance myself straight away.

When I look back, there's so much to beat myself up about. So many things I should have done better. More importantly, things I should have avoided. Once I start, the list is endless. Nic ending up in my room at Cally's wedding, those half-naked brush-pasts in the attic, letting him drive me home last Thursday. If I'd made myself all stern and frosty we might never have made the progress we have. But I'd never have got into this mess either.

The 'should've' list is very long. I should've been firmer, I should've made my boundaries more obvious, and I should never have started enjoying his company. I mean, when the hell did that happen?

When I think back over every single meeting, I'm shuddering with shame at every one. I know none of the accidents and blunders were planned, and I never had any intentions other than to be completely upfront and honest and honourable. But the only option is for me to step back from this immediately and hope that's soon enough to stop the fall-out. And if there's a silver lining to this, it's that after today I won't have to be near, so I'll be spared the agony of another three months of rubbing shoulders – and anything else – with Nic.

Just to make sure I'm taking my own advice, I jerk my chair a couple of feet to the left and push my laptop towards him across the table so the keyboard is at arm's length.

We should really be making the most of the lovely spring sunshine by sitting out in the shelter of the courtyard, but for this last meeting I've taken the precaution of staying inside. I look through the glass doors across the outdoor terrace, fix my eyes on the little triangle of blue that's the sea, and make my voice brusque. 'The faster you get these save-the-dates out, the more guests will be able to make it. So I've kept them simple, just the date and first names in handwritten fonts. A plain cream card might work and rose gold lettering would add a classy twist.'

'Great.' Nic grunts even though I'm not sure he's looking at the screen.

I'm giving Nic plenty of options, so I go out on a high. 'You could go with a funny one like 'Shit Got Real' or 'Free Cake', or else there are the straightforward 'We're Getting Married', or 'This Is The Day' ones, or even just two names with a heart between?' Of course, it wasn't hard to write Pixie and Nic. It's happening, I won't be anywhere near. And I need to get over it.

Nic's forehead wrinkles. 'What's rose gold again?'

However many times I say it, he never gets this either. 'It's gold with a pink tinge, like copper, but softer.' I let that sink in. 'It's very current.'

He slides me a grin. 'You always say that, every time I ask.'

I squirm as my heart clenches in response to that smile, but I keep my tone firm. 'Are you winding me up?'

'As if I'd do that.' His grin widens. 'You know me too well, Milla Vanilla.'

Shit! Milla Vanilla! I never even got to that one. I die again inside this time with a very loud moan. 'Possibly.'

He lets out a squawk. 'Possibly? What kind of head mistress-y reply is that? You sound like that awful Thisbe mate of yours.'

'You mean Phoebe.'

He's laughing. 'Come on, loosen up, Mills. No one's called me Captain Kirk since last Thursday and I'm starting to miss it.'

How could I have been so stupid? And I'm wondering why this has gone pear-shaped. 'So do you have a preference?'

As he laughs his eyes light up. 'Probably not vanilla, thanks for asking though.'

I should not be automatically thinking he means his bloody sex life, either. 'For the cards.'

'If you'd told me you'd left your sense of humour in the attic, we could have got on with this so much faster.' He sits up and squints at the screen. 'Definitely the one with the two names linked, Pixie loves hearts.'

I'm sure she does. 'Thanks for the quick decision.' I'm approximately two questions away from the end of my work here.

He's biting his lip. 'They're all great ... apart from the one glaring error, that is.'

'Excuse me?'

He's pursing his lips. 'You've got the name wrong.'

I'm ready for this. 'We'll simply change Pixie for Elfinor before we print.'

This time he lets out a full-blown snort. 'It's way funnier than that.'

I'm not smiling. 'And are you going to let me in on the joke?'

His eyes are wide and his cheeks look like they're going to pop. 'I don't know how we got so far with this so wrong. Pixie's not marrying me, she's marrying Ewan.'

My voice is high. 'Who the hell is Ewan?'

Nic's explaining slowly. 'Ewan is Pixie's fiancé. That is what you call the soon-to-be-groom?'

'So where ... the hell ... do you fit in?' I need time to pick myself up off the floor.

He's sounding so matter of fact. 'Pixie's my sister and Ewan's another best mate.'

'Ok-a-a-y.' It's simple but it's still taking a while to sink in. Nic isn't going to marry Pixie, he's just her very devoted brother. It's as if someone just lifted a weight off my chest. In fact, I feel so light that if I weren't clinging on to the table, I might just float away. I didn't kiss/dry hump/throw myself at/spend the night with anyone else's partner.

Nic's carrying on. 'Ewan's in the navy, they're both a ten-hour drive away, north of Glasgow, which is why I'm looking after things this end.'

I'm back to my hedgehog squeak. 'So, whatever happened to the *Don't Tell The Bride* thing?'

'Well, that part's still right.' He takes a breath. 'The less she knows about it, the less likely she is to get cold feet and pull out. Pixie really wants to marry Ewan, but she's not a diva, she's shying away from being the centre of attention. I probably should have been clearer about this to begin with. But when I asked Jess for help to sort out a wedding on the quiet because the bride is working away she jumped on it, and that was that. We didn't discuss it any further.' Knowing Jess, she'd have been so intent on landing the job, the rest of the details wouldn't have come up.

I let out a groan. 'Oh my days, you don't make it easy do you?'

As he looks at the screen again, he gives a visible shudder. 'Brrrr, could you close that down? Seeing my name on those is freaking me out.'

Now I've heard it all, but what a turnaround. 'Don't tell me. Another guy terrified of commitment?'

He's back to looking pleased with himself. 'I'm the world's most confirmed bachelor, destined to stay single forever and all that.'

I'm muttering. 'I'm sure George Clooney said the same at one stage.' But I have to ask. 'So what made you commit to a life as an eternal playboy?'

His smile fades. 'It's not quite like that, Milla.' He sounds hurt, then he blows out his cheeks. 'It's another one of those long stories you're so fond of.'

I shake my head. 'So if ever I've got a spare hundred years you'll tell me you're too busy building your business.'

His voice rises in protest. 'I have a great life. Most of my mates would give their right arm to be as free as I am.'

'Sure they would, that's why they're all getting married.'

I'm not sure why I'm giving him such a hard time over this. I mean, my first thought wasn't even *whoopee, he's not taken, I can have him for me*. I was simply relieved that no one had unwittingly cheated. As it sinks in, I'm mostly thinking that if my theories about why I wanted to grab him were true, I should have instantly stopped fancying him because he had suddenly become available. But I have to be honest, I haven't quite reached that place yet.

There's another thing niggling me. Whenever Elfie was in the picture, there was always an outside chance that she would turn out to be a mean-faced bride who didn't deserve him, a teensy chance that she would turn up and they'd decide for themselves – with absolutely no input from me – that they really weren't suited. So what I've got to honestly ask myself is: was I secretly wanting that to happen?

If that's the case, I need to stop and take a reality check. Because now that he's defiantly, stubbornly, happily, ecstatically single, there's actually even less chance of him being available than there was when he might just have turned out to be a reluctant groom who had nothing in common with his fiancée.

And right now, my mind is a blur of questions. But rather than seeing things more clearly, sitting here in a sun spot, watching a tiny fishing boat chugging across the turquoise water in the distance, all I'm feeling is horribly confused. And though I was soaring when I first realised, I now feel like I've crashed back down and my chest's collapsed. All I know is that I don't have to resign right now. In fact, if I did resign now it would look terrible.

But one thing's for sure, I'm going to seize this chance to rewrite the rules so I can make sure in future my behaviour is beyond reproach. From now on, if Poppy or Ivy looks at me interacting with any client, all they'll see is serious, dedicated, professional communication.

I push back my hair and re-cross my legs, being super-careful not to flash anything I shouldn't, then clear my throat and prepare to launch my new initiative. 'In any case, I've been thinking it would be useful to realign our working relationship.'

Nic's squinting at me. 'What's this? Another thought from Thisbe?'

I keep my smile very serene. 'Simply that as we move forwards from here it should be on a more professional footing.'

'You mean you'll be getting drunk less?' He's shaking his head. 'Don't feel you have to do that for me, Milla. If getting hammered is your style, I really don't mind looking after you, since you seem to get results. I actually like it, it gives me a sense of purpose.'

I can feel my nostrils flaring, which is never a good look. 'That's the part I'm not comfortable with. It's completely inappropriate.' As for him enjoying it, that's even worse. It makes me feel like a project.

He's sending me a bemused stare. 'Well someone's got to do it. What happened? Have you had a visit from the fun police?' He rubs his hands together. 'I'm starving, how about we talk about this more over homemade pancakes at mine?'

I'm shaking my head. 'That's exactly what I'm trying to avoid, Nic.'

He's staring up at the ceiling. 'There could be whipped cream and banana with rum and orange?'

I swallow because my mouth's watering so much. 'I'd still rather not, thanks all the same.'

'Damn, you've turned into Frisbee again.' He narrows his eyes. 'If it makes you feel better, we could talk about colours. Or groom's suits. Or bridesmaids.'

'Do you know how desperate you sound?' I manage to bite my tongue before I call him Captain Kirk. Under any other circumstances, I'd be whooping at his enthusiasm, but somehow today I can't. I feel like my heart's been through the wringer ... and the tumble drier too.

'I'm not desperate, just hungry. And how about we borrow

Merwyn so we can take him for a walk along the beach to work off the calories ... and then we can talk about lanterns.'

'Nic ...'

'What?'

He'd have had the old me at colours. But I'm not that easy anymore. 'I'm flat out for the rest of this week getting ready for a last-minute wedding fair that's coming up on Saturday.'

His eyes narrow. 'A wedding fair – should I be going to that?'

I've no idea where his sudden interest has come from, but as it's my first with Brides by the Sea and without Phoebe, I'll need all my mind on the job. The last thing I want is Nic hanging around judging, or worse still, jinxing it.

I wrinkle my nose. 'It'll be more productive if you come to one where I'm more available to show you around and talk you through it all.' I'm getting the hang of sounding kick-ass and serious. 'So once we've got the cards sent out I suggest you look through all the information Poppy gave you, study your wedding file until you know it off by heart. And we'll meet up again this time next week.' I bite my tongue before I say, *and smash it!* 'Is that okay with you?'

'Sounds like it'll have to be, Princess Milla.' He sniffs and as he stands up he's towering over me. 'You're the one who said this was urgent. If we don't get this done, you're the one who carries the can.'

And the next thing I know he's striding back towards the desk and the door, hands in his windcheater pockets, without so much as a backwards glance.

Chapter 23

Sunday, twelve days later.
At The Winery at Windy Point.
Amens and April showers.

'What an outlook! And all those lofty inside spaces with those big vats ... it's industrial and modern all at the same time. And such a brilliant setting to show off everyone's wedding items.'

This is me, in the courtyard outside our very first joint Brides by the Sea and Brides Go West wedding fair, and I'm gazing across at the undulating fields in the little inland valley where the vineyards are planted. In the distance there are rows of vines running right across the hillside, their poles and wires so neat they could have been drawn on. Actually, this is a smaller try-out fair that we've slipped in for practice at a brand-new venue, and if I'm gushing it's with a mixture of excitement and relief that after a really early start everyone has arrived and set up without any hitches.

The first couples are beginning to arrive, and Poppy's carrying a stack of cupcake boxes in from the car park. 'Isn't it great here? And so original holding the ceremonies in the barrel store!'

Like most great business done in St Aidan, this is all due to word of mouth. Ten days wasn't much time to get ready, but as the winery's just started opening for weddings, they had a spare Sunday, and are eager to get themselves on the map. All I had to do was email my regular exhibitors to see who could come. And the last-minute social media publicity blitz paid off with loads of couples pre-registering to get goody bags.

It's still early, but there's already a stream of people making their way towards the entrance where my Brides Go West camper is parked and Jess is handing out flutes of Prosecco and elder-flower fizz in return for people's details.

As the forecast is good and the air is already warm, we're making the most of the lovely outdoor spaces. The winery build-ings have big glass doors opening out all around a courtyard, and we've got exhibitors in all the spaces to showcase the venue to the maximum. The ever-popular Roaring Waves brewery gazebo out in the main courtyard is already crowded with grooms and beside it there's a bicycle cart with homemade ice cream that I will be visiting again later. The organic burger barbecue with ethically-sourced charcoal is already smoking, and they're also lighting up some fire baskets for marshmallow toasting.

Holly's here, too, with her photographs and stop-motion videos, and Ivy's brought the whole family. Merwyn, Bill, and his daughter Abby are looking after the Cockle Shell Castle gin stall, while Ivy's on hand for style consultations at the different themed tables she's decorated.

I'm nodding at Poppy. 'With so many people it's a shame I haven't got my Brides Go Wild signage sorted.'

Her eyebrows shoot up. 'A banner would be well worth the investment.'

I'm staring at my van in the distance. 'Or I could just change the roof sign on my camper.'

She nudges me with her shoulder. 'Good thinking, super-woman! West to Wild! Three letters would make it yours rather than Phoebe's.'

I'm liking that a lot more than I should. 'Remind me to ask Nic, he might know where I can get the letters made up.'

Her face relaxes to a grin. 'But the rest is amazing. We've done these fairs at the farm before; believe me, they don't happen on their own.'

I have to say I've barely slept this week worrying about it all. 'All I've got to do now is hold it all together for the next six hours. This is the bit Phoebe usually takes care of.'

Poppy pulls me into a hug with her spare arm. 'I should have lent you my "Feel The Fear and Do It Anyway" playlist.'

'My mum always used to tell me if I took a deep breath and pulled myself up to my full height, it would make me feel as empowered as eating a chocolate muffin. I might just give it a try.' As I drag in my stomach, I add at least four inches to my height. Then I smooth down my green flowery tea dress and remember the sign on my desk back in Bristol. 'Okay, do I look ready to "Go forth and be fierce"?'

Poppy gives my arm a play punch. 'You've got this, Mills, and we're all here to catch you if you need us.' Then she leans across to me. 'Hey, is that a vicar talking to Jess?'

I nod. 'Here to advise on church celebrations.'

'You really have thought of everything!' She wiggles her eyebrows. 'I bet the hot priest in *Fleabag* has done a lot for his take up.'

It's only fair to warn her. 'This one's a couple of cassocks cooler. Probably a good thing – if he was as sizzling as Andrew

Scott, some brides would never move on to the floral displays or the stationery.'

I must be waving my hands too enthusiastically because Poppy grabs my left wrist and lets out a shout of protest. 'What's this, Mills? You're surely not wearing your old engagement ring?'

It was too much to hope she wouldn't notice. 'It's my fake one from Next.' I bought it last year after I'd given Ben my old one back, and I kept having palpitations every time I felt my empty finger and thought I'd lost it. Then, when I was in the bathroom this morning, my ring finger looked so thin and I'd slipped it on before I knew I'd done it. 'It's only for solidarity – to show today's brides-to-be I've been through the same as them and can empathise.'

Poppy frowns. 'Isn't it strange wearing one again?'

I sigh. 'It's actually lovely pretending my life's sorted. I still miss that blissful state of blind optimism you get when you're engaged.'

She pulls me into a hug. 'It's the hardest business for you to be in when your heart's still not mended.'

Which is exactly why I should be moving on to a different area. Except today has reminded me all over again why I love the buzz of being around these fairs even if it does scare the crap out of me being the one in charge.

I stare at the cubic zirconia rock on my finger. 'I've completely accepted I'm better off without Ben. But I'm still pining for that settled future, stretching out ahead of me.' As I've no hope of trusting anyone again, that particular door's slammed in my face. But every time I think what I'll never have, it feels like there's a stone in my chest where my heart should be.

Poppy snorts. 'After all that confusion, it's a damn shame Nic's hell bent on sailing off into the sunset single-handed.'

It's the perfect time for me to set her straight on this. 'If I was stuck on a boat with that man, I'd have to swim.' Even if I hadn't been hurt, I'd know better than to get involved with Nic. I know my judgement hasn't always been the best, but even I have more sense than to go within a mile of a dedicated singleton. It's a simple sense of self preservation. It's hard enough to risk rejection at the best of times, so if you know in advance you're guaranteed a 'thanks, but no thanks', well, why would you?

She grins at me. 'As we said the other day, not every maddening guy stays that way. There's this rule – the more they annoy the hell out of you, the hotter they are once you get their clothes off.'

When Poppy's in this mood you just have to ignore her. 'Now might be a good time for me to check in with Casper, who doesn't annoy me at all. Just saying.'

She laughs. 'Which probably means that despite his very pretty face, there's zero chemistry between you.'

I'm shaking my head. 'How about "happy on my own, not looking for a man to complete me"?'

She sniffs. 'You know that's not completely true.'

'But I'm learning fast; I'll get there very soon.'

Her look as she turns tells me she's not buying it. 'I'll see you later then. Drop by my table any time you need a sugar rush.'

As I punch the air, Poppy and I both know I'll be taking her up on the cupcakes in approximately two minutes from now. But as I've already checked up on all the other exhibitors, once I've seen Casper I can move on to welcoming the visitors. As I walk over to where his cars are lined up, I can't help admire the sleek shine of the paintwork glistening in the sunlight and the inky perfection of the tyre black.

'Nice suit, and I love your choice of cars, Casper.' If he was looking sharp the day in the shop, this morning he's off the phwoar scale.

'There's only three of those electric blue cabbies in the country. Then we brought the Aston along in case anyone's looking for super-smooth, and of course the ever-popular VW camper.'

'So how many weddings have you done so far, Casper?'

'Er ...'

I'm staring at the pale blue paint on the flat front of the van with the matching flower garlands hanging in the windscreen when it hits me. 'Casper, you've forgotten your ribbons.'

'My what?'

His blank stare makes me think that people as young as him might have a next-generation name for them. 'Those strips of satin that drape across the front of the bonnet on every bridal car across the entire world.'

'There should be ribbons? Really?'

I nod. 'Wedding cars usually have them.'

He lets out a low groan. 'Oh shit, that's me busted!' The throat cutting sign he makes should be crass, but the way he does it it's cute. 'Okay, I hold my hands up, I'm a total wedding virgin who hasn't ever had a booking – but my cars are amazing, my tux is Armani and I'm desperate to make a go of this. What's a bit of ribbon between friends?' Despite those startling blue eyes and that agonised smile, he's also got the cheek to talk himself out of a tight corner. At every other fair I've done he'd have been having this awkward conversation with Phoebe.

I clear my throat and try to sound like I'm not a pushover. 'As your cars are the first thing couples see, we need to get this right.' Another thought hits me. 'If they don't have ribbons on you'll definitely miss out on bookings.'

He's screwing his face up in the bright light. 'So where would I get these ribbon things from?'

'They have them at the shop.' Not that that's much help, seeing as most people from there are here, and the people back in St Aidan will have back-to-back appointments.

His expression's a lot like Merwyn's as he watches you eat the last bite of your biscuit. 'We brought the cars yesterday, but I'm here on my own today.'

'Is there anyone you know in St Aidan who could drop by the shop and bring it over. Then I'll help you put it on.' My heart's squishing for him in the same way it would if he were a small boy who'd dropped his ice cream.

He rubs his forehead. 'Good thinking, I'll get Nic Trendell onto it.'

Worst idea ever. 'I'm sure he'll be busy.'

He digs in his pocket for his phone. 'The amount of work my dad gives him, he won't be able to refuse. It's ringing!'

However much I feel like putting a pillow over his face and not letting go, I manage to smile. 'If that's you sorted, I'll go and see if everyone else is okay.' In other words, I'll go and hide inside until Nic's been and gone. If this is the worst it gets I can just about cope.

I reckon I'll have at least an hour before Nic arrives so first I give out some fizz, then I do another circuit. Then I have to find a phone charger for someone who's forgotten theirs and take trays of coffees round to the stall holders. Then I stand in for Jess by the dresses while she goes off to talk to a couple interested in a wedding at the manor.

By the time I realise Casper's cars are still without ribbons, it's three in the afternoon and I'm in the courtyard being handed the biggest ice cream cone in the history of the world, piled high with strawberry, lemon, and blackcurrant scoops. I'm wondering where to begin when a voice behind me makes me jump so hard I nearly lose the whole lot down my front.

'You've got time to eat ice creams?!' It's Nic, his voice rising in disbelief. 'If that's the size of them, I'll have what you're having.'

Somehow, I get control of the wobble on my cone and smile too. 'Nic, what a surprise!' I'm telling the truth – when he hadn't arrived by now, I'd assumed he wouldn't be coming at all.

He's giving me a hard stare. 'I heard you needed ribbons.'

I take the bag he's pushing towards me and hand him my ice cream. 'Here, you have this, I'm actually not that hungry anymore.'

He laughs. 'What, have you eaten too many free samples?' He gives me a nudge. 'Hey, you're wearing my favourite dress. If you need help holding it down in these gusts, just give me a shout.'

There's definitely something about making yourself your tallest. From somewhere I find another couple of inches and a whole load more arctic for my attitude. 'I'm not even going to answer that.'

'However much you're doing giraffe stretches with your neck, you're still quite mini.' He takes a bite of my ice cream then wrinkles his nose as he concentrates on swallowing. 'And how about Casper – didn't I tell you he was faking it?'

I'm rising above it. All of it. 'He's a new start up, we could negotiate a great price for Pixie.' It's funny how much easier it is to say her name now.

He lets out a snort. 'The way Casper's had me running around today he should be doing it for free.'

'I'll leave you to negotiate that one, then.'

He's pursing his lips, staring around the courtyard. 'You know, these open doors flowing straight outside might have worked for Pixie too.'

Now I've heard it all. 'Well, luckily you're committed to the castle now, so finish your ice cream and then you can go.'

He's sniffing the breeze. 'On second thoughts, maybe the prevailing wind isn't right, it's getting a bit smoky out here. Great if you're a kipper, but if you're a wedding party, not so much.' He takes a long lick of his cone and then looks up. 'Now I'm here it would be great to have a look round if you've time?'

More fool me for stopping for the first time since six this morning. And worse for letting his hopeful expression melt me. As for the barbecue people, they're piling on the wood, but it's probably just to save taking it home.

'I could whizz you around quickly before it's time to pack up.' I'm still slightly doubtful because I'd hate to tempt fate by showing off too soon.

He grins. 'If you'd said that before I'd have come earlier.'

I'm leading the way through the tall open doors, taking in the space still full of customers looking at glass cases of rings, tables of bottles, and flowers on crates. I point at the first table we come to which is surrounded by chairs decked in every kind of fabric and style of bow. 'Take a Seat are showcasing their different covers here. It's a fully inclusive service which means they press and install them too.'

Nic grunts. 'Am I allowed to say I prefer my chairs without clothes?'

I nod. 'Once you've seen a roomful of ugly chairs, you might think differently.'

'Hey!' As he leans forward, his nose is practically resting on my wrist. 'What's that?'

I prise my left hand free. 'Just a ring.'

His eyes are boring into me. 'On your *significant* finger.'

'And?'

He sounds jubilant. 'You could have fooled me two months ago, but now you can't. I thought you said you didn't have a groom anymore?' His scowl darkens. 'If you've had a reconciliation and got back together, don't you think it's only fair you should tell people?'

'What people? Why?'

He's straight back. 'Well, otherwise you're just misleading everyone, making them think you're single when you're not.'

I'm opening and closing my mouth but he gets in before me.

'I've got time for the explanation.' His jaw's clenching and he spins his chest to face me. 'I'm not moving until you've told me.'

'There's really nothing to say.'

Then his eyes flash open. 'Shit, Milla.' Even for Nic he's sounding way too dramatic for the situation. 'Look outside ...' He's shouting now, jumping forwards. 'Where the hell's the fire extinguisher?'

He answers his own question by finding one and wrenching it off the wall. A second later he's diving across the courtyard towards a sheet of flame outside. The next thing I see, he's at the barbecue, firing a stream of foam at the fire that's flaring high above the drum. Then as the dark orange and blue flames die down, clouds of black smoke billow up instead and a massive wind gust blows it straight through the open doorway into the room we've just come from.

As I follow the smoke inside, the acrid cloud engulfs me and stings my lungs. Then it hits me – I'm in charge here. This is down to me! I have to waft the smoke outside before it chokes anyone else.

I'm waving my arms, staring around for something to flap

when there's a sudden beeping that sounds a lot like what I hear in the attic when I burn the toast. As I look up to see where it's coming from, a few drops of water fall on my face. The drops build to a trickle, then a gush, and suddenly it's as if there's been a cloudburst and I'm standing with the downpour hammering down on my head – except, that can't be right, because I'm still inside.

I'm scraping a river of water out of my eyes and staring around wildly. Then, beyond the minimal florist and the tropical plants, I catch sight of Jess's mannequins and I let out a moan. I'm about to set off towards them when I hear Nic's voice in my ear.

'The smoke has triggered the sprinklers, Mills.' So that explains the water torrents and why he's looking like that famous photo of a soaking wet Matt Bomer coming out of the sea. And it's really not the time to be thinking how hot he looks.

With thousands of pounds worth of displays about to be ruined I can't help my shriek. 'Well don't just stand there, we need to find someone to turn the damn things off!'

He grabs my wrist. 'I'll do that, you get the stuff out!'

As I hurl myself towards the dresses I'm howling inside and thinking what Phoebe would do if this were her crisis. She always loves a microphone, so I cup my hands around my mouth and yell. 'Okay, any items that may spoil, please, *everyone* help us carry them out into the courtyard.'

I pick up a mannequin, and shove it into a guy's arms, do the same with another, then grab hold of the rail of dresses. By the time I've wheeled it to the open door, people are already picking up entire tables and walking them outside.

Five minutes later, as the sprinklers drip their last drips, all that's left in the Corking Room are a few sopping palms. The courtyard, on the other hand, looks like a rummage sale, and

I'm dashing from pile to pile handing out industrial-strength kitchen roll and bin bags from the winery's cleaning store along with huge apologies and promises of compensation to anyone who needs it. It's a couple of hours later by the time all the customers have drifted away and the last business people are carrying their boxes back to their vans. I'm sharing the last of my leftover cupcake with Merwyn, when I realise that not only is Nic is still here, he's standing watching me.

His shoulder is propped against the wall, and he's got a bottle of Roaring Waves alcohol-free beer in his hand. 'Good thing I came when I did, Milla Vanilla, I knew my onboard fire-fighting techniques would come in handy eventually, I just never imagined it would be at a wedding fair.'

'Great job back there, Nic, and thanks for staying around to help.' I have to add, 'You really didn't have to.'

He's narrowing his eyes, running his fingers through his hair which is extra tousled now it's dried. 'You surely didn't think I'd run out on you?'

I'm counting my lucky stars that for now he's so caught up with the adrenalin he obviously hasn't had time to add this to the Milla Disaster List yet. And it hasn't escaped me that, yet again, in a crisis, he didn't mess about and he couldn't have been any more helpful. I know on a personal level I'd much rather he hadn't been here at all because I'd so much rather he saw things going right for me rather than wrong. But at the same time, if he hadn't been here, I'd have really missed his cool head, fast action, and capacity for quietly sorting things out while reassuring me it wasn't my fault and that I had this under control.

Looking at the bigger picture, if this was going to happen anywhere, it was better that it happened at this small pop up fair rather than at one of the much bigger flagship events that are coming up next. And I'm just hoping this is the last time an event I'm at ends up in ruins. Since the first night I set foot in St Aidan, every single thing I've been involved in has ended with me falling flat on my face either literally or metaphorically.

He takes a swig of beer. 'On the upside, at least we ruled out bows on the chairs for Pixie.'

And it might have been a bit extreme, but at least it saved me from explaining about my ring. Not that I'm going to remind him of that now.

His face breaks into a grin. 'So how are we fixed for tomorrow? I thought breakfast pancakes on *Snow Goose* at ten, and we can talk about seating plans.'

'Seating plans?' That has to be the most random choice of topic.

He gives a shrug. 'It's in the file. We might as well do it sooner rather than later.'

We usually do that right at the end when the guest list is finalised, but after the way he's pitched in today, if he's showing willing, I'm hardly in a position to argue. But I may have to draw the line at breakfast.

I just hope he's not picking up that he's getting his own way, because if he senses he's taking control, who knows where this will end.

Chapter 24

Monday, the next day.
On *Snow Goose* in St Aidan harbour.
Sea legs and butter fingers.

'So that's the batter done, and now it's got to rest for five minutes.'

This is Nic at ten the next morning, and we're in what he calls his galley and I'd call his floating kitchen diner. And I know I didn't intend to have breakfast, but once he'd helped me cross the gap above the brown harbour water onto the bobbing deck of *Snow Goose*, I was already breathless. By the time he'd led me down some steep teak steps and I squeezed into a bench seat, I was so giddy all I could do was watch the puff of flour as he cracked eggs into a bowl and hang on to the table top so tightly my fingertips turned white.

Then, as he gently stirred the mixture, I made myself concentrate on the pale grey checks of the cushions, the dove grey paint on the walls, and the miniature size of the kitchen appliances. I manage to swallow down my sour saliva and croak. 'Resting? What's that about?'

He unfolds a clean black tea towel and spreads it over the bowl. 'It's the secret to light and fluffy pancakes – it helps the batter hydrate, smooths out the lumps, and lets the gluten relax.'

I'm rolling my eyes because only a guy would be that pedantic. Or Phoebe. When I think back to my mum in our tiny cottage kitchen in the years before she got ill, the butter sizzling in her age-blackened frying pan, slopping in the mixture and turning out pancakes by the dozen, there was no time to mess about with resting. What I remember is the air thick with the burning oil, my mum's shouts of, 'Pancakes up'. Me and my brothers diving across the red and black chequered quarry tile floor, falling over the dog, fighting to make sure ours was the empty plate under the pancake flopping off the slice. Then the grittiness of the sprinkled sugar. The tang of the puddling lemon juice. The golden syrup, sticky and melting on our chins, mopped away with squares of kitchen roll. The satisfaction of being so full you couldn't eat another thing.

As Nic slides into the seat at right angles to me his brows knit. 'Are you okay?'

'To be honest ...' For once I'm going to say it how it is. '... I've felt less dizzy after ten straight gins.' And even though he claimed the boat was big enough for entertaining a crowd, with my knees rammed up against his under the table it feels way too small for two of us.

He sends me a grin. 'Don't worry, the queasiness will pass. Let's talk about something to take your mind off it – like how grateful the winery is that we accidentally highlighted the problem of their over-enthusiastic sprinkler system.'

It seems a bit ambitious, but I attempt a nod. 'Imagine if that deluge had cascaded onto a wedding.' It's such an awful image I can't actually make my mind flash it up. 'And apart from some soggy stationery, and the dresses needing a trip to Iron Maiden's cleaners, no one lost too much.'

He's nodding. 'All thanks to your quick thinking getting everyone to help with the evacuation. You definitely have a gift for averting crises.'

I manage a faint smile. 'I'm not sure about that.' I mean, I was the one who had the brilliant idea to site the ethical barbecue right next to the open door where the sprinkler smoke detector was.

'Anyway, now we're here there's something more important I want to clear up.' He lets out a breath. 'This whole upcoming wedding of Pixie's is so stressful, I can't cope with you being distant too. I want to go back to how we were before.'

'Before what?'

'Before you stopped laughing and turned into Mrs Freezer Pants.'

This is all my fault for not being more guarded at the start; I went in way too casually and now it's impossible to backtrack. 'You seem to be forgetting that what we have is a professional working relationship, Nic.'

He lets out a snort. 'I know originally I didn't want to work with you because you were too pretty ...'

I let out a squawk. 'What total bollocks! You rejected me due to my lack of qualifications.' That could have been put in a more office-y way too, but it's too late now.

His lips are a straight line. 'That may have been an excuse. I wasn't sure I could see you crossing your legs every day without thinking of the kittens on your pyjamas. I might not want a long-term girlfriend but I'm still a guy. For my own self-preservation, I was simply trying for someone less drop-dead sexy.'

I let my groan go. 'All of that – so not appropriate.'

He shrugs. 'I'm simply being honest so we can get back on track. I thought planning a wedding was going to be awful, but we ended up having fun and I want that to carry on. It's a great stress buster.'

I blow out my cheeks, because I have to stand my ground on this. 'For the sake of the shop's reputation, I can't be seen to be ...' I hesitate to use the word, then I let it go anyway. '... flirty or over-familiar with clients.' That last bit made it more how Phoebe would have put it.

His eyes narrow. 'But it can't possibly be flirting with me, because we're both very clear that I don't do relationships.'

'Right.' I'm not sure it is.

'Flirting's completely the wrong word anyway, with us it's just banter – that's what mates have, isn't it?' His face lights up. 'If you keep me entertained at the same time as you make Pixie's choices, it will be so much easier.'

I'm not sure where he's going with this.

He's spreading his fingers on the table. 'You just be your normal, hilarious self, and I'll be my usual serious self with an ironic twist. Maybe with a bit of heckling too.' He stares at me. 'So, are we happy that's how we'll take things forward?'

I sigh. 'We'll give it a try.' That's as much as he's getting for now. Truly, if I'm even a tiny bit funny, I'm definitely not hilarious.

'And one more thing ...' He's really making the most of grabbing the reins here. 'I shouldn't have to practically abduct you to get you to eat with me. I should be able to suggest a casual working lunch without you running for the hills. Okay?'

'Nic ...' I'm staring him straight in the eye – then when my stomach dissolves, wishing I wasn't. 'There are lines, you just crossed a hell of a lot of them.'

His lips twist. 'I'm about to cook you light and fluffy pancakes. Surely you can say "yes" better than that?'

I think being on the boat must have gone to his head. 'Does "Aye aye, captain" work for you?'

'Keep going.'

'Aye aye, Captain Kirk.'

He's looking suitably pleased. 'And now that's settled, tell me what's going on with the ring.'

Oh crap. 'Surely your gluten must have hydrated by now? If you leave it too long your lumps will relapse.'

'Nice try, Milla Vanilla, the batter will be fine. I thought we just agreed to be open and honest.'

I'm not sure we did, but I might as well get this over. And if there's an opportunity to get back in the driving seat I might as well take it. 'Listen up, because it's complicated and I'm only saying this once, okay?'

He nods. 'Fine.'

I brace myself and launch. 'So, I run Brides go West with my business partner and bestie in Bristol ...'

'That's the awful Frisbee, isn't it?'

It has to be said. 'If you interrupt it'll take too long.'

'Okay, I'll shut up. Go on.'

With any luck I can say this in one breath. 'Phoebe was married to Harry, and I was engaged to Ben. Ben and I bought a flat together, and had been planning our wedding for five years, then one day Harry suddenly walked out on Phoebe. And then Phoebe and Ben went off together.'

Nic's eyes flash open. 'Oh shit, I'm so sorry. How bloody awful. It doesn't get any worse than your partner going off with your best friend, does it?'

It actually does, but I'm not going into the details here. But now I've started, it's hard to stop. 'Unlike you, I had no interest in being single; I absolutely adored the idea of having a home and a partner, and dogs by the fire. I loved everything being engaged stood for, the promise of a wonderful future, our whole lives ahead to look forward to.'

He wrinkles his nose. 'I'm not sure that's always true, I wouldn't buy into all of it.'

'The point is however much I wanted all that, now I'll never be able to trust anyone enough again, so I won't get to have any of it.'

'Poor Mills.' He's stretching out his hand towards mine.

I pull mine away just in time and snap, 'Banter is questionable, touching is definitely off limits.'

He closes his eyes briefly. 'Sorry, it was only because of all the shit you've been through.'

I'm almost done here, so I press on. 'And I was only wearing the ring at the wedding fair to show the engaged couples I knew what they were going through – and for that one day it was fab to remember how it felt to have everything to look forward to.'

'Oh crap. And sorry all over again for that. And for doubting you. You're sure I can't give you a hug?' He tilts his head and looks at me. 'It might make you feel better?'

'No, absolutely not! It totally wouldn't. Thanks all the same.'

His voice is low. 'I'm sorry I asked. What must you think of me, sticking my nose in?' He rubs his jaw. 'But it's really good to get this straight so I don't put my foot in it in future.'

And for me, even if I'm not saying it, it's lovely to feel that Nic truly cares. That he wants to take the time to understand. That he came in so gently and said all the right things to make me feel better. How achingly comforting it would be to rest my head on his chest. To feel his arms close around me. To let him gently rock me until all the hurt has gone away. Even if there isn't any future in it, just the warmth would be lovely.

'Sooooo ...' It's down to me to fill the gap here, but it's fine because I've been meaning to ask this for ages. 'This might be a good time for me to see a picture of Pixie?' Staring around for photo frames and not finding any, I can't believe I still don't know what she looks like.

'Yes, great idea.' He really doesn't sound like he thinks it is.

I'm backing this up to make it sound less like stalking. 'Now we're moving onto the styling, seeing her will give me a better sense of what she'd like.'

He pulls out his phone from his pocket and flicks through, then hands me the screen. 'There you go. This is her with her basketball team.'

Oh my. After two months of near obsession, I'm actually about to see her. The Elfie in my head at first was super-toned, tall, and slim with beachy blonde hair. Once I knew Nic was her brother, her hair went darker and I let myself add in an Insta-pretty face. So I was possibly expecting an engagement shot of Pixie and Ewan, probably on a beach with some wind and perhaps a sunset. Or maybe just a close-up of their faces and the ring. If it's athletic bodies in shorts draped around a ball, I can still work with that.

Talk about being wrongfooted. When I finally focus on the screen I'm staring at women in sports kit sitting in wheelchairs and two coaches with whistles around their necks standing at the back. It's just so unexpected I'm stuttering.

'W—w—wheelchair sport? Somehow when you said basket-ball I assumed she'd be playing not coaching.' I'm staring from one blonde coach to the other, trying to find a resemblance. 'So which one is she?'

He gives a sniff as he leans over and points. 'There, front row, third from the left.'

As his finger stops at the girl in the chair with long dark hair who looks just like him my stomach's shrinking because I've got this so wrong. And then my shock twists – it's not something I can be annoyed about, but at the same time there's a voice in my head screaming, what the eff? Pixie's in a wheelchair and for two whole months *you didn't think to mention it*!

I blow out a breath, make my voice low and measured. 'Why didn't you tell me?'

There's no need to say any more.

His jaw is clenching, and his mouth has hardened to a defensive line. 'Pixie refuses to be limited or defined by her chair. She lives her life focusing on everything she can do, not what she can't.' He lets out a sigh. 'If I'd told you earlier, you'd have seen the whole day in terms of her limitations. In your head she'd simply have been a disability, not a person.'

It might have led to a more practical way forward, that's all. At least now I can see why he's been such an awkward client. And this explains his obsession with floor coverings and why fields and cliff-top paths were out and why a handy bathroom was so vital in a tipi.

I let out a sigh because, though he doesn't know it, he couldn't have got me any more wrong. If he'd only told me, no one would have understood the problems better than me. Not that he'll ever know, but however much my mum's body let her down, she was always herself. It's hard to explain unless you've been there and seen it. But the more her body failed her, the stronger the very essence of who she was shone out. Because in the end that will, that beautiful, creative, argumentative, bloody-minded fighting spirit was all she had left. And I know for myself how other people's thoughtless acts or comments can pierce straight through to your heart if they catch you wrongly.

I'm kicking myself as I think back to my time with Nic. 'If I'd known, we'd never have gone to the Harbourside Hotel, or all those other places with a million steps or narrow doors.' It's not only the time we've wasted, it's that every unsuitable venue I dragged him to must have been a painful reminder to him of everything she couldn't have.

He pulls down the corner of his mouth. 'Endless tours of facilities for the disabled would have been way more depressing.' And I suppose he has a point. 'I knew if you showed me enough beautiful venues we'd find the right one in the end. And we did.'

So he's right again. But this time rather than minding, I'm pleased for him. I know it's made my job a thousand times harder, but he read the situation, and found his own way through. And I really can't fault him for that. In fact, it shows remarkable good judgement on his part. I'm admiring him for sticking to it because this particular way forward must have caused him a lot of painful moments.

I'm dying inside to think I actually suggested a Cinderella staircase for Pixie to walk down. I'm flicking through my brain to think what else I need to ask so I don't go putting my foot in it again. 'Has she always been ... er ... the same?'

His eyes are strangely blank as he speaks. 'She wasn't born like that and she's not ill. It's a spinal cord injury from an accident on a go cart track five years ago.' He's staring across the harbour and out to the navy blue expanse of sea that's sparking like diamonds where the sun's hitting it. 'She was twenty-six with her whole life in front of her, and in a split second it was all taken away.'

My mouth's gone dry with the desolation in his voice. At least with my mum it came on slowly. There were difficult times –

tears and anguish and shock – when the hospital told us what to expect. But at least we had the luxury of crying in anticipation. Watching the changes creep up on us. We didn't have the shock of an instantaneous change.

'Was Ewan with her then?' All I want to do is wrap my arms around him. To hold him for as long as it takes to make the hurt in his voice go away.

He's still examining the floor. 'She was seeing someone else when it happened but he didn't stick around, and she didn't want him to. She and Ewan used to hate each other growing up, but a few summers ago he went as her helper on a tall ship voyage when none of the rest of us could make it.' He finally looks up and gives a rueful grin. 'I guess she found out he wasn't so bad after all.'

This puts me in my place, bleating about a little thing like losing my fiancé.

At least now I understand how much pressure he's under to get her wedding right. And it explains the torture lurking in his eyes and makes me understand why his laughter so often tails away to nothing. 'And this is why it's all got to be perfect?'

He's nodding. 'She's so brave and she never complains. After everything she's been through ...'

I cut in as he swallows. 'Don't worry, you've already bagged her the princess castle; we're going to give her the most amazing day.' I reach across, put my hand over his, and squeeze. And I wish with all my heart I could do more.

His eyes pull into focus. 'She'd never have been a typical bride, even when her legs did work. No offence, but she'd have a fit at most of the gear at your fairs.'

I'm biting back my smile, getting exactly what he means. 'Napkins folded like swans aren't for everyone.' I laugh. 'Don't worry, there's lots of choice for the chilled-out bride. We'll stick to nachos and jumpsuits.'

He slumps back against the bench. 'It's a relief we've sorted that out.' It's not clear if he's talking about Pixie's aversion to wedding paraphernalia or the fact she can't walk. Worse still, somehow my hand's still on his and now he's squeezing mine back. 'I know you've got this, Milla Vanilla. There's no one in the world I'd trust more with this.'

Which he could inadvertently be right about, although he has no idea why. And it might be great for him, but for me the stress just went off the scale. With my record lately, I've had a lot more stuff-ups than successes, and he's just given me every reason why this has to be absolutely flawless. And wonderful. The kind of faultless that's got my heart racing already. In fact, my mind's galloping so fast, I already know I'll barely have time to sleep between now and then.

And as I can't afford to miss a single detail, I have to check. 'So is there anything else you haven't told me? Anything more I need to know?'

I mean, for two months I had no idea who the groom was and now I find out the bride is in a wheelchair. It might not be deliberate, but Nic does have a habit of concealing vital information.

He rubs his chin. 'No, I reckon that's you fully briefed and up to speed.' His lips slide into a smile as he pushes himself up to standing. 'Shall I get cooking, then?'

'Cooking?' It comes out as a scream. 'There's no time to eat, Nic, we've got a wedding to sort out!'

MAY

Chapter 25

Tuesday, the next week.
At the camper van on St Aidan harbour.
Comfort zones and clean breaks.

'What the hell is going on?'

Arriving at the harbour with half an hour to spare before meeting up with Nic, mostly I'm trying to remember where I left the camper. As I finally spot it along the quay edge by a stack of fishing nets, the last thing I expect to find next to it is the guy himself at the top of a stepladder on the cobbles between the side of the van and the water. As he wipes his hands on his jeans and turns around, I can't help smiling at the smudges of pink paint on his backside.

He's resting his elbows on the roof and he sounds just as perplexed as me. 'More importantly, what the hell are you doing running around the harbourside waving a cordless vacuum and asking awkward questions when you should be at the shop, Milla? Our meeting isn't until ten.'

'I'm here for a quick tidy.' Believe me, those words don't often come out of my mouth naturally, but this is the new super-energised version of me – the upcoming fairs and Pixie's big day are working like a mahoosive kick up the bum. 'What's your excuse? And it'd better be good, Trendell! You can't just clamber all over people's expensive paint jobs without asking. And you're horribly close to the edge of the quay too!'

When he holds up his hands it's obvious where the pink paint on his jeans has come from. 'You know I like to live dangerously.' He lets a grin slide out.

I give a snort. 'If this is your idea of banter, it's not very funny.'

He stares over the top of the van for a second, then looks down at me again. 'It was meant to be a surprise. I'm doing the rooftop makeover you were asking about in time for Sunday's wedding fair.'

I'm blinking at the bright blue sky behind his head. 'Excuse me?'

He's pointing at my Brides Go West roof sign. 'That West to Wild you mentioned, it's not going to take long.'

'B—b—but ...' When I mentioned the letters, I was thinking I'd build my courage up slowly.

'It's a brilliant idea – Brides Go Wild is so much more you.' His lips twist into a smile as he looks along the roof. 'Great van, by the way. Where did you pick it up?'

If he's trying to distract me it's worked. 'It belonged to this lovely old guy called Sam-the-van who bought it new back in 1972. He lived two doors down from us in Rose Hill and always parked it on the patch of ground belonging to our cottage.' I'm watching as Nic lines up the 'L'. 'If you haven't got time, I don't need to ...'

'No, I like hearing about your long-lost past.' He grins at me again and fishes a screwdriver out of the pocket of his padded waistcoat. 'Carry on, and I'll fix this lot into place.'

I'm more likely to put him to sleep; I just hope he knows

not to wobble when he does. 'When we were kids, whenever my mum baked she'd always send me round to Sam's with some for him. Poppy's mum was good at cakes, mine was better at pastry, so mostly she made pies. Then when she was too ill to bake, and I was at home looking after her ...'

He pulls a handful of screws out of his pocket. 'Hang on, you didn't say anything about this.'

And damn that it's slipped out now. I don't usually talk about this part of my mum's life because that kind of illness is so far outside people's experience, no one can ever relate. 'You can't have my entire life story; you said this wasn't a big job.' That's the trouble. Once I start, it's all too involved. But when I do talk about her it makes her feel more real. Less like I dreamed her.

'Give me the shortened version then.' He lines up his screwdriver but he's still looking at me. 'So you must have been young to be looking after your mum? How did that work?'

Somehow, standing here on the quayside, with the call of gulls overhead and the lap of the water against the harbour wall, surprising as it feels, I know I'm completely comfortable sharing this with Nic. Whenever he's heard about my mum, he doesn't judge; he just listens. And quietly understands.

'She had motor neurone disease. In the end it took everything away from her except her mind. She knew exactly what was going on, but as it got worse she couldn't be left alone. So as a teenager I mostly stayed home with her instead of going to school. That's how I missed out on my exams. And why I have a good insight into negotiating the world in a wheelchair.'

There's a pained expression on his face. 'Poor Mills, it sounds awful.'

That's not what I want him to think. 'It wasn't that bad. It went on for years, and only the very end bit was really hard.

The rest was about making the most of everything we could do, not dwelling on everything we couldn't.' As I look up, there's so much compassion in his eyes and it's nothing to do with pity. And there's no need for any words. I can just feel he cares. I swallow back the lump in my throat and carry on. 'Sam had trouble with his sight, and my mum wasn't great at going out, so Sam would come round and I'd read to them both. Sam had a subscription to National Geographic and an attic full of detective novels so there was always plenty to choose from. It seems like a lifetime ago now. We might have been trapped in one room, but my mum was determined to have fun and we were all great at living in our heads. But when it was all over, and I was moving to Bristol because that's where my brothers were, Sam made me take the van.'

'He gave you it?' Nic's eyes soften even more. 'I like that he did that. It makes it very special.'

I shrug. 'He couldn't see to drive it anymore and when our cottage was sold he wouldn't have had anywhere to park it. He didn't have kids of his own, so he said to think of it as payment for all the Bakewell tarts and the crime novels and articles I'd read him.

'At the time I didn't know how much he was giving me. I was just glad to have wheels. I'd learned to drive so I could take Mum around, but her old car gave up not long after she did. And then a couple of years later Sam died too.'

Nic's rubbing his thumb along his jaw. 'The world has a way of making things right. After everything you gave up for your mum, you deserved something good for yourself.'

I can't hold back my smile. 'That's a very "peace and love" attitude from a hard-headed businessman.'

He pulls a face. 'Don't be fooled. On the inside I'm squishy as baked Alaska. So I take it you were the one who did the van restoration?'

There's an extra heartfelt sigh for that. 'It was beaten up but I was happy running it round as it was, then Phoebe decided it would be great for our brand if it were shiny and new. But doing it up nearly broke me; I'm still paying back the money I borrowed.' And that's another heap of detail I never meant to give away and which I'm hoping Nic will instantly forget.

'There you go, another example of Frisbee taking advantage. Poppy and Jess were talking about that too.' He gives a cough. 'For what it's worth, they seem to dislike her as much as I do.'

'You haven't even met her.'

He lets out a splutter. 'I don't have to. She stole your fiancé, and from what I hear she doesn't lift a finger. You've been here months doing all the work ... where the hell is she?'

'But that's because she's on mat leave.' It's out before I can think.

His forehead wrinkles. 'Isn't that when you have a baby?'

I sniff. 'As an employer you should know that, Nic.'

He lets out a shout. 'Shit, Milla, don't go all Frisbee on me. If she's just given birth, whose child was it? It surely can't have been ...?' And good on him for stopping at that.

I blow out a breath. 'It's Phoebe and Ben's baby. That's why I'm here. I watched the bump grow, but when it came to the due date I ran. I'm hiding out here until it blows over.'

He's come down the steps now 'Oh, Milla Vanilla, you surely can't go back to that? Babies don't go away, they just get bigger. Haven't they offered to buy you out of the business?'

I'm back to grinding my teeth. 'It's the company I put seven years of my life into building, it's all I have left.' I take in his stare that says he's not buying it. 'I'm trying to extend the business into this area. That's what the Wild is about. But it's very early days.'

'Then I'm extra pleased I'm doing this now.' He's staring at the letters on the roof, blinking in the sunlight. 'I haven't quite got the pink right, have I?'

Phoebe would have thrown him in the harbour for less. And it's true, the vibrant paint is very different from the almost-white of the other letters.

He's frowning. 'Why did I choose that colour? When I thought of the van it was the only pink that came to mind.'

'I have no idea but I like it – and it pops!'

He laughs. 'It makes the wild even wilder somehow. Don't worry, it's only temporary, I had the letters knocked up in the chandlery workshop, you can swap them back any time. But, for what it's worth, I really hope you don't.' He glances at his phone. 'I'll just pop your light bulbs through the holes, then I'll make us some coffee.'

After everything he's done I feel I should be offering. 'Shall I put the kettle on?'

'I thought you'd never ask.' It's a guy's voice, but Nic didn't move his lips and as I watch him his face darkens.

'Casper.' Nic's voice is stony. 'What can we do for you today? I take it you're only here because you want something?'

As I whip round to see him standing behind me, Casper buries his hands even deeper in the pockets of his smart wool jacket and lets his smile go. 'We could start with that coffee you just mentioned.' He looks to me. 'I'm just dropping by to get ribbons from the shop for Sunday.'

Nic stares at the clouds. 'Well, at least that might save me running halfway across the county on the day.'

Casper ignores him and grins at me. 'Don't worry, I'm not

going to get caught without a second time.' He swoops in and, before I know it, he's dropped a kiss on both my cheeks and whipped the cordless vac out of my hand. 'When it comes to car valets, I'm your man. How about I whisk this around your camper, while you get the drinks?' Casper's laughing. 'And then I'll take you out for lunch, Mills.'

Nic's straight in there. 'Sorry, Casper, Milla's tied up with me – *all day*!'

And that's not true either. I'm about to tell them both to butt out but Casper gets in first.

He pulls a face at Nic. 'You're sounding very Fifty Shades and last decade, Nic. In any case, you're far too old and dull for lovely Milla. I have it on good authority she's looking for fun not a father figure.' He pauses to let that sink in. 'Maybe someone who doesn't have bright pink paint all over the back of their Levi's, too. It's not a great look.'

'Okay guys, that's *enough*!' I'm pointing at Nic. 'You, get back on the roof.' I dangle the van keys in front of Casper. 'If you're sure you don't mind?' Then, as I back along the harbourside towards the jetty, I growl. 'And if either of you dares throw the other in the harbour while I'm away … I will personally mash you.'

Nic's lips are twisting as he looks down at me from the top of the steps. 'There's a box of pastries from the bakery on the counter. As long as we watch out for the seagulls you can bring those back too.'

I'm marching away across the cobbles towards *Snow Goose* when I have a thought. 'And Casper, if you make my van spick and span I might just have some good news for you too …'

Chapter 26

Later on Tuesday.
At the camper van on St Aidan harbour.
Empty promises and splashy landings.

Half an hour later and I'm back on the harbourside, bottom on the edge of my camper van floor, my back leaning against the open sliding door, soaking up the sun. I sip my coffee and sink my teeth into my almond croissant, but every time I remember there's a Brides Go Wild sign above my head, a shiver of pure terror runs down my spine. But then as I gaze around the lino floor Casper has left spotless, I couldn't be any more blissed out.

Casper and Nic both declined my offer of a folding chair, so they're standing with their backs to the harbour, while I have a secret smile at the random mugs we've ended up with. Mine says 'Whatever', Casper's says 'Life Begins at 40' and Nic's just confirms he's a 'Grumpy Old Git'.

Casper takes a bite of his apricot Danish, then frowns at me. 'Hey, watch where you're dropping your pastry flakes, Milla, I just cleaned in there.'

'Oops, sorry.' I pick up the two tiny offending crumbs on my finger tip and smile at him. 'So, how about you pencil in a wedding booking for your camper for July 2nd.'

Nic chokes on his coffee. 'But that's Pixie's date.'

I'm beaming at him. 'So it is. Which also means we've got a bride, bridesmaids, groomsmen, and guests to transport! I'm asking Casper to bring along one very versatile and photogenic vehicle. What's not to like?'

It's been weeks since we finalised the booking at the castle, but rather than making decisions Nic still hasn't got any further than musing over name cards and frowning about cocktails. I've been flat out, sorting the layouts and advertisers for the BGW glossy magazine we sell at fairs, which is why I've let things slide. So by forcing his hand here I'm hoping we'll break the deadlock.

Nic glares at Casper. 'Scrap that, mate.' As he shoos away a couple of seagulls hopping around on the cobbles, we all know he's metaphorically flapping Casper away too. 'Watch your croissant, Milla, they're very persistent.'

I turn to Casper. 'Ignore Nic for now. He'll see sense in a bit.'

Nic's voice goes high. 'You can't say that, Milla, I'm the client.'

I know better than to back down. 'I just did say it. You're also paying me for my expertise.' I grin at him. 'So tough shit, I'm overruling you.'

'I—I—I ...' Nic's opening and closing his mouth and Casper's waving his Danish at me, cheering me on.

'Happy to argue all day on this one.' I'm smiling through my clenched teeth, getting ready to dig my heels in, when there's a whoosh of air, a loud squawk, and a huge flap.

Then Casper lets out a howl. 'What the eff! That bloody bird swiped my pastry right out of my hand.'

Nic lets out a low laugh. 'I did warn you. You could say that's natural justice.'

Another swoop, a flash of beak and bird's feet and Nic's croissant goes too.

Nic growls. 'Damned seagull!'

Except this time, Casper takes a stride backwards to avoid the seagull as it wheels away from Nic. But instead of landing on the pavement, Casper's foot hits the handle of the cordless vacuum lying on the floor behind him. As his second foot goes backwards, his ankles get completely tangled with the pole.

'Hey, Casper, cordless vacuums are made without cables so you don't fall over them.' It's so funny seeing him staggering around, his cool shattered as his eyes pop wide with surprise. I'm starting to laugh, and at first he's joining in. But instead of stopping, he carries on lurching, back across the quayside. Then he flings his arms outwards, his mouth opens wide and he lets out a yell as he topples backwards over the quay edge.

As he disappears from view, I let out a low 'oh crap' then a howl. 'Nooooooo …'

A second later there's an almighty splash. And then nothing.

As my eyes lock with Nic's his face cracks into a huge grin, then he yells too. 'Man overboard! Casper's in the pond!' Then he kicks off his deck shoes, throws down his phone and padded jacket, springs to the edge of the harbour, sticks his arms up over his head, and with a graceful dive he follows Casper in.

And I'm left on the quay, staring at the ripples on the water, waiting. Then as the two heads bob up and break the surface a couple of yards apart they both shake the water from their hair, scrape the brine out of their eyes and start to swim for the harbour steps. Nic gets there first, hauls himself out, then offers his hand to Casper and drags him up beside him.

As they crawl back up to the harbourside, Casper's sputtering. 'Why the hell did you jump in too?'

The water's sluicing off Nic's shirt and there are slices of dimples in his cheeks. 'I didn't know for sure you could swim.'

As Casper shakes his head, a thousand drops glisten like diamonds in the sun. 'That's a laugh. I was in the bloody Olympic development squad.'

Nic's frowning. 'I thought you were a skiing champion?'

'That too.' Casper rolls his eyes. 'Trying to save me? Bollocks! Your hero act was to impress Milla.'

As they come towards me, I laugh. 'Just saying – I am right here.' I step back to avoid the drips. If the fabulous view of Nic's inky blue soaking-wet T-shirt clinging to his six pack takes my breath away, it's my own fault for looking. 'You're like two wet dogs.'

Nic laughs. 'I'll grab some towels then we'll head straight for the harbour master's showers.' He turns to Casper. 'Can I lend you some dry clothes?'

Casper gives a grimace. 'If it's a choice between being wet or wearing old man jeans – thanks all the same, but I'll take the water every time.' He slicks his hair back and dips in towards me for an air kiss on each cheek. 'So I'll be off, but I'll be back soon for that lunch, and thanks again for the booking, Mills.'

I'm wiping a stray drip from my chin. 'You're very welcome, Casper. Thanks again for the van-clean. See ya 'round.' I'm hoping that sounds youthful enough.

Nic is apoplectic. 'He falls in the harbour, and you're still giving him the business?'

I'm glossing over this one. 'Accidents can happen to any of us.' I should know – I've had enough of the damn things myself lately. I'm thanking my lucky stars it wasn't me in the water earlier. I smile at Nic and pull the vac close against my chest. 'And on the upside, Jess's Dyson's still on dry land.' Lesson learned. At three hundred quid a shot, I won't risk it getting stamped on in future.

Nic gives a shudder. 'Damn stupid place for Casper to leave it. Do you know how late he's made us?'

I'm not going to point out that if Nic hadn't been so keen to get in on the act with Casper, he'd still be dry. If he'd actually stop protesting, we may have nailed another item on the to-do list. And better still, Casper's camper is wheelchair-friendly too.

Wedding transport: tick.

Chapter 27

**Later still on Tuesday.
On the beach at Cockle Shell Castle.
Winkles, sea foam and men with muscles.**

'You can't make a booking with Casper just because he hoovers your camper.'

It's Nic, and I can't believe it's late afternoon and he's still talking about this.

We've spent the afternoon testing the castle by going around in two ancient wheelchairs Bill had in his coach house store – circling the rooms, wheeling ourselves in and out, through every door, manoeuvring, noting every lump, bump and flooring transition, every unsuitable area to be avoided. We've made lists of where temporary ramps need to be added and sorted out which bathrooms and bedrooms work best.

In fact, as Nic instinctively picked up on during that first day we visited, the castle is a natural fit for accessibility because of the wide doorways and large living spaces and the spectacular lack of steps on the ground floor. And when Bill was doing the restorations, the council insisted that the accommodation included a downstairs bedroom and bathroom suitable for wheelchair use, so that's the bridal suite sorted. And, unusually for accessible accommodation, this room has wonderful views straight out across the bay rather than the car park.

Then we met up with Bill's dad, Keef, and his silver surfer friends, who've offered to construct a boardwalk to extend the solid garden paths on through the dunes and right down onto the hard sand so that will be wheelchair-friendly too.

And now we're walking back to St Aidan the same way we came, along the beach. But on the way back we've got some extra special people with us. Merwyn is here, without his coat, because the late spring sun's unseasonably warm today, but with a snazzy blue and red checked necktie, because that's the kind of doggy fashion-icon he is.

And we're also looking after Abby, Bill's daughter, who's visiting from London, who's wearing yellow spotty wellies and a red body warmer. And due to being on the beach we've used my scarf to hitch up the long, flowing, *Frozen* dress that she refuses to take off, to keep it out of the shallows when she dashes in and out of the waves. As the wind blows off the sea and wraps the turquoise blue tulle skirt tight around her calves, with her long dark plait and her sea-glass bangles she looks more like a mermaid than a princess from a snow kingdom.

When we first arrived at the castle Abby was perched on a high stool at the kitchen island, quietly colouring while Bill cleared up the baking they'd been doing together. Blueberry muffins – delicious to graze on as we worked too. But the second Nic offered Abby a ride in his wheelchair, she ditched her rainbow felt pens and clambered onboard, whooping as he did wheelies and handbrake turns.

Then because she's one of those truly delightful kids who spreads her favours around all the adults, she insisted that I shouldn't miss out on my turn with her either. And as she's also enjoying having Ivy around, being a savvy six-year-old who knows exactly what she wants, the minute she found we were heading back to where Ivy would be finishing work, she hitched a lift on the walking bus back to St Aidan to meet up with her.

After filling our pockets with equal amounts of shells and pebbles and doing some writing in the sand, she and Merwyn run off to dodge the rushes of foam as they sweep up the beach, which gives Nic the perfect opening to hark back to this morning and Casper's cleaning.

I shrug. 'Casper found a nifty way to my heart and you're getting the benefit too, why all the protest?'

Nic's come to a sudden halt and he's staring at me very hard. 'Has he offered to sleep with you?'

My eyes go wide, and the shock has me shouting. '*No*! Totally not – it was only lunch and the van-clean.' Not that it would be any of Nic's business if he had.

'At least that's a relief.' Nic blows out his cheeks. 'But, in my expert opinion, I wouldn't trust him an inch with the wedding.'

Now I'm the one who has to protest. 'It's not fair to discount him just because he's young. People must have supported you when you were starting out.'

Nic rubs his nose. 'It's not his youth, it's his entitled attitude I object to. And you must have heard how ageist he is?'

I allow myself a mental eye roll then go in to tease him. 'Might you be a teensy bit jealous of his sense of style and how good-looking he is?'

Nic stares at me like I've lost it. 'You are joking?'

'You're the one who asked me to be entertaining.' I pause to give the audience time to laugh, but he doesn't. 'You'll see when the time comes, we'll prove you wrong.' I'm completely confident on this one, or I wouldn't be using him.

Surely that has to be the end of the argument, but just in case it's not I run a few steps so I'm further away from him, pick up a shell, and examine it as I walk along.

Then I let my gaze slide back down the beach to Abby and Merwyn. I'm watching as Merwyn divebombs a seaweed pile, while Abby's skipping after him, trailing a stick behind her. It's all set against the backdrop of a glittering green sea, with a pale aqua sky above. And Nic's a few strides away from me. I know the individuals aren't right at all, but this is like a trial run of the family I thought I was going to be getting, but now won't be.

And somehow, as I think this, my legs have stopped moving, because a moment later I'm standing still and Nic's at my shoulder.

'Are you okay, Milla Vanilla? Not worrying about the ramps are you?'

His tone is so deep with concern, I can't help laughing at how wrong he is. 'For once it's nothing to do with work or weddings ...'

His eyebrows go up in question. 'If they've run out of raspberry sauce by the time we get to the Surf Shack I promise we'll find something equally yummy to dribble on your cone.'

I let out a sigh. 'I'd actually forgotten about the cafe.'

'What the eff, Milla? If it's serious enough to eclipse the ice cream you definitely need to share this.'

For once I'm too tired to pretend any more. 'It's nothing really. Except this walk on the beach reminds me of everything I signed up for when I got engaged to Ben.'

Nic's standing beside me staring out at the waves as they break on the shore. 'That's a lot more than nothing.'

As I rationalise in my head yet again, it has to be for the millionth time. 'I'm know I'm better off without Ben ...'

Nic does one of his choking coughs. 'Ben's a bastard – you deserve so much more.'

I let out another sigh. 'But the dog and the child and the home and the husband are what I wanted and won't ever have now.'

Nic nods. 'But Phoebe will.'

I sniff. 'It's not just the baby ... they're getting married too.'

Nic gives a groan. 'I hate those two.'

'And then they'll be buying the cottage in the country. I know I loved the city, but that was another of my dreams that Phoebe stole.'

Nic's nodding. 'Seriously, that woman is such bad news.' He stares out to where a fishing boat is bobbing towards the horizon. 'If we're completely honest, a lot of us would secretly settle for a glass of wine, a dog or two, and a woodburner.'

I can't hide my surprise. 'And to think I had you down as a space captain who wouldn't give up until you'd toured every galaxy and ocean.'

He gives a shrug. 'When I'm sailing and the storms are at their roughest, it's the thought of the cosy fireside that always gets me home again.'

There's something solid and reassuring about standing next to Nic when he's being so honest. I hadn't expected his dreams would be so simple and down-to-earth. And it's surprising and fascinating that our secret fantasies are so similar. 'I mind about all of it a lot less now than I did when I got here.'

Nic's eyes are dark and thoughtful as he looks down at me. 'It sounds like a cliché but the Cornish sea air can be very healing.'

I know I'm rambling. 'If it hadn't been for Pixie's wedding I might have rushed back to Bristol. I won't ever be looking for those things in life now. But maybe Poppy's right. Maybe I should stay here until I don't mind about the past anymore.'

His voice is low and measured. 'Sometimes if you get to know yourself better, that helps too.'

'It's funny, when I got here my emotional life was falling apart, but I still had my professional confidence. When I was bigging myself up to you that first day, I was so certain of my ability to deliver you the perfect wedding. But maybe I'm not all that after all.'

Nic gives me a nudge. 'You surely aren't going to tell me you've lost your magic?'

I have to level with him. 'I'm only being realistic. Since I've been in St Aidan, everything I touch turns to shit.'

Nic's frowning. 'That's not true. In any case, real life isn't ever perfect; the imperfections are what make it interesting.'

I have to disagree. 'These last couple of months it's been one disaster after another for me. Cock-ups, epic fails and catastrophes. Monumental mistakes and enormous failures. Eff-ups and dog's breakfasts.'

Nic's lips are lilting. 'Think about all the things you do succeed at, rather than the bits that don't work out. You have so many amazing qualities, Milla, those are what you need to focus on. No one's good at everything, remember. Accepting yourself as you are can set you free.'

'In my case it might just finish me off.'

He's giving me a sideways look. 'Or it's possible you've been trying to be someone else for too long, and this is the real you finally breaking through.'

'Bloody hell, Nic, you sound a lot like my mum in her Hari Krishna phase.'

That really makes him smile. Which makes it all the worse

for me because when he does my stomach instantly dissolves. He clears his throat. 'The point is, we don't all get the lives we plan for. Take Bill – for a long time he was in a relationship that didn't make him happy and after they split he hadn't seen Abby for a year. Then Ivy came along, and here he is, back with Abby again.'

'When did you find this out?' Nic's full of surprises this afternoon.

'We guys aren't all strong, silent, and non-communicative.' He laughs. 'Ivy told me, but Bill filled in the gaps.'

'Oh my.' Nic turned my legs to jelly before, but with this open, soft-centred version, it's ten times harder to think clean thoughts. Picturing him naked is nothing – right now I've knocked him onto the sand, jumped on top of him, and I'm about to pash the socks off him. But actually, it's more than that. I'm thinking how lovely he'd be to come home to, sitting on the sofa with his feet on the coffee table, Merwyn on his knee ...

But he breaks in. 'You're doing it tough now, but you have to trust that when the time is right, all the pieces of your life will fall into place.'

'You really think my life will click, like it did for Bill and Ivy?'

He smiles at me. 'So long as you keep believing, you'll get those "his and hers" matching slippers and the comfy sofa and the dog.' He can have no idea right now that the feet I'm picturing in those slippers are his.

I laugh because he sounds so certain. 'Back at you, Captain Kirk.'

Instead of grinning, he purses his lips. 'Not everyone deserves a happy ending as much as you. Some of us won't ever get there.' As he turns towards me, he's smiling down at me, but his eyes are dark and shot with pain.

'Are you going to tell me what's wrong?'

'Probably not.'

The way he hunches his shoulders and lets out a long sigh, all I want to do is throw my arms around him. To rock him and make him feel better. He looks so sad and lost, my heart aches for him. It's as if there's an invisible cord between us, drawing me to him. But before I can move my legs, he takes a step towards me. One tiny step. It's a small patch of sand, but he's crossed an unspoken barrier to a whole other place. As he arrives in my space, my heart clatters against my ribs so hard I'm jolting.

He's so close I can feel the heat radiating out of his body. See the individual hairs on his forearms. So close that when I reach straight upwards, my palm is grazing his jaw. Rubbing his cheek. My thumb is following the line of his cheekbone. And he's tilting his head, pushing so hard against the pressure of my hand, I can feel the scratch of his stubble on my fingers. Then he's closing his eyes. Biting his lip. Turning. He slides his mouth to gently brush the skin of my inner wrist. I hold my breath, letting out the smallest whimper as I sense the flicker of his tongue.

My whole body is screaming. Primed. Bursting with anticipation. His eyes darken as he dips. Slowly, gently. It's completely unexpected, yet completely right. My mouth's already watering, anticipating how he'll taste. I'm listening to the pounding of the waves, telling myself this is real. Then, as I part my lips and close my eyes, there's a scuffle. A bark. And as Merwyn collides with my knee I jump sideways and Nic lets out a shout.

'Merwyn, what the eff?' As Merwyn gallops away again, his tongue lolling out, Nic lets out a groan. 'Well, thanks for that mate.' He pulls a face at me. 'Probably for the best. That wasn't very professional of me, was it, Milla Vanilla?'

As I rub at the tingling skin on my wrist, Merwyn dashes back with Abby who's panting even harder.

She tugs at Nic's denim jacket and points along the beach to the higgledy-piggledy wooden building with the deck in front. 'That's the Surf Snack. Me and Daddy have our hot chocolate there.'

I'm staggering as I realign myself. I just manage to get it together enough to smile as I think how much cuter Abby's name for The Surf Shack is than the real one.

And then the moment moves on and from the way Nic's grinning down at her, I can tell he thinks so too. 'I heard they do a great *Frozen* sundae in there.'

I'm blinking in surprise. 'You did?'

He gives me a nudge with his elbow. 'Keep up, Milla, I thought ice cream was your specialist subject – and comforting miserable sailors.' He holds out his hand to Abby. 'How about we race Milla?'

Abby gives him a hard stare. 'Actually, Daddy carries me on his shoulders for this bit.'

I can't help laughing at her. 'Hitch up your princess dress, and we'll ask if Nic will do the same.'

Nic's smiling down at her. 'It's a few weeks since I carried a princess in a long dress, isn't it, Milla?' He grins at me over the top of her head. 'Let's see what we can do.'

As his eyes widen for a moment and lock with mine again, it's like he's acknowledging what we just missed. I've got Merwyn to thank there ... nothing to do with how awkward it might have made the run up to the wedding. I should be grateful for the lucky escape. For saving myself from a guy whose life statement means, however delicious his touch is, he'll always walk away. And I suppose back there I caught him at the same kind of weak moment I had the day he was making pancakes on the boat. When all he wanted was some human touch to make him feel better. Nothing more.

Abby's eyes are so wide I'm laughing again. 'The princess Nic carried was much heavier than you, Abby, but I'm told he did a great job.' I whistle for Merwyn. 'Good boy, come and have your lead on.'

'If your royal highness is ready?' Nic sends Abby a wink.

Then he swings her into the air, wedges her on one shoulder and strides off across the shingle as if he's done this every day of his life.

And all I can think as I hurry after them is not that I'm going to smother my triple vanilla ninety-nine in raspberry sauce and then totally demolish it. It's that, looking at how natural Nic is with Abby, he wasn't born to be an effing playboy. What a waste that would be. He was born to be a dad. And if there's a tiny voice inside my head as Merwyn and I bounce up the broad bleached wooden steps to the Surf Shack, screaming, *pick him, grab him, jump him and have his babies*, well, I really didn't hear it.

Chapter 28

Sunday, ten days later.
The Potting Shed, near Okehampton, Devon.
Gone fishing.

For our first proper wedding fair we've not only come two hours from home, we're actually over the county border, in Devon. But the change of area means that as well as the regulars we've also got new exhibitors too, and the walled-garden location couldn't be prettier, in the most low-key, on-trend way.

The Potting Shed is a newly-opened restaurant venue with a kitchen filled with starry chefs, set in a cluster of simple single-storey stone farm buildings below wide, shallow-pitched slate roofs. What makes it so special isn't just the converted cart sheds with their hewn-timber roof trusses, and the scrubbed stone walls that set off the simple designer furnishings. On the entrance side there's a wide gravelled car park, with Casper's fleet in a shimmery line on one side of the doorway, and the Brides Go Wild camper on the other, looking totally amazing parked side-ways on to maximise the signage.

But the best is at the back, where the buildings open out onto a secret walled kitchen garden that was originally for the nearby manor farm. There are ancient apple and pear trees trained along the tall sheltering boundary walls, and the borders echo the origins. Here, the bursts of delphiniums, roses, peonies, and sweet peas are interspersed with sage and golden marjoram, with feathery leaves of dill and fennel growing next to climbing beans. And at the far end there's a long rectangular stone-edged pond with lily pads and flashes of orange fish in the depths.

What's even more special is that this is their first wedding fair since opening, and there's so much buzz that people are coming in crowds, from all around.

I was so worried about not waking up for my 5am start that in the end I didn't dare go to bed. Instead, I got ready then snatched a couple of hours' sleep sitting upright on the sofa. But in spite of that, I'm not actually tired – in fact, there's so much adrenalin pumping around my body, at this rate I might well stay awake until July. Driving into the sunrise was magical, chasing away the night-time shadows along the roadside hedge-rows as I sped inland, with the scarlet ball of the sun coming up over the moorland horizon. Even though the air from my open van window blasting over my face was chilly enough to turn my nose pink, the pale cloudless sky and soft morning light as I wound my way along the narrow lane to the smart gravelled entrance was a promise of the warm day to come.

It's almost as if Phoebe was watching Nic swap the signage on the roof, because I've had missed calls from her at the most random times. And as I arrive this morning and pick up my bag from the van floor there's yet another, but my head's too full right now to take on Phoebe too.

I might have been shivery early on with my optimistic bare legs and sandals, but by lunchtime as I make my way past the snowy display of Sera's bridal dresses, and out of the huge open doors towards the pretty open-sided marquee out on the lawn and thread my way through the couples wandering outside on the grass, in the shelter of the garden I'm pushing the sleeves of my soft denim shirt dress up beyond my elbows, and undoing the top and bottom buttons for extra ventilation.

Now I'm getting into my stride as the person in charge of sorting the exhibitors out, instead of looking for trouble, I'm finding that if I keep walking around with my tray, the difficulties come to me as I pass. And if I'm handing out goodies as I go, people are much less likely to grumble, and easier to help.

As I go in through the open doors for my umpteenth circuit, I'm heading for Immie and Poppy who are standing by one of her lovely three-tier cakes. This one's covered in pink ombré frosting and topped with white chocolate drips, and getting shedloads of attention.

'Cupcake, Milla?' Immie's nothing to do with Poppy's cake-making business, but she said she was damned if she was staying home for our first big fair.

I put down my empty tray and sweep my finger through the soft chocolate buttercream swirl she's passing me. 'I've been saving myself for this. It's only my sixth.'

Poppy's lips are twisting. 'Don't worry, they're only a bite each, and you're walking them off.'

'You keep telling me that, and I'll keep eating them.'

She catches hold of my free hand. 'No ring today?'

I'm staring at my thin left finger. 'Damn, in the rush I totally forgot all about it.' I catch a glimpse of my reflection in the ring cabinet I'm standing next to. I pull the belt of my dress tighter and smooth out a crumple in the skirt. 'Can you see I slept in it?'

Immie gives a chortle. 'You're so much my kind of woman.'

Poppy's smile widens. 'Oh, Mills, how did that happen?'

'I got ready at midnight, then didn't go to bed, that's all.' I pull a face. 'But on the plus side, Casper's remembered his ribbons, the canapés coming out of the kitchen are to die for, and there seem to be lots of people here.' If I sound hesitant it's because I can't quite believe it.

Poppy's grinning. 'According to Jess, there are so many couples, Rory's already rung Huntley and Handsome HQ and asked them to send more fizz.' Her eyes are shining. 'How does that make you feel?'

I think for a second. 'Great … but worried it could all still go wrong.' I smile, because this isn't just about me. 'There are so many amazing exhibitors, they deserve a fabulous day.'

Poppy nods. 'Don't forget to try Clemmie's Little Cornish Kitchen afternoon teas out on the lawn.'

I give her a teasing nudge. 'Are you bigging-up the competition?'

She laughs. 'She's done some fabulous weddings for us at the farm – her meringues are to die for.'

I'm scrunching up my cupcake wrapper and picking up my tray. 'I'll try them next time I'm outside. I'd better be getting on, I'm taking iced elderflower cordial round next.'

It's one of those days when there's so much going on that my head feels like it's going to explode. And because my phone never comes out of my pocket and I'm passing the clocks on the wall at a run, I lose all track of time. When I finally get a chance to head for the pretty cake stands and curly metal tables and chairs under the white canvas tent on the lawns, the shadows are getting long, so it has to be late afternoon. And when I pull my phone out to check, there are four texts from Phoebe that I don't have time to open.

Out on the lawn, the strings of ditsy floral bunting are

swinging in the breeze, and beyond the marquee poles there's the Little Cornish Kitchen owner, Clemmie, in a pretty orange tea dress, her auburn curls caught up into a bun on top of her head, handing out samples. As I head into the shade, I'm making bets with myself on how likely it is I'll find a meringue to sink my teeth into rather than concentrating on where I'm walking. So when I run slap bang into a denim-shirted chest I'm kicking myself for being so careless. As a very familiar scent engulfs me and my head starts to spin, I'm silently cursing for not having checked my face or topped up my perfume since this morning.

'Nic, what are you doing here?'

There are deep shadows in the stubble on his chin and his voice is low with laughter. 'Looking for a free shower?'

I allow myself a full eye roll. 'Not funny. Try again.'

This time the ends of his lips are hinting at a smile. 'It's your big moment, Milla Vanilla, what kind of a guy would I be if I missed that? I had to be here to support you.' His full smile finally breaks loose. 'Don't worry, I brought my umbrella.'

I hiss at him under my breath. 'Like you'll need that in this star zone, Captain K.' Then I grin at him. 'Have you been here long?'

'You could say that.' He blows out his cheeks. 'At first I raced after you. When I was too knackered to run anymore and still hadn't caught you, I decided to have a look around and wait for you to bump into me.'

If I can't hold back my grin it's because I'm suddenly feeling really bouncy when I thought I was whacked. 'I can't believe how at home you look.'

He shrugs and shuffles the stack of flyers he's picked up. 'I'm that kind of a guy – easy wherever I am.' He's biting back his smile. 'Or it could be because I'm wearing the team uniform.'

'Excuse me?' Obviously, apart from Jess with her linen trousers and Gucci loafers, we don't have one.

He gives me a nudge. 'Pure coincidence. Have you noticed how similar our denim is.' His smile widens. 'And please note, I'm wearing a shirt today.'

I'm pursing my lips so this banter stops there. 'And moving on, how about we take a look at Clemmie's afternoon tea? I'm told the dainty sandwiches are spectacular.'

He nods. 'They absolutely are.'

'You tried them already?'

'Yes.' He takes in my surprise. 'I was waiting a while. And before you ask the question, the answer's yes, yes, and yes again ...'

I'm frowning. 'Yes, what?'

His eyebrows rise. 'Yes, that's what we'll have for our wedding.'

We have to keep this straight. 'You mean Pixie's wedding?'

When he smiles this much, the dimples slice up his cheeks. 'Isn't it the same thing?'

I'm aware there's something more important to root out here. 'What will you have?'

He smiles. 'The afternoon tea ... and Poppy's cake with petals sticking to it ...' He wafts his hand towards the country-garden blooms in bottles on Clemmie's tables. '... And flowers like those ones.'

I'm opening and closing my mouth. 'Just like that ... you decide three things all at once?'

He's looking pleased with himself. 'I'm not deliberately awkward, I just hadn't seen anything right for Pixie before.' He's raising a finger. 'And the woman from The Deck gallery in St Aidan ...'

I'm narrowing my eyes. 'You mean Plum?'

He nods. 'That's the one – we'll have her sea-glass key fobs, and invitations with the shells painted on. And Rory's person-alised Mr and Mrs beer.'

I'm picking my jaw up off the floor. 'So, twenty minutes' browsing and you're almost done?'

'Hell, no, Milla.' He's looking at me like I'm the amateur here. 'There's some serious tasting to do on that last one. You have no idea how many beers there are to choose from. And I'm no closer to deciding on the cocktails.'

'But great progress otherwise?' As Clemmie passes with a plate of mini cream-filled meringues, I take one and pop it in my mouth. Then as I crunch and the powdery sweetness explodes onto my tongue I let out a soft moan of pleasure.

Again, Nic stares at me like I've gone mad. 'You saw the thickness of that wedding file. We're barely scratching the surface. There's still all the clothes to do.'

I'm mentally comparing his laid-back country choices today with his weakness for slash-to-the-waist dresses at Cally's wedding. 'I may need a word with the bride about the dress.'

His eyebrows shoot up. 'You think?' It's obvious he doesn't.

'The dress can make or break a bride's day, so it's important Pixie feels amazing and relaxed.' It could be a big part of the budget too – not that he ever mentions that. But with the extra considerations of her wheelchair combined with her reluctance, we might struggle to get this right. 'If I have a chat with her, I promise not to give any of the other secrets away.'

'Great, we'll sort you some FaceTime.' He's staring off into the distance. 'In the meantime, what the hell is that huge red thing over there?'

I peer at where he's looking, but fail to see over the heads of the crowd. 'Please tell me it's not a fire engine.'

He coughs. 'It's *way* bigger than that. More like the Starship Enterprise on wheels. It's possibly a pushchair being steered by a woman with full eff-off four-by-four-driver attitude who embodies the whole resting-bitch-face thing.'

My wail is for women everywhere. 'You shouldn't say that say about anyone!'

He shrugs. 'I'm sorry, but you didn't see the dead-eye she gave me. She's gone now, but from the way she was mowing people down, I hope you're insured for third party injuries.'

I'm turning to go and check for myself when Clemmie comes over, a plate in each hand.

She smiles. 'I promised Nic a taster but he wanted to wait for you, Milla.'

I'm hesitating. 'Is it okay if I take it to eat on the run?'

Nic's tilting his head on one side as he stares at me. 'I bet you haven't stopped since breakfast.'

'Breakfast? There was no time for that! But I have been grazing.'

Nic's hand is behind my back. 'Five minutes – I promise the world will keep on turning, the fair will keep on buzzing – and then you can go back to work.'

As we leave the crowds behind and reach the far end of the garden by the pond, Nic's looking at the ground. 'Shall we sit down?'

'Absolutely not, or I'll never get up again. Let's stand and watch the fish.' I know that standing like this I've got my back to the action, but Nic's right about stopping – it's blissful. I turn my attention to my plate. 'Aren't the teensy jam tarts adorable?'

Nic's holding up a small goat's cheese and tomato flan. 'Mini-quiches and pizzas, brioches with ham and cheese, and then scones and muffins too. It's all delicious.'

'I'm on my third meringue.' Even as I say it, I know I'm mumbling through my mouthful.

Nic's licking his fingers beside me. 'Careful not to drop crumbs in the water – do fish eat sausage rolls?'

I've no need to grin as widely as I am. 'Why do you always ask me the hard questions?'

I'm hoovering the last sugar crumbs off the meringue paper when there's a jab in my back, then a squawk. 'It is you, Milla, isn't it? No one else would be out with a skirt that creased.'

My heart stops. There's only one person I know who'd say that.

'And why the hell aren't you answering your phone?'

And that's the giveaway. I have zero idea what the hell she's doing here when she's on her baby-popping sabbatical but the pointy, suede court shoe I'm looking down on matches her, as well as the parrot shriek. My stomach has dropped faster than a five-ton weight, but as I turn I know exactly who I'm going to see.

'Phoebe!' I'm less ready to be rammed in the shins with a pram so humungous it looks like it's built for giants, but I peer in anyway. 'And this must be Hunter?' The child I'm staring at is in full rugby kit, giving furious kicks with his Nike trainers, and his beady eyes are a lot like Phoebe's when she's intent on snaffling the last chocolate biccy for herself. To my untrained eye, he looks closer to teenager size than the teensy bundle I'd imagined cradling, which just proves how little I know. If I tried to cuddle this one he'd most likely smother me.

The big surprise for me is that I'm staring hard at a little human and my tummy isn't squishing even a tiny bit. And the pangs of jealousy I'd expected to find belting me in the chest aren't there at all. As I take in large ears and a lolling mouth that's a lot like Ben's when he's come off the spare-bedroom treadmill, and a nose pointing at exactly the same angle as Phoebe's, it's like that game where you make faces out of strips. I can't say he's cute at all.

I know I have issues with Hunter's mum and dad, but he's only a baby; he can't help his parents. I give him a little wave and when he doesn't wave back I try for an ice-breaking age-appropriate greeting instead. 'Great intergalactic transport you've got there, Hunter. I'm Aunty Milla.' I turn back to Phoebe. 'How did he get so big?'

The fact that Phoebe towers above me as she looks through the curtains of her Kate Middleton hair could be a clue to the size. She's simpering. 'Hunter's a ninety-fifth-percentile child. He's off the top of every graph in the baby handbook.' This is Phoebe; of course he has to be bigger and better than anyone else's baby. As she shakes back her hair again, her chin juts and her eyes go all flinty. 'By the way, baby-name etiquette changes faster than the top one-hundred names. First to the labour ward gets first dibs now. Not that I'd expect you to know that, being so far away from childbirth. In any case, they were my wellingtons, you know.'

'That name's dropped off my list anyway.' Since I've seen the baby, it's put me off big time.

Nic's turned with me, and he gives me a nudge. 'None of us are ever more than nine months away from a baby. Nine is right, isn't it Milla?'

Phoebe's spluttering. 'Who the hell is this?'

Nic's grins at me. 'Nic Trendell, happy to meet you. I'm Milla's fiancé.'

I'm watching Phoebe's jaw drop so I rush in to put her right. 'He's joking, obviously.'

Phoebe's face recomposes. 'He'd have to be.'

Nic's voice is gravelly and full of laughter. 'She didn't say that when I asked her.'

Phoebe's looking from Nic to me and back again. 'But she can't be engaged. She's barely been here five minutes.'

Nic gives one of his famous shrugs. 'When cupid's arrow hits, you can't fight it. Especially when you're as smitten as Milla and I are.' He's going to fall flat on his face any minute, and it won't be so funny when he does. But he's still not stopping. 'Working as closely together as we do, we were bound to be on fast-forward. But when you're as certain as we are, why wait?'

I can't believe how much he's going for this. He did seem to have taken an irrationally large dislike to Phoebe before he even met her, but even so.

When Phoebe's left eyebrow shoots up she doesn't look funny like Poppy does, she's just plain scary. 'So where's the ring?'

Nic turns to me with a frown. 'That's a good question. Why aren't you wearing your ring today, Milla Vanilla?'

I'm about to fall flat on my face, but I can't resist playing along. 'You know me and early mornings – I left it in the bathroom.'

Nic's staring me straight in the eye. 'I'm sorry, that's going to cost you a kiss.' He has to be kidding. And crazy.

I'm so panicked the only voice I find is my squeaky hedgehog impression. 'With so many people around?' Knowing Phoebe's feelings on PDA she'd be appalled.

Nic's laugh is low and husky. 'Don't worry, our audience will be way smaller than the one we kissed in front of at the Valentine's fireworks display. Anyway, aren't wedding fairs all about the romance?' His grin spreads wider. 'We're hardly likely to get thrown out when you're the one in charge here.'

With each of Nic's statements, Phoebe's face is pinching tighter. My mistake is, I'm so busy watching the size of her final grimace that I take my eyes of Nic. So by the time I realise what's happening, he's already spun to face me, taken away my plate and balanced it on the little wall behind me.

As his arm slides around my back and his mouth dips towards me, I'm opening mine to protest but before the words come out his lips are melting into mine. And that's the funny thing – it's not jerky and awkward like it's only our second ever time. It's as smooth and natural and delicious as if we did it a hundred times a day. As my hips slide against his, the fit is perfect enough to leave me in no doubt how much he's enjoying this and to confirm that the size of what he's waved in front of me quite a few times already is totally genuine.

As every bit of breath leaves my body, I sag against him; the only thing that saves my collapsing knees is his arms tightening around me. And who knows how, but my hand's already behind his head pulling him in further, my fingers entwined in his hair. Then there's the heat of his body and his whole dark velvet cocoa taste making me bury myself deeper. And the thump of my heart, the rush in my ears as loud as the tide crashing up the beach on a stormy day, and warm rainbow shivers flowing all the way from my scalp to my toes.

When we finally break apart, I'm blinking away the X-rated images, and pressing my hand to my mouth to hide the fact that any all-day gloss I had left from this morning is probably smeared all over my face now. Then, as I catch Nic's eye to warn him that the bad-boy behaviour has to stop here, I spot a smear of toffee-coloured gloss on his upper lip. I know I intended to stay away from him for the rest of time, but the only thing for it is to dive across with my hanky to wipe it off.

And then I lean in for one last brush of his lips, simply because I can't resist it.

As I leap away again, I grin at Phoebe. It's not like I can hide what just happened, so the next best thing is to come out and own it. 'As you can see, they're quite good kissers in Cornwall.'

She snorts. 'Well, I've just spent three months tied to a newborn; there's no need to ask what you've been up to when you should have been holding the business together. And I know your geography's abysmal, but even you should know this is Devon.'

Nic jumps in. 'Milla's been working her butt off for your company. And over the past three months I couldn't have asked for a more perfect navigator.'

Thinking of the day I ended up driving into a field, we both know that's not true.

Phoebe sniffs. 'You really must be blinded by love if you think that, Nicolas.'

Nic holds up a finger. 'If you insist on being formal, it's Nicolson.' His lips are twisting as he holds back his smile. 'I also answer to Captain Kirk.'

I flash him another look, this time to properly say shut the eff up. 'And moving this on, how great that you've brought Ben too.' As he's doing his best to hide behind Phoebe and the pram, it's especially pleasurable to give him a name check and watch him squirm. I'm also wondering how I ever actually looked at that blond stubble mixed with a touch of shaving rash every day for all those years without realising dark beards are so much sexier.

Phoebe's purring like a cat who got a strawberry sponge cake as well as the cream. 'This is a family outing; we have them all the time.' She stretches out the fingers on her left hand and lets her huge engagement diamond catch the sunlight. 'We're paring down the shortlist for our wedding day. My own Brides Go West wedding fair at the most talked-about new venue in the area was enough to tempt me away from the nursery and it's certainly paid off – we'll be making a booking before we go.'

The strangled choke coming from behind the pram has to be Ben. I've heard it too many times at too many venues not to recognise those first throes of an oncoming panic attack. And do you know what? All I feel is a rush of sheer relief that this time around I'm not the one trying to make him sign 'I do' on the deposit cheque.

I'm still smiling at Nic. 'Well, good luck with that one, Phoebe.' As for her, it's a stunning venue, but other than it being bang on-trend, it's not what she goes for at all. She's much more of a wall-to-wall-marble-with-hot-and-cold-running-doormen kind of a person than a cart-shed-and-cow-parsley girl.

'Which brings me round to the next topic.' Phoebe's pulling herself up to her full height, which is approximately seven feet ten. 'What the hell are you wearing, Milla?'

'Before you start, it's not from Primark.' If I tell her it came from St Aidan Cat Protection she may just expire on the spot.

Her eyes are flashing. 'Truly, I've seen wrung-out dishcloths with more quality. You're completely letting our corporate side down! How have you gone so far downhill so fast? Toenails on show too! That's a complete betrayal of our brand.'

With every word I'm shrivelling in front of her. By the end I'm feeling slightly less significant than a worm. Then, in the distance, in the space beyond her elbow, I spot Poppy and Immie powering across the lawn. Nic's grinning at me from the side. And suddenly I remember that I'm not on my own here. And I'm not the same, meek, do-as-I'm-told person that Phoebe used to batter down and boss around. Surrounded by good, loyal, supportive friends, who'd do anything to fight my corner, I'm strong. More than that, I feel loved. And the love of my friends isn't just wrapping me up and protecting me, it's making me powerful too. More important still, I don't have to take Phoebe's taunts. In the last three months, I've learned it's okay to stand up for myself. One look at Immie – as wide as she's tall, pumping the air with her hands, her short legs stomping – and my courage gets a reboot. Instead of diving for cover under the nearest rhubarb leaf, I'm re-inflating. And with no apparent input from me, I'm answering back, in Phoebe-speak too.

'Our customer base has a very different vibe here, Phoebe. It's more about the wind off the sea and the salt in our hair than ladies who lunch at other people's expense.' I have no idea where the hell that came from, but for the first time in my life I've thought on my feet. And you've no idea how good that feels.

Phoebe's snort explodes from her nose. 'I don't give a damn if you've got sand blowing out of your ears, Milla, you look like the old woman who crawled out of the sea.'

Nic's opening his mouth, but I'm too quick for him. 'Forget what I'm wearing, Phoebe, at least I'm not trying to make myself look better than I am by undermining people. And unlike you, I try not to be mean or to bully people. And I won't be letting you do that to me anymore.'

Phoebe's never one to back off, and now she's shouting so hard she's spraying us with spit too. 'I have no idea what you're talking about, Milla. But *what the hell's with Brides Go Wild when it should be Brides Go West?*'

Nic's grinning at me. 'See, I told you your new signage would get a reaction, Milly Vanilly.'

As Phoebe turns to Nic she looks like she's about to eat his head. 'For the last time, *stop calling Milla those ridiculous names*!'

I'm looking at her through narrowed eyes. 'If there's so much to criticise here, why not buy me out of Brides Go West and get the hell back to Bristol.' I can't actually believe I just said that, but now that I have, I feel so much better. And glancing down at the grass as I get my breath back, I'm handed another gift. 'Is that mud on your Manolos?'

Phoebe's hands are on her miniscule hips. 'I don't know where you got this attitude from, Milla, but it's completely unacceptable!'

Poppy's eyes are bright, and her hands are clenched. 'Go on, Millsy Vanillsy, tell her where to get off!'

I pull myself up to my full height and for the first time in my life I'm almost on a level with her. Brilliant doesn't begin to cover it. And better still, I know exactly what I'm going to say.

'Let's revisit this at a time and place that's more appropriate. And as you're spoiling things for the other guests, not to mention the brand, I suggest you either stop your shouting or leave.'

There's a hush in the huddle by the pushchair. Phoebe's mouth wrinkles under her pointy nose, but she stays silent.

In my head I'm already punching the air for making her shut the eff up. For saving a situation which was careering off the edge of a cliff. But most of all, for stopping her in her tracks when she was hell bent on ruining this wonderful wedding fair with a scene. I've told her where to go and I still have my dignity. I'm already anticipating Immie's thump on the back. Poppy's hug. Nic's high five. Clemmie's excited hand clapping ...

But then the film reel in my head stops. As I tumble back to reality, Phoebe takes a big step towards me.

Her lippy's flawless, her nails are beautifully shaped and painted russet brown, her dress and her stomach are as flat as the board it was ironed on, and I can see she thinks every single thing about her is better than me. But for some reason, I'm not intimidated any more. And I really wouldn't want to be like that anyway. I feel liberated.

I've still got this. All I have to do is take two steps away so I can see her better. And this time, I'll be so quietly fierce that she won't dare come back for more.

But as I take my giant strides sideways the lull is broken by a strange gurgling rumble.

I catch Nic's eye. 'What the hell is that?' Not being alarmist, but it sounds major enough to wreck a wedding fair.

His eyes narrow. 'Drains being unblocked? A farmer pumping slurry?' There's another muffled explosion and his puzzled frown deepens. 'An elephant that's overdosed on laxatives?'

Behind the pushchair, Poppy's holding her nose and Immie hoots. 'I know that noise blindfolded at a hundred yards – that's a nappy being filled.'

We all turn to look at Hunter, his popping cheeks as red as his chariot.

Phoebe lets out a squeal. 'Hunter's done poopies, Ben.' Her voice rises to a shriek. 'Poop, Ben, I *said poooooooop! This one's yours.*'

Ben takes a leap backwards down the lawn. 'I *don't think so!*'

'It *totally* is.' Phoebe grits her teeth and shoves the pushchair at him. Somehow, the force that hits him is so strong, it accelerates his backwards leap. His arms are spread-eagled as he flies over the grass, straight over the little wall, and he drops like a stone, and flops straight down into the pond.

He hits the lily pads and the pond surface with such force that the water flies up into the air, splats Phoebe, and soaks her from neck to calf.

As Ben groans and disappears under the lily pads, Phoebe stiffens and shoots bolt upright as the slick of pondweed slimes her cream linen dress.

She lets out a shriek and staggers forwards holding out her arm to Ben. But instead of hauling Ben out, she face-plants in there beside him.

There seem to be a lot more arms and legs in the water than just Ben and Phoebe's, and they're lashing out in all directions.

Not that I'm mean or have ever been looking for payback, but standing there watching them flailing together in the murky water, knowing how much they'll both hate it, it finally feels like I've found some kind of closure.

I can see Nic's enjoying it as much as I am, but eventually he steps forward. As he starts to haul them out, Phoebe's shaking her head so violently the drops are flying off her like diamonds in the late afternoon sunlight.

Nic steps back. 'Is there a problem, Phoebe?' Then he laughs and reaches for the high neckline of her dress. When he stands back he's holding up a goldfish and grinning straight at me. 'Definitely better back in the water than down a customer's top. Starfleet captain to the rescue, call again any time, Thisbe.'

By the time Ben and Phoebe are side by side and dripping like waterfalls, I'm back in organiser mode. 'Can I get you some dry clothes? Or some elderflower cordial?'

Phoebe's squeezing out the dripping rat tails of her hair. 'Don't you think you've done enough damage for one day, Milla? We'll leave you to your sex-crazed fiancé. See you when you get back home to Bristol.'

On the upside, the reek of pond algae is totally overpowering every bit of Nic's heady scent as he comes to put his arm around me.

There's an unconscious jarring in my head when I hear the words home and Bristol. And in a way, Phoebe's right – guests in the pond is another spectacular catastrophe to add to my list. But this is one I'm extraordinarily happy to live with, in a wouldn't-have-missed-it-for-the-world kind of way. Ben's shout brings me back to earth.

'Hurry up, Phoebe, we don't want to get any more contaminated.' He's already by the doors. If it wasn't for Hunter and the Starship Enterprise pram, I suspect he'd have vaulted the wall in his rush to get them all out to the car park.

I'm calling after Phoebe as she struts. 'Whatever! We're definitely waiting until we're married to have sex, but he's the whole package … and he owns a shipping line.' Not that I care but Phoebe will.

Nic coughs. 'It's more of a navigation agency, remember?'

As she gouges a new trail of heel marks across the lawn I'm shouting after her. 'And he's spending humungous amounts on the wedding too.' I haven't claimed it as mine, so it isn't a lie. I'm still going, cupping my hands as she reaches the building. 'This is the bit where you say you hope we'll be very happy …'

As I turn back, Immie's standing, hands on her hips and beaming. 'I've waited my whole life to see you stand up for yourself. Good job, Mills.'

Poppy's laughing at me. 'Yay to that. You certainly gave her plenty to think about there.'

I'm feeling slightly guilty now. 'I didn't mean them to fall in the pond. And I hope it hasn't wrecked the wedding fair.'

Immie delivers the thump to my back I was waiting for. 'But I'm damned pleased they did.' She's chortling to herself. 'You should have seen her face when she toppled. I can't think of anyone I'd rather see get a soaking.'

Poppy's smiling. 'I've got a feeling all the people Phoebe rammed on her way out here will be very happy too.'

Nic's giving me a nudge from the other side. 'Not that I'm trying to get you naked yet again, Milla, but you seem to be pretty wet too. I've got towels in the car and some spare jeans and T-shirts. You're welcome to borrow them.'

I'm running through the alternatives in my head. 'It's either that or a visit to the bridesmaid's rail.' I send Poppy a wink. 'Thinking about last time I raided the Bridesmaid's Beach Hut for Valentine's Day sequins, I'll maybe take you up on the T-shirt, Nic.'

Nic's face brightens. 'The little pink mini-dress – that was another bridesmaid's dress I liked. We might want to note that in the file.' Then he shakes his head and blinks. 'Sorry, I'll go and get the towels.'

I look beyond Poppy and Immie who both looking like they're about to pop with laughter. 'Thanks, Nic, great plan.'

Nic's halfway across the grass when he turns and grins at me over his shoulder. 'This might be the part where you tell me you love me, Milla?'

'In your dreams, Captain Kirk.' I wave my middle finger at him. Then I remember how he's helped me wipe the floor with Phoebe. 'Okay, I give in, I totally do.' I turn to Poppy and Immie and give them my sternest stare. 'And you two – it's a towel, nothing more.'

And then, very firmly, I tell myself the same.

But there's another thing too. My mum was a strong, independent single parent. After an upbringing like that, the last person I'd turn to in trouble is a man. So letting Nic help me fight my battles really isn't my style. But just this once, I have to secretly admit how great it was to have a prince on a charger on my team. So long as I don't let it happen too often.

Chapter 29

Tuesday.
Jaggers Bar, St Aidan.
Sand between the toes and bottomless lemonade.

'Your wedding fairs do work, don't they?'
This is Nic, musing as we sit on the beachside terrace at Jagger's Bar, where we're sipping our cocktails, nibbling our on-trend snacks, and watching a tangerine sun slide down towards a glistening turquoise and silver sea.

I wrinkle my nose. 'I'd be out of business if they didn't.' Then I laugh, because I have to be honest. 'We'd be in trouble for Pixie's wedding if you hadn't found so much to like at The Potting Shed.' As we're finally ticking off the outstanding choices, I'm determined to make the most of Nic's decisive mood.

Originally, we'd planned an evening meet-up over pancakes on *Snow Goose*, to fit in with when Pixie was free for a call. But as Jagger's were doing Gin's Up! Tuesday we switched to here hoping Nic might have another lightbulb moment and decide about drinks.

As for Jagger's, the downsides are the teenage clientele, the migraine-inducing red and purple Perspex tables and chairs and the giant signs announcing the two-for-one Sex-on-the-Beach happy hour. So long as you can live with those, the cocktails and the sea views from the deck are excellent.

'So what's Pixie like?'

He sends me a wink. 'Fun, lively, nervous about the wedding – a lot like me, I suppose.'

'What, stubborn and impossible?' I laugh as I think of him as my original nightmare client. When he's properly relaxed there are crinkles at the corners of his eyes when he smiles, and despite the stress of putting a wedding together I'm seeing them more and more often.

His grin widens. 'Not anymore. These days I'm very easy to please.'

And he's right again, but this time I really don't mind because after three months of progressing more slowly than a sea snail, we're finally storming ahead in every area. Even the theme's sorted. Nic's still in denial about having one, but for everyone else, it's Seashore Castle Rainbow Garden.

I peer in at the herb sprigs in my Rosemary and Grapefruit Comet and pick up my jar. 'Cheers then, Nicolson. Here's to lots more decisions and a lovely wedding.' We've each been taking a different choice of cocktail, to get through the maximum number on the board.

Nic lifts his Cockle Shell Gimlet. 'Back at you, Ms Vanilla. They sell these in pitchers as well as glasses, if you'd like to go large. Having met Ben, I reckon he'd drive most normal people to hit the bottle.' His smile fades. 'Not judging, but how did an amazing woman like you end up with him, Milla? Unless you've been hiding a frantic hand-washing obsession from me, you two can't have had much in common.'

Obviously, I'm glossing over the compliments. But I'm so surprised by his directness that instead of telling him to butt out, I'm replying. 'I met Ben after I went to Bristol when my mum died. We packed up the rented cottage where we'd lived our whole lives and I went there to be near my brothers.'

His fingers are closing around mine. 'It must have been awful.'

I stare into the distance to where the shimmer of the water smudges into the sky. 'At first I went out all night, every night, to take away the pain. By the time I got together with Ben, I was partied out. But I still felt as if I was drifting without an anchor.' I'm blinking. 'You'd have had to see our cottage to understand how secure and enveloping it was – thrumming to the soundtrack of Mum's Greatest Hits collections, with all her vibrant colours. And, despite the chaos, there'd always be her latest hotpot concoction bubbling on the stove, her jam tarts steaming from the oven ...'

There's such warmth in his eyes as he looks at me. 'I can almost smell the pastry from here.'

I'm so grateful, because him buying into this makes it feel less like it's lost forever. And of everyone I've ever met, Nic's the one person I've found who makes me feel comfortable talking about Mum, because he seems so interested and in tune with what he hears. 'She made Bakewell tarts to die for. That hot raspberry jam and sticky sponge ... I wish you could have tasted it.'

His enthusiasm is so real. 'Me too. I'm gutted that I missed meeting her.'

And so am I, even though I have no idea why. 'She'd have loved anyone who'll dance to Jon Bon Jovi.' I drag in a breath. 'We had this wonderful feeling of family and belonging. Her being ill and us being homebound made that stronger still. It took years to come to terms with the shock of losing her, but once I did I was desperate to recreate that home all over again for myself.'

Nic shakes his head. 'Be honest, it was never going to work with contagion man was it?'

I watch the foamy wiggle of the tide rushing up the sand and pulling back again, and decide. I'm not hiding it from him. 'We got engaged before we really knew each other. We even bought a flat, but in five whole years of looking he'd never settle on a wedding venue.' When I used to tell people, it came out as a pathetic wail. This time it feels more like I'm claiming my badge of honour for coming out the other side. 'That's going to be my claim to comic fame forever.'

Nic's wrinkling his nose. 'Oh, Milla Vanilla, that explains why you're such an expert on venues.' His eyes narrow. 'But then think what a life of hell he saved you from – by not getting married.' And he has got a point.

'On the upside, Phoebe's got all that to look forward to.' This has to be the first time I've laughed about it.

He blows his cheeks out. 'What I can't work out is how you got involved with a taker like her in the first place?'

'She was my boss when we worked at Costa.'

Nic shakes his head. 'I bet she made the most of making you feel small there too?'

I can't believe how right he is. 'I had a bit of money my mum had left me, and my camper van and I suppose she picked up on that and became a bit of a limpet bestie.' I'm under no illusions now that if she hadn't accidentally found out about my cash by peering over my shoulder when I was checking my bank balance at the cash machine, she wouldn't have noticed I existed. I shrug because I have to face facts here. 'Since I've been doing Brides Go West on my own, I've got a whole new respect for what she did as a frontperson. I mean, I've worked my bum off and I still haven't had a trouble-free fair. It's damned hard making everyone do what you want and keeping every-body happy. When she wafted about making it look effortless, she must have been nailing it.'

Nic's staring at me. 'But you're so much better at it than she could ever be. People know the difference – you genuinely care. She doesn't even bother to fake it.'

I have to laugh. 'Maybe you're just blinded by your dislike of Phoebe. If I hadn't had my assets, she'd have been best friends with someone else. But it's fine. It really hit home when Phoebe turned up at the fair. I'm back with people who love and look out for me. It's time to let go of the bad stuff and move forwards.' I can't hold back my smile. 'Seeing Ben and Phoebe floundering in the pond water at the wedding fair, they didn't feel like part of my life at all. And as I watched them walking away with Hunter's pram, I didn't feel anything. I wasn't even jealous. I just had a huge sense of relief that I don't have to deal with them anymore. They're welcome to each other, their life, and their giant baby. It's as though these last few months have truly set me free.'

'Being ready to let go of the past is a huge achievement. Believe me, I know, you can't get on with your life until you have.' His sigh is heartfelt, and when he gazes out to sea his eyes are far away. And the silence he drifts into isn't the sort I'd intrude on.

Which leaves me back in my own head, remembering what Poppy said about me moving on that first night in St Aidan. I'm probably still light years away from that, but just to try it out, I take a sideways glance at Nic.

I know the wedding fair kiss with Nic was pretty full-on. And I completely accept he never intends to get tied down. But if Nic were the one I moved on with, how awkward would it feel bumping into him down at the quayside if the last time he saw me I'd been naked and groaning in his bed? It's a million times worse than him knowing I wear pants with kitten prints on. But looking at him now, it's hard to imagine ever finding someone who smells as nice and looks as nice and makes my tummy flip or my blood rush like he does.

But while he's so obviously thinking about something else, I might as well just mentally run it past myself. Just to try out how far I've come. Very quietly, in my head, I let him murmur the words:

Milla, if you'd like someone to bonk your brains out, for one time only, just say the word …

And my imaginary self is unexpectedly opening her mouth, about to say 'Hell, yes! Thanks so much, that would be lovely.'

But before I can tell myself off for being so outrageous, shocking, and out of touch with reality – not to mention unprofessional – there's a vibration.

Nic shakes away his daze, pushes his hand into the pocket of his denim jacket, and eyeballs me as he pulls out his phone. 'Here we go … and finally … it's Pixie!'

I close my mouth and force it into a really bright smile and make myself concentrate.

'Hey up, Pix, how's it going? Milla's here. She can't wait to say hello.'

As I watch her face on Nic's phone screen, there's a moment where she's just like her picture. Then she moves and immediately she's a living, breathing, talking, feeling person, with a real personality and an unlimited number of dimensions.

'Hi Milla.' She does a little finger wiggle to the camera then does a three-sixty swivel on her wheels, throws back her nut-brown waves, screws her face up, and groans. 'It's all happening so fast and I've no idea how I'm going to get through a whole day when all the focus is on me! I'm really not a limelight person, I'm much more of a team player.'

In two seconds flat, she wipes out three months of preconceptions and becomes a strong, determined woman who has the same dark grey eyes as Nic and who is having a minor wobble. As for her whirling around the floor, there's very little to tell that she's in a wheelchair and not an everyday executive office one.

I don't stop to think I might be going through exactly the same for her. 'Don't worry, Pixie, most brides feel exactly the same as you.'

She puts her hands over her ears. 'Go easy with the wedding jargon. Every time I hear the "B" word my tummy drops through the floor.'

Nic's rolling his eyes. 'Stop being such a drama queen.' He turns to me. 'Hang on in there, we might get some sense in a bit.'

And Nic's changing in front of me too, getting new layers. Because here he is, kidding around with Pixie. And where before we've just assumed he must really love his sister because of the lengths he's going to, now I'm watching the reality. How he is with his family isn't something he can put on or pretend. Right in front of me, there's the living proof of what a kind, deep, caring, genuine, funny, loving, tender guy he is.

Pixie wrinkles her nose. 'So long as you don't tell me anything in advance, I reckon I'll be able to turn up on the day.' When her face breaks into a grin, she has the same dimples as Nic. 'I bet he's driven you crazy with his prevaricating, Milla. Don't take any shit and watch him like a hawk!

Given half a chance, he'll sail off into the sunset and leave us without a best man.'

Nic lets out a shout of protest. 'I gave you my word that I'll be in St Aidan until your big day is over.' He turns to me. 'And in case you're worried about your parking permit, that's safe too. *Snow Goose* will be here well into next year.'

It's one small sentence, but the ripples from it set my mind racing. It isn't until my body suddenly relaxes that I realise I've even been worried about the time when Nic will sail out of the harbour for good. It's inevitable there will come a time when there's a gap on the dock where the hull is and an empty space in the sky where *Snow Goose's* mast and rigging should be. How it's totally crazy that I'm really hoping it will be later rather than sooner.

As I pull my eyes back to Pixie, I can't help laughing at how well she's summed Nic up. 'After four months racing around the whole of Cornwall, I reckon I'm getting the measure of him.'

Despite the time lag I can tell her eyes are twinkling. 'It's lucky he likes you so much, or we might have lost him already.' She laughs. 'You're even prettier than I gathered.'

Nic lets out a cry of protest. 'Shit, Pixie, why not spill all my secrets?'

Even though I love the way she's winding him up, I'm hurrying this on before it turns into a full-blown family barney. 'Nic may have said—' it doesn't sound like he's been holding back on the information exchange '—I thought a quick a chat about the dress might be useful before he goes shopping?'

Pixie's shaking her head. 'He hasn't told you, has he? I'm avoiding the obvious clichés. A friend is lending me a navy satin dress she wore for her prom.'

I'm stifling my surprise for so many reasons – that it's sorted at all when I'd expected it to be outstanding, but most of all the colour. 'Brill. That covers your *borrowed* and your *blue* then.'

She pulls a face. 'It's a lovely dark indigo, perfect for me to blend into the background.'

I'm letting out a silent phew that it fits with the Seashore Castle Rainbow Garden plans. 'And are you having ... ahem—' I'm finding a way to say bridesmaids that won't put the wind up this very uncertain bride. '—close girlfriends in coordinated outfits?'

Her face splits into a smile. 'I seriously doubt it. Ordering them around the basketball court is one thing, telling them what to wear is something else entirely.'

Lucky for me we've got the word rainbow in the theme then. 'So you won't need to come to the shop then?'

'Which shop is that?'

I think how best to put it. 'It's near the beach, it sells clothes and – er – other items for people in your position.'

Pixie sounds intrigued. 'What, wheelchair users ... or sailors?'

Nic lets out a sigh. 'No numbskull. Milla's talking about Brides by the Sea. It's a wedding shop, for people getting married. Obviously not anywhere you'll be visiting any time soon.'

Pixie's enjoying his frustration. 'Oh, right. So what does that sell, then?'

Nic looks at me. 'She's a total wedding virgin. She knows even less than I did when I started.'

Pixie gives him an indulgent smile. 'Listen to you – how hilarious is my big brother the wedding expert!'

I bite back my smile at the double act and give her a short

version. 'The shop has wedding dresses, obviously, but you don't need them, bridesmaids' stuff, you don't need that. Nic's sorted the styling and I take it the guys have chosen their suits. Flowers are already sorted.'

Pixie stiffens. 'Flowers! Where the hell are they for?'

Nic sighs. 'No need to flip out, they're mostly for the tables and the window sills.'

Pixie's eyes are like saucers. 'We're having *tables*?'

Nic's lips are twisting. 'To rest your drinks on. That's okay isn't it?'

Pixie laughs nervously. 'Yeah, I s'pose.'

Nic pulls a face at me. 'You have no idea how hard she's making this.'

I'm aiming to say the least possible and get the hell off the phone before I make it any worse. 'Other than that, probably just hair slides. Oh, and shoes.'

'Shoes?' She's leaning into the screen. 'What *kind* of shoes?'

'The usual.' I'm thinking of the glass cabinet in the White Room. 'With ankle straps, labels, sparkly bits. And wellies for meadows.' That just about covers it.

'Labels? In St Aidan? Which labels?' She's suddenly concentrating. 'Don't stop!'

I'm reeling them off. 'Rachel Simpson, Manolo thingy, Alexander McQueen, Gucci, Louboutin, Dior, Jimmy whatsit ...'

Pixie's face is so close to the screen she's practically bursting out of Nic's phone. 'You have *Jimmy Choos*?'

Nic's laughing. 'Well done for finding Pixie's Achilles' heel, Milla. She must be the only sailor I know to have more cupboards full of shoes than ocean-going kit. How many pairs have you got now?'

She gives him a dead eye. 'I don't ask you how many boats you own, or how many staff you have on your books.'

His whoop is gleeful. 'Enough to have taken over an entire spare room from Ewan.'

She sniffs. 'My legs don't work, but I still have feet. Shoes are essential.'

'Great reasoning.' I shrug. 'Not that you ever need an excuse for another pair.'

'Exactly, Milla.' Pixie wheels herself backwards and grins. 'Well, some of us have work to do. If that's everything, I'll let you two bunnies get on with your evening.'

Nic holds up his jam jar. 'We're doing a hard night of cocktail selecting.'

'My heart bleeds for you.' Pixie lets out a throaty laugh. 'Don't let him give you a hard time, Milla. He's very well trained, find the right commands and he's like a lamb.'

Nic shouts. 'Stop shattering my manly image.'

Pixie's looking gleeful. 'Okay, make safe choices, see you soon – oh and that itinerary you're sorting, Nic, make that shop my first stop when I get off the plane.'

'Okay, bye-eeee.' I'm waving madly, then the screen goes blank and I turn to Nic again. 'The name Pixie really suits her.'

He's blinking. 'She's always been the same – a total handful, making it up as she goes along.'

I can't help smiling. 'I can see she runs rings around you.'

He gives a hurt sniff. 'And what the hell happened to sibling loyalty?'

'I suspect sisterly solidarity won out.' Then it hits me what I've just said – because if he takes that the wrong way, me implying I could ever be her sister-in-law is like the biggest gaffe ever. I'm so mortified I'm colouring up under my freckly wind tan and I've gone so sweaty my shirt is sticking to my spine. I'm blurting to cover my confusion. 'I can tell she's a woman without limits.'

Nic's face falls. 'You didn't see her before. The world is a much smaller place for her since ...' He tails off, then he pushes his gimlet jar across the table and gets up. 'I'm sorry, I can't do this now.'

It's like a switch has flipped and I'm floundering to help, kicking myself for being so thoughtless. 'How about we get fish and chips?' I'm thinking of the hole in my stomach where I skipped lunch because I was too busy writing copy. But mostly I'm thinking that it's comfort food for Nic. From the hunch of his back as I follow him towards the harbour, it's going to take a lot more than cod in batter to fix this.

Chapter 30

Tuesday, a week later.
The beach, St Aidan.
Broken dreams and free lunches.

As the weeks go by and the sun climbs higher in the sky, there's only a month to go until the wedding. The fresh spring days are turning warmer and St Aidan's narrow winding streets are filling with visitors. On sunny weekends the beach is thronged, and the car parks are so full it's only thanks to my beloved boat-owner parking permit that I'm saved from hiking for miles from the van to the shop.

We've got a few more wedding fairs under our belt now too. Sure, every one throws up unexpected challenges – but I'm learning to run with the problems rather than letting them trip me up. Instead of falling flat on my face, I'm slowly picking up the art of winging it. I'm still coming down from yesterday's Bank Holiday Monday fair in a converted Lifeboat Station further to the north. The more I do, the more I find that instead of being wrung-out by the worry, by the end I'm flying with the adrenalin of giving the exhibitors and the customers a wonderful time.

At Brides by the Sea, as well as keeping on top of the details for Pixie's day we've been working on other requests too. There's a couple from London who want to marry with just the two of them, ideally on a cliff top in August. It was only after I'd been emailing them for a few days that I realised I'd originally planned to have moved on by then. If there's a tiny whisper in my head telling me I'd hate to leave town while *Snow Goose* is bobbing up and down in the harbour, luckily there's always a more sensible shout ready to drown it out.

As Jess said back in February, bespoke work comes in all shapes and sizes. Last week we had to drop everything and make a whole new four-tier cake when some poor bride's dad didn't know the cake was in boxes in the car boot, opened it, and let a Labrador the size of a tank jump in on top of the lot.

Once you listen to the stories, you'd be surprised how many wedding cakes come to grief somewhere between the cake maker's kitchen and the cake cutting table. In fact, the more I'm around the live side of weddings rather than the supply side, the more I'm appreciating that a wedding plan is the starting point, not the blueprint. That the world is full of random hitches that will force you to rethink. But the key thing to remember is, in the face of disaster, the world is also full of other amazing options which let you carry on.

Looking down from the Style File terrace at lunchtime today I could see the beach was almost empty, so I've come out for a quick wander. I've brought Merwyn along for company and a leg stretch. I admit that the Milla who arrived in the winter avoided exercise like a hole in the head, but over the last few weeks I've found that after a morning at my laptop, a stomp along the beach and a blast of sea air helps to clear my brain.

And I know that when I first looked down on the beach four months ago the vast stretch of wintery ocean made me shudder.

But now I find I'm hurrying down the alley short-cuts, skipping down the cobbled steps, anticipating the sense of release I get when I reach the sand that stretches around the bay as far as I can see. I'm looking forward to the frills of tide rushing towards me. Hurrying to check how big the waves are, listening for the sound of them breaking on the shore before I see them. And then there's the colour of the sea, which constantly changes with the light as the clouds scud across the sky. I can leave the shop courtyard looking out over turquoise shimmer, yet if the sun goes behind a cloud, it can be iron grey by the time I arrive. It's funny to think that in all those years growing up I never noticed a time the sea was ever pale blue with navy patches.

Back then I loved the beach because it meant days out and picnics. Dayglow jelly shoes, and plastic buckets filled with treasures. It meant wonders like sea anemones in the rock pools and crabs washed up on the shoreline. But now it's as if the roar of the water and the wind snagging at my hair, the soaring seagulls and the red and blue fishing boats, the white and grey cottages stacked up on the hillside, are all a part of my being. It's as if by coming back as a proper adult I've finally woken up to how much I always loved them. How much they belong to me and I belong to them.

And today I'm loving it all the more because when you're with Merwyn it's impossible not to have a good time. His latest obsession is his Donald Trump rag doll which he turned up with after a frantic dig in the sand dunes last week and won't let out of his sight. As he drops it at my feet for the fiftieth time I shake off the sand and seaweed and fling it back into the shallows for him. 'Quick, Merwyn, we don't want Donald to get washed out to sea.' I jump as I hear a laugh behind me.

'Not everyone would agree with that, Milla Vanilla.'

I'm sounding grumpy to cover up that my stomach just dropped so far down it's probably in my new-to-me super-practical Converse trainers. 'Do you enjoy creeping up on people?'

Nic rubs the stubble on his chin. 'I haven't had much chance lately. Apart from our meetings, I've been busy in the office down the coast.'

I stare at him and wonder how he always manages to make me flustered and hot, even when there's a stiff breeze. It's even worse since I had that ridiculous moving-on moment. 'I thought you drove boats?'

'Sometimes there are loose ends on land that need tying up too.' He smiles. 'I see you've finally got the hang of beach walking?'

I shrug. 'It's great for clearing my head.' My life never felt quite so broken when I looked at it from the shoreline. And that aching, gaping hole in my chest that was here in February has gone now. 'You know, since I decided to let go of the past, I've actually had a final revelation.' At one time Nic would have been the last person I'd have shared it with, but lately he seems to understand so well. And this one's a biggie.

'If there are any ghosts left to lay, I'm always happy to listen.'

I blow out a breath because I feel so guilty. 'I've realised I wasn't actually ever in love with Ben.' Out loud it sounds even worse than it was in my head. 'I grabbed him because he was there and I needed a comfort blanket to help me through.' It's funny to think that at the time I assumed finding someone house-trained and okay-looking was all that being suited as a couple was about.

If I'd got out and about more as a teenager, I'd have had more kisses to compare. If I'd had a dizzy first love at fourteen – even an unrequited one – I'd have known to keep on looking. It's strange how one kiss through a van window changed my whole outlook on love and life. Once your eyes are open to the possibilities of super-hot, lukewarm doesn't get a look in. With Ben, neither of us had been around enough to know any better.

I'm staring out at the waves racing towards the shore in parallel lines. 'What I was in love with wasn't Ben, it was the home and the family Ben was going to let me have.' It feels good to finally admit the truth. There's a natural thought that follows. 'That makes the break-up my fault just as much as his. If we'd been properly happy, he wouldn't have looked at Phoebe.'

Nic wrinkles his nose. 'It's not about blame.' There's a flash of a grin. 'From what I've seen, Ben and Frisbee are ideally suited – they're both super-anal about things that don't matter, they both have inflated opinions of themselves, they both get immense pleasure from putting people down, and they're both great at ordering people around and taking advantage.'

I can't help smile at how accurate he is, and that he hasn't held back. 'That's a very comprehensive list considering you've just come up with it.'

A flicker of guilt passes across his face. 'I've been thinking about it quite a lot too.'

'When Phoebe used to list the reasons why Ben was with her and not me I could never see it. But I can now.' I kick the sand. 'People say time heals, but I stood still for a whole year in Bristol, seeing them both every day. It's only since I moved away that I've worked my way around to the truth.'

There's another throw of the rag doll, then Nic blows out his cheeks. 'You know, time's supposed to heal. But it hasn't helped me.'

'Sorry?' This is the first time he's ever volunteered anything. I jolt to a halt so I can concentrate better.

He's stopped walking and he's staring at the horizon. 'Pixie's accident at the go-cart track ...' His face is set. 'Her spinal cord injury was entirely down to me because I booked the go-carts. I couldn't have chosen a worse way to celebrate my thirty fifth.'

Oh shit. I'm feeling sick for him. And no wonder he closed up that day at Jagger's when I mentioned her life without limits. 'And you still feel that was your fault?'

He gives a grimace and his voice is empty. 'It's hardly anyone else's is it?'

'And does Pixie think that?'

He shrugs. 'You saw Pixie. She's fiercely independent, she takes ownership of everything including this. But I'll always know that if it hadn't been for me she'd be okay – I'm always going to carry that guilt.'

His face is so sad, I want to wrap my arms around him and not let go. 'But wasn't it just an awful accident?'

He sighs. 'Whatever you call it, she was twenty-six, she had her whole amazing life ahead of her – and now she doesn't. She won't ever trek in the Himalayas, or run the mothers' race at sports day, or walk down the aisle like every other woman does. And I won't ever forgive myself for that.'

I'm swallowing back my saliva. 'But despite all that, she really is going to have the best wedding day.'

'I hope so.' He dips for a pebble and throws it into the water. 'That's all down to you, Milla Vanilla, I'll never be able to thank you enough. And I've had such a good time with you these last few weeks putting it together.'

I shrug. 'Happy we could help.' I don't need to be a mind reader – I can sense from his hesitation there's a 'but' coming.

He throws another pebble. 'That was okay, somehow, because I was doing it for Pixie.' He frowns. 'I'd never be comfortable enjoying things that much for myself though. The only way I can live with my conscience going forward is by making sure I never get too happy.'

Here we were, two broken people washed up on the same shore. Except, after weeks of hanging around with him and having the support of all my friends here, I'm almost mended. While he never will be. I'm staring up at the hollows in his cheeks, the darkness of his eyes, that tousled hair blowing, tangled with salt from the breeze off the sea. His beautiful tanned wrists sticking out from his rolled-up shirt sleeves, his strong hands. And I'm aching to grab those long, lean fingers, smother those scuffed knuckles in kisses. I want to wind my fingers through his hair, slide my hand up inside his shirt, and pull him towards me. And not let go until I've pieced every bit of his very broken soul back together and made him whole again. However long it took it would be worth it. Because that's how much and how deeply I've come to care about him.

I'm squinting into the sun, trying to work out where he's going with this. 'So what are you saying?'

He blows out his cheeks. 'Well, you sound like you're almost ready for your dogs on the hearth rug.' He clears his throat. 'This is me explaining why I never will be.'

My heart is breaking for him. 'Because this is so big and awful you won't ever be able to let go?'

He nods. 'Exactly. If I ever thought there was the smallest chance I was falling in love, I'd have to walk away.'

I swallow hard. 'Great.' Seeing as he's staying around until next year, it's obvious that me feeling like my heart's going out to him has to be one-sided. But wasn't that my unconscious brain's plan all the time? To fancy someone unavailable, to prove to myself that I still could. I just never counted on the fancying part getting so intense. I make a mammoth effort to move this on. 'So long as Pixie likes mini sandwiches and jam scones and cupcakes and castles, she's going to love what you've put together.'

My distraction has worked, because he pulls a face at me. 'I still haven't found the right cocktails.'

I feel so inadequate on every level. For totally failing to help him out of his emotional chasm. For being helpless to change anything to make life better for Pixie. So all I can do is check. 'Apart from the alchemy with the gin, is there anything else you'd like me to do for the wedding?' I pick up the doll and let Merwyn tug it as we start to walk along again.

Nic throws his denim jacket over his shoulder. 'Actually, I've been thinking about Pixie's blue dress.'

I've been thinking about that too. It's a measure of how in tune he is that he's picked up on this. 'Indigo is unusual, but when a bride decides to break with tradition it's helpful if her family respects that choice.' I have to ask the biggie. 'How does your mum feel about it?'

'She knows Pixie's head-strong. It's not so much her – I'm remembering how fabulous Cally looked when she came towards us down the aisle in her lovely white dress.'

I have to agree. 'She did look amazing.' It feels so special that we both shared that moment. And not that I'm in any doubt, but it shows one more time how thoughtful and in tune with his emotions Nic is. And what a waste and a damned shame it would be for him to live a life where he closes them down.

Nic nods. 'There was no doubt, and no half measures with Cally. She didn't look like she accidentally got lost on her way to a prom. Categorically, the only thing she was there for was to marry Nigel.' He pulls a face. 'It's a shame for Ewan and Pixie to miss out on that just because Pixie hates the idea of being the centre of attention. I thought maybe you could help?'

'Me?' My jaw's dropped so far it's practically on the sand. 'It depends on why she's gone for the blue. If it's always been her dream it's completely different from her wanting to wear it so no one looks at her.'

'When Pixie comes to the shop, maybe you could check that out. Persuade her to think about whether she'd rather be a proper bride? It's a once-in-a-lifetime moment, I'd hate her to throw it away.' He's taking in my hesitation. 'Jess did say you'd tackle any job?'

I'm groaning inside simply because I already know he could be asking the impossible with this. Then I remember – he's not just a very good friend I've grown to rely on more and more, he's here for professional reasons. And he really needs my help with this. 'Leave it with me.' I'm not holding out much hope, but I'll do my best. 'So long as I get her on my own for a casual glance at the shoes, maybe, just maybe, I'll be able to have quiet word.'

He comes in and gives me a squeeze. 'Did I ever tell you how much I love you, Milla?'

'No, but I told you that the day you pretended to be my fake fiancé and lent me a T-shirt.' I force out a laugh, try to make it ironic. 'Not long now.'

He grins. 'When it's over, I'm hoping I'll know so much you'll take me on as a wedding consultant.'

I laugh. 'You'd have to get the right qualifications.' Seeing as he was so generous to me earlier, I'm happy to return that. 'Truly, Captain Kirk, you have to take the prize for the biggest turnaround in the history of weddings. In the end, you've astonished me with your aptitude for the business.'

'Thanks for that. I have to say, I had the best teacher.' He sends me a wink. 'I'd better get on, I'll leave you and Merwyn to your walk.'

And I'm left with yet another impossible job. And a bruise on my leg where I've been kicking myself for even imagining he's looking at me. But most of all, I'm kicking myself for not holding on tightly enough to my heart. Me growing to like Nic so much? Of all my blunders so far, that has to be the worst. It's just a good thing no one will ever find out about it. And hopefully, once I don't have to see him every day, I'll have time to come to my senses.

Chapter 31

Monday, three weeks later.
The White Room at Brides by the Sea.
Old and new.

'So it's between the diamanté strappy and the suede with feather tassels.'

It's three weeks later, the white-painted wood plank floor of the White Room at Brides by the Sea is covered in open boxes, and Pixie is holding a shoe in each hand, frowning with the effort of deciding.

Pixie was as good as her word; with three days to go to the wedding we're her first call after touching down from Glasgow. And as Monday's a quiet day, I booked out the entire shop for the whole afternoon so the two of us could have a long, girly chat over the Jimmy Choos, totally undisturbed. Between us, that bit could have gone better.

'Have another macaroon while you're mulling it over.' Poppy whooshes over with the biscuits, each topped with a butter-toasted almond. From the size of the platter and the six different pastel colours it's no last-minute ambush; this one's backed by Poppy's usual flawless logistics and impeccable long-term strategic planning.

Jess follows her with a tray of Hendricks, ice, mini bottles of tonic and lemonade, and lime and lemon slices. 'And I'll top up everyone's G&T's.' There are leaf sprigs too which is telling – if Jess reaches for the mint, it's a serious occasion.

Sera's sitting on the bottom step of the spiral staircase that leads up to the studio fiddling with the holes in her threadbare denim shorts. As she pushes back her mass of streaky blonde curls there's a dreamy look in her eye. 'It's like me when I'm trying to decide between an exquisite tiny sequin, or a seed pearl. Sometimes it's impossible.'

I mean, Sera? Sera always hides in her studio. Yet here she is, hanging out with a bride. Which is a measure of how special Pixie is and how much everyone wants to chip in with this. This last week I've talked to all of them individually, getting their take on how I might tackle this. And this is why I love it here. Because in St Aidan generally, and in Brides by the Sea in particular, every difficulty is faced together. So me suggesting Pixie might change her mind about her dress has become everyone's challenge, not just mine. Which is why they've all turned out in force to support me now.

As for how Pixie looks in real life – beautiful and amazing don't begin to cover it. She spun in here in her wheelchair, tossed back her nut-brown waves, and lit up the room with her wide, warm smile, the sparkle in her dark brown eyes, and her energy. Not that I'm an expert, but her chair's not like any other wheelchair I've seen. This one has a tilt to the wheels, sparkly rims, apparently no sides and a tiny Gucci backpack hanging off the back. And even though you'd expect her to get her fingers caught in the wheel spokes, her polished nails put mine to shame.

Immie chomps on a macaroon and holds her tumbler out to Jess for a refill. 'When I'm at the bar trying to decide between

Rolling Wave or Half Pipe, quite often I have to have a pint of each.'

I mean, Immie doesn't even work here. But she's been such a force willing the wedding plans along, and as she's in charge of the housekeeping team at the castle, there was no keeping her away.

I'm hoping Pixie's not feeling overwhelmed with so much unexpected bustle. 'I'm sorry there's such a crowd of us, but everyone's been so committed to putting your day together, they all wanted to come and wish you luck.'

Jess is smiling the beatific smile she saves for her proudest moments. 'Under normal circumstances we'd have been working with you hand in hand all the way, not meeting you just before.' Jess has carefully avoided the bridal words Pixie's so wary of. And at least people have arrived one by one to introduce themselves.

Possibly because she's sitting in a sea of gorgeous stilettos, Pixie looks completely at ease as she smiles around the room. 'Even though Nic's kept the details a secret he's told me how much you've all done. It's lovely to see you so I can thank you in person.' She turns to me. 'As for you, Milla, you're a total star. If there's anything I can ever do for you in return, you'll have to let me know.'

I'm swallowing back the lump in my throat, fanning my face with my fingers like a teenager in an American High School movie. I manage to mumble. 'Our pleasure ... you're very welcome ... any time.' And then it hits me. 'Actually ...'

'Yes ...?' Pixie's smiling at her over the glint of the strappy sandals, gently stroking a feather with her finger.

'I'm hoping it's not too much to ask, but I'd love to feature you on my Brides Go Wild blog.'

'Really?' Pixie tilts her head.

I'm rushing on while I can. 'One of the most popular blog features is Six of the Best where different, interesting women try on half a dozen dresses and give their reactions. Sometimes we focus on dresses for a certain kind of venue, or a certain budget or, or by a featured designer.'

Jess is picking up the baton. 'It would be brilliant to feature you trying dresses from the shop, Pixie.'

I'm grinning at Pixie. 'We've never had a basketball player before.'

Pixie shrugs. 'You want me to try on dresses from here?'

Holly's clasping her hands. 'If I took some quick pictures of you wearing them, it would help you to relax in front of the camera too.'

When Pixie wrinkles her nose she looks even more adorable. 'I never considered trying on proper wedding dresses.'

Jess smiles at her. 'It must all look very over the top to you on a first visit.'

Immie puts her hand on Pixie's. 'I know how you're feeling, Pix. It took me a year and seven visits before I dared to try one. In the end they ambushed me with a blindfold, but I was so glad they did.' Immie's eyes are shining with tears. 'The trouble was, I didn't believe I could ever look beautiful. Not that you'd ever have that problem – but even if you aren't wanting one, Sera's dresses are so special they're worth trying once in your life.'

Jess nods at the spangly sandal in Pixie's hand. 'On one unsuccessful dress appointment, Immie fell off some heels very like those and took the entire bridal display with her.'

Pixie laughs. 'With my legs, I'd likely do the same. I'm warning you, it'd take quite a few of you to get me into a dress like the one in the window.'

I'm smiling because she's picked on the biggest, most voluminous dress in the shop. 'Luckily, there are plenty of us to help! And I promise you, most dresses will be easier to put on than that one.'

She gives a shrug. 'It would be good to wave the flag for women in wheelchairs. We do get married too – not that anyone ever mentions it.'

I'm wary of offending her but I can't skirt around it anymore. 'There's simply nothing out there. Women who can't walk are entirely overlooked in the wedding world. It sounds fake if someone not disabled tests the dresses out, but you making the dresses look so good too will be really encouraging to people. And you're the perfect person to talk about how the different styles work and which are most comfortable.'

Pixie gives a little shiver. 'I've been dreading all the attention a bride gets, but this would be different somehow. It's more of an opportunity.' Her nose wrinkles as she considers. 'If it would help other woman like me see the possibilities and feel better about themselves I'd be doing it for them, not for me.'

Jess only ever purrs like this when she's winning. 'You'd make a wonderful ambassador, Pixie.'

Pixie sighs. 'I wanted to try on my blue dress anyway to check that the shoes go. I'm up for trying on a few more, if you are.' As she looks around the room, we're all holding our breath. 'So what are we waiting for? Let's go for it!'

We don't want to scare her off, so we start with a simple oyster satin shift that slips over her head and could easily be a bridesmaid's dress.

Verdict: lovely feel, it looks fab, and the skirt stays well away from the wheels. But the impeccable satin's not very forgiving for spills or small children climbing on her knee.

Then we move on to a variation in cream and add a champagne lace overdress, caught with a slim ribbon belt, which is very pretty and gets the thumbs up because it's both gorgeous and less prone to showing marks. By this time we're all getting into this. Not only is Holly jumping around taking pictures, I'm also filming Pixie's reactions and comments on my phone.

Next we decide to try a much bigger dress, by a different designer, for the bride who wants to hide the chair under her skirt. When Pixie catches a glimpse herself in this in the mirror she lets out a scream.

'Totally not for me.' Then she gets more objective. 'But for anyone looking for a Cinderella vibe who wants to make a statement *and* cover up the chair, this would be a dream.'

I can't help smiling at her.

She pulls at the boned bodice. 'On the down side, it's less comfy, and you'd never find your pants with so many petticoats.' She sniffs. 'And if I did a wheel spin, I reckon there would be some serious lace carnage. Moving on ...'

For Meghan fans, she attempts a fitted raw-silk dress with a Bardot neck, but even undone it's too much like a straightjacket. So then we try one of Sera's which is a silk and lace all-in-one flowing dress, but that loses a lot of the 'wow factor' because Pixie's sitting down. And after that we move on to Sera's mix-and-match separates, putting tulle skirts with different silk underdresses and tops and adding tiny jackets, which all work much better. Then Immie wheels the chair back towards the fitting room curtains to help Pixie out of a floaty tulle overskirt covered with tiny silver stars.

As Pixie reaches to unwind the pearl wires we slipped into her hair along the way her smile is rueful. 'Thank you for showing me that wedding dresses don't all have to be like meringues or nylon body scrubbers.' She gives a wistful sigh. 'If only I'd known these were here earlier.'

As I follow her behind the curtain, I'm not going to push it. 'Your dress sounds lovely too; we can try that next.'

She leans forward so Poppy can undo the back of her skirt. 'With an injury like mine, intensive physio can make a huge difference and I'm still in my golden time. That's why Nic sorted out the wedding down here. But it does mean I was less in touch than I should have been.'

'Apart from missing out on the dress, the rest worked fine – fingers crossed you like everything.' As Immie and I lift Pixie forwards Poppy eases the skirt downwards.

Pixie sighs. 'Nic took the accident so badly. Even now, all he thinks about is that I can't walk.'

It only seems right to share. 'He mentioned that he blames himself.'

Pixie nods. 'I know. He thinks my life is wrecked, but I just don't see it like that – I actually feel truly lucky because I still have some feeling in my legs, and everything above that is in tip-top working order. It's different for me though – without the accident Ewan and I would never have got together. I have the downside of legs that won't ever run again, but they also let me meet the love of my life. Ewan's made me the happiest I've ever been, I feel like the luckiest woman in the world to have that.'

We're all smiling around at each other.

Pixie pulls a face. 'Nic's so weighed down by the bad things, but I really don't want his life to be ruined because of me.'

'So you prescribed a spot of wedding therapy?'

She nods. 'I hoped he might come to understand how much Ewan and I have. Is it too much to hope that by the time it's all over, he'll be ready to move on?'

I don't want to be the one to dash her hopes, but I have to be honest. 'He's certainly been busy. I'm not sure about the rest, though.'

She gives a grimace. 'We'll see. There's still a long way to go to the end of our wedding day.'

I've been waiting all afternoon for a chance to say this line. 'It might help reinforce the happy bride message if he saw you in white rather than blue?'

Her brow furrows. 'You think so?'

I'm not lying. 'I really do.'

As the curtain tweaks and Sera's head appears, it's obvious she's been listening in and had taken her cue. 'Stay as you are, Pixie, there's one more dress I'd love you to try.'

I can't help feeling exited. I raise my eyebrows at Pixie. 'That's the amazing thing about Sera, everyone has a dress that's perfect for them and Sera has this amazing sixth sense for knowing what it is.'

And then the curtain parts again, and Sera's there holding out a skirt on one hanger and a top on another.

'So, this is a simple soft gathered lace skirt, with a matching long-sleeved cropped top that holds off the body. It reads as a dress, but it'll accentuate your tiny waist. The teensy flashes of tanned midriff it gives from the side will be just sexy enough and the three-quarter sleeves are unlined so they show how delicate the lace is. And the slightly short top will be a perfect length for you sitting down – what everyone will see is the line of the lace edge across your waist, standing out from the skirt.'

Pixie's holding her hands out. 'I already love it, for all those reasons.' She turns to Poppy, Immie, and me. 'Can we try it?'

We put the soft skirt on first, and even before we've done up the rouleaux loops and pearl buttons down the back of the little top, Pixie's breathless, stroking the elbow-length sleeves. 'This is it. This is what I want to wear. Please tell me I can?'

As we throw back the curtains to let everyone see, Sera lets out a soft sigh. 'When I first did my sketches I had a picture in my head of how it would be, but on you it's even better.' Her eyebrows close together as she considers. 'We might replace the buttons with flatter ones. You do know it's a sample – other people have already tried it on?'

Pixie huffs. 'Like I care about that.' She's looking past us to her reflection. 'Even from here, I can see it's perfect. And you know what, when I look at myself in the mirror, all my eyes are drawn to is me in the wonderful dress.' As she scrapes a finger under her lashes her eyes are wet with tears and she's biting her lip. 'Much as I love my chair for everything it lets me do, I'm not seeing that at all. And because the top isn't attached to the skirt and isn't tucked in, I'm completely free to move.'

I give Sera a silent double thumbs up as I dip down and squeeze Pixie into a hug. Then Poppy bobs across the room and comes back in with the mother-of-the-bride tissue box and we all take one and blow our noses very noisily.

Pixie finally scrunches up her tissue, then takes anther to pat her eyes. 'I don't even mind not having the shoes. Just the dress is more than enough.'

Sera's beaming as she leans in to examine the waistband. 'We'll check the length and maybe add a little elastic so there's a bit more give then you'll be good to go.'

I'm smiling at Pixie. 'Nic's going to love your choice.' As I look at her lovely face and her generous, eager expression so full of courage, I understand why Nic's been ready to go to the ends of the earth to make her happy. And I feel exactly the same. Perfect won't be enough – it's got to be even more than that.

And the pressure on me just ramped up so far with that realisation that I'm almost struggling to breathe.

Pixie lets out a groan. 'Poor Nic, he's insisting that the whole thing is his treat. I've just added even more to his bill. I know what he's like, if he hears about them he'll want to get the shoes too.'

Jess is waving away Pixie's concern. 'Don't worry, we'll do the best we can with the price.' She gives a throaty laugh. 'Nic got his picture on the Valentine's board, plus he's one of our best customers, he always gets a great deal.'

Pixie's frowning. 'What was that?'

I laugh. 'It was a great move on Nic's part, grabbing Jess's special Valentine's Day offer.'

Jess goes across to the desk, comes back with the Polaroid from the board, and we all crowd in, but after the first glance I have to drop back. It seems like such a long time ago now. That pale, uptight woman with her wonky laurel crown, squashed next to Nic on the love seat, is barely recognisable as the smiley, messy-haired sun-tanned person I say good morning to in the bathroom mirror every day now.

Pixie's nodding. 'It must have been after this that Nic offered to help out.'

Poppy's laughing at me. 'He's squished in between us, Milla, but from his smile you didn't need to stab him with your Cupid's arrow.'

When I look at the picture it's true, he's facing my way with the goofiest grin. Which had to be pure chance. 'Total bollocks, Poppy.' To put the brakes on this I'm going for a subject change that's still on topic. 'We had such fab cocktails that night. Do you have any favourites, Pixie?'

She wrinkles her nose and nods at her glass on the carved

console table. 'We might be uncool, but forget the fancy stuff, Ewan and I love our triple-X G&T's – extra straight, extra strong and extra long. With ice and lemon.'

It's a relief we haven't settled on anything more exotic. And Pixie and Ewan's Mr & Mrs Three Kisses has to be the perfect name. It was a useful diversion, but it hasn't got me off the hook.

Pixie's squinting at the Polaroid then looking back to me. 'I'd say, looking at this, that's one big brother just waiting to be set free.'

Which is just what I don't want to hear when I've got a wedding to deliver – with no hitches.

My biggest test is coming up. My first wedding. I can't blow it. My whole future depends on this.

JULY

Chapter 32

The next Thursday.
Early morning in the attic bedroom.
Empty seats and spare tyres.

'Merwyn! What the heck are you doing here?'
When I open my eyes on the morning of the wedding
it should be because my phone is beeping to tell me it's 7am. I
admit it's a bit earlier than needed. But maybe, just maybe, I
was planning to make the most of Nic accepting my offer to
drop by to use the bathroom. To accidentally (on purpose) bump
into him wearing nothing but a towel as he dashes across the
landing to grab his tux from the living room.

Okay, I know I'm totally lame and sad, but it hit me yesterday
– it could be my last chance, in the world, ever to see the Trendell
torso unwrapped. It would be crazy not to take advantage one
final time.

But getting woken by a wet brown nose pushing in my ear,
followed by an entire floor mop of a dog landing on me and
pinning down the duvet, I'm struggling to make sense of what's
going on when Merwyn should be a mile away fast asleep on
his bed at the castle.

As I hear a knock on the bedroom door and Nic's voice softly saying 'Milla?' I'm kicking myself again. I wanted to have my hair properly tonged by the time he saw me, not be doing an impersonation of a haystack. As it is, with Merwyn on my chest licking my face I can't even get my hands free to rake my fingers through my hair. So all I can do is brace myself for the fabulous view of tanned chest.

'I hope it's not too early for breakfast?' As he pushes through the door, a full tray comes first, so at least the huge pile of almond croissants and the pot of coffee make up for the disappointment that he's fully dressed.

I take in a T-shirt and jeans, the strands of damp hair hanging over his forehead, and do my best to enjoy the consolation prize of his lovely forearms and bare ankles. 'You showered already?'

He nods. 'I tried not to wake you. I know I'm earlier than we agreed, but there's been some last-minute changes to our schedule.'

'Really?' We talked about this yesterday – how everything would be fine so long as we stuck to the plan like superglue. So I'm slightly anxious that he's already veering off course. Then, as I run Merwyn's silky ears between my fingers, I take in the wiggly tension lines crossing Nic's forehead and my stomach drops. 'Is something wrong?'

'Nothing to worry about, it's all in hand.' He puts the tray down on the end of the bed. 'But Abby fell out of an apple tree at her mum's and she was asking for Bill and Ivy, so they rushed off to London early this morning.'

'Oh no, poor Abby.'

He shrugs. 'In the meantime, we've got Merwyn, and we're covering for them at the castle.'

I let out a whistle. 'Phew, if that's all, you're right, we'll manage.'

'Actually, it's not.'

It's hard for your whole body to go tense when there's a dog wriggling on your belly, but mine does. 'There's more?'

'I had another call late last night – from Casper's dad.' Nic blows out his cheeks. 'Sorry to be the one to break this to you, but someone smashed the headlights on the wedding camper.'

I can't believe this is happening. 'I only saw him on Tuesday to give him the ribbons. Go on, you're allowed to say, *I told you so.*'

Nic shrugs. 'You couldn't have known this would happen.' He's being very generous. 'Casper's been posting pictures of his sex partners online and someone's brother paid him a visit with a hammer.' His grin is slightly shamefaced. 'I did my best to warn you off him. I'd have hated to see your kitten knickers going viral.'

I shudder and move this on. 'We'll use the Brides Go Wild van. Keef has insurance, he told me that night at the distillery when he offered to run the van back. We can ask him to do the bride's side pick-ups.' I'm mentally checking through. 'So what else? Please don't tell me the groomsmen's boat has sunk?'

'The groomsmen will still be arriving via the beach.'

'So it's all sorted before breakfast!'

There are crinkles at the corners of his eyes when he smiles. 'Before your breakfast. I had mine after I took Merwyn for his walk, then we called in at the bakery on the way up. So if you'll let me have the keys, I'll go and give the van a quick wash and you can bring me the ribbons down when you're ready.'

'All the more for me and Merwyn then.' There's no reason to feel disappointed. I have breakfast on my own every day – what's not to like?

'And by the way ...' He's already halfway to the door. 'I spoke to Nigel yesterday. He and Cally are having a baby.'

I take a moment to make my face surprised. 'Wow, that's *so* fab.'

Nic's eyes narrow. 'But perhaps not *entirely* unexpected? I also heard about your valiant efforts to cover for Cally. Off your face and you still managed to keep her secret, that's what I call a true professional.'

I groan. 'It all went so wrong. But at least now you know I won't be drinking all the drinks today.'

He laughs. 'All the same, nice job. Nige was very appreciative.'

Now I'm more awake, my mind's racing ahead. 'So is there anything else you need to tell me before you go?' It's one of those questions I already know the answer to – if there were he'd already have said.

His face crumples as he hesitates. 'Actually, there is.' He's standing in a shaft of bright sunlight from the porthole window that's making him even more dazzling than usual. 'Great Auntie Di's messed up her hotel booking, so I'm giving her my room at the castle.'

My lips are twitching. 'And you need me to lend you my festival tent?' I'm kidding to cover how I gutted am. He's best man and brother of the bride, there's no question what I have to do here. I just didn't realise how desperately I was looking forward to staying in a princess bed myself until it's been taken away. 'No, you have to take my room. I'll be finished by then, I'll easily get a lift back to St Aidan.'

He jumps straight in. 'Absolutely not. That brilliant breakfast menu was all down to you. The whole thing is, I want you to have your night at the castle,'

Two people, one room. It doesn't take Einstein to work out the solution here.

I make it sound a thousand times more casual than it feels.

'You didn't keep me awake with your snoring at the Waterfront.' Being forced to share a room with the hottie – it's the stuff of teenage fantasies. Sure, I've played this exact scenario over in my head a few hundred times, but only because I'm temporarily obsessed and a sad person. But I'll get over it. And lastly, I haven't engineered this on purpose. I definitely have not been ringing round all the hotels to bribe them to make this gift happen. Honestly. Because it's as terrifying as it is thrilling. And my throat's so dry my I'm croaking. 'We could ... share again?'

This is how easy we are with each other now. How good I've got at concealing my galloping heartbeat, how skilled at blanking those dragonflies. There's not even a hint of innuendo.

His eyes go soft. 'Maybe I didn't snore because last time I stayed awake to check you were okay.' And that's what a sweetie he is, looking out for everyone without ever making a fuss about it. And in the end, it's not how edible he looks in his plain white T. What counts much more in real life is someone looking out for you at every turn without even questioning, like Nic does. Then he blinks and re-boots. 'If you're sure you don't mind, that would be great. I'll have the sofa, obviously.'

I can't let him get away with that. 'I take equality for women over chivalry every time. I'll toss you for it.'

'Tails I lose, you get the bed.' And not a coin in sight. There are those slices in his cheeks he gets when he really smiles. 'You do realise this could ruin my reputation as a sad loner.'

Lucky I made it super-clear to Pixie that the Polaroid of us on the loveseat meant nothing. Less than nothing.

I have a go at wiggling my eyebrows to show how much of a joke this all is. 'Best make sure we sneak you out well before breakfast, then.' I can't help pulling a face as the full implications sink in. How much I'm going to have to restrain myself. How hard it's going to be to have him so close yet so unavailable. How very much of a last parade this is going to be in every sense. But it's another one of those times when the best way of hiding things is to bring them out in the open and shake them around. 'Last time I was unconscious; this time – hopefully – I won't be. Just don't go looking too drop-dead gorgeous in that tux of yours, okay?'

His laugh is low and husky. 'Back at you. In any case, Merwyn will be there to make sure we behave.' He looks at his watch. 'Great. In that case I'll be back for you and Merwyn just before nine.'

And a moment later he's gone.

I ease Merwyn off my chest and onto the duvet. 'Come on, Merwyn, we'd better have some croissants to build our strength up.' However testing today was going to be, it just got a whole lot harder.

And as I listen to the sound of his footsteps fading as he winds down the four flights of stairs, I can't help thinking how quiet life will be when I no longer have any reason to go looking for Nic.

Chapter 33

Later on Thursday.
Outside Cockle Shell Castle.
Cornflowers and embroidered hankies.

As I wander out of the huge front door of the castle, the bright July sun straight overhead is shining out of a cobalt blue sky. I can't believe it's already time for Pixie to arrive and we've got this far without any more major hitches.

When we got here earlier, Nic and I took two seconds flat to drop our overnight bags in our room up a narrow flight of stairs behind the spacious castle kitchen. There was just enough time to take in wonderful views across the white sands to the light aquamarine expanse of the bay, catch a glimpse of the double shower in the en suite, and have a two-second pretend fight over the dreamy and inviting king size bed with its downy duvet and light-grey Egyptian cotton covers. Then we shot back downstairs to get on with our pressing jobs.

First on the list was finding Holly and her cameras, then shooting down to the beach to pull the groomsmen ashore as they chugged towards the beach in their inflatable. If the size of Holly's whoops were anything to go by, the photos of Ewan and a dozen groomsmen in their tuxes sitting in the boat in the shallows, then all leaping out onto the sand and high fiving their way up the beach swigging bottles of champagne are going to be amazing.

She laughed at me as she jumped out of the way of a wave. 'This is exactly what a wedding by the sea should be.'

I was shouting at Ewan as he hung back to talk to Nic. 'Salt spray in your stubble and sand in your jacket pockets makes for an extra handsome party. Don't forget your buttonholes, they're waiting in the hall of the castle for you to pick up.'

He pushed his fingers through his light brown hair, blinking in the bright light as he stared up the beach at the turrets beyond the shrubbery. 'Tell me again, am I dreaming, or are we really getting married in a castle with views across the bay?'

Nic's face dropped. 'You wouldn't rather be getting married in the distillery?'

Ewan opened his arms wide, and flopped a hand over each of our shoulders. 'I don't know how you two have pulled this off. Brilliant doesn't come close, I can't thank you enough.'

Nic grimaced. 'I just hope stroppy tomboy Pixie's up for being star of the show for a day.'

Ewan gave him a wink. 'You watch, she might just surprise you.'

Pixie and the girls are staying a mile up the road and are currently enjoying the help of the Brides by the Sea dedicated hair and make-up team before being whisked over by Keef in the Brides Go Wild bus. Thanks to their light airbrush foundation, and deftness with the hair tongs, the make-up team are legendary across the county for making brides and their parties into the most fabulous versions of themselves, with a look that will last all day.

Meanwhile, Poppy and Immie and the rest of the Daisy

Hill gang, have been putting in the final touches at the castle and checking the bedrooms, welcoming the guests, and directing them through to the spacious ground-floor room where the ceremony is going to be. The right entrance music is ready to go, and after that there's a day-long playlist compiled by Nic. There are tall pots all around the edge of the room with pink and white and purple sweet peas and bright pink cosmos and blue cornflowers and vibrant orange marigolds and larkspur spilling out of them, all from Lily's garden at Rose Hill Manor.

Whatever Nic might once have said about chair covers, the folding chairs borrowed from the manor's wedding store are looking very well-dressed. The simple cream silk covers with chiffon bows that are lighter than air look gorgeously understated and are a perfect contrast for the rugged bare stone walls of the castle. And mostly they're already filled with waiting guests, chattering excitedly, standing up to hug each other or wave as new ones arrive. I have to say, every second word I overhear is probably *castle*.

Due to Pixie's preference for a relaxed day, and the number of wheelchairs coming, rather than rows we've set the seats out in clusters for guests to arrange themselves, with the aisle marked with smaller pots with the same tumbling masses of colourful flowers as the big pots around the edge. The ever present three-foot-high Brides by the Sea letters spelling out *love* are propped up by the monumental stone fireplace, and next to that, at Nic's request, Merwyn is curled up on his best blue velvet cushion with the gold braid edging and he's wearing his diamond studded collar.

At last we're at the stage where everyone's moving into their places for the ceremony. The registrars are standing together in a shaft of sunlight slicing the air from the small paned window, shuffling their papers for the fifty-seventh time. Ewan and Nic are at the right-hand side at the front too, sitting side by side, Nic flashing me a smile and a nervous thumbs up over his shoulder, grinning at his mum and a couple of grandmothers who I was hurriedly introduced to earlier as Nic helped them pull up their seats.

On the left-hand side at the front, there's space for the basketball team to wheel themselves down the aisle ahead of Pixie and make a front row.

As I make my way back through the castle entrance hall, I can see the glasses lined up ready to be filled with their Mr & Mrs Three Kisses cocktails and my stomach is churning like a washing machine on a 1400 spin. If I were getting married myself, I think I'd be breathing more. As it is, I'm so nervous I'm not sure I've inhaled any air since I left the flat this morning.

Then I push my way through the monumental castle door, and I'm outside in the sun with the chattering cluster of friends-who-aren't-bridesmaids, who, like me, are all here waiting for Pixie.

I smile at Holly, who's got Rory behind her carrying her cameras. 'You're back again?'

She nods. 'Just made it. The groomsmen coming in by boat wasn't on my original schedule, but it was too good to miss. I'll get Pixie arriving now, then we'll head inside to catch her big entrance and the ceremony.'

And then there's a scrunch of tyres on the gravel, and my van is sweeping in. Set off against the cream satin wedding ribbons, I'm falling in love with the paint colour all over again. Holly leans across to me and whispers. 'This has worked out so well for all of us, yours is so much prettier than Casper's.'

And then as Bill's dad and Keef the Reef are opening the doors of the front seats, Pixie's waving at us from the back.

Holly's snapping away and then Keef and Bill's dad go one on either side of Pixie and lift the chair, and a second later her wheels touch down on the ground.

Pixie's sitting blinking, staring at the lovely façade, her eyes wide as she takes in the little windows and the towers at each end. 'Oh, my days, it's a real live castle, right by the sea.'

One of her bridesmaids laughs. 'It's better than any of the dream houses we send each other off Rightmove.' Now they're waiting in a row, I'm getting the full benefit of their dresses – all different, but all lovely bright flowery cotton prints.

Pixie's sigh is dreamy as she turns to me. 'Oh Milla, it's beautiful ...'

There's a big lump in my throat as I take in the pleasure spreading across her face. Her dark hair falling across her shoulders, and the simple cream lace of her dress makes her look slender and more vulnerable than ever. 'You're beautiful too, Pixie.'

She murmurs. 'Thank you for all of it, Milla. But especially for making me into a bride.'

As she holds out her arms towards me I dip down and give her some air kisses. 'Hey, don't smudge your lippy!'

As Pixie finally lets go of me, she's tugging her dad's sleeve. 'Dad you really need to say hello to Milla. She's the one who made this happen and, you know ...'

'Milla ...' When he turns to face me, I'm looking at Nic thirty years on, his dark hair shorter and threaded with silver, his face more lived in. Then his eyes go wide. 'You're *Nic's* Milla!'

Them accidentally thinking I'm any more than an employee is too complicated to explain right now. I jump forward and grab his hand. 'Lovely to meet you, Pixie's dad, and now, if Holly's got all the pictures she needs, we really must be moving this on. Everyone's waiting inside.'

As Holly snatches up her bag of cameras and dives ahead of us, Rafe appears in the open doorway raising his eyebrows and asking for bridesmaids.

Pixie's calling to the women in the wheelchairs. 'Okay, you guys, lead the way, we'll follow.' She takes a bag from Keef, balances it on her knee, and then with her dad walking beside her she wheels herself into the hall. She calls out to me. 'You come too, Milla, I need you next.'

By the time I catch them up outside the ceremony room door, Poppy's there resting a posy of flowers on the knees of each of the bridesmaids as they line up ready to roll in and down the aisle.

She wiggles her eyebrows at Pixie. 'All ready?'

Pixie hisses. 'Roll on through, ladies, let's knock them out of the park.' Then, as the music begins, she turns to me and hands me her bag. 'Okay, my sandals are in here, I want you to carry them, and push my chair.'

Poppy flashes me a nod from where she's guiding the line of bridesmaids onto the aisle. But it's one of those moments where I already know – on the day, whatever they say, the bride's always right.

I'm already tapping my feet, thinking what an apt choice *All You Need Is Love* is for the entrance music. I'm also saying a silent thank you to my mum reclining on her fluffy cloud above the castle roof for getting it right this time. I'm lining myself up to hold the wheelchair handles, bracing myself to push, to keep in step with Pixie's dad, when there's a lurch, and suddenly the chair in front of me is empty. As my heart drops I let out a cry. 'Pixie, are you okay?'

For a moment I close my eyes really tight and don't dare to open them. Brides faint, brides fall. Pixie sliding out of her chair would be exactly the kind of calamity I'm expecting here. So when I finally force myself to open them I'm expecting to see her crumpled in a white lacy heap on the floor. But instead she's hanging onto her dad's arm, and – what the eff! She's flaming well *standing up*!

She shoots me a glance. 'Follow close behind with the chair, Milla, I need you there in case I don't make it all the way.'

I'm screwing my face up because I don't believe what I'm seeing. 'You're walking down the aisle?'

Her eyes are shining. 'That's the idea. I'm not sure how far I'm going to get. It suddenly looks a very long way.' Her forehead's already shining with the exertion. 'I'll be sitting down again the second we reach Ewan, so don't hang around, make sure the chair's there ready.'

And then she goes. One faltering step after another. Her dad leaning in to support her. Pixie looking slender enough to break, but there's so much strength of will in that spine. She's gritting her teeth and I'm following straight behind her, getting the same view she is. All the faces turning to see the bride in her chair, and instead they're seeing Pixie putting one tentative, wobbly foot in front of the other. Walking. Yes, walking. For the first time in four years. And as the realisation hits, the guests start to clap, then gradually the clapping rises to a cheer, and in the end the noise is so loud that *All you need is love, love, love is all you need* is totally drowned out under the stamping and the whooping and the roar.

And we're going towards Ewan at the front, his face turned towards us, looking so proud and happy and in love. And he's holding his arms open to catch his bride. But beside him, Nic is standing, tears streaming down his face as he watches Pixie making her faltering way down the aisle.

And then it's over, Ewan sweeps Pixie into his arms, and her dad steps aside. The roar of voices and applause is so loud my ears are hurting. But then it gradually subsides, someone fades the music and in the silence Pixie's turning to me. 'That's enough showing off for one day. Pass me my chair, Milla, before I expire.'

And as Pixie sinks down into the chair again and smooths her dress over her knees, the registrar smiles at her. 'All ready to begin?'

Pixie frowns up at her. 'Hell no! I'm not getting married wearing trainers. Milla's going to put my Jimmy Choos on for me first.' She gives me a prod. 'Aren't you Milla? Then we'll do the marrying bit after that.'

I jump to my senses, drop to my knees, undo her trainers and whip them away. Then I take out each spangly sandal in turn, push them onto her feet, and do up the straps. Then I inexpertly place her feet on the foot rests, and, more expertly, rearrange the lace folds of her dress edge so the diamond straps are just visible. Then I grab her trainers and the bag, scramble to my feet, and I'm just about to make a run down the aisle to safety when Pixie's hand lands on my arm.

'Sit next to Nic.'

She must sense me pulling away, because her grip tightens but her face breaks into a grin. 'Bride's orders, okay?'

As I shuffle around to stand next to Nic, he bends and breathes into my ear. 'Great dresses – you and Pixie.'

Somehow I'm forgetting my floaty skirt with the sprigs and the handkerchief hem, because I'm still catching up with what just happened. 'She walked. Did you see that? Pixie just walked ...'

Nic lets out a low laugh. 'Ewan said Pixie was going to surprise us, and she has.' He rubs his eyes. 'It's barely begun, and it's already the best day.' His arm comes around me and he squeezes me into a hug, his chin is in my hair again, and his low laugh resonates in my ear. 'Promise you'll dance with me later? And let's keep the chocolate puddings in the bag this time?'

And as the registrar finally looks over her glasses and coughs to get everyone's attention, my head's spinning from the heady scent of Nic mixed with a double dose of swoon due to how meltingly hot his tux is against the stubble shadows on his chin and the hollows of his cheeks. And for the next half hour, as the ceremony takes place, I'm metaphorically waving at my mum, knowing she'll be up above me looking down. But I'm also reclining on my own little cloud of happiness, because it's one of those moments when it feels that life is so perfect nothing can ever go wrong again.

Chapter 34

Later on Thursday.
In the reception room at Cockle Shell Castle.
Tops and tales.

'Have you got a second, Milla?'

It's Nic, and it's funny he should say that. We've come out of the ceremony room now and all spread out in the sun patches in the lovely reception space at the other side of the castle to pick up the Mr & Mrs Three Kisses G&T's while Holly carries on taking the photos of Pixie and Ewan with various groups of friends and family. The big open room is scattered with easy chairs and sofas for anyone who wants to sit down and decorated with similar cascades of cottage-garden flowers tumbling out of tall pots. But, rather than sipping my rhubarb and elderflower cordial watching the other guests knocking back their gin while nibbling on Clemmie's delicious bite-size savoury snacks and thinking about Pixie and Ewan's lovely, heartfelt wedding vows and how in love they are, ever since we got here I've been non-stop troubleshooting.

First there was a skirt with a small side-split that had accidentally ripped thigh high. Nic's young-at-heart Great Auntie Di was very grateful for the sewing kit in the emergency basket

I had tucked away in the downstairs cloakroom. A few stitches and some safety pin reinforcement was all it took to make her look like an on-trend seventy-nine-year-old again, rather than a teenager on the pull.

Next up was three-year-old Maisie who'd been given her first stick of bubblegum by an unsuspecting well-wisher, chewed it thoroughly during the ceremony, then promptly stuck it all over the top of her head. Let's just say, Maisie won't be having a pony-tail again any time soon.

As for the gluten-free vegan having a panic attack and trying to tear out her tongue after she failed to see the six-inch-high letters on the contains-meat-and-wheat-and-traces-of-nuts sign – as problems go, if I'm giving ratings, the sprinklers soaking the entire wedding fair were marginally easier to deal with.

As I lick the last of the spinach and goat's cheese puff pastry parcel flakes off my fingers, I'm smiling up at Nic. 'Right, I'm all yours.' I wiggle my eyebrows at him wildly. 'Just for today, obviously.'

I know it might sound way too much, but playing for laughs is the only way I can handle this. Not that I'm broadcasting it any further than a little sigh to Poppy, but I'm having a seriously hard time keeping my hands off the goods here. Nic turns my toes to syrup at the best of times. Trendell, the tux-clad version, is so smoking hot there have been times today standing next to him when I've felt like I've literally been about to vaporise. For this one last day, I'm not going to fight it – I'm just going to let those rainbow shivers zip up and down my spine, and let my skin tingle without beating myself up. And then after tomorrow, unless I ever take him up on that ongoing offer of those pancakes of his that he's never managed to cook yet, we'll be back to waving across the harbourside car park.

It might wring my heart out for a while, but I have to be honest – giving this a positive spin, it could turn out to be a whole lot more comfortable and a lot less agonising than the last few months have been.

'So?' I meet his gaze, then as my stomach starts to disintegrate I wish I hadn't.

'One of the groomsmen's just been out to the car park. He spotted a bit of a ...' He hesitates then coughs. '... A ... situation ... by the pergolas.'

This turns my wavering stomach back to rock again. 'Go on?'

He lowers his voice. 'One we need you to sort out rather than me, if you don't mind hurrying ...'

His hands are already on my shoulders and as he turns me around he's whistling Merwyn who comes careering off his cushion and scuttles out of the room ahead of us. He steers me out of the front door, into the salty breeze and the sunshine, along the path at the side of the castle, and round the corner towards the pretty terrace decked with unlit fairy lights. Beyond the box sprigs is the hot tub, but instead of the covers being on, the steam is rising. And sitting neck-deep in bubbles, there's a whole crowd of women, laughing and waving glasses in the air.

He's laughing in my ear. 'See those bikini tops on the floor along with their towels? That's why it has to be you not me.'

I groan and catch hold of Merwyn's collar. 'Who are they?'

'They're definitely not on our guest list.' Nic pulls down the corners of his mouth. 'We just need to move them on.'

As I march into the open across the daisy speckled lawn I'm pleased I've had practice at the fairs. 'Excuse me, ladies, can I help you?'

The first woman pushes her sunnies up as far as her streaky blonde messy bun. 'More bubbly would be nice, please. And if you see Bill, tell him Miranda's girls have arrived for the well-being weekend.'

My mouth drops open. 'But surely, that's tomorrow?' Then I close it again and take a breath. 'I'm sorry, we have an event here today.'

'So you're the reason we couldn't get our camper vans parked!' The way her chin is jutting, she's not happy and she's not backing down either. 'I was here in December, so I know that can't be right. Bill never has mid-week guests.'

'He does now. We're Cockle Shell Castle's first wedding.'

Miranda snorts. 'It's a shame Bill didn't share that with us before we set off at five to get the extra day in.' Her annoyed tone softens to a purr. 'Maybe we could bring our picnic and join you? You can never have too many people for a confetti shot.' She flutters her eyelashes and wiggles her cleavage straight at Nic. 'Obviously we'll get dressed for that. I promise you we're equally gorgeous with our clothes on. We might be on the golden side of fifty, but we all still appreciate hotties like you in tuxes.'

Nic's smiling at her. 'A lovely idea. But we're already very full.'

Miranda's eyebrows shoot up. 'Fine, in that case we'll head to the beach. That's private too, you know.' There's a wicked twinkle in her eye. 'It's our mission this weekend to open Bill's eyes to the joys of naked sunbathing. There's nothing like a sea breeze on your bare butt cheeks.'

Nic's hissing at me from behind his hand. 'Looks like they're staying for the day then.'

I murmur to Nic. 'Give me a minute.'

I dash through to the stores beyond the kitchen and pull open the wine fridge. Then with my arms full I hurry back to the terrace and wave a bottle of chilled fizz at the hot tub. 'To make up for the disappointment, how about you have a drink on us, somewhere in St Aidan. Then come back to the castle again tomorrow – late afternoon would work well.'

Miranda's narrowing her eyes. 'One bottle's not going to go very far between eight of us is it?'

I'm smiling at her cheek, nodding at what I'm clutching in my other arm. 'That's why I've brought you four.'

'In which case, you have yourself a deal.' She's out and wrapped in her towel before you can say 'over-exposure'.

As we finally watch them all skip across the lawn along the path that leads to the distillery, I turn to Nic. 'If that's Bill's festive lot back for a revisit, I can see why he was reluctant to do weddings.'

'Good job, Milla Vanilla.'

I lean in to Nic's high five. And unlike the last time I tried to high five him and ended up in his arms, this time our hands meet perfectly in mid-air. I'm laughing, mostly with relief that Miranda's gone. 'We make a great team, Captain Kirk. What a nightmare they were.'

He's shaking his head. 'It could have been worse, at least they weren't playing naked Twister. Come on, we don't want to miss that confetti shot.'

And seamlessly, the day is back on course again. And if I'm hanging back a little, just to enjoy how easily those words rolled off Nic's tongue, after everything we've been through to get here, you can't blame me for taking a moment. There's the castle with its chunky towers etched against the billowy white clouds behind us, the sea shimmering into the distance around the bay. The sound of the waves ebbing and flowing on the sand out beyond the lawns, the faint movement of sea air across my cheeks. Then, walking away, there's the man who's so beautiful and broken that my heart breaks all over again for him.

And sometime tomorrow I'll walk away from him too and nothing for me will ever be quite the same again. There will be no excuses to text him to tell him off for being indecisive about gin garnish. No reason to call him and summon him to the shop to see my latest find. I know it's going to be hard. But I'm getting through it by telling myself he'll still be there to wave to when he's out on *Snow Goose's* deck every evening, propping his back against the mast as he watches the sun go down. Not that I'll be stalking him. But if I time it right, we'll still manage a cheery hello most mornings as I'm getting in my van and he's nipping across to the harbour master's offices for a shower. If I leave the shop on the dot of twelve thirty, it's likely I'll pass him on the cobbles on his way to the bakery to buy his lunchtime sandwich as I take Merwyn for his run on the beach.

I've thought it all through. It isn't going to be easy. Call me my mother's daughter, but I've got my Spotify playlist ready – all the songs that have formed the backdrop to the last few months. That will be my crutch to get me through the hard times of my withdrawal. If I stick at it for a few months, it should be completely do-able. What matters is, he's still going to be there. He just won't be there with me so much. And it may take a while, but I'll have to learn to live with that. Learn to be happy expressing my one-sided adoration and concern from a hundred yards away instead of across a table or the front of a car.

But for now I need to let myself be. Soak up every moment. Make the day last as long as I can.

Chapter 35

Even later on Thursday.
On the terrace outside at Cockle Shell Castle.
Cake faces and long afternoons.

So much for willing time to stand still.

Where Cally's wedding day seemed to last a lifetime and then some, Pixie and Ewan's whizzes by. Maybe it's because of the fun or perhaps it's the party vibe. Nic looks relaxed as well as edible as he jokes around with the groomsmen, whose names I should know but end up forgetting because there are so many of them. Clemmie's afternoon teas go down well as everyone sits in the sunshine with their cake stands popping exquisite sandwiches and scones and pastries and cakes into their mouths, drinking fizz at the curly painted metal tables or lazing on brightly checked picnic rugs with our vintage china plates from Bill's barn. This rolls seamlessly into a gentle wander or wheel down to the beach on the carefully constructed boardwalk made out of railway sleepers.

And when everyone has had enough of collecting shells and throwing stones into the water, making sandcastles, and paddling, it's back to the castle for more lazing on the lawns, an ice cream van and another consignment of fizz in ice buckets. Then, just because we could, impromptu games of croquet, hopscotch, boules. The kiddies darting in and out of the lovely wooden playhouse at the lawn edge. Then the evening emphasis changing to the terrace on the hot-tub side of the castle, with vans serving burgers and nachos, a not-too-smoky barbecue, and a horse-box bar, followed by Clemmie's amazing pudding-fest laid out in the castle kitchen.

It's relaxed, it's laid-back. But best of all, Pixie and Ewan look as if they're having a truly wonderful time. Even as it's happening, I know when I spin the day back in my head, it's going to be like looking through a wedding album. By the time they cut Poppy's prettiest cake of all time – four tiers with the palest lilac ombré buttercream covered in tiny pressed viola flowers – the bright orange ball of sun is sliding downwards towards the sea. As we move on to disco time it's already dusk, and as the dusty blue sky fades to grey, the fairy lights swaying on their strings in the breeze are pricking the gently enveloping darkness.

With everyone gathered around the wide outside terrace that opens off the kitchen, with the hot tub steaming in the background, Pixie and Ewan are ready for their first dance. Nic and Kip haven't stinted on the techy stuff either, so Pixie is sitting waiting in her chair waving a mic. As she taps the end and clears her throat there's a squeak of feedback out of the tall speaker stacks around the garden, and everyone stops talking.

She pushes her hair back into the twists of pearl wires, smiles that wonderful broad smile of hers and begins. 'We said no speeches, because we didn't want anything formal. And in case you're wondering, I know I walked before, but I'm not ready for Strictly yet, so tonight I'll be dancing in my trusty chair.'

As everyone claps she pauses, then carries on. 'But before we hit the dance floor for our first dance I'd like to thank everybody who has made the day wonderful. So thank you to Poppy, Rafe and the Daisy Hill helpers, thanks to everyone from Brides by the Sea, to Nic for having the inspired idea to step in to organise this for us, and thanks to his fabulous partner in crime, Milla, for all your expertise and insisting he made the right choices. You simply couldn't have done a better job or made us any happier.'

There's lots of clapping, and two of the children run in with wrapped presents and hand them to Nic and me, then give out posies to all the other helpers. We run over and give Pixie hugs and kisses, then she carries on.

'Okay, guys, open those later, because we need everyone to watch what's coming next.' As she grins up at Ewan standing beside her, she couldn't be any more confident or at ease with herself. 'For our first dance we've chosen a track that was a very significant part of us getting to know each other. Believe it or not, before he met me, Ewan was a confirmed non-dancer.'

Ewan grins at her. 'Luckily, for both of us, Pixie changed my mind.'

Pixie laughs. 'For a long time, this first dance track was our signature tune. But when you see his moves tonight, I think you'll agree he's shaping up nicely.' She breaks off and laughs. 'Practising this is why we didn't have time to sort our own wedding.'

All the guys do a hand clap and call 'Ewan, Ewan, Ewan.'

Pixie laughs. 'And when we've finished, don't go away, because me and my basketball besties have organised a little celebration dance of our own too.' She gives Ewan a wink. 'Just to show Ewan how it should be done.'

She passes the mic to Nic, then we watch Ewan take her hand. And then as the words begin I smile at Nic. 'The Scissor Sisters,

I Don't Feel Like Dancing. Great choice for anyone with a reluctant dance partner.'

Nic laughs and starts tapping his foot as he leans against a pergola post. 'Plenty of irony and shedloads of rhythm.'

We're watching as Ewan holds Pixie by the hand and twirls her around in her chair. And then she's wheeling her chair towards him and he's running away. Then she's zooming after him and when she catches him they go into another spin.

I let out a breath because it's so full of life and fun and laughter. But what hits me most is that they're so together, and such a team. 'They couldn't be any happier or any more in love, could they?'

Nic swallows. 'And today is the day she walked in front of everyone too.' He shakes his head. 'I can't believe she kept that quiet.'

I can't help smiling at his injured tone. 'She wanted to surprise everyone.'

He lets out a grunt. 'She certainly did that.'

I've been to a lot of weddings, but this has to be the most exuberant and original first dance ever. It ends with Ewan taking Pixie into a spectacular spin, then dropping onto one knee and kissing her hand.

Everyone goes wild with the clapping, and when it finally subsides and Ewan and Pixie have taken their bows, Ewan skips off and four of the besties zoom on.

Pixie takes the mic again. 'Okay, so this is our little Dance Monkey routine, never done before in long dresses, so cross your fingers we don't get our skirts wrapped around our axles.'

The track is one of those really catchy tunes with repetitive lyrics that stick in your head. *Dance for me, dance for me, dance for me* makes the perfect backing for choreographed spins and wheelies they're doing in their chairs. Somehow they're also managing to throw a basketball around at the same time and catch it too. When the music ends, Pixie's shouting again. 'Okay, no excuses, *everybody* has to dance tonight, just watch you don't get your toes run over.' Then she's calling to Ewan, and he goes onto the dance area to join her again and as the first notes of *This Is It* echo off the castle walls everyone goes bonkers.

I pull Merwyn to a safe distance and rest my bum on the edge of one of the stone planters.

Nic comes too and a second later his hip lands next to mine. 'And what about you? You must have got your wedding confidence back after how well today's gone?'

I pull a face. 'If you ignore the topless bathers, your mum getting stuck in the disabled loo, and the kids finding the condom supply in the emergency basket and using them as water bombs?'

'They're what made the day legendary.' Nic laughs and looks down at me. 'Before I go, you have to promise me you're going to stay at Brides by the Sea and carry on with weddings?'

I have no idea where he's planning on disappearing to, because the castle isn't that big, but I smile at him anyway. 'You know, I think I will.'

'It's the best wedding I've ever been to.'

I wrinkle my nose. 'Me too. Well done for holding out to have it here. It's so lovely being at the castle and hearing the sea. I love the way that in every room we go in you can look right out across the bay. And it's worked so well for the wheelchairs.'

He raises an eyebrow. 'Would you like to dance?'

As I look at his Adam's apple moving as he swallows and hear the up tempo beat of *Don't Look Back Into The Sun* beginning, I'm very torn. However much I'd love to, I am technically working. 'If I take my eye off the wedding ball, that'll be when it spins out of control. Thanks for the offer, but I'd rather not risk the carnage.'

He nods. 'I thought you'd say that. That's why I've put our dance track on almost at the end. That way you can relax and enjoy it.'

'We have our own dance track?' It's ridiculous how much that makes my stomach contract.

He laughs. 'We do – and before you ask, I'm saving it as a surprise. In the meantime, we can sit and enjoy the playlist. I hope your mum would approve, I was thinking of her when I put it together.'

My heart was already full, but after that it's bursting. 'You've got *Tiger Feet*?'

He nods. 'Of course. And *Uptown Girl*, obviously.'

'*The Summer of '69*?' I see another nod. '*Every Time We Touch, All By Myself, Amarillo* ...' I take in more nods. 'Bon Jovi's *Always, My Heart Will Go On*?'

His eyebrows arch into a smile. 'They're all there, with a few well-chosen recent tunes I know she'd have liked too.' He gives a shamefaced shrug. 'I have to admit, I went through your CDs when you weren't looking. But the upside to that is I rediscovered *The Time Warp*.'

I nudge him. 'In that case I'll forgive you.' It's not that I'm going soft on him, it's just too late to give him a hard time.

It's one of those evenings when even though I don't see the hands on my watch moving, hours flash by in the space of minutes. It's a whole lot later when Immie and Poppy wander over.

Nic stiffens next to me. 'Don't look now ... but watch out for flying masonry!'

The 'hello again' punch on the arm Immie gives Nic nearly

sends him off the wall. 'You have to agree, Nic, we nailed it with our team work here?'

His mouth twists into a genuine smile. 'So long as you don't demolish anything in the next twelve hours, I might recommend you to my friends and colleagues.'

She chortles and punches him again. 'You can trust me and Pops, we're looking out for you all the way.'

Poppy joins in. 'And we've come to say, after everything you've done today, you two are due some down time, so we'll be sorting out any problems from now on.' She bends and breathes into my ear. 'When we replaced the condoms in the emergency basket, I dropped a few in your bathroom, just in case.'

My eyes go wide as I hiss back at her. 'Why would you do that?'

Her low voice is full of laughter. 'However determined you are to keep your hands off the sizzling space captain, it might be the ideal opportunity ... to cross the bridge properly this time.'

'Absolutely not – but thanks for thinking of me.'

She laughs. 'You're welcome.' She gives me a wink. 'Thank me again tomorrow if they come in handy.'

Nic stands up, and a moment later he's back with a tray of full glasses. He hands them to me, Poppy, and Immie and takes the last himself. 'There you go, Milla Vanilla. You can allow yourself a glass of fizz now.'

'Cheers.' Poppy and Immie are staring at me as I take my first sip.

Poppy smiles. 'You've come so far since Valentine's Day, Mills. We're all very proud of you.'

Immie's waving her glass at me too. 'Brides Go Wild is already big – by next year it's going to be huge.'

Poppy's brow wrinkles. 'What we're saying is, you have to tell us you're staying on with us in St Aidan.'

Nic's looking at me like I'm his protégée, not the other way around. 'She's just promised me that she will.'

As I sip the fizz, the bubbles are pricking my nose. 'I can't actually think of being anywhere else now.' I really should be thinking of my lunchtime walks along the high-tide mark with its tangles of driftwood and pebbles and cockle shells. Falling asleep to the rush of the surf, waking to the view from the tiny porthole in the bedroom, of the sun sparkling off the water. The clatter of Poppy baking in the kitchen, the buzz of the wedding shop down below. But for now, the clearest image in my mind is the outline of *Snow Goose's* rigging against the sky at sunset. I push that out of my head and smile. 'It's all thanks to you two and all the friends who've helped me.'

This time Immie pulls me into a hug and Poppy follows. 'No arguments. You're on Team St Aidan with us now.'

As *Don't Worry, Be Happy* drifts out of the speakers, Nic catches my eye. 'Not wanting to break up the friend-fest, but this is our cue – three minutes, and we're on.'

I'm frowning across at the dance area. 'This was never on my mum's list. It's too wet – look, everyone else thinks so too, they're all leaving and heading for the horse-box bar.'

He gives a low laugh. 'All part of my plan. Wouldn't you rather dance when it's not too crowded?'

Then he passes my glass to Poppy and takes my hand, and, as I hurry behind him, a moon that's almost full slides out from behind a cloud and covers the garden in silver light that makes me shiver.

Chapter 36

Even later on Thursday.
On the dance floor at Cockle Shell Castle.
The last dance.

As I stand facing Nic on an almost empty dance floor, the last track fades and there's a beat of silence. Then, as a few slow tinkling piano notes and some slow humming spreads across the terrace, he pulls me towards him. As I let myself lean in, the warmth of his body is radiating against my skin.

His voice is low in my ear. 'I hope Ellie Goulding is okay?'

I listen as the lyrics hang in the air. *How long will I love you? As long as stars are above you – longer if I can …*

As the sound echoes back off the walls of the castle there's something about the haunting tone of her voice, the stark simplicity of the words, that somehow wraps up all the emotion of the day. And here I am with a few minutes to legitimately run my hands over the man I've been aching to have permission to touch for months. And then as the words sink into my head, it hits me why it's all been so very hard. What I'm feeling isn't mistaken. It isn't fake, it's actually real. What began as a tingle as he took my hand is building to a tidal surge, rushing through my entire body. That feeling isn't just crazy, uncontrolled lust

– it's love. This is the man I've loved for months. It's just that I haven't been tuned in enough to recognise it.

I let out a sigh. 'I love Ellie ... and this song.' And if that's how it is, I can't let my feelings leak out now. I need to add something more concrete to hide the rest. 'You know she had bell sleeves on her wedding gown.'

'You're so funny, Mills.' I can feel the reverberation of Nic's laugh through his chest. 'And I have two minutes and thirty-four blissful seconds to hold you – are you okay with that?'

Blissful? That's Nic being ironic. 'Ahaaa ...'

But for me it's the very last waltz – I'm not proud, I'll take what I can get. The distant swish of the sea in the background is lulling me and I know that tomorrow, when this wedding is over, for a while my heart will be aching like nothing I've ever known before. But so long as I stick to my plan of distant appreciation to wean myself off and readjust gently, it should be totally containable. But for now, I should be soaking up every bit of the bliss.

There's such tenderness in Nic's touch as he wraps me in his arms, his cheek resting softly on the side of my head, his stubble gently snagging my hair. Enveloped in his heat, that scent he has. Inhaling and exhaling together as if, just for now, we are one person not two. My eyes are tightly closed, keeping the real world out, sealing me in my own very private bubble of happiness.

There's also an unnerving storm of sexual need that, given we're in full view of eighty or more wedding guests, I'm trying to rise above. The feel of his back muscles flexing under my fingers, our bodies merging where they touch like molten metal. Some bits eye-wateringly hard and other parts startlingly soft. I'm willing these hundred and fifty-four seconds to last my whole life. Truly, if I had to float on this particular tiny cloud until the end of time, I would not be grumbling or getting off.

But as we stand almost rooted to the spot, there's a terrible poignancy to the notes we're hearing too. Those sweet simple words floating out into the night with the single piano accompaniment feel like they're loaded with a particular unfathomable anguish.

And at the end when the very last note fades and drifts upwards, all the way to the stars, we finally part. As the heat where his body pressed against mine ebbs away and is replaced by the chill of a gust of air from the sea, I slowly open my eyes and let in the world again. When I look up into Nic's face it's lined with sadness and I'm scraping tears I didn't know were there from under my lashes.

As he sees me, he shakes his head, sniffs, and blinks himself. 'Earth to Starship Enterprise ... how about we take Merwyn down to the beach for a run before bed?'

As I give a silent nod of agreement, there's a whistle, a scuffle of paws, and Merwyn's damp nose on my knee followed by the thud of Trump, the rag doll on my thigh. The silver of the lawn is soft under our feet as we move across it and behind us the dance floor is already full again with dancers jumping around to the twangy guitar chords of *Dancing In The Street*. As we head for the space in the juniper bushes at the edge of the lawns that links the garden to the beach, the moonlight is splashing a line across the sea beyond and we're leaving the beat of the music behind us. And my shoulder is still wedged inside Nic's open waistcoat, with his arm firm and strong around me.

As the beach opens out, Nic bends, throws Trump for Merwyn, then puts his arm around me again. 'The thing is, Milla ...' His voice is so low it's grating. 'I've been trying to find the right time ... and now it's running out ... and I'm sorry, but I haven't been completely open with you.'

As I'm the same, I can hardly complain. 'So are you going to come clean now?' I have no idea what he's about to say.

He sighs. 'When I offered to sort out Pixie's wedding, it was a crazy impulse after Valentine's night – but it wasn't just about grabbing Jess's discount. Mostly it was an excuse to bump into you around the shop to get to know you better.'

I can't help laughing. 'And it totally backfired when Jess put me on your case and we were joined at the hip?'

He sniffs. 'It was a challenge, and I haven't come out of it very well.'

My heart is sinking. 'But I thought you liked the wedding?'

'The wedding couldn't have been better.' There's another sigh. 'It was the rest that was the disaster – I hadn't counted on liking you so much.'

In the space where my heart should be banging there's just a gaping void. I suspect my heart stopped dead when my stomach dropped through the floor. 'You *like* me? Why the hell didn't you tell me?'

Not that I'm ever going to get ahead of myself, but maybe this being a two-sided thing rather than a figment of my lust-brain explains my pulse racing at a million beats a second for the last six months every time I've come within a hundred yards of him. Why even touching him casually now feels like someone's directing a flame thrower on my skin.

He clears his throat. 'It's much worse than that, Milla.'

'Worse – worse how?'

He blows out a breath. 'By the time I realised what was happening was more than over-excited male hormones with a mind of their own, it was too late ... I'd already fallen in love with you.'

'Excuse me? When was this?'

He's shaking his head. 'By Cally and Nigel's wedding I was already in over my head. I tried to deny it, I went away and tried not to come back. But that didn't work either.'

The unnerving thing is, he's not talking about it like it's anything good. Or even anything that actually involves me in the emotional sense at all. 'It needn't be a problem.'

He picks up Trump and hurls him along the beach. 'If you're saying that it's because you have no idea how I feel about you. And why should you? That day on the beach when I tried to explain why I could never allow myself to be in love, I knew there was only one way out.' He lets out a sigh. 'So the thing is ... I'm solving it in the way I always vowed I would if this ever happened to me and I couldn't shake it off – by going away.'

I try not to let my legs give way. Then gulp in a breath. 'But ... *Snow Goose* ... the harbour ...?'

He blows out his cheeks. 'Don't worry, *Snow Goose* is staying. You get to keep your permit.'

I can't believe he thinks that's all I'm interested in.

As he goes on his voice is more level again. 'My friend's parents have a yacht moored up the coast north of Sydney waiting for their retirement. I've agreed to go over and skipper it for them until they feel more confident sailing it on their own.'

'Sydney ... in *Australia*?' If I'm screeching, it's because that's a hell of a long way to go. I try to sound bright. And interested. 'So, how many weeks will that take?' If there's a good side to this, at least he has no idea how I feel.

Nic's voice rises in frustration. 'Milla, this isn't ten days in the sun. This is me removing myself from the problem until it goes away.' As he stares out to sea, he's calmer again. 'I've agreed to six months initially. With an option to extend.'

'Great.' What else is there for me say? And I do it very brightly.

'I've sorted the business here to carry on without me. It's a traditional yacht, with no modern technology. We'll be totally off-grid. Unplugged and out of reach. There will be absolutely no opportunity for me to relapse.'

Oh my days. Fuck, fuck, *fuck*. 'Even better.'

'I'm just really sorry ... for involving you, for not telling you earlier, for being such a screwed-up mess ... for all of it ...'

I blow out a breath. 'There's nothing to apologise for. It's not as if you ran out on me and broke my heart or anything hideous like that.' Any collateral damage is all of my own making. That much is obvious; he's kept this completely to himself. Fought it every inch of the way. He doesn't ever intend this to involve me. And if I begged him to let me in, I'd be setting myself up for the biggest fall.

He shakes his head. 'If I'd hurt you as well as all the rest, I could never have lived with myself.'

My mouth fills with sour saliva, and I swallow it away. All the more reason to show him I'm completely unscathed. That's how I finally know what I'm feeling for him is love – because my overriding feeling, all I want, is for him to be okay. And my mind is racing. To think there was once a time I fleetingly imagined he might help me move on. Although again, this kind of explains what I was picking up on, thinking it at all. And back then, I knew I had to steer well clear because I couldn't face bumping into him afterwards. But suddenly he's taken that out of the equation.

He's frowning again. 'I know I persuaded you to have fun

rather than keeping our distance. That was a bad call on my part, so I'm sorry for that too.'

I give him a hard stare. This is so screwed up, I need to take it a little bit further. 'You were playing a very dangerous game there.' I'm not going to mention the bit about making out for Phoebe's benefit, because that was such a good call on his part and such a help to me. But the rest ... I have to ask. 'What if I'd fallen for you?'

His face pales. 'Seriously, look at me. There was never any chance of that.' There's another long pause. 'But when you really love someone, all you want is to do the best for them. All along all I wanted was to help you to believe in yourself again, to get you to realise your worth, to see how wonderful you are. I want you to have the future you dreamed of, even if it kills me to think I can't be part of it. But, believe me, you deserve someone so much better than me.'

In my head, I'm playing Russian roulette. Either way, I'm going to get the bullet. That Nic's going is certain; nobody's going to talk him out of it. I can let him go and always regret it. Or I can snatch one more kiss before I wave him goodbye forever.

But even as I stare up at the anguish in his face, I know I could never manipulate him like that. As I let out a sigh, it's for everything that didn't go our way. But more, it's for this lovely, selfless, deserving human who works so hard for everyone else, who will never feel it's okay to be in love. And how hopeless I have been at changing that. I've let him help to rebuild me. And sure, I've helped him with Pixie's wedding, but on a personal level I've done nothing to help him at all. Unless you count causing him to run to the other side of the world. As I look up at the shadows on the face of this guy who despises himself too much to ever accept he's worthy of being loved, my heart is breaking for him.

I clear my throat. 'It's ironic. Everything we've done together these last few months has allowed me to heal. Even better than that, I've become a whole new version of myself. I'm not that old scaredy-cat I used to be. I don't want to hide. I don't feel worse than everyone else anymore. I can hold my head up. I'm happy to be me.' It's not lost on me that a lot of that has happened with his support.

He reaches out and brushes the hair off my face. 'Of everyone I know, you're the one who most deserves to be happy.'

I step towards him, and slide my hand over his cheek. My main job here is to reassure him I'm okay. 'That's the funny thing – I'm actually fine as I am, I don't need any more than I have now – but thank you for helping me. I'm just really sad the last few months haven't done the same for you.'

His laugh is hollow. 'I'm too far gone to save.'

He might be right, but I have one chance here to open his mind. 'You've been so busy working on your escape plan, I think you've missed the bigger picture.' It looks like this is down to me, so I brace myself. 'You do know Pixie hoped that planning the wedding would cure you?'

His voice rises in protest. 'You are joking? This isn't something I'll get better from.'

However hard it will be for him to hear, it's time he knew the truth. 'You've got her accident on your conscience, why shouldn't you be on hers? She hates feeling responsible for your guilt. All she wants is for you to start being normal again.'

One small grunt is all that comment gets. 'I never thought of it that way.'

I've got a few fleeting moments to make him look at this

differently. 'Pixie hasn't just made the best of it. She and Ewan wouldn't be how they are without the accident. She probably wouldn't swap back to her old life if it meant giving up what she has now, because they're truly, properly happy. They love each other as they are. That's such an amazing thing to find that the rest doesn't matter.' I stop and take a breath before I fire the biggest gun. 'The cloud on her horizon isn't that she can't walk anymore – it's that her brother is wrecking his life on her behalf because he won't let go of the past.' It feels like I've gone too far, but it's my one chance to save him from himself.

He lets out a groan. 'Oh shit.'

'There's something else too.' Now I've started, I might as well give him all of my insight. 'When my mum was ill, she didn't ever grumble about how hellish it was not to be able to move a finger to scratch herself, not being able to swallow. She was never resentful about what she was losing, that bit by bit, day by day, her body wouldn't work anymore. What made her apoplectic was when she saw someone who was lucky enough to be well, wasting their life.'

Nic swallows. 'She'd have been furious with me, then.'

I'm nodding. 'Too right. Circumnavigating the globe like an albatross looking for a pity party when you could have been living your best life? For four years now, too. That's such a lot of your life to waste. If she could still have talked, she'd have given you such a bollocking you'd have heard her all the way to the village green.' I'm hearing the words so clearly, it's as if Mum's saying them herself. I put a hand on his arm and squeeze it. 'Everyone here, including you, helped me learn to love myself. Maybe it's time for you to let the guilt go. Learn to forgive yourself.'

He lets out a sigh. 'Until I do, I'm no use to anyone, am I?'

He shakes his head. 'Okay, I accept I've got a problem, now I need to address it. Six months is a long time to do that. Now it's happening, it feels more like forever.'

I'm parroting it back at him. 'With an option to extend.' I'm shaking my head because I want to support him as much as he's supported me. 'No one blames you, Nic. We all care about you, we all want the best for you. But you're the only one who can make this happen.' Maybe I need to clarify that for one last time. 'If you sort yourself out, you'll be the best guy for someone to love.'

He blows. 'You're the one person who's dared to say this. Thanks for being brave enough to tell me the truth, Milla.' He takes a breath. 'I love you. For this, as well as the rest.'

I thump my fist onto his biceps. 'Back at you, Captain K.' And I'm really not lying. 'Let's hope I'll catch you in another universe.' Another life. And I'm not lying there either.

We've had our chance, and we've missed it. Spectacularly. But I'm not deluded either. He's flying to the other side of the world. Once he's thousands of miles away, surrounded by beautiful Aussie surfing babes, all helping him work through his problems, the likelihood of him coming back is zero. Seriously, wouldn't you hit on him if you saw him on the beach?

His eyes narrow in the shadows and his voice is low, urgent. 'Maybe you could come to visit – check out Sydney, we could sail up the coast, see the coral reefs. I could treat you ...'

I'm blocking out how blissful it sounds, because I think this is desperation kicking in. 'As if that's going to fit in when I've got wedding fairs all the way to Christmas.'

He's shaking his head now. 'No, you're right, of course you wouldn't want to. Bad idea. It's not fair of me to ask that either. You've just spent six years with a guy who wouldn't commit.

Me asking anything of you is like pushing you to make that same mistake all over again.'

It's sad that this is so hopeless. If the last few months have taught me anything, it's not to waste my time on anyone reluctant. And Nic is so much more decided than that – he's in total denial. 'If ever I try again ...' and right now I feel like I never will, but at least I know the theory '... I'll be waiting for that special person who wants me every bit as much as I want them.' Even as I'm saying the words, it's reinforcing the message. A guy who's running to the other side of the world to avoid me really isn't that person.

Nic reaches out and rubs his thumb over my cheekbone. 'You don't deserve anything less, Milla Vanilla.'

'No hard feelings, though?' After all of this, I'd hate to part on bad terms. Phoebe and Ben have taught me that bad feelings bring you down; happiness comes from a positive place. And Nic might be ripping my heart out here, but it's not deliberate. He's never led me to believe he was available. He's never been less than open and honest about it. As heartbreakers go, he's very honourable. And endlessly caring. And considerate.

His chest heaves. 'I'll only ever have the warmest feelings for you.'

I'm swallowing back the lump in my throat as it's slowly sinking in he's not going to be anywhere near. That if there's anything to ask, or say, time's running out. 'Do you still have your scar ... from my arrow?'

As he tugs his shirt out of his trouser belt, and holds out his arms, the white fabric hangs luminous in the moonlight. 'Why not take a look?'

My fingers are shaking as I fumble with the buttons. As I pull back the fine cotton, and tentatively slide my fingers over his taut tanned skin I feel him tense. 'Is that ticklish?'

His voice is very low. 'No, just very nice. Have you found it yet?'

As my fingers come across a small knot of skin, I smile. 'It's still here.' I put my palm on his ribs, and stretch out my fingers as I peer into the shadows to find the mark. 'You'll be taking that with you, wherever you go.'

'To remind me of the woman who stole my heart, then stabbed me.' As he laughs and shivers again he reaches out, cupping my face in his hands. 'That day at Jagger's you were talking about being ready to move on.' His voice is so deep, it's vibrating below the rush of the surf and the wind. 'Are you still thinking that would be good for you?'

My lips are parted, and my heart is banging so hard all I can say is 'Ahhhh ... I could be ...' I reach up with one hand, slide my fingers through his hair, and pull his head towards mine. Because I really do have nothing to lose here.

He's breathing into my ear. 'If you'd like me to help ...' His head is tilting as he looks at me. Then his jaw is lining up with mine, and just before his lips slide onto mine he says 'Just say the word.'

And then as I find those familiar lips and get swept into the molten chocolate fountain of his mouth, it's as if the world stops turning, and the sea is rushing through my head. And it's like the first day in the van, and the day at the wedding fair, but because no one's watching, it's supercharged with an energy and an urgency so forceful that by the time we break apart, I feel like a rag doll that lost its stuffing.

When I finally get to talk all that comes out is a breathy gasp. 'For definite ... absolutely ... totally ... please ...'

'So long as you're sure it's what you want.' There's a low laugh in my ear. 'I'll take that as a yes then.'

This is the bit in the movies where I'd sinuously slide my body up against his to reinforce that. Then sweep him into another earth-shattering snog.

But this is me. Things in my life have improved. I didn't say I'd had a total personality transplant and become entirely perfect. I'm guessing I'm always going to have my catastrophic moments.

Sure, I'm trying for super-slinky, but what actually happens is that halfway through the move I catch the raggedy bit of my long chiffon sleeve on Nic's belt buckle and end up with my hand jammed – for want of a better description – against the rock hard bulge in his super-sexy tux trousers.

He's laughing more. 'Feel free to check that out for as long as you want – as you can probably tell, that's an extra-large yes please from me too.'

He isn't wrong there. After quite a long time, I have to agree. 'It totally is.'

'So would you like fast and rough on the beach ... or slow and smooth in the king size bed with champagne ... standing in the shower ... or something else entirely?'

To be honest, after months of anticipation, I'm likely to pop in about two seconds whatever we do. 'Maybe there's too much sand and water around here ... and as Immie's stuffed our en suite full of condoms ...'

'It's official. Whatever Immie did in the past, this overrides all of it.' He sweeps me into a hug. 'Team St Aidan look out for you all the way, don't they?'

I'm laughing. 'Absolutely.' That might have been Phoebe talking, but I don't even care. 'It would be a shame to waste them.'

His arms are wrapped tightly around me. 'Will you be walking upstairs this time, or would you like me to carry you?'

It's so easy because we know each other so well. 'Why not surprise me?'

'Shall we have a few more salty kisses before we go?'

If he'd asked me to walk on my hands to St Aidan I'd have agreed. And I can't even do handstands – that's how much I want this. For now I'm not even thinking that he's leaving; because if he wasn't we wouldn't even be here. I'm simply thinking of this as a gift to go with the whole wonderful day. One night I'll hold in my heart that will get me through. That will have to last me the rest of my life.

This time my sexy body slide goes like a dream. And a moment later, my mouth is buried in his, and as I wriggle inside his shirt with him I'm already spinning, and counting the rainbows.

Chapter 37

Friday.
Our bedroom at Cockle Shell Castle.
Bed heads and block heads.

When I wake next morning it's to the patter of soft rain. There's pale light seeping through the muslin curtains and my aching brain tells me three things: I've had approximately one hour of sleep; when I finally get up, I'm going to need the strongest coffee known to mankind; and it's going to need to work miracles. But with any luck that won't be any time soon. I'm guessing that rolling down to the kitchen for breakfast at nine would be completely respectable. We could maybe even push it for brunch at eleven. Another four hours then. I can't help a sleepy, self-satisfied smile at that as I stretch my hand to touch the linen-covered headboard.

As for my body, it's in a blurry and very unfamiliar state of feeling satiated, euphoric, super-relaxed, but also like I've done Joe Wicks' biggest workout twice. Not that I ever do those, but seriously, they're exhausting even to watch. But in spite of me having the kind of supreme inner glow you'd usually only get from eating four large tubs of Haagen Dazs back to back, there's a desperate undertone crying out for more of what made me feel like that. Maybe this is what it's like for sex addicts. If this was any more than a one-off, I can see I might have to go into recovery.

I'm mumbling to Nic as I turn over to him. 'Can you actually get addicted to sex after only one night?' Not that we've done much talking up to now. Mostly we were just lying in ecstatic silence, soaking up that it was actually happening. Getting our breath back before we started all over again for another wonderful round. When Poppy said *cross the bridge*, I'm not sure she meant me to go over it four times and then some.

As I flop over and extend my arm into the space on the pillow where Nic's tousled hair should be, I let out a shout as my hand lands on some very soft, silky ears instead.

'Merwyn?' His nose finds my hand and he gives my finger a little lick. 'Why aren't you on your bed?'

And as I run my palm across the pillow and my fingers close around an envelope my heart freezes. Then my body goes rigid.

I'd leap out of bed and search the bathroom, but there's no need. Because I'm staring at my name in Nic's regular handwriting on the front of a very white envelope.

Milla.

And there's a hole where my heart should be that's larger than Wales, because that can only mean one thing.

I'm easing up the flap, pulling the sticker off the small tissue-paper parcel inside to find a tiny silver starfish on a slender chain. It's simple. Beautiful. Perfect. I close my fist around it because I already know I'm going to look at it every day for the rest of time.

As I open the white paper note, I'm staring at the same gently rounded letters, the blue ink they're written in barely dry.

Milla – my very favourite space cadet and wedding planner,

I'd meant to wake you before I left but looking down at you now, you've not long gone to sleep and you look too peaceful. And if I did wake you, I might not ever leave.

So instead I'm writing this, to say sorry – for running away and all my other blunders. And thank you – for the wedding, everything else, and more. And lastly, goodbye.

Six months is a very long time. I'm not sure I know enough about forgiveness or the state of my tortured soul to guarantee an outcome.

So, for now, all I can do is make you a promise – I'll love you for as long as stars are above you, Milla Vanilla. I hope sometimes you'll look up at them from your little attic port-hole and think of me.

Yours forever, (in every galaxy),
Nic xx

'Back at you, Captain Kirk.' I'm whispering as I swallow back my tears. And just before the flood gates open I see his tux still hanging on the hook on back of the bedroom door.

Then I hear the distant slam of the huge front door, and as

it sinks in that I've missed him by seconds, I bury my face in his pillow. As the distant sound of a car revs up the drive, I let the sobs come. As the engine note fades to nothing, my body convulses and I let my howls go free.

Chapter 38

St Aidan in July.
Reruns and rewinds.

Poppy was the one who came in and found me the morning Nic left, when she heard my sobs through the door. Then Immie whisked me out by the kitchen door, and back to my own comfy bed under the sloping attic ceiling so I didn't have to face anyone.

And as I woke again later that day, after a sleep ruptured with tears and desperate re-runs in my head, it felt like I was leaving something very significant behind. It was about much more than crossing Poppy's proverbial bridge. As Nic left, I waved away my old life too. And whatever happens, I owe it to Mum to smile no matter how sad and broken I feel inside. After the straight talking I gave Nic, it would be hypocritical of me to do anything else.

Then Bill and Ivy came back again bringing Abby with her arm in a sling and a bump on her head. And there were a couple of days of post-wedding excitement when the flat was bursting with flowers sent from Pixie and Ewan, and Pixie's mum and dad. Both bunches were so big I had to borrow flower buckets from the basement to display them in.

Holly had filmed Pixie's amazing and emotional walk down the aisle, and with Pixie's permission, that was loaded to YouTube where it got loads of attention. Then we shared it across the Brides by the Sea and Brides Go Wild platforms too, and it also got picked up by the local press. Thanks to that and the blog we did about Pixie trying on wedding dresses, the hits and followers for Brides Go Wild literally did go crazy.

I have to admit, at least five hundred of those thousands of YouTube views of Pixie taking her first steps are mine. The first time I watched it was with the excuse that I had seen it all from the back not the front. Even so, it was gut-wrenching watching Pixie make her halting, yet amazing way down the aisle, *All You Need Is Love* in the background, seeing all the guests' eyes going wide as they realised the enormity of what she was doing. Ewan, looking so very proud and in love, Nic with tears streaming down his face. And then after it was over and she's back in her chair, there's me, fumbling to get her shoes on, and Pixie telling me to sit next to Nic. And just before the clip ends, there's Nic with so much love in his face, stooping to whisper to me about the chocolate puddings. It's impossible for anyone who knows Pixie to watch it without sobbing buckets, and it's been the best excuse for me to be bawling my eyes out. Again and again.

Pixie FaceTimed me from her jet-skiing honeymoon near Newquay. What was meant to be a thank you call quickly moved on to Pixie first apologising, then going ape about Nic. Her saying 'What a knobhead! I promise I'll run him over then mash him!' is great. But realistically, right now he's well beyond the reach of Pixie and her studded tyres.

With the old life gone, I am here at the start of a whole other new one, with an unfamiliar landscape. One crowded with friends, all gently tiptoeing around me, delicately checking in to see how I am. But it's one that's filled with unexpected obstacles that fell me every hour, as reminders of Nic leap out from every crack between the cobblestones and alleyway end. Spring up everywhere from groomswear to the furthest rockpool out along the bay, where Merwyn and I still walk every lunchtime.

But it's not just life that's different; I've changed too. I'm not the same woman who tottered around in her six-inch heels, squeezing myself into pencil skirts and John Smedley jumpers because Phoebe told me to. This version of me wouldn't have fallen apart over losing Ben, who should never have been mine to start with. But even though I'm grounded by my certainty that I had to let Nic go, it doesn't stop my heart breaking. After throwing all my efforts at him and his quest, day and night, for five months, there's bound to be a huge void in my life now that's gone. Now he's gone.

Two weeks after Pixie's wedding, an envelope arrives with a koala bear on the stamp. Inside there's a postcard with a picture of fireworks over Sydney Harbour Bridge. And on the back, Nic's relaxed yet even handwriting, and the words:

Saw this and thought of you, Nic x

I prop it on the tiny table next to my bed. Then I move on with my next wedding fair. And getting together the copy for the glossy magazine to go with the fairs for the autumn, which I've decided I'll go ahead with independently. The idea is, if I make sure I never stop, there's less time to think. Less possibility of jerking to a halt every time I remember I feel like there's a gaping hole in my side where someone wrenched my heart out.

As for Nic's tux, I have to come clean – it's still here waiting to be returned to his office. Sometime – when I'm far enough down the line that I no longer have to bury my face in it every night before bed, when I can pass the bedroom door where it hangs without stopping every time to breathe in his smell.

With any luck, the smell will fade to nothing around the same time I forget to stop and sniff it. Just like when I was grieving for my mum, so long as I'm patient and wait enough years, there will be a time when my heart will finally stop aching. When every little task I do doesn't feel like it's taking the same effort as if I were moving an elephant across the room.

Then, as July wears on and the season builds towards its peak, my own accidental groans that escape past my smile are masked by everyone else's moans about the streets and the beaches being rammed with holidaymakers, and the lanes around Cornwall being clogged with what feels like one continual traffic jam. Lucky for me, having to set off for wedding fairs at an even earlier crack of dawn than usual fits in well with me waking up at stupid o'clock every day. For some reason, since Nic left there's so much high-alert adrenalin coursing around my body, when I've had two hours sleep that seems to be enough.

And more good news – when Nic's cash and bonus from Jess finally hits my account there's enough to pay back my brothers the money I borrowed to finance the first Brides Go West magazine and the van renovations. With that debt cleared, I put it to Phoebe that it makes sense for her and Ben to buy me out of Brides Go West. Before July ends, I'm in Trenowden and Trenowden's solicitors office by the quayside, on first name terms with George, going through the final contract agreements. In the end, it turns out that letting go isn't hard at all; a couple of signatures is all it takes. And I'm free.

I'm throwing myself into the Brides Go Wild blog too, filling the pages with dreamy stories of lovely summer weddings as they happen. And little by little, if I say it often enough, I'll be able to persuade myself that I'm doing fine.

But my favourite part of every day is at night, just before I go to bed, when I look out at the navy blue sky, studded with tiny, bright white stars. There's the slivery splash of moonlight on the inky water, the arc of lights curving out around the bay, and if I open the little porthole window and lean out into the warm evening air, I can just make out *Snow Goose's* tall mast and rigging, etched against the night. And I try not to remember that the stars Nic's looking out on are in a totally different sky. Because when I stand and will my love for Nic to travel into the night and right across the ocean, it feels less like he's gone forever.

AUGUST

Chapter 39

Saturday, five weeks after Pixie's wedding.
Birds nests and flowers on doorsteps.

When I say the last thing I look out at before going to sleep is *Snow Goose's* mast, it's also the first thing I see when I wake too. Today is Saturday and because, for now, I'm still counting, that's five weeks and two days on from Pixie's wedding. When I ease forward on my pillows and peer out of the porthole window at six, the clouds are washed with the pale apricot of dawn and a solitary seagull is perched at the top of *Snow Goose's* rigging.

And then, as my eyes slide downwards, my body jerks upright – because for a second, there in the distance, through the mist rising off the water, I swear I see a figure on the deck. Hand propped against the mast. Just like ...

I screw up my eyes and scrape away the sleep. And when I look again it's gone. But when you're as wired as I am, nothing's completely rational. And it's not like I can turn off the possibility in my mind. So I'm already across the room, shrugging on a cardi over my sleep-shorts and T-shirt, leaping down the stairs, wincing as the wind chills my skin.

I dive into the stepped alleyways and skid out at the bottom

by the dune path. Then I'm curling back towards the harbourside cottages, scrambling over fishing nets, and leaping a pile of
lobster pots. By the time I'm finally racing towards the jetties,
my throat is burning and my lungs are bursting and as I get to
the walkway where *Snow Goose* is moored, I'm pulling to a halt.
Standing. Staring. And I already know what I'll be looking at.

It's the same empty space I've seen every other time I've rushed
down here chasing moonbeams, only to stare out across the
deserted deck.

I sag against a lamp post and blink back the tears pricking
my eyelids. When my gasps finally subside, I'll wind my way
back up the long route by the empty cobbled street, past the
brightly painted cottage doors, the windows with closed blinds,
the early morning smells of freshly-baked bread from Crusty
Cobs bakery. Past the Deck Gallery.

But for now I'm kicking myself for being so stupid. So reac-
tive. So raw. Seriously, if I'm going to find myself half asleep
down at the harbourside on a regular basis, I need more substan-
tial pyjamas. Ideally ones with whole legs. And maybe that
counselling Poppy keeps talking about – for people who've
totally lost their shit.

I pull my cardigan closer around me. I'm scraping every last
bit of energy together ready to walk back up the hill when a
noise behind me makes me jump.

'Milla?'

I glance down at the expanse of thigh on show, try to slide
behind the lamp post and pretend I'm not here but it comes
again.

'Milla ... are you trying to hide? It is you, Milla Vanilla ...?'

And as I turn I'm blinking because, silhouetted against the
streaky orange sky, there's a figure hurrying along the quayside.

Tall. Muscled. Dark wavy hair. A dusky tan. Jacket tossed over his shoulder. 'Captain *Kirk*?' I screw my eyes closed in case I'm dreaming but when I open them again he's still there. Those faded jeans and those soft grey-brown eyes with the crinkles at the edge when he smiles – even through the blur of my tears, it couldn't be anyone else.

I'm stammering. 'W—w—why aren't you on Hamilton Island?' It's only as he slides in beside me that it hits me quite how much I've been dying inside, how much I've been longing for the smell of him.

He's staring down at me. 'What about you, out in your cardi? You're like Bridget Jones on her snow run.'

I sniff hard so he won't see I'm crying. 'I thought I saw you from the window, but when I got down the hill you'd gone.' It's such a huge flip from that worst, crushing disappointment to the whoosh of elation that he's here. Then it hits me that I could be taking too much for granted. 'You do want to see me?'

There's a smile playing around his lips. 'I didn't come twelve thousand miles to see anyone else. I nipped to the bakery to give you time to wake up.' He's holding up a cake box, then his eyes narrow as he stares down at the hem of my T-shirt skimming my thighs. 'Please make my day and tell me there are kittens under there.'

I'm feeling like a wrung-out dishcloth, and that's all he can say? 'For eff's sake, Nic.'

He gives me a nudge with his elbow. 'And ...?'

Two seconds in his company and I'm already rolling my eyes. 'There are kittens. And pompoms too.' It's sad to watch how much he visibly relaxes. 'So how come you're on deck at six in the bloody morning?'

He blows out a breath. 'I flew in to London late last night, picked up a car, and here I am.' He runs his fingers through the tangle of his curls. 'I really needed to talk to you.'

I'm trying not to let my heart sink as I hear that, and to re-twist my hair so I look less like a seagull built its nest on my head as I slide onto the nearest bench. 'Is here okay?'

'Anywhere is good.' He slides his jacket around my shoulders. 'It's still quite cold. Why not put this on.'

It still doesn't feel real. I'm inhaling his scent from the fabric, tucking my knees up, hugging them to my chest as much for comfort as for warmth. I hate to admit that the jacket is one small gesture; I'm a strong independent woman, but it's still the loveliest feeling to have someone looking out for me. As I pull the edges closer around me, my eyes are randomly leaking, so I'm mopping them with my cardigan cuff. And even though he's come all this way, it still feels as if there's a very large chasm he hasn't crossed yet. That in spite of the nudges and the kitten jokes, as he sits down beside me, he's still keeping his distance. Now that he's here, however much he's respecting my boundaries, I don't want to let him too far out of reach, so I shuffle towards him.

He pushes the open cake box towards me. 'I hope you still like almond croissants. They're just out of the oven.'

'Great choice, Nicolson. And you know me, six won't be a challenge.' That's total bullshit. Right now, the dragonfly explosion in my stomach is making my mouth drier than sawdust; I couldn't manage a bite. Instead I take one, and wave it around, trying to divert attention from my lack of appetite. 'So how's your new job? It must be good if they're already giving you a holiday.'

He pulls a face. 'Mostly brilliant. It's a great boat, fabulous sailing, lovely employers.'

My eyes are wide. 'Lots to like then.' No downsides at all. And I'm reminding myself, most business guys don't have carbon footprints as teensy as mine; they fly long-distance without a second thought. There are heaps of reasons he could be here, other than me – for family, or an emergency with the company.

He wrinkles up his face. 'I have to come clean. Sailing off into the blue didn't work out quite as I'd planned it.'

'What went wrong?'

He's staring down, watching the ripples on the inky water of the harbour. 'That night on the beach you said you'd changed, but I hadn't. But actually I had. I only discovered how much when I tried to go back to how I was before.'

'I see.' I'm not sure if this is good or bad but I nod anyway.

He's biting his lip. 'Doing Pixie's wedding was the first time since her accident that I'd done something truly positive. You were the catalyst to me doing that. I didn't realise it at the time, but just being around you and working with you changed my thought processes. I assumed I'd take myself off afterwards and find my same old refuge of negativity, that if I denied my feelings for you, buried them deep enough, I could carry on with life as it used to be. But I couldn't. The new version of Nic ran away. But he couldn't go back to being how he was before.'

As he stops and gazes out to sea, staring at the pale horizon, his voice is low. 'There's a lot of time to think when you sail. There were a couple of other big problems I hadn't foreseen, too.' He turns to meet my eye. 'First was how much I missed you. And then there was your mum ...'

My eyes pop open. 'My mum?'

He nods slowly. 'Everywhere we went, she was up there, looking down at me from her cloud. She just kept telling me over and over again not to throw my life away.'

I'm swallowing back my tears. 'But you were unplugged on the Great Barrier Reef. Wasn't that enough for her?'

He shrugs. 'Apparently not. Not compared to the size of the love I was walking away from.'

I'm sniffing and apologising at the same time. 'She can be very persistent if there's something she doesn't approve of; she does the same to me. It's just strange that she's doing it to you.'

He's staring at the water. 'That night on the beach, you put the idea of your mum in my head. And I knew what she'd said was so true. For the first time in four years I didn't feel guilty about Pixie. I was feeling guilty for everything I wasn't making the most of.'

He's rubbing his jaw with his thumb now, looking at me quizzically. 'I told you at the castle that I'd fallen in love with you, didn't I? I know those feelings might be very one-sided. But now I've finally come to my senses, I realise that's too important to ignore – I've got to put every bit of my effort in and try to make you love me too. I have no idea what I've done to deserve this, but now that I'm in love with you I see that you and your mum are completely right. I can't run away, I've got to fight for you. I'm hoping that now I've shaken myself up, I might be good enough for you too. Because I certainly couldn't want you any more than I do.'

I'm gulping so hard I can't actually get any words out.

He's turning to me with a wistful smile. 'So that's what I've come here to do – to work until I'm good enough to deserve your love.'

All I can do is dissolve into my sleeve. I manage to stretch out a hand and grasp his.

He gives a sigh. 'And this time, as I sailed back down the coast, there was one thought guiding me home. On the beach when I told you I loved you for the last time, you said "back at you".' He's looking at me through narrowed eyes. 'You did say "back at you", didn't you?'

I'm mumbling my excuses into my sleeve. 'It's thirty-seven days ago now ... that's quite a long time to remember ...'

He's scrutinising my face. 'When Pixie rang to give me a bollocking, she also said she heard you crying before you left.' He leaves a pause. 'Inconsolably. So I do have a vague idea ... you wouldn't have been that upset if you hadn't cared.'

And finally, I decide it's time to own it. 'Actually, I did cry ... and I did say that ...'

His lips twist for a second, then he looks serious again. 'But did you mean it? And if you did, how the hell have I missed it? I mean, if you loved me too, how did I not know?'

'Where do you want me to begin?'

He gives a low laugh. 'I actually fell in love with you way before the Valentine's cocktails. Even before the kiss through your van window.'

'Really?' I'm blinking at him. 'So it wasn't my Love Potion No. 9 or my arrow?'

'Nope.' He's shaking his head. 'When the fireworks were on I was leaning on my mast, and I looked across and saw you crying. All I wanted to do was help you, and make you feel better. If I have to pinpoint one moment in time when you grabbed my heart, it was then. That was the moment when my whole world pivoted.'

I'm biting my lip. 'I'd just heard Hunter had been born. I was wailing because Phoebe had stolen my baby name.' It seems so long ago now and matters so little to me. But at the same time, it's somehow momentous that that awful moment from my past was so important in shaping my future. It's strangely satisfying and significant that at my worst moment of my old world falling apart, my new one was also coming together. 'I remember looking across and seeing you standing on your own in the dark, and suddenly feeling less alone.' It's sending shivers down my spine to think that was when we both felt that first connection.

He laughs. 'That's why I came storming over to you with my parking permit. The wardens aren't that bad. They've been really lenient with me, parking without one since.'

I'm picking my jaw up off the floor at what he's revealing here. 'But you said it was a spare.'

He's laughing. 'It was my one chance to connect with you and I was desperate. And when Poppy came over, it felt like cupid really was looking down on me.'

I'm shaking my head. 'Did she tell you what a loser I was?'

'Not at all. She said you needed one small kiss and asked if I had any friends who might help. I wasn't hanging around to ask questions, I was straight in there, and the kiss only proved me right. So by the time you hit me with your arrow, I'd already been in love with you for quite a few hours.'

Now it's my turn to laugh. 'This might be where I say "back at you" again. When you turned up and I thought you were marrying Pixie I struggled. But then when I found out you weren't engaged after all, but were slightly less available than a monk, that was even worse.' I take a deep breath, because it's okay to tell him. 'I had such a hard time keeping my hands off you those five months. All those times you were naked ... But I convinced myself it was misdirected lust, all the way to our first dance. Then, as I listened to Ellie sing, with my head on your chest, it hit me – everything I'd been feeling all along was because I was completely in love with you.'

'And then straight after that I went on to tell you I had to go away ... because I loved you.' He's shaking his head. 'What terrible timing that was. I'm sorry I messed up so badly.'

'I knew it would only upset you more if I told you the truth, and I didn't want to do that. But I did try to give you a way to understand. And I did get to have the best night of my life.'

He laughs. 'Me too, Milla Vanilla.'

'And then you went away, and I've tried really hard, but I've been so miserable.' It comes out as a wail.

He blows out his cheeks. 'I'm so sorry. Pixie was right to want to run me over. But thanks to you, and your mum, I've finally got here in the end. So, do you think I could have a kiss now?'

He gets up, grasps me by the wrist and pulls me into his arms, and a moment later, my mouth is buried in his, and the world slides out of focus for a very long time.

As I finally let him go and push myself back again, Nic's pupils are dilated. He's holding on to me very tightly, and I've got my hands on his chest, looking up at the dreamy smile on his face. 'I was looking out at the stars every night, willing you to come back.'

He lets out a low laugh. 'And I was looking up at the stars, knowing I had to. And now that I have, I'm here to stay.'

I'm smiling now, but still sniffing back my happy tears. 'Five months to get to know each other properly is good – so does that mean we're officially going out now as well as being in love?'

He drops a kiss on the top of my head. 'If that's okay with you?'

My head's racing, looking for the catch. 'But what about your friend's mum and dad in Australia?'

Nic smiles. 'I found a very good skipper to step in for me. As for us, not wanting to resort to bribery here, but maybe we could get our very own puppy to sit by our fire with us. Or better still, find another Merwyn from a rescue?'

'I do love you so much, Nicolson Trendell.' I'm laughing across at him. 'For all of that. Somehow I doubt we'll ever find a dog with quite as much side-eye as Merwyn. But yes please to all of it.'

He's smiling down at me. 'And you do want babies too? Kids of our own?'

I'm laughing at how, after all the holding back, he's all over this now. 'You do realise you'll need a whole new manual for those?'

He's grinning back at me. 'And a cottage to keep them in might be handy. With a view of the sea, obviously. And maybe a jetty to tie up the boats.'

'So long as we're together and in love with each other, I don't mind about any of the rest.' My face is aching with all the smiling. 'You know, Jess said Brides by the Sea works its magic, and it has done for us hasn't it?'

'It has.' He gives a shamefaced grin. 'I really won't mind helping you with Brides Go Wild rather than delivering boats.'

I can't help laughing at the change in him. 'You really love your weddings, don't you?'

He grimaces. 'I haven't given up on boats altogether. In fact, I've got something to show you, over there.' He takes my hand, leads me down towards the end walkway, and stops by the second largest boat in the harbour. 'So what do you think of her?'

'That's not *Snow Goose*?' The rigging and the mast are similar, but the shape and the colour are different. For a non-boat-y person, I'm proud of that summing up.

There's a smile playing around Nic's lips. 'No, this one's got a better bathroom and a much bigger bed. It came in a couple of days ago and, so long as you like it, it will be ours.' His face breaks into a beam. 'See what you think of the name.'

I'm walking along the quayside, and when I come to the back of the boat and read the neatly painted letters, I let out a cry. 'Milla Vanilla? How cool is that? You called it after me!'

'I hope that's okay? You know what a boat fiend I am. It was the best way I could think of to show you I was here for good, that we're going to be forever.'

I've got tingles running up and down my spine. 'It's amazing. How am I ever going to get back at you for that?'

He laughs and pulls me into another kiss that leaves my knees collapsing. Then, when he finally lets me go again, he grins down at me. 'I can think of a way, but let's leave the serious stuff for further down the line. There are so many things we need to do before that. First, I need to kiss you some more ... and take you to bed, like, *immediately* ... And, back in February, I offered to make you pancakes and you still haven't had those.'

As I rub my palm over his face, I feel like I'm going to burst with happiness. 'And best of all, I think my mum would approve of all of that.'

He laughs again. 'Are you ready for me to carry you onboard then? I reckon it's time to try out this enormous bed.' He sends me a wink. 'Luckily for me, you came in your pyjamas. Unless you'd rather have breakfast first?'

I'm laughing back at him. 'After so long keeping my hands off you, breakfast will have to wait!'

And as this wonderful man who almost slipped away takes me by the hand and leads me down to the jetty, I feel like the luckiest woman in the world. I know we couldn't be any happier or more in love. And I know I'm going to love Nic as long as there are stars above us. And longer too.

P.S.

Happy endings come in all shapes and sizes. For anyone wanting a home-shaped happy ending, Nic and I move into Anemone Cottage on the Harbourside just in time for Christmas. We're really sad to say goodbye to the little attic flat at Brides by the Sea, but it's worked its charm for us, and we know we have to move on. And hopefully someone else will move in there and enjoy the same fairy-dust luck in love as we have.

Our new cottage is a few doors along from Sera's, and is so tiny that the bathroom on Milla Vanilla is actually bigger than the one in the cottage. And there's lots of work to do on it, but it has views of the sea, and a wood burning stove, which is perfect for our very own hearth-rug rescue dog, Tiller, who sits beside it whenever he's not sitting on Nic or me.

And anyone who likes babies in the future is going to be happy too. No, Nic and I aren't that quick! But when Pixie and Ewan fly down for Christmas they come with their own very happy baby news. And I know from the way Nic looked at me with his eyes all out of focus when he heard that it won't be too long before we'll be thinking about that too.

As for anyone who likes happy endings with rings, Nic and I came across a beautiful topaz one, with a stone that changes colour like the sea, at a vintage stall at a Christmas market. It wasn't expensive, but it's beautiful, and for some reason it reminds us both of my mum.

He keeps it until Valentine's night when we stand on deck on Milla Vanilla, watching Jess's firework display, which has already become an annual event in St Aidan's calendar. And in the dark, as the crackling red hearts drift down into the sea, he quietly whispers in my ear and asks me to marry him. And obviously I say yes and grapple him into a huge kiss. Then as the last volleys of bangs echo around the bay, he pushes the ring onto my finger and it shows how far he's come that he gets it on the right one. It's a very quiet moment, but it's filled with love. Because for us, Valentine's night will always be extra special. And we couldn't be any happier.

Acknowledgements

A big thank you ... To my agent, Amanda Preston for her warmth and brilliance, her vision and encouragement, for sparkling and for always being there. To my publisher and friend Charlotte Ledger, for her inspiration, support, brilliance and all round loveliness. After twelve books together it never gets any less exciting. To my totally brilliant editor, Emily Ruston, with her unerring eye and fabulous sense of what's needed and what belongs on the cutting room floor – I love what you do to my books. To Kimberley Young and the team at HarperCollins and One More Chapter, for their fabulous covers, and all round expertise and support.

To my writing friends across the world ... To the fabulous book bloggers, who spread the word. To all my wonderful Facebook friends.

To my wonderful readers ... these books are all for you, thank you so much for enjoying them – I love hearing from you and meeting up with you.

And last of all, huge hugs to my family, for cheering me on all the way. And big love to my own hero, Phil ... thank you for never letting me give up.

Favourite Cocktails from *Love at the Little Wedding Shop by the Sea*

In case you'd like to try a taste of Brides by the Sea at home, it's become a bit of a tradition to include a few recipes at the end of the story. So here's how to make some of the drinks mentioned in the *Love at the Little Wedding Shop* book. Don't stress too much about the quantities. Just like Milla, Poppy and the gang at the Cockle Shell Castle design your own cocktail evening, it's much more about sloshing it in and having a good time.

MR & MRS THREE KISSES G&T's

This was Pixie's choice for her wedding cocktails at Cockle Shell Castle. A gin and tonic sounds easy peasy, but here are a few extra tips to give you the very best results.

- **Getting the perfect balance of gin to tonic** will avoid a drink that's too strong, and also avoid drinking something that tastes so weak you might as well just drink straight tonic. 2oz gin to 4-5oz tonic is ideal.
- **A good gin** will make a much better G&T than a cut-price one. There are lots of fab designer gins around now in the prettiest bottles, you can experiment to find your own favourite.
- **Choose a good tonic**, in small bottles, **and use it freshly**

opened for the best the fizz. Fever tree do an excellent plain version, but their aromatic tonic is also great if you fancy a pink G&T.

- **High ball glasses or balloon shape glasses** both work well but give a very different feel to the drink.
- **Make sure all the ingredients are really cold**.
- **For extra-special results chill the glasses** in the fridge, or pre-chill by filling with ice cubes before you begin.
- **For the garnish** choose nice, ripe, juicy fruit or fresh herbs. Limes, ruby grapefruit or lemons all work well sliced. Sprigs of thyme or mint are also good.
- **Have your ice cubes large** so they last longer before they melt and dilute the drink.

So here goes for the recipe for the perfect G&T with lime...

- 2oz gin
- 4–5oz tonic
- 3 lime wedges
- Take a chilled highball glass and add the gin.
- Fill the glass with large ice cubes, then squeeze in one of the wedges.
- Add the tonic, squeeze in the second lime. Then float the third lime slice, or attach to the glass rim.
- Then sit back and enjoy.

RHUBARB AND ROSE COCKTAIL

I love pink drinks and I also love rhubarb and raspberries, so for me this is a triple winner. This delicious drink couldn't be any more simple to make either.

- 125ml Fentimans rose lemonade
- 25ml rhubarb gin
- Raspberries to garnish
- Take a decorated stemmed glass. Add the gin, top up with the chilled rose lemonade. Then toss in some raspberries. Sigh at how pretty it is, and enjoy.

RHUBARB AND ROSE COCKTAIL
(The non-alcoholic version)

At the Valentine's night party Milla and Poppy are drinking non-alcoholic rhubarb and rose drinks. Not that they're party poopers, but sometimes it pays to keep a clear head, and this is a delish way to do that.

- 125ml Fentimans rose lemonade
- 25ml rhubarb cordial (using Bottle Green rhubarb and ginger cordial will give you a kick and some extra warmth if it's February!)
- Raspberries to garnish. (And mint too if Jess is around!)
- Mix all the ingredients in a stemmed glass, or alternatively, mix larger quantities in a glass jug so you can come back for more.

TIE ME UP TIE ME DOWN

This is one of the hilarious but embarrassing cocktail names Milla was shouting from the chalk board on Valentine's night. Very tasty, yet simple to make.

- 1.5oz vodka
- 1oz sugar syrup, infuse the syrup with a rosemary sprig for an hour before using

- .75oz lemon juice
- Rosemary sprigs

Combine the liquid ingredients in a shaker, add ice shake thoroughly, then strain and pour over ice in a glass. Garnish with a rosemary sprig or two. Down in one (only joking!) and wait for the fun to start.

LOVE POTION NO.1

At the cocktail evening Milla mixed Nic an off-the-cuff cocktail which she called Love Potion No. 9. This is the original recipe for a Love Potion cocktail.

- 3oz gin
- 3oz lime juice
- 1oz elderflower cordial
- 6oz pink champagne
- Ice cubes made from water with rose petals floating in it. (Imagine how pretty they will be!)
- Combine the gin, elderflower cordial and lime juice in a cocktail shaker, and shake thoroughly. Put the rose petal ice cubes in an empty cocktail glass, and strain the mixture over the ice cubes. Then top up with pink champagne. Sit back, sip ... and wait for Cupid's arrow to hit.

Cheers!

Love Jane xx